The Water Nymph

ALSO BY MICHELE JAFFE

The Stargazer

Published by Pocket Books

The Water Nymph

MICHELE JAFFE

POCKET BOOKS

NEW YORK LONDON TORONTO SYDNEY SINGAPORE

POCKET BOOKS, a division of Simon & Schuster Inc.
1230 Avenue of the Americas, New York, NY 10020

ISBN: 0-671-02741-7

First Pocket Books hardcover printing June 2000

10 9 8 7 6 5 4 3 2 1

Designed by Lindgren/Fuller Design

Printed in the U.S.A.

This book is dedicated to Emily Goldner and Michael Humphries.

From the shores of the Sea of Cortez to the banks of the Thames,
may your life together be filled with happily-ever-afters.

Prologue

He was being followed.

There were two of them, a short one with a strange cap, and a tall one whose bald head reflected the early morning sun. He had tested them, leading them back and forth through the bustling colonnades of Saint Paul's, studying their reactions, looking for weaknesses. He noticed that the little one had a slight blind spot, and that the tall one was quicker on his left, but he could not shake them off, even with his best tricks. They were good, he had concluded. Very good. And that made him smile. Because there was nothing Crispin Foscari, the Earl of Sandal, liked better than a challenge.

Coming out of Saint Paul's, he turned right, then right again. He smelled his objective before he saw it, the warren of makeshift stalls on the bank of the Thames that served as London's main fish market. The shouts of the stallholders filled the air, offering trout fit for the Queen's own table on the right, the Sultan's favorite kippers on the left. Crispin stopped to inspect a slab of something pinkish that was promised to be every bit as delicious as a woodcock, never losing sight of his companions. Short was right behind him, and Tall was moving parallel along the next avenue of stalls. Crispin consulted his pocket watch and decided that it was time.

Without giving a sign, he dove under the counter of a particularly rickety stall, tossed a half dozen coins at the proprietor, grabbed a basket of eels, and disappeared. With his slippery companions perched on his shoulder he was able to move unobtrusively down the pathway that ran between the stalls and reach the edge of the market undetected. Before leaving, Crispin made a present of the eels to a gaunt-looking boy with a dog, and then plunged himself into the thicket of alleyways and narrow lanes that marked this quarter of London. Four turns took him within sight of the rendezvous place, five minutes early. He had just entered the alley that led to it when a gentleman stepped out of a doorway and held a knife to his stomach.

Crispin nodded at him politely. "Is there something I can do for you and your"—he looked down at the knife—"friend?"

The gentleman smiled. "Did you hear that, boys?" he said over his shoulder to the three large men, daggers out, who entered the alley behind him. "His Lordship wants to know if there is something he can do for us."

"I suppose," Crispin said with an apologetic sigh, "I should have made it a statement rather than a question. There *is* something I can do for you." Before the man could respond, Crispin had him distracted, disarmed, and disjointed. "Much better," he said, looking at the unconscious figure at his feet. "Who would like to be next?"

The three other men fell on Crispin simultaneously and in less than two minutes were arrayed against the alley wall next to their leader. Crispin was just checking the fabric and stitching of the clothes of the last of them, confirming his hunch that they were all English, when the bells of Saint Paul's began to ring. As they tolled for the ninth and final time, a black-lacquered coach without a coat of arms on the door pulled up before him. None of the coachmen looked at him, but kept their eyes focused on the middle distance, like all good servants who serve a secretive master.

The door opened from within, and, entering, Crispin found himself in almost complete darkness.

"That was very neat, Lord Sandal. Those were some of our best men," a voice said from the far end of the vehicle. "I hope you had an unremarkable journey and have found London everything you left it."

That was the first code phrase specified in the letter. "The sea was flat and the keel even," Crispin replied, giving the appropriate key-phrase as he had been instructed.

"Very good," the voice commended. "Although with the performance you just gave out there in response to Our little test, your identity is hardly in question. There is only one man in Europe who could have done that. Perhaps," the voice went on, sniffing delicately, "perhaps next time the Phoenix will not choose to spend quite so much time in the fish market."

Crispin murmured the requisite thanks for the compliment and apology for his piscine scent, but he had really only attended the remarks with part of his mind. The other, larger part, was distracted by the tingling sensation that had begun at the base of his spine. He always felt it, and only felt it, when something extremely important or extremely dangerous was about to happen. He had gotten an inkling of it eight days earlier when a messenger had burst into the small apartment he was occupying in Spain with an urgent summons to London. He had spent months establishing himself as Carlos, a *pescador* so notoriously stupid and bumbling that the Spanish admiralty did not even bother to punish him when he accidentally rowed his boat around their munitions storehouse, and no longer paid attention when he was found floating, dead drunk, among their newest and most secret warships. In this guise he had been able to provide information that would be vital to England in the country's inevitable clash with Spain. Only something very important and probably dangerous, he had surmised, could account for his abrupt recall to London.

He was about to receive confirmation that he was not wrong. There was a rustling in the carriage and a flame sprung into life, bobbing on the end of an oil lantern. Even in the jiggling shadows thrown by the lamp there could be no mistaking the person across from him. Or the importance of the meeting. For facing him was not merely one of Her Majesty's most trusted secret operatives. It was Her Majesty, Queen Elizabeth I, herself.

Crispin sank to his knees, bowing his head over the fingers that were held out to him. The Queen gave him her ring to kiss, a thick gold band with an enormous knot just under the knuckle, and then motioned him up. She began speaking as soon as he was reseated, not wasting time with a preamble.

"We have summoned you, Lord Sandal, to thank you for your fine work on Our behalf. The attempt on Our life by Our Cousin the Queen of Scots would never have been uncovered without your efforts, and the end of that smuggling operation in Turkey has been a blessing for Our Exchequer. Not to mention that it has been a pleasure not to have to worry about an attack by the Dutch, since their fleet was so cunningly destroyed." The Queen held a pomander before her nose as she spoke, making her words slightly muffled.

Crispin nodded. "I did nothing more than my duty, Your Majesty. I could—"

The Queen cut him off with a gesture. "Indeed. We hope you shall continue in this vein even after your retirement."

"Retirement?" Crispin repeated. "But I do not wish to retire. King Philip of Spain is about to invade—"

"Yes, We have read your reports about the Spanish, and are taking them under advisement, given what We now know. But your work for Us is finished. The Phoenix will not serve Us any longer."

The tingling at the base of Crispin's spine now extended itself all the way to his neck. "May I ask why?"

"We fear that the burden of Our trust has been too much for you."

"Are you accusing me of betrayal?" Crispin's eyes darkened.

"We accuse you of nothing. Your recent record speaks for itself."

"What record? I have been disguised as a fisherman in Spain these many months and out of communication with everyone."

"Of course," Her Majesty said in an unapologetic tone. She now removed the pomander from her nose and looked at Crispin with the penetrating gaze that had brought so many men to their knees. "We refrain from mentioning the specifics of your actions, for your case is still under consideration. The judges will meet about it in a fortnight, and We would not like for any of the witnesses to be unduly influenced. For the time being, you should be content that you have merely been retired. Out of respect for your fine service and your aunts, Our dear friends, We have forborne to arrest you, but Our clemency is not boundless. If you rectify your behavior and act as you should during these next days, We may still deign to grant you your life."

"May I at least know who has maligned me this way?" Crispin asked with deceptive calm.

"We cannot say who is behind these accusations, and We advise you not to inquire or find out why they are making them. Do not do anything to thwart them, Lord Sandal, and do not make any long-term plans. Make no mistake—it is your life which hangs in the balance."

The Queen held Crispin's eyes for a moment, using her gaze to underscore her words. "We trust you understand what we are telling you, Lord Sandal."

"I understand," Crispin said, his expression grim.

The Queen scrutinized him closely for one last moment, nodded curtly to herself, and then reached up with her pomander to bang on the roof of the coach three times, bringing it almost immediately to a halt.

"Good day, Lord Sandal," she told Crispin. "You shall hear from Us in fourteen days. Do not let Us hear of you before that."

Crispin stood in the middle of the narrow street and watched the coach recede until it was nothing but a bouncing black dot in the distance. As it disappeared, the words *fourteen days* echoed in his head, repeating and rearranging themselves endlessly. Fourteen days to salvage an identity he had spent years creating. Fourteen days to find out who was trying to destroy the Phoenix and why. Fourteen days to defuse a powerful threat. Or fourteen days until his death.

Crispin Foscari, the Earl of Sandal, liked challenges. But he was not smiling anymore.

Chapter One

"Are you aware," the voice whispered into Sophie Champion's ear, "that your mustache is slipping?"

Sophie was having a very bad week. Her cook had quit, twice. Her beekeeper was hearing voices, in particular that of the queen bee suggesting that they run away together. She had been compelled to suffer through two balls to model Octavia's newest gown designs, which had led to three new marriage proposals. Her godfather, Lord Grosgrain, had been killed in a mysterious riding accident. Her upper lip was numb and her nose itched from the false mustache she had been forced to wear for two days in her desperate attempt to infiltrate the Unicorn—London's most exclusive, and exclusively male, gaming establishment—in the hope of tracking down the one man who possessed any information about the real cause of her godfather's death. Her attempts to look inconspicuous while she waited for that man had cost her a small fortune at the dice tables. And now, unless she misunderstood the tone of his comment, the individual next to her was threatening to undo all her efforts and turn her in as an impostor.

Sophie raised the dice cup to her lips, appeared to whisper a good-luck prayer to the ivory cubes, and let them fly across the table. Without waiting for the dice master to announce that she had lost, she tossed a silver coin onto the table, turned to the man who had addressed her, made a short bow, and spoke in her best Spanish accent. "Don Alfonso del Forest al Carmen, gentleman of

Seville, thanks you for your interest in his mustachios, *señor*, and begs you not to trouble yourself about them further."

The man acknowledged her bow with a tilt of his head. "Very nicely done," he said, smiling slightly. "Pretending to whisper to the dice so you could fix your mustache, I mean. The accent, however, is atrocious." As he spoke, the man carelessly threw the dice across the table, gathered his winnings, and motioned her to follow him into a less populated corner of the chamber.

Sophie was furious. Not only was she not in the habit of following men around, but she had practiced her accent for hours and thought it quite good. When they arrived at their corner, she pulled herself up to her full height—which, she noticed with surprise and then annoyance, did not even bring her eyes level with those of her adversary—and addressed him. "Don Alfonso del Carmen al Forest—"

"—al Forest del Carmen," the man corrected helpfully.

"—will not stand here and listen to your insults, *señor*." Sophie bent her head back and glared at the man ferociously.

The man met her glare with calm silver-blue eyes. He studied her for a moment before he spoke, and when he did his voice was low, calm, and slightly menacing. "Perhaps Don Alfonso will listen to a message from his friend Richard Tottle?"

She was good, he thought as he watched her quickly suppress her surprise. He would have to ask her whether it was Cordova or Von Krummen who had trained her as soon as he had her well locked away.

Sophie's heart had begun to pound. This was exactly what she had been waiting for. She was so excited she almost forgot that she was furious, or that she was supposed to have an accent. "A message from Richard Tottle? What is it?"

Damn good, the man reiterated, and damn dangerous. "He wants to meet with you again."

"Again?" she repeated with only a whisper of a Spanish accent.

"Yes. Again. Right now."

Her tone, even through the accent, was different when she asked, "What does *Señor* Tottle want to see me about?"

"I am just the errand boy, Don Alfonso," the man said, pronouncing the name with only the vaguest hint of irony. "Most likely whatever you discussed before."

"Then I am afraid I cannot accompany you. Our conversation, señor, is over." Sophie began to turn from him, but was stopped by the man's hand on her elbow.

"I am afraid it isn't. At least as long as you do not want me to announce that Don Alfonso is a woman." There was no menace now in the man's tone or his eyes, but the words held their own threat. As Sophie was acutely aware, under the newest laws impersonating a man was a treasonable offense, carrying the punishment of hanging. The man let his first suggestion sink in, then leaned closer to whisper, "Or that he plays with loaded dice."

For an instant, Sophie's composure ebbed completely away, and her eyes grew enormous. How the devil did he know about the dice? She had been sure that no one would suspect anything. After all, what kind of idiot would play with dice that had been altered to allow her to *lose* every time rather than win?

"I have to say, the dice were rather ingenious," the man commended her. "They are probably the only thing that kept you from being seen for a woman from the beginning, because no one pays close attention to those who lose, only those who win. Nobody would bother to suspect a loser."

Exactly. That had been Sophie's exact surmise. And it had worked splendidly during the two days she had been loitering around the Unicorn, waiting for Richard Tottle to appear, worked without a flaw until...

"Until you came along," she said aloud without realizing it. She looked up at her companion in the dim light, seeing him for the first time. He was undoubtedly the tallest man in the room, but despite his height he was not lanky. Instead, she noticed as she lowered her eyes from his face, his body was beautifully proportioned, from his broad shoulders, all the way down to the remarkable curve of his—

Satan's knockers, what was she thinking? Sophie Champion did not spend time ogling men, particularly not infuriating men who lied and used threats to coerce her to go with them. Nor men who criticized her Spanish accent. Nor men in general. Nor any man, ever. The paste Octavia had used to adhere the mustache had been making Sophie feel woozy for the past two days, but she had not previously realized that it was interfering with her thinking as well. It was, however, the only reasonable explanation for her unusual and unacceptable flightiness.

With that resolved, she addressed the man in as pronounced a Spanish accent as she could produce. "*Señor,* I have assessed my options—"

"Yes, I noticed you assessing," the man interrupted, laying extreme emphasis on the final word.

"—and have decided to accept your invitation to meet with Richard Tottle again."

The man only nodded his acknowledgment, and steered Sophie down the stairs to a wide mahogany door at their base. He watched with interest as his companion hesitated on the threshold, then put her fingers on the handle, took a deep breath, and passed through.

At first Sophie thought it was the effect of the deep breath, a sort of mustache-paste-induced hallucination, but then she saw it was real. Very real. And very dead.

Sophie had no eyes for the sumptuous decoration of the Unicorn's smoking chamber, the dark red brocade walls or the beautiful gold carpet that covered the floor. She did not notice the wall of tobacco-filled ebony boxes or the smoke that hung in the air. Only much later did she remember the sugared almond crushed into the carpet. At that first moment she saw simply the body of the man sprawled across one of the couches and the dark hole where gunpowder had scorched the satin fabric of his doublet.

"That is Richard Tottle," she said, and the man could not be sure whether it was a statement or a question.

"Yes. Or rather, was. He is dead." He observed her closely as she approached the corpse, then asked, "When you were here before, did Tottle give you anything?"

I did not see him before, Sophie almost said, but caught herself just in time, recollecting simultaneously her Spanish accent. "I cannot say, *señor*. I have never been in this room before." She was momentarily flustered, and became more so as the man said nothing and merely stood looking at her. Not only did Sophie Champion not ogle men, she did not permit them to ogle her. "What?" she demanded finally. "Don Alfonso al Foren del Carmest is not in the habit of being stared at."

"I am trying to decide which you are worse at. Lying. Or impersonating a Spaniard." He circled around her slowly, letting his eyes scour her, then faced her with their chests less than a hand's width apart. "I know you were here tonight. I know you met with Richard Tottle. I entered this room as soon as I saw you leave, and I found Tottle dead. The obvious assumption, Don Alfonso, is that you murdered him, but I am willing to forgo that if you can give me an adequate explanation. To begin, what did you take from Richard Tottle?"

Sophie was having a hard time marshalling her thoughts. It was becoming more and more clear that the mustache paste was dangerous stuff, because she could not remember either her fake name or her real one. All of which would have been unacceptable under any circumstances, but in the presence of the dangerous man in front of her, it was completely unthinkable.

He was playing with her, but she could play back. Let him ask all the questions he wanted, hundreds of them even. She was under no obligation to answer them, or at least, not helpfully. In fact, given his presumptuous behavior, it might almost be her duty to aggravate him. She had settled this definitively when he resumed his interrogation.

"Don Alfonso. I am waiting for your response."

Sophie cleared her throat, inhaled through her mouth—hoping to mitigate the effects of the paste—and said, "Suppose you are correct. Suppose I was in this room, tonight, with *Señor* Tottle."

The man examined her. "And? Did you take anything from him?"

"Nothing," Sophie replied in a fishily innocent tone.

"Where was he sitting?"

She gave a slight smile. "I cannot say."

"What did you and he discuss?"

"Nothing."

The man tilted his head back and regarded her through slitlike eyes. "Was he alive?"

"I cannot say."

"You will have to do better than 'nothing' and 'I cannot say' if you want to stay out of jail, Don Alfonso." As he spoke, the man moved away from her and toward the corpse.

She had clearly annoyed him, but Sophie did not feel any real joy at the victory. Her eyes kept returning to the body on the divan, the literal dead end of her investigation. Her godfather, Lord Grosgrain, had been on his way to Richard Tottle's the morning he died, carrying in his doublet a bill of credit for twelve hundred pounds and on his face more obvious signs of worry than Sophie could ever remember seeing. There had been something strange about the meeting, something that upset Lord Grosgrain terribly, something Sophie thought might be connected to his death, or at least might give a reason for it. Richard Tottle had been her only hope for information about what really lay behind her godfather's accident—which she was convinced was no accident at all—and with him gone she felt completely lost. Even more lost than she had felt that morning four days earlier when she saw her godfather's dead body being carried into the stable yard.

Lord Grosgrain had been both more and less than a simple godfather to her. He had been her whole family for more than ten years; but he had also been her responsibility. Not only had his death removed the only person she had ever entirely trusted, but she also deemed that it was, somehow, her fault. She should have stopped him, should have asked him more questions the morning of their last meeting, should have wondered more at his recent behavior. She felt at once desperately, achingly alone and horribly to blame.

She did not allow herself to wonder whether it was the echoing hollowness inside her or a rational quest for truth that drove her to question his death, because each time she wondered, she found herself biting her lip and swallowing back tears, as she was now. She was simply determined to find out what had caused his horse, a completely reliable and untemperamental animal, to lose its footing on London's best thoroughfare and hurl her godfather headlong to his death. Now, with Richard Tottle dead as well, she had nothing to go on.

Except the fact that the annoying man in front of her, whose muscles showed through his leggings each time he moved, had used threats of exposure to force her into the smoking room with the corpse, apparently to interrogate her.

But Sophie Champion would not allow herself to be threatened. "Now it is my turn to ask questions," she announced in a voice that challenged him to deny it. "Why did you insist on bringing me down here? What did you hope to learn? Who do you work for? Why do you keep asking what Richard Tottle gave me?"

It was one of the man's professional axioms that you could learn more from the questions that a subject asked than from those they answered, and with this slippery specimen that was doubly true. She was not in the least disturbed by his threats—they seemed simply to make her mad—nor did she seem frightened. Indeed, it was only when he had ceased speaking that she showed any weakness at all, and then it had vanished almost as soon as it had come. Clearly getting her to give up the piece of parchment that he suspected she had removed from Richard Tottle's dead body was going to require unusually devious scare tactics. He was about to test her, to find out whether she would be more susceptible to force or cunning, when one of her battery of questions cut into his thoughts and gave him the answer.

"I cannot say," the man replied smoothly to her interrogation.

Pompous caterpillar, Sophie thought to herself, her irritation intensifying as the suggestion of a smile flashed across his lips. Sophie had made a fortune by trusting her instincts, and they now told her that there was more to that almost-smile than the mere pleasure of throwing her unhelpful responses back at her, something far more ominous and sinister. They also told her that she should leave as quickly as possible.

But she could not go and let this arrogant beetle of a man think he had intimidated her. The prospect of appearing to be bullied overrode all of Sophie's instincts. "I am not afraid of you," she told the man, standing with her legs apart and her hand on the hilt of the dagger at her waist.

The smile suggested itself again. She was reacting beautifully. "It is not I you have to be afraid of, Don Alfonso. I told you, I am just the errand boy."

"Who do you work for?"

The man shrugged. "I cannot say."

Sophie's irritation turned to anger. She had neither the time nor the energy to stand around trading evasive answers with a tick. The game they were playing was pointless, her mustache was itchier than ever, her godfather was dead, and between her grief and her investigation she had not had a chance to either eat or sleep for three days. She was torn by conflicting desires, to challenge the man in front of her to a duel, or to go home and eat a hundred of her cook's candied-orange cakes dribbled with honey.

But then she saw that flicker of a smile, and the choice was clear. Puffing herself up in her best Don Alfonso style, she announced, "I am a very busy man, and I am unaccustomed to chatter with mere messengers. You have smeared the name of Don Alfonso Al Corest del Farmen with your accusation of murder, and I demand satisfaction. Either explain yourself, or prepare to fight."

The man shook his head. "Both engaging offers, particularly the challenge to duel, but I fear I shall have to decline. Frankly, Don Alfonso, you are much too wily for me. The way you flit from one identity to the other, one accent to the other...I dare not trust myself on the field against such an opponent. Indeed," the man went on, watching the play of anger over her face, "I rather find myself at a disadvantage here. I believe the time has come for me to take my leave. And while we are speaking of it, I should warn you that I am about to alert the authorities to Richard Tottle's plight."

"Is that a threat? Do you threaten to turn me in?"

The man shook his head. "On the contrary. I tell you so you may leave. I should not like you to confess anything to the authorities before you have confessed it to me."

"And if I decide to stay and cooperate with the constables?"

"Then I am afraid the next time I see you shall be on the gallows. Really, Don Alfonso, I should choose to talk to me rather than the authorities if I were in your shoes. Nice shoes, by the way," the man added casually. "Brooker?"

"I beg your pardon?"

"Are they by Brooker? Did he make them? The shoes?"

"Yes," she said through clenched teeth. Sophie was furious now. Brooker was the most famous and selective of the shoemakers in London, but that scarcely seemed relevant in the context of their conversation. Because the shoe-obsessed man had just effectively told her that she had two choices: to speak to the authorities and hang within a few days, or to do what he said, to put herself in his power and, she thought bitterly, hang within a few weeks. Then, in a flash, she saw an option he had not named. "I am afraid, *señor,* that Don Alfonso is leaving England for good tonight."

"Don Alfonso may be," the man said with a negligent shrug, "but I doubt that whoever bought those boots from Brooker is. All I need to do is ask him where the red velvet Spanish-style riding boots reside, and I will know where to find you."

He watched her eyes fill with angry astonishment at his ruse, but he was impressed by the steadiness of her voice. "If I were in your shoes, *señor,*" she pronounced carefully, "I would hardly trust in my responses. I can assure you that Brooker did not make these boots."

The smile flickered again. The man was really enjoying himself now. "I believe I mentioned that you are a wretched liar." He had moved toward the door as he spoke, and he turned to face her. "This has been a most interesting evening, Don Alfonso, and I can only console myself for the loss of your company with the knowledge that we shall meet again soon. I look forward to that pleasure." He bowed low and stepped across the threshold.

"Pleasure," Sophie repeated after him, pronouncing the word as if it might grow scales on her tongue. She could not remember having spent a less pleasant quarter of an hour in many, many years. If she had her way, she would never set eyes on that arrogant, horrible, shallow, annoying, conniving, tricky, handsome, dimpled, asset-rich, upsetting, lousy louse ever again.

As soon as she had the thought, she knew she was wrong. Indeed, she saw that she was reacting exactly as he had hoped she would. His plan had obviously been to annoy and antagonize her so efficiently that she would tell him anything and then let him wander off unhampered, with her fate in his hands. And she had fallen for it entirely, even giving up the name of her shoemaker. As she thought about this, thought about how docilely she had walked into his trap, her anger at him was transmuted into cold, hard rage against herself. She had behaved like an idiot. No, she *was* an idiot.

What made it worse was that she did not know into whose hands she had actually fallen. The man was just the messenger, he had said, and she needed to learn for whom he was working. His questions suggested that he believed she knew something or, rather, that she had *taken* something from Richard Tottle. Something important. Probably important enough to require that he report to his employer right away. Before she had even finished the thought, she was closing the door of the smoking chamber behind her and making for the servants' door of the Unicorn.

She had only been lingering in the shadows in front of the club for a minute when she saw the louse come out and turn right. Never having pursued a man on foot through London before, Sophie was too preoccupied with following unobtrusively to notice the old beggar woman camped inside the doorway of the building opposite the Unicorn, or the curtain in the club's second-floor window flutter slightly as she and the man went past. The thunderclouds that had blanketed the city earlier in the day were gone now, and a bright moon shone, making it easy for Sophie to keep the man in view but hard for her to stay in the shadows.

It became even harder after they had turned out of Hanging Sword Court and on to Fleet Street, because the entire road was thronged with people, most of them barely clad and very sociable women. Sophie was astonished by their careless comfort and confidence in their bodies, but astonishment turned into something much less clear when she saw the louse approach one of them, a blonde, whisper a few words to her, and then disappear through a doorway with his arm entwined in hers. Suddenly concerned that the meeting might be taking place within those doors, Sophie crossed the street and entered.

It looked like a tavern, but instead of food, each table was topped by a completely naked woman, extended to her full length here, sitting cross-legged there, all of them joking with and teasing the male patrons who surrounded them. As Sophie watched, a plump brunette brought her lips to the ear of a well-dressed young man, allowing her breasts to brush his chin as she whispered something to him. Her skills as an orator must have been quite overwhelming, for the man was so moved that he lifted her from the table and accompanied her up a ramshackle set of stairs, apparently wishing to pursue the subject in more private quarters. Sophie then watched as another woman stood atop a table, slowly rotating her hips in front of an increasingly large group of spectators, using a long string of pearls to do something that she indicated loudly was very pleasurable. Before the climax of the performance, however, Sophie saw the man from the Unicorn descending the stairs. When he reached the bottom, he turned and blew a kiss up toward a voluptuous blonde standing naked at the top and then made directly for the door.

Sophie pressed herself into the crowd around the pearl woman until he had passed, then fled back into the night, relieved to see her target continuing straight down Fleet Street. The experiences in the tavern had left Sophie addled, and it required all her concentration to keep her mind on the man she was following. She forced herself to study his movements, watching for a sign that he would veer left here, or a flicker that he would look over his shoulder, until she discovered to her horror that she had unwittingly amassed a catalog of the comparative differences between him BW—Before the Woman—and after (including walk: jauntier; whistling: louder; loathsomeness: greater).

She had just added, swaggering: increased, when he turned abruptly into a narrow passage and ducked through a door. Proceeding as silently as she could, she followed him through the door and found herself standing in a small paved court. Directly in front of her, there was another door, slightly ajar.

Sophie swallowed hard and hoped her racing heart did not sound as loud outside her body as it did inside. She crept across the court and pushed the door open with one hand, keeping her other on the hilt of her rapier. She waited, listening intently. Nothing.

When what felt like two years had passed in unbroken silence, she ducked under the low lintel and into a pastry kitchen. Remembering the food she had not eaten in days and the orange cakes she had been dreaming of, her stomach did an imitation of a sawmill. There was only one other door in the kitchen, and Sophie proceeded through it, stopping at intervals to listen and to give her stomach severe warnings about talking out of turn.

After weaving through two more kitchens, three pantries, and a labyrinth of twisty hallways, Sophie finally arrived in an immense entrance hall. The wood paneling glowed in the moonlight that streamed through the tall windows of the façade, filling the hall with an ethereal radiance and making the broad staircase at its center appear to float. From somewhere deep in the house came the ticking of a clock, and in its somber regularity Sophie could have sworn she heard the words "Take heed. Go back. Take heed."

If she had not heard the voices above her at the same time, Sophie might have taken the clock's very good advice. Instead, she ascended the staircase and alighted in front of an inlaid door. It was not entirely closed, and from within she could hear faint sounds of conversation.

One of the voices she recognized instantly as belonging to her quarry. The other, a sort of angry rasp, was new to her, and its words created a cold knot in her stomach.

"Get the girl," it growled harshly. "I want the girl."

"I tried," the familiar voice replied. "I did all I could."

She heard the other voice mimic comically, "I tried. I did all I could," then snort and command again, "Get the girl."

The familiar voice sounded annoyed. "There is nothing we can do tonight. We will just have to wait."

It was the perfect time, Sophie decided. She would catch them off guard, take them by surprise. Drawing an enormous breath, she pushed open the door—

And froze in her tracks.

"Ah, Don Alfonso. We have been expecting you," the familiar voice told her while the other cackled in delight.

Horrified, Sophie looked from the smiling face of the man to the piercing gaze of his companion, and understood for the first time what she should have known hours earlier.

She had been playing a game. Her opponent was cunning and ruthless. The stake was her life.

And there was no end to her losing streak in sight.

Chapter Two

"—**a**n arrogant, blustering, contemptible, disgusting slug," Sophie concluded triumphantly, leaning forward in her seat as if to hurl the last word across the desk at the man. "Or rather, slugs. You and your vulture."

"It is a raven," the man answered smoothly. "And I have to admit, I am disappointed. 'Slug'? Surely you could do better. What about 'clever devil'?"

The raven, on its perch at the man's shoulder, repeated "clever devil, clever devil," in its rasping voice, and executed a jig.

Sophie sneered at the bird, then at its owner. "I think you overrate yourself. Dragging women against their will to your house for your entertainment hardly counts as clever."

The man regarded her paternally. "Let us review. *You* followed me of your own volition. *You* broke into my house at your own initiative. And so far, you have not been very entertaining at all."

That was not strictly true. Indeed, he had to admit that the two hours he had just passed with her had been more diverting than any in his recent memory. Because Crispin Foscari had been having a very bad week. He had been forcibly stripped of his status as the Phoenix, accused of treason, and for all intents and purposes, dismissed from the Queen's service. He had been given only fourteen days to find out who was angling for his destruction and stop them. He had already spent six days investigating, with no appreciable results. And his best source of information had been shot dead in the smoking room at the Unicorn. But despite all that, he now found that he was enjoying himself immensely.

He could not decide which was more entertaining: watching the woman in front of him or antagonizing her. Fortunately, he could do both at the same time.

"You know, you still have not really fixed your mustache," he pointed out sweetly.

"Not fixed your mustache," the raven intoned, less sweetly.

In her outrage at being tricked, Sophie had forgotten that she was still wearing the mustache, but this double reminder made it suddenly ten times itchier than it had been earlier. "And you," she replied, her voice tight with the struggle to resist the urge to scratch her upper lip, "still have not explained what you want with me. Or, for that matter, even who you are."

"Why, this is my house," the man answered simply, as if that settled everything. Then, seeing that the woman looked uncomprehending, he added, "Sandal Hall." When she continued to regard him blankly, he quickly explained, "I am Crispin Foscari. The Earl of Sandal."

Satan's knockers, he was a pompous termite. "The Earl of Sandal? I have never heard of the Earl of Sandal." She was focusing hard on keeping her voice level, but not so hard that she missed the look of astonishment on the man's face. She decided to push him farther. "How do I know you are not making the title up? That you are not one of those rakes who invent a noble-sounding name in order to con others out of their money or property?"

"Like Don Alfonso del Forest al Carmen del Farmen al Carest?" Crispin suggested in a voice slightly tighter than usual.

"Exactly." Sophie pretended to cough then, in a desperate effort to keep from bursting into laughter. It was the first time in hours that she held the upper hand, and she found it so pleasant that the mustache ceased to bother her at all. "How can I even be sure this is your house? Given the way you have behaved tonight, with unscrupulous disregard for the truth, I would not be shocked to learn that you had purloined it."

Sophie did not know it, but she had done something quite incredible: she had surprised him. Indeed, as one of Queen Elizabeth's most secret operatives, surprise was something Crispin could ill afford if he valued his life. He was not a vain or haughty man, but he had assumed that his name and title would be well known to her. After all, it was well known to everyone. It had been years since he had been able to go anywhere incognito, to remain unrecognized or unacknowledged in any locale from a seedy quayside tavern to the papal court unless he was well disguised. And yet here was this woman, challenging not only his right to his house and title, but the very existence of the title itself.

As she watched his bemusement, Sophie was thinking that her bluff seemed to be working admirably. It alone provided an antidote to the stinging mortification of her failure to recognize him at the Unicorn. For she would have had to be dead or locked deep inside Bedlam not to have heard of the Earl of Sandal, given the frequency with which his rakish exploits had been detailed in printed broadsides and ballads—complete with collectible engraved portraits—during the two and a half years of his exile. According to these newssheets, where he was retitled the Earl of Scandal, there was no challenge to which this peer of the realm would not rise, no woman he could not possess, no bedroom door that would not fly open at the merest hint of his smile, nothing he would not casually wager for the bare thrill of it. A recent number related how he had bid an outrageous sum for a stable of racehorses one morning, only to hazard them at cards that night against a worthless necklace to which his mistress had taken a fancy. (As usual, he won the necklace, but gave up the horses to the loser anyway in what was described as a wildly gallant gesture.) Other editions touted his prowess with arms by pointing out that only one of Europe's leading swordsmen could seduce so many married women and live to tell about it. It was just such behavior, in particular a duel over one of the Queen's ladies-in-waiting, that had gotten him exiled two and a half years earlier, and all London was alive with speculation about his current reinstatement in Her Majesty's good graces.

Everyone knew that as one of the Arboretti, the six co-owners of the most successful shipping company in Europe, the Earl of Scandal had to be worth at least as much as Queen Elizabeth herself. This information, coupled with the general opinion that the earl had renounced his Scandalous ways and returned to England to be married, caused deep stirrings in the hearts of every English mama with an unbetrothed daughter between the ages of two and forty. Indeed, Sophie had herself invested in silk and lace that week on the Royal Exchange, correctly assuming that such rumors would prompt a flurry of dress orders from the scheming mamas hoping to catch the Sandal eye by outfitting their daughters in yards of the latest continental fashions. But she was certainly not going to tell *Señor* Scandal about the one thousand pounds in profit she had reaped from those investments, any more than she was going to admit that he was better looking than the engravings had led her to believe. And also smarter.

In fact, this was the most annoying part of all. What was goading Sophie so painfully was that she had been tricked—twice—by, of all men, the one she had always regarded as a brainless, pleasure-obsessed tick. Who, she realized with further annoyance, was again addressing her.

"So you see, Don Alfonso," Crispin was saying, "it really does not matter whether you believe in my identity, because the constables certainly will, and will have no qualms about arresting you for the murder of Richard Tottle on my order." He smiled that annoying smile. "Now, you asked why you were here. I need some information, and it seems likely that you have it."

Sophie tried to keep her eyes off his smile, and especially his long dimples. "I have already answered all your questions," she told him haughtily. Then she had an inspiration. "In fact, I will not say another word to you."

"How gracious. Your wishes tally with mine exactly. I have always been partial to quiet women." He almost laughed when he saw her struggling to pack all her emotion into the glare she leveled at him. "Besides, what I am looking for is not the answer to a question, but rather an object. An object removed from the murdered man. I suspect you have it somewhere on your person, so you will oblige me by removing your clothes."

Sophie's glare turned to a disbelieving stare.

"That is right. I am asking you to strip," Crispin replied firmly to her unspoken question.

The raven, who had been quietly cleaning itself, suddenly chimed in "Strip! Strip, strip, strip!" and then resumed its preening as if nothing had happened.

Sophie treated it to a glance that would have killed a lesser bird, then broke her vow of silence. "Why should I comply with your wishes?"

"Because otherwise I shall turn you and this"—Crispin held an object up for her to see—"over to the constable."

Before realizing what she was saying, Sophie blurted, "Where did you get my pistol?"

"Where you left it."

Sophie was horrified. "You stole it from my house?" Only then, when the words were out, did she remember the silver plaque on the hilt of the weapon. The pistol had been presented to her by the gunsmith, a gift of gratitude for dowering his bride, and he had recorded his appreciation on the plaque.

"'For Sophie Champion. In Everlasting Thanks,'" Crispin read aloud. "In the future, Miss Champion, you might remove all identifiable markings from your murder weapon. It takes all the fun out of trying to learn your name."

"Murder weapon?" Sophie repeated breathlessly. "Richard Tottle was shot with my pistol?"

Crispin nodded, noting how convincing her surprise sounded. "I found it right next to the body, and it was still hot from the explosion. But you know all that. Now, Miss Champion, if you will please remove—"

Sophie interrupted him. "Why, if I were the murderer, would I leave my pistol lying next to the body?"

"Why indeed?"

"Clearly this proves that I did not kill Richard Tottle." Sophie leaned forward in her chair. "Surely even you can see that is obvious."

Crispin leaned toward her across the desk, as if speaking confidentially. "I am not familiar with that particular use of the words 'clearly,' 'proves,' and 'obvious.' I would say the evidence points in the opposite direction. The *obvious* assumption is that the owner of the murder weapon is the murderer. Your gun was the murder weapon. You are its owner. And constables are notoriously obvious minded. So, while I might agree with your more figurative take on the situation, I am afraid they will see the pistol with your name on it as clear and obvious proof that you *are* the murderer."

Sophie ignored his sarcasm, leaping instead on the hint they contained. "If you agree with me, that means you do not think I committed the murder."

"I have reservations." The room fell silent except for an occasional grunt from the raven, and Crispin's words hung between them. After a long moment, he continued, moving closer to his objective. "There is a way you can prove it to me. Or at least, make me relatively certain. You see, if you do not have the object I am looking for, I shall be forced to conclude that you did not murder Tottle, or at least not alone. I could hardly turn in a woman I knew to be innocent, even one as bothersome as you are."

"I told you. I did not take anything from Richard Tottle, dead or alive."

Crispin caught her eyes with his own and stared at her steadily. "Prove it."

Sophie's eyes continued to meet his, but narrowed. "I did not think the famous Earl of Sandal would have to stoop to such tricks to get a woman out of her clothes."

"I did not think you had heard of the Earl of Sandal."

Sophie was too angry now to be upset by her gaffe. Her only interest was in provoking him, as he had provoked her. She strove to keep her voice neutral as she said, "I am not at all impressed by your means of seduction."

"I assure you, I had no such intention. I would rather seduce a porcupine than you, Miss Champion. Now, are you going to remove your clothes, or must I do it for you?"

Sophie leaned across the desk again. "I would rather have a dozen of Her Majesty's lewdest sailors touch me than you, Lord Sandal."

"I don't doubt it," Crispin replied, unconcerned. "Even animals are most attracted to their own kind. But your predilection does make me wonder why you are so afraid of me."

"Afraid of you?" Sophie repeated, appalled.

"Clearly. If you are innocent, as you claim, and do not have what I am looking for, your refusal to remove your clothes obviously proves that you are afraid of me."

"I am not familiar with your use of the words 'clearly,' 'obviously,' and 'proves,'" Sophie mimicked.

Crispin pretended not to hear. "Be honest, Miss Champion. Is it that you don't think you can trust yourself around me? My charms are famously hard to resist."

He knew he had won then, even though it took another few moments for his victory to manifest itself. The striptease that followed was the least erotic striptease Crispin had ever witnessed, possibly the least erotic striptease ever, probably the only one conducted to the snores of a sleeping raven.

And yet it nearly undid him.

Sophie rose from her chair and, her eyes never leaving his, proceeded to remove her red velvet doublet. Her boots came next, then her leggings, until finally she was standing in only her hat and a thin linen shirt that ended just below her bottom. Reaching over her head, she deftly removed three pins and the hat, liberating a riot of long, ruby-colored waves that reached to her stomach. Finally, she loosened the ties at her neck and cuffs and pulled the shirt over her head. Her gaze left Crispin's as the fabric passed across her face, and he had his expression back under control by the time she was done, so she never saw what passed through his eyes that first moment she stood before him completely naked.

During his service for Queen Elizabeth, Crispin had learned that impulses, like emotions, made people vulnerable, which was only a half-step from making them dead. Containing his emotions was easy, and he had trained himself rigorously to overmaster the impulses of his body as well. He could hold his breath underwater for ten minutes, slow his heartbeat to appear dead, and stand stock-still for twelve hours. Compared to these feats, curtailing amorous urges was child's play, and he had become so good at it that he had begun to wonder if he had not eradicated them entirely. He had completely lost interest in seducing women, finding the thrill and adventure of his secret commissions far more exciting than any-thing he experienced between the arms of even the most talented courtesans.

Until now. Now it all came rushing back in a torrent that threatened to overwhelm him, to burst all his carefully crafted restraints, unseat all his rigorously upheld rules.

Sophie stood before him, conscious only of his intense scrutiny. "Are you satisfied?"

"No," Crispin replied, but he was answering a different question than the one she had asked. When he realized what he had done, he cleared his throat and elaborated. "I want to look through your clothes as well."

It was the mustache that saved him. Only the mustache kept Crispin from forgetting what he was doing there, what his purpose was, what, for that matter, his name was. And even the mustache posed problems, particularly the way it drew the eye to her wide, sensual lips. Would they feel like silk brushing against his neck, or like velvet? Crispin found himself wondering and immediately instructed himself to stop. He had much more important matters to consider, he reminded himself, than whether the mark over her lip was a birthmark or a shadow, and how the gentle curve of her waist would look from the back, and whether her head would reach to just under his nose so that he could rest his cheek on the crown of her hair, and what it would feel like to cup her full breasts in his hands, or have her legs twined around his waist or...

Crispin rose so abruptly from his chair that it fell backward, startling both Sophie and the sleeping raven, who immediately began shrieking, "Get the girl!" while hopping on one leg. It took Sophie a moment to figure out what was happening, and by that time Crispin had crossed the room and disappeared through a set of double doors.

Blazing with indignation, Sophie began to follow him, then stopped on the threshold. She had never felt so humiliated and foolish in her life. It was the first time she had stood like that, completely naked, in front of a man, and he had found it so distasteful to look at her that he had stormed out of the room. That was bad, but what was worse was how vulnerable it made her feel. Sophie Champion did not care what anyone thought of her, even in clothes, she reminded herself, and she certainly did not care for the opinion of an irksome tick like the Earl of Scandal. It must be the unsettling effects of the damned mustache paste again, she reasoned, and immediately felt better.

Buoyed, she addressed him through the open doors. "If you are trying to lure me to your bed, it will not work."

Crispin emerged from the room carrying a red-and-gold silk robe. "I assure you nothing was farther from my mind," he lied. She noticed that he did not look at her at all but kept his gaze firmly on something just past her right ear as he held the robe toward her and commanded, "Put this on."

Sophie hastily wrapped herself in the silk sheath. It was not until she was completely covered that Crispin returned his gaze to her, hoping that with her body not so palpably before his eyes, he might be able to control the direction of his thoughts. Such control was more important now than ever, since Tottle's demise.

Richard Tottle had long been a source of information about the goings-on behind the doors of the Palace, both official and unofficial. He had been printing, "By Order of The Queen," all official laws, speeches, and proclamations since he had become a master printer eight years earlier. He was so well-informed, in fact, that the Queen herself consulted him to find out what was stirring in her own court, and it was therefore to Richard Tottle that Crispin had gone to learn who was trying to turn Her Majesty against the Phoenix. From Tottle, Crispin was supposed to have gotten an encrypted list of those close to Queen Elizabeth who might be behind the destruction of the Phoenix. He had found half a piece of parchment containing such a list clutched in the dead man's fingers, but the other half was gone, crudely torn away as if during a struggle. Recovered by the wrong person—one who could decode it—the lost half of the list would be a clear signal that someone was looking into the Phoenix's detractors. A clear signal that Crispin, whose investigation had to be completely clandestine, could ill afford.

If this devilish Sophie Champion woman did not have the piece of parchment, as it appeared she did not, then it was in somebody else's hands, and he had better take steps to invalidate it as quickly—and secretly—as possible. Which promised to be difficult if she was roving around unsupervised, undertaking an inquiry, arousing people's suspicions before he had even talked to them, as seemed likely given the interest she had already evinced by following him home. Running through these thoughts, Crispin picked up first her red doublet, then her leggings, then her hat, halfheartedly searching each for secret compartments and double linings. He was about to return to his seat, vanquished, when he saw Sophie glance anxiously at her right boot.

Despite this clue, he almost missed it. He slid his finger around the inside of the shoe, tugged at the laces that looped up the front, and had just decided that she was trying to trick him, when he felt the heel give way. It pivoted, and from inside it he lifted a gold medallion and a piece of paper. He set aside the medallion, apparently an image of the goddess Diana, and unfolded the paper.

There were only three words on it, but their juxtaposition made his stomach tighten. The first two, which had a thick, black line through them, were "Richard Tottle." The next was "Phoenix."

"Is this your marketing list of murder victims?" he asked coolly, waving the paper in front of her face.

"Certainly," Sophie replied, equally coolly. "There are more names in the other shoe." When she saw him glance in the direction of the other boot, actually hesitating about whether to try it or not, she laughed aloud.

The laugh brought the raven half out of its renewed nap, just enough for it to chant, "Get the girl," once, and resume snoring.

Crispin returned his attention to her. "I know who Richard Tottle is—"

"—was," Sophie corrected helpfully.

"Was." Crispin bowed his thanks. "But who is the Phoenix?"

"A mythical bird." Sophie's tone was pedantic. "From antiquity. Each time it is killed, it rises anew from its own ashes and therefore would be a very unsatisfying murder victim."

"Thank you for the lesson in classical mythology. Why is it on your list? Do you presume to travel through time?"

"Why should that matter to you?" Sophie eyed him keenly, then wished she had not. After she had reviewed all the reasons that she hated him that could not be erased by his long dimples, she spoke again. "Lord Sandal, I have done everything you asked. I have answered your ridiculous questions. I have stripped off my clothes. I have waited patiently while you ruined my boots. But now I must go. I am hungry and thirsty and I have not slept in three nights. Or rather, four. And, unlike you, I am interested in finding out who murdered Richard Tottle." She had not realized that this was the case until she spoke the words, but she immediately saw it was true.

Before, Richard Tottle's death had been an ill-timed inconvenience, one that put a stop to her investigations into Lord Grosgrain's accident. Since Lord Grosgrain had been killed on his way to his strange meeting with Richard Tottle, Sophie had thought it possible that the two—the meeting and her godfather's death—were connected. And now that she knew that someone had left her pistol alongside Richard Tottle's body, now that it was clear that someone was trying to implicate her in his death, possibility turned to probability. What was more, this was strong evidence that Lord Grosgrain had been murdered. For if Lord Grosgrain had really died in an accident, her inquiries would not have excited anyone to action and certainly would not have threatened anyone so much that they tried to entangle her in a crime. Whoever killed Richard Tottle, she suspected, had killed Lord Grosgrain as well.

The last time she had seen Lord Grosgrain, when she had given him the bill of credit made out to Richard Tottle for twelve hundred pounds, he had said he would be able to repay her soon and then added, in a voice with a tinge of fear, "unless the phoenix gets me first." He often used phrases like that, referring to the "black dragon" or the "red lion" or the "green bear," all of which Sophie knew were alchemical terms for the potions he was always concocting in his unflagging attempts to produce gold from lesser metals. At first she had assumed the phoenix was merely a potion she had never heard of, but after Lord Grosgrain's accident she had thought better of it. She and Octavia and Emme had spent a day and a night skimming through his books and papers, reading everything that was not in his strange personal code, but found no mention of a chemical called the phoenix. It was then that she realized the 'phoenix' must be a person. Probably a person with information about her godfather's death. In her initial message to Richard Tottle, which went unanswered and forced her to track him down at the Unicorn, she had asked both what Lord Grosgrain was supposed to be paying him for and who the Phoenix was.

Crispin studied her as she sat wrapped in these thoughts, lost in thoughts of his own. The paper in her boot was a clear sign that she knew something, something he needed to know, something he was determined to find out. It was no use asking her questions, he saw, and simultaneously saw how he could get answers without them. He liked his plan so well that he almost had difficulty repressing a smile. Almost.

Crispin's tone was lazy as he broke the silence of the room. "Why are you so interested in uncovering Richard Tottle's murderer? I do not recall him mentioning you. Was he a friend of yours?"

Sophie countered with a question of her own. "Was he a friend of yours? What were you doing in the smoking room anyw—" She stopped speaking abruptly and her eyes grew large.

"You only just thought of it?" Crispin chided her. "It only just occurred to you that I might have murdered him?"

"But why did you use my pistol?" Sophie blurted. "Or rather how did you use my pistol? And why, if you wanted to frame me, did you take it away? And what were you looking for?" The demands toppled out, one after another.

"All marvelous questions," Crispin lauded. "Unfortunately, I'm not really in the mood to answer them. Oh, perhaps one: I took the pistol to use as leverage against you. So I could induce you to answer my questions."

"Leverage," Sophie repeated under her breath, and then leveled her eyes at him. "It won't work. I've answered all the questions I plan to. Now I am going home." Sophie rose, and as she did so the silk robe fell open at the neck, revealing the swell of her breasts.

Crispin shook his head slowly from side to side and concentrated on her mustache. "I doubt you could solve the murder of Richard Tottle without my assistance."

Sophie, suddenly conscious of the feeling of his eyes on her body and annoyed with herself for this consciousness, sat back down clutching the robe closed. "I need nothing that you have to offer. As it seems to me, your entire method consists in luring women to your home so you can torment them. If that is the best you can do to find the murderer..." She let her voice trail off with disdain.

"And just how would you set about it?"

"I might try searching Richard Tottle's quarters. Perhaps he left whatever you were looking for there." She leaned forward, and the robe slid open again. "If you were even looking for something and did not manufacture that merely as an excuse to order me out of my clothes."

"If that is the best you can do to find the murderer..." Crispin met her disdain and raised it.

It did the trick. "The worst that I could do, Lord Sandal, is undoubtedly superior to your best," Sophie growled. "From what I have read of your adventures, you are better equipped for pursuing coquettes than murderers."

If Sophie had known him longer, she would have known that the glittering of Crispin's eyes boded ill for her. They were the eyes of a predatory animal, ready to pounce and sure of a victory. "Even if that were true," he purred at her, "having observed the feeble quality of your mind, I bet that I am still a thousand times better equipped to find the murderer than you are."

Her reaction was instantaneous and satisfying. Sophie barely recognized her voice through her anger as she said, "Would you care to wager on that?"

Crispin leaned back in his chair to gloat. "Wager on the fact that I can find the murderer before you can? Certainly."

"Very well. What about a thousand pounds? One for each time you are better equipped than I am to find him."

Crispin appeared to think for a moment, then shook his head. His eyes were still shining. "I would not like it to be said that I bankrupted a lady." Sophie was about to assure him that her coffers were more than adequate to the challenge, but he went on. "Besides, monetary wagers lack excitement. Why bother to strive for something you already have? Instead of stating now what we are willing to *lose,* I propose that we each write down what we want to win. Something marvelous, our secret, deepest desire. The wagers will be kept locked away, so neither of us knows the stakes, until the murderer is caught. Then the loser must provide whatever the winner asked for." He saw her hesitating, then added, "I do this only out of courtesy to you, so you will not be bored. I suspect that losing is much more interesting when you do not know what you will be expected to give up. Of course, since, unlike you, I never lose, I can only guess."

"In the interest of making your first time as thrilling as possible, I accept the terms of your wager." Sophie took the quill and the piece of paper he slid across the desk to her, thought for a moment about what she might possibly want from him, let the quill hang in the air, thought again, and then, with a sly smile on her face, carefully wrote a dozen words. When she had folded her paper in quarters and he had done the same with his, she asked, "Who will hold on to these?"

Apparently by magic, a slender man somewhere between the ages of thirty and eighty materialized in their midst. "Good evening, my lord," the man said, as if there were nothing the least bit unusual about his master sitting in the library in the middle of the night with a barely clad woman wearing a mustache. "I took the liberty of bringing these," he continued, lifting two silver goblets and a glass carafe of glimmering red wine from the tray he carried. "Would you like me to lock those papers in the safe?"

Crispin spoke not to him, but to Sophie. "This is my steward, Thurston. I propose we entrust the bets to him."

Those who knew Thurston had long since ceased to be astonished by his ability to appear without ever making a noise and to anticipate every command before it could be spoken, but Sophie, new to his talents, was staring at him as if he were some sort of apparition. She nodded mutely and kept her eyes on him until he had, noiselessly, disappeared through the door.

When she turned them back to the plaguesome man behind the desk, she saw that he was extending one of the goblets toward her. "Let us drink to our wager."

Sophie raised her vessel to him, then drank the contents down in three swallows.

That was a mistake.

Crispin leapt from his seat but was still not quite fast enough to keep Sophie's head from grazing the corner of his desk before she lost consciousness.

Chapter Three

I have always been a connoisseur of Beauty. From when I was a child, I understood that Beauty was the true and only good. Who can deny the evidence of their eyes when every day the old, the poor, the ugly, are removed from our world by death, in order to make it better and more perfect for the young, the rich—in a word, the beautiful? Everything I have done, and everything I will do, is for the sake of Beauty alone. She sanctifies my actions, ~~washes the blood from my hands,~~ and praises me for my ~~ruthlessness and~~ loyalty.

I knew I had been elected when I was very young. ~~I was a striking child~~ I was a very striking child, and from the earliest age, I harbored a repugnance for the ugliness of my family's poverty that even my mother deemed unnatural. She, ~~curse~~ bless her memory, had married for love beneath her station and had thus condemned me to a life of unadulterated horror, of watching others ride the fine horses I deserved to ride, wear the rich velvets and furs that I deserved to wear, wield the power I deserved to wield.

I understood then that, of all things, poverty is the enemy of Beauty. It destroys her, covers her in its filth, drags her down so that

The servant heard his master's pen drop with annoyance as he entered the room and knew he would receive a stern lecture for this interruption, but he had no choice. "A man to see you, Your

Excellence," he announced, then rushed to explain, "I would not have broken in on your writing like this, but he says he has important information for you. He told me to show you this."

He extended a gold signet ring for his master's perusal. He watched as his master ran a finger over the single feather embossed into the otherwise smooth surface of the ring, then finally said, "Send him in, Kit. The usual precautions."

Kit returned leading a tall, blindfolded man with his hands bound behind his back. His clothes were slightly too small for him but well made, and he had a livid scar across his forehead. Kit pushed him into a chair near the desk, then stepped back two paces.

The blindfolded man turned his head from side to side as if trying to scent out the presence of the person he had come to see. He jumped slightly as a voice quite close to his ear whispered, "What do you have for me?" It was a voice the blindfolded man did not recognize, and he frowned, trying to decide if it came from a young person or an old one, a man or a woman.

"I sent my calling card," he answered finally.

"Your calling card." The whisper was tinged with amusement. "Where did you get it?"

"That does not matter. What matters is that I got it. I know how to find him. I can get you the Phoenix."

"What makes you think I want the Phoenix?"

The blindfolded man squirmed against the restraints on his hand. "I beg your pardon for my mistake. Give me back the ring and I will go." He rose to stand, but a powerful hand on his shoulder stopped him and shoved him back into the chair.

The man shifted uncomfortably as the whispering resumed, right in his ear. "You are overhasty. I did not say that I did not want the Phoenix. Do you mean to tell me that you know who he is?"

"I know how to find him," the man replied, not answering the question. "I know how he thinks. He has already fallen out of favor with Her Majesty, so he does not have the power he is accustomed to. Weakened, he is easy prey. And I can get him for you."

A hand touched the man's shoulder, pulling him forward. He had the feeling of eyes boring into him, studying him, his scar, his clothes. Then he felt warm breath on his neck. "I believe you can get the Phoenix." The hand on his shoulder relaxed somewhat. "And I believe we shall get along very well together. Contact me when you have destroyed him. And do not be slow about it. The time is ripe for our undertaking now." The hand left his shoulder completely. "You are dismissed."

The blindfolded man did not move. "We have not yet discussed my compensation," he said slowly.

"You will get your share when our undertaking is successful."

"I want one third of the profits."

"What?" The pitch of the whisper rose precipitously. "One third? Are you mad?"

The man leaned forward, this time of his own accord, and lowered his voice. "Do you want the Phoenix or not?"

There was silence, during which the man heard only his adversary's short, angry breathing, and then, in a staccato whisper, "One quarter of the profits."

"One quarter," the man confirmed, adding, almost offhandedly, "And the girl."

"What girl?"

"Sophie Champion. The girl you are trying to frame."

A new tone crept into the whisper. "Why? Why do you want her?"

"Why do you want the Phoenix?" the man challenged.

"That is none of your business."

The blindfolded man nodded. "Precisely."

Another long moment passed in silence. "Very well, you shall have Sophie Champion. And one fifth of the profits."

The man turned his face toward his invisible companion. "You said one quarter."

"I changed my mind. I have no tolerance for weaknesses of the flesh."

"You cheating bastard," the blindfolded man said through clenched teeth.

"No names, please. A simple yes or no. Do you accept? The girl and one fifth of the profits?"

"Yes." The man's jaw was still tight. "Yes, I accept."

"Good decision. "For one fifth of the profits, I shall have the Phoenix—"

"And I," the blindfolded man interrupted, "shall have Sophie Champion." A slow smile spread across his face as he spoke. He was still wearing it when he left the workshop a quarter of an hour later, a strange, inscrutable smile.

A smile, the old beggar woman slouched in a doorway outside Sandal Hall thought to herself, that she never wanted to see again. A smile that chilled her blood and haunted her dreams for days to come.

Chapter Four

"Where have you been?" the stocky deputy demanded as his boss strode through the door. "I have had the boys looking all over London for you since daybreak."

"'My lord,'" Lawrence Pickering suggested to his second-in-command.

"My lord," the deputy repeated with a clumsy bow. "I have had the boys looking all over London for you since daybreak, my lord."

Lawrence Pickering was not, in fact, a peer of the realm, nor even distantly related to a gentleman by birth. But he was as rich as four earls put together and had far more influence over Alsatia—the quarter of London many referred to as "Little Eden" because of the endless proliferation of earthly pleasures available there—than most landed gentry had over their larders. People who dared to flout his control, or his will, were said to disappear, sometimes forever, more often for as long as it took for their bodies to wash up on the lower shoals of the Thames. He had originally been dubbed Lord Pickering by his enemies in an attempt to mock his ambition to rule London's underworld, but as that ambition was realized, the title changed from taunt to truism, and he was now addressed that way by his loyal followers—and all others who valued their necks.

The deputy, whose neck was a short, thick, ugly one but none the less valuable to him for that, cringed under his master's look of displeasure.

"Surely my men have better things to do than chase me around," Lawrence said, handing his cape to the footman who had followed him in. "And surely I am allowed to run private errands."

"Of course, my lord. It is just that something has happened and I thought you should know and I needed advice and..." He wilted under Lawrence's unwavering displeasure and finally croaked out, "Your Excellency."

"Let us not get above ourselves. 'My lord' will do," Lawrence instructed, turning from his deputy so the man would not see the smile on his face. Grimley was a very good man, loyal and trustworthy to a fault, and he had somehow contrived to terrify every one of Lawrence's fiercest henchmen, so that they did not dare oppose his orders. Lawrence had never asked what his deputy did to achieve this, but he was glad to capitalize on it, entrusting to Grimley the management of his army of informers and thugs. But the main reason Lawrence kept Grimley around was because of the pleasure he derived from making him crumple. It was really too easy, and he knew it was unkind, but there was something about cowing the little toadlike man that he found distinctly entertaining, especially on a lousy day like the one he was having.

Which seemed, if Grimley's words were anything to go by, about to get lousier. Lawrence seated himself behind his wide desk, caressed its smooth mahogany top as if it were a beautiful woman, and brought his eyes once more to those of his deputy. "What exactly happened?"

"It's Richard Tottle, my lord. Dead, my lord. In the smoking chamber at the Unicorn."

The deputy took a step away from the desk when he saw his boss's jaw tighten. "Do we know who did it?" Lawrence asked.

"No."

Lawrence cursed under his breath. It was damn inconvenient, having one of his informers knocked off, and at his most profitable club. The last thing they needed were constables and the Queen's guard roaming around the Unicorn, poking their noses into the business and requiring a share of the profits in exchange for their silence. "Who else knows about this?" he asked finally.

"No one," Grimley replied. "Yet. A boy arrived shortly after midnight with this anonymous note." Grimley held the crumpled paper out to Lawrence.

"'*Look in the smoking room of the Unicorn,*'" he read aloud, then handed it back to the deputy. "Where did the boy get it from?"

"He said one of the Fleet Street ladies handed it to him, but he had difficulty recalling which one, even with persuasion."

Lawrence glowered at him. "You did not hurt him, did you?"

"No," Grimley replied sheepishly. "Not much."

"What have I told you about hurting young boys? It achieves nothing, and it only adds to our list of enemies. Perhaps you never had to live by your wits on the street, but—" Lawrence broke off. "Never mind. Find the boy, give him ten pounds, and offer him a job. A good job. I guarantee that will restore his memory."

Grimley moved grimly to the door, summoned a footman, gave a few, brisk instructions, and returned to face his master.

"What has become of the body?" Lawrence asked when the door was closed.

Grimley looked nervous again. "We left it there, my lord. I did not know where you wanted it, but no one will go to the club before three bells, so it is safe. I did not want it to be discovered before I had your orders about Tottle's apartments."

Lawrence nodded and gave a resigned sigh. "We may as well make use of the body. Leave it on the doorstep of whoever owes us the most money, and let them draw their own conclusions. In the meantime—"

The deputy was nodding briskly. "I know. Is there anything in particular we want from Master Tottle's chambers, my lord, or should I just take it all?"

"You are, as ever, overhasty. It is your gravest flaw, Grimley. As I have told you before, it is not what you take from a room that matters, it is what you leave behind. And I have not yet decided what that ought to be."

The deputy frowned. "But, Lord Pickering—"

Lawrence put up a hand. "We would not want to hinder the constabulary in their work. You know how my brother gets annoyed when we interfere with his cases."

Grimley gave a resigned nod. Bull Pickering, Lawrence's older brother, was a man of few words, few thoughts, and great strength. He had worked his way up from debt collector in his brother's corps to the exalted role of London's hangman, and he took his job very seriously. The last time Bull suspected his brother of having deprived him of a neck that was rightfully his, it had taken two days to put Lawrence's office to rights again. In order to avoid such chaos, which Lawrence abhorred, he saw to it that every crime had a deserving neck attached to it.

"However, we should not be too generous to the constabulary," Lawrence was going on. "Send someone to Tottle's to empty his safe. And tell our other men to be on their guard in case someone is targeting our people."

Grimley was opening the door to issue these new orders when a flustered footman pushed past him, apparently propelled by an otherworldly force.

"My lord, I am sorry. I tried to stop him, but there was nothing—"

The otherworldly force was soon revealed to be the shiny blade of a rapier, held by a very tall, blond man with cold blue-gray eyes. "It is true, my lord," the man said. "I insisted on seeing you. I believe we have some unfinished business to discuss."

Grimley did not waste a minute, but had his own rapier out of its sheath and was pointing it at the intruder, ready to protect his boss to the death. "You go no farther, sir, if you value your life."

With a single, deft movement of the wrist, the intruder had the deputy disarmed and prostrate on the floor before the footman had time to flee. Grimley was stunned by this performance, and then more stunned when he heard his boss practically cackling with merriment.

"Crispin, I see your sword skills have improved some since the time I got you in the arm. When did you get back?" Lawrence asked, brushing aside tears of laughter from his eyes as he moved around the desk to embrace the other man.

"Earlier this week." Crispin returned the embrace warmly. "I would have been by sooner, but business kept me occupied."

Lawrence raised one eyebrow, a trick he had learned from Crispin when they were ten. "What is her name? Anne? Mary? Or is she one of those French mademoiselles you used to tell me stories of?"

Crispin grinned noncommittally, then bent down to help the stunned Grimley to his feet and returned his sword to him. "I am sorry about that, my friend. I cannot resist a challenge."

Grimley tried a smile, found that it did not work, and made a bow instead. "It is a pleasure to be disarmed by the Earl of Sandal," he murmured finally, then turned to his boss. "Will you need me, my lord, or should I see to the business we were just discussing?"

"Please do that. We can resume our talk later."

Grimley bowed again to each of the men and left the room.

"If I am interrupting something, I can come back another time," Crispin offered, but Lawrence shook his head.

"Nothing important. Now come, tell me everything. Or rather, let me guess. She is slender and delicate, with hair so light it is almost silver, and small, round breasts the size of two ripe oranges." Lawrence described to perfection every woman he and Crispin had fought over since the beginning of their friendship twenty-two years earlier.

They had met at the age of ten, and despite being from radically different backgrounds—Lawrence from incredible poverty, and Crispin from incredible wealth—the two had grown up together and shared a relationship that Crispin's cousins, the other Arboretti, envied. Crispin could still recall the day they met. From the river steps of Sandal Hall, he had been studying the churning brown water of the Thames and trying to decide whether to swim for Venice on his own or return to the house and face the torture of two more weeks with The Aunts. He had just opted for swimming, reasoning that even a watery grave was better than another lecture about gentlemanly deportment, when he heard a shout and saw a head bobbing in the river. The next moment the head was gone, replaced by a pair of flailing arms. Without stopping to think, Crispin leapt in and dragged the flailing arms to the river steps.

The arms turned out to belong to a boy of about his same age, who, as soon as he had coughed the water out of his lungs, demanded, "What did you do that for?"

Crispin stared down at him. "You were drowning. I saved your life."

The boy glared up at him. "And lost a three-ha'penny wager." Then he looked around, noted the immense house looming behind his savior, and smiled genially. "But you can make it up to me for a pound."

Crispin, whose allowance had been stopped by The Aunts when he failed to observe The Appropriate Method of Eating a Squab (which did not, it seemed, include spearing it on your fork and having it perform a song-and-dance routine with the turnips, despite the approbation of the pretty housemaid), had countered that Lawrence owed him at least that for saving his life.

"I like you," the waterlogged boy had replied. "You are a man of sense." And from that moment on, the friendship was cemented. Crispin taught Lawrence to swim, and Lawrence taught Crispin to live. Crispin found in Lawrence the perfect antidote to The Aunts' teachings, and Lawrence found in Crispin a pattern of the gentleman he was ambitious to become. As the years passed, the Sandal cook ceased to be surprised when Crispin's consumption of mutton, pigeon pie, roast pig, and especially cream pudding doubled every summer, and the steward came to expect the haberdasher's bills for two identical sets of every item of clothing Crispin ordered.

At first, the economic disparity between the boys meant that Crispin had to subsidize all their activities, but by the time they were fifteen, Lawrence had begun piecemeal to acquire the properties that would soon turn into his empire. While even then Lawrence refused all offers of financial help, he was happy to accept the assistance of the Arboretti in managing his growing portfolio of gaming houses and taverns. Crispin, his brother, Ian, and his cousins Miles, Tristan, and Sebastian would spend the summers they passed in England watching from behind invisible sliding panels as men entered and left gaming houses, each cousin computing the potential profits and losses at different tables; or they would sit, struggling to contain their thirst, as they observed the flow of traffic and ale inside Lawrence's newest inn. Late at night, they would argue together heatedly about the advisability of having a gaming house where all the tables were overseen by topless women (yes), an open-air tavern where cream pudding and only cream pudding was served at all hours (no, too many bees), a drinking establishment where the servingwomen wore jewels and nothing else (yes, yes, yes), and whether red or black velvet upholstery encouraged people to spend more money (red).

This advice, and the polish Lawrence acquired by rubbing shoulders with the Arboretti, had proved invaluable for the building of the Pickering empire, giving him an edge over his competitors and earning him their respect, but Crispin knew that the two most important keys to his friend's success were Lawrence's incredible intelligence and his network of informers. Very little happened in London that Lawrence did not know about or somehow profit from. His sources of information rivaled those of the Queen, and indeed, one of the ways in which he had managed to evade the hand of the law for so long was through carefully orchestrated collaborations with the Crown.

It was information that Crispin had come for that day, and as he still had several other places to go, he decided not to waste time. "You are wrong," Crispin said with a smirk. "She is not small, nor fair, nor orange-endowed."

Lawrence looked concerned. "I have long feared this. All that time on the continent has ruined your palate. We shall have to commence retraining at once."

Crispin laughed and shook his head. "No, no, you need not worry. My tastes are constant, as ever. This one is not, thank god, my mistress, but I need information about her. Do you know any-thing about a woman called Sophie Champion?"

Lawrence frowned, then crossed to a door in the far wall and hollered, "Elwood!"

Before he was even reseated, a tall, thin, serious-looking young man with scraggly dark hair that flopped over a scar on his fore-head, loped into the room carrying a red leather-bound volume. "Yes, my lord?"

"Elwood is in charge of the alphabet from A to F," Lawrence explained to Crispin, then turned to his employee. "What do we know about Sophie Champion?"

The man rolled his eyes to the ceiling and tapped a finger on the red book. "Sophie Champion," he began, as if reciting a chroni-cle of her crimes. "Age, about twenty-six. Height, too tall. Sup-posed to be very wealthy, but the source is unknown. Not," Elwood rushed to affirm, lest his master think he was slatternly, "for lack of trying. Familiarly called the Siren."

"The Siren?" Crispin and Lawrence countered, in unison.

Elwood brought his eyes down to his audience to explain. "Yes. I am not sure if it is because her beauty has the power to lure men from their destiny or because her tongue can lash them to death. Both are said to be true." The young man blushed slightly and rushed on. "Those who do not call her the Siren still claim that she is some sort of sorceress or, rather, witch. She does things to men, it seems, which make them behave strangely. It is said that she curses those who dare to touch her or, worse, propose to her, but that does not stop them."

"Has she had many proposals?" Crispin asked casually.

Elwood consulted the red leather volume. He flipped one page, then another, his lips moving as he counted the names. "Forty-three," he replied finally, then paused and turned another page. "No, I beg your pardon, forty-six. There were three in the last week."

Lawrence whistled slightly. "What odds are we offering?"

Elwood moved back and forth among the pages. "At first the bets were very safe, with an equal payoff. When Thomas Argyle proposed, one pound would get you one pound if she accepted him.

Then, by the time Lord Creamly proposed, one pound would get you ten if she accepted. On these most recent two, we are offering one hundred pounds for one pound." He looked up at the two men, his eyes wide. "That is the highest the payoff has ever been, for anyone, in the marriage wager."

"You know"—Lawrence leaned toward Crispin—"if you could pull it off, you would be very rich."

"I am already very rich," Crispin pointed out. "Besides, she is not my type."

"Ah, so you have seen her. What is she like? Perhaps I will try it myself."

Elwood look concerned. "If I might venture, my lord, I would not suggest it. She is a very dangerous woman."

"Dangerous?" Crispin and Lawrence repeated, again in unison.

Elwood nodded solemnly. "We were asked to investigate her on behalf of Her Majesty, but despite our best labors we were able to learn nothing of her background or family. We got as far as the fact that she was born somewhere near Newcastle, but the parish records were locked away or destroyed, no one knew which, and there was a new priest who had never heard of her. She first appeared in London society roughly two years ago, introduced by Lord Grosgrain. Your neighbor, Lord Sandal. It was then that the Crown consulted us for information. Lord Grosgrain claimed she was his goddaughter, but there were questions about that, questions which were left unanswered at his death last Monday."

There was something in the man's tone that piqued Crispin's interest. "Do you think she killed him? Her godfather?"

"I do not think, my lord, I merely report," Elwood said humbly. "Lord Grosgrain's death appears to have been a riding accident. But there have been intimations of other sorts. There were rumors, even before the accident, that his relationship with Miss Champion was not exactly what it seemed. Shortly after he presented her as his goddaughter, he remarried."

Lawrence cut Elwood off here. "That's right, he's the one who married Constantia Catchesol."

"Yes, sir. At one and a half pounds to the pound. It was a very likely thing." Elwood turned to address Crispin directly. "I believe, Lord Sandal, that you were once involved with the lady?"

Crispin, who had learned long ago not to be astonished by the thoroughness of Lawrence's information network, nodded. "I was. But don't put my name into your betting book as her next suitor just yet. One must observe a respectable mourning period."

One day earlier, the news that Constantia was again available would have filled Crispin's heart with joy. She had been the most beautiful woman he could imagine ten years earlier when, at twenty-two, he had proposed to her. She had been beautiful as she fluttered her hand to her breast in surprise at his clumsy proposal, and still beautiful as she laughed sweetly and told him that although she adored him, she could never think of marrying him because he was far too young. He probably would have married her after the death of her first husband, three years earlier, if he had not left for the continent before her period of mourning ended. At that point, older, wiser, and rich, she had given him strong indications that he could easily win her hand, if not her heart, and he suspected the same conditions still held.

She would make an ideal wife for him, he knew, beautiful enough to enjoy making love to, conceited enough not to require large doses of his admiration or affection, and shallow enough not to need too much stimulation. After their marriage he could go on with his life as he liked it, so long as he saw that she was provided with jewels and gowns and whatever other pleasures she desired. They would appear together stunningly in public, stay out of each other's way comfortably in private, and perhaps share an occasional interaction between the sheets of the marriage bed. It would be the perfect marriage of convenience for both parties. What was more, he knew, The Aunts would be overjoyed with his choice.

But Constantia was not the woman he had come for information about. Shaking off his reverie, Crispin asked, "What does Lord Grosgrain's marriage have to do with Sophie Champion?"

"It is said that after the marriage, Lord Grosgrain and his god-daughter grew apart," Elwood explained. "People drew the obvious conclusion that she had been expecting to become the next Lady Grosgrain and was disappointed, or rather, enraged. This is generally offered as the reason she rejected all her previous proposals."

"But it would not account for her rejecting the three proposals this week which must have come after his death," Crispin interposed before he realized he was speaking. "Or even those offered after Lord Grosgrain wedded Constantia."

"No, indeed it would not." Elwood shook his head. "However, it has been suggested by the more coarse-minded that Miss Champion's wealth derived from blackmailing Lord Grosgrain for breaching their betrothal contract. Accepting someone else's proposal would have negated her claims on him." Seeing Crispin poised to ask a question, he rushed on. "There is no evidence for such a contract, it is merely rumored. We have nothing on our books"—he tapped the red leather volume—"to indicate it existed. His name was never listed among those who proposed to her."

Crispin looked confused. "If she was blackmailing him, why would she kill him?"

"There are those who say she was unable to stop at blackmail, and that, a passionate woman, she resorted to murder. Others scorn the blackmail theory entirely, and say that her disappointment alone caused her to do it. The opinions are not very clear. 'A woman scorned,' you know."

Crispin frowned. "This makes no sense. If she resented the marriage, why not kill Constantia instead of Lord Grosgrain? Besides, I thought you said it was an accident."

"The Sirens of mythology," Elwood began, "were able to lure a man to his death merely by singing to him. Many people would not hesitate to assign Sophie Champion similar powers."

"She sounds like quite a woman," Lawrence said as Elwood fell silent.

"She is," Crispin answered to himself, then asked aloud, "Do you know where she lives?"

"That is another reason people think she is a witch," Elwood resumed. "She lives in the old convent of Our Lady of the Whispers, just adjacent to her godfather's house and across from yours, Lord Sandal. People call the place 'Hen House' now because she lives there with two other women, Octavia Apia, the famous dressmaker"—Elwood paused and looked at Lawrence, who flinched almost imperceptibly—"and Emme Butterich, the late Lord Elsley's daughter. All the servants are female as well."

"Even the cook?" Lawrence and Crispin asked, once more in unison.

"Yes," Elwood confirmed. "And she is said to be very good. Apparently, the Duke of Dorchester tried to hire her away from Miss Champion after merely hearing her 'cake of candied orange peels' described, but he was unsuccessful."

Lawrence looked hard at Crispin. "Why did you want this information, anyway? Are you after the cook?"

"No, I am quite happy with Castor." Crispin shook his head and hoped his smile looked genuine. "Actually, a friend of mine asked me to make inquiries. In return for your help, I'll be sure to have him enlist in your book if he moves into the proposal stage. Although I am not sure that in good conscience I can recommend he betroth himself to such a monster."

"Monster," Lawrence repeated. "That reminds me of something I meant to ask you about, Crispin. Elwood"—he faced the *A*-to-*F* man—"you have been invaluable. Thank you very much."

Elwood bowed awkwardly to the two men, then loped out the door clutching his red leather volume.

Crispin's eyes followed him across the threshold. "He is remarkable. Where did you find him?"

"He picked my pocket," Lawrence said, laughing. "Or attempted to. He was desperate, trying to feed his mother and four sisters on scraps and fish skeletons from the sewers around the Palace. Her Majesty's courtiers would scurry by him every day, heaping their stinking trash on his head, without giving him a second thought. I could tell he would never be a first-class hand man, but he was intelligent and it seemed somehow just to give him the power to heap the stink of ill repute on the heads of Their Lords and Ladyships if he should feel like it."

Crispin shook his thus-endangered head. "I suppose I should have given him my purse, then, just to be on the safe side."

Lawrence assumed a mock swaggering tone. "Don't worry. I might be able to put in a good word for you with his boss. So long as you do me a favor in return."

Crispin spread his hands wide. "Whatever you wish, Your Lordship."

"Not a favor, really. Just a question. While you were on the continent, up to no good, did you ever hear about a fellow named the Phoenix?"

A crease appeared on Crispin's forehead as he tried to remember. "The Phoenix. Isn't that a mythical bird? The one that regenerates itself constantly from the ashes of its own destruction or some such nonsense?"

Lawrence was nodding impatiently. "Yes, but it is also a man. A fairly mythical man. He got the name because, like the bird, he seems to be impossible to kill. Every government on the continent, as well as the Emperor of China, has offered to pay a bounty to whoever does him in irrevocably. The bounty has been collected four times by people claiming to have killed him, and then returned four times when he reappeared unscathed. Everyone assumed he was working for dear Queen Liz, but someone in London is offering a bounty fit for a king for the Phoenix's identification and capture, and, from the size of it, it would appear to be the Royal Highness herself."

"And you would like to collect this regal reward," Crispin hazarded.

"Exactly. I thought you might have heard something about the man while you were abroad, or noticed someone here that you had seen over there. He has been operating in Europe for the past two years, but rumor has it that he is back in England now."

"Back in England? Has he been here before?"

Lawrence nodded. "He crushed a counterfeiting ring a few years ago. That was the first that anyone heard of him, and also the beginning of his myth. A bystander saw one of the counterfeiters—Damon Goldhawk, a damn good shot—fire at him four times. Instead of getting shot, the bullets apparently ricocheted off the Phoenix and returned to Damon, all of them going straight into his heart."

"How do you propose to capture him, then?" Crispin asked with unfeigned interest, and was disappointed when Lawrence only shrugged.

"First I must find him. Then I can worry about trapping him."

Noticing that he had already stayed far longer than he intended, Crispin wished his friend luck and took his leave.

"Be careful," Lawrence advised Crispin as he reached the door. "With this menagerie of mythic beasts running around, London is hardly safe."

Walking down the stairs, Crispin chuckled to himself as he remembered Lawrence's words. It had been three bullets that were fired at him, not four, and only two of his had gone into the counterfeiter's heart. After all, the Phoenix was not *completely* infallible.

Chapter Five

"Where have you been?" Octavia demanded when she opened the front door of Hen House and found Sophie there. Without waiting for an answer, she gently steered Sophie toward the library and into a green brocade chair. "You really look dreadful," Octavia continued despite herself. "Where did you get those leggings? And that shirt. The fabric is beautiful—it looks too fine to be English—but it is much too large for you. What did you do with the suit I made you? Are you aware that your mustache is slipping?"

Sophie just stared at her friend through this torrent of questions, and had begun to think of trying to compose a response, when Emme burst into the room.

"Where did you find her?" she demanded of Octavia.

"On the front walk. She was sort of teetering there when I got back from my workshop."

Sophie resented the word "teetering." She was sure she had been more perching than teetering, and she planned to tell them so, probably next spring.

"You look dreadful and that stupid mustache is crooked," Emme told Sophie, circling around to face her. "What happened to your head?"

"Orange cake," Sophie replied, squeezing the words out.

"You were hit with an orange cake?" Emme's tone suggested incredulity.

"No." Sophie found her strength coming back in the all-important pursuit of orange cake. "But I will hit you with one if you do not stop badgering me. Providing there are any in the house. Are there? I could eat about ten of them."

Octavia and Emme exchanged pained looks. "You know that Richards will quit again if you refuse to eat anything but her candied-orange cake," Octavia reminded her. "And we do not want that to happen."

"But this is an emergency," Sophie pleaded, and she really felt it was, considering the state of her head, her nerves, and her unfed stomach. It was not every morning she awoke naked in a man's bed. "I promise, if she lets me eat ten, no, make it twelve of them, now, I will never do it again." Sophie reached her hand toward her heart pathetically as if taking an oath.

"Your word of honor?" Emme asked.

Sophie looked alarmed. "Has it come to that?" When Emme and Octavia nodded in tandem, she sighed. "My word of honor."

Emme moved off toward the kitchen, the domain she shared with Richards the cook and whose borders no one else was allowed to breach, while Octavia shuttled Sophie toward her bedchamber. Sophie loved this room, indeed it was the reason she had purchased the abandoned convent of Our Lady of the Whispers two years earlier.

That day, a hazy early summer's day like this one, she had entered the abandoned convent at dusk. Wandering alone through its long halls and deserted rooms, she had found herself, as if magically, in a chamber that dazzled her. It was filled with light, in hundreds of colors, streaming in through five tall stained-glass windows at its far end, bouncing off its yellow stone walls. The windows had once belonged to a private chapel, but had later been built into the abbess's private chambers. The two pairs of windows on either side contained portraits of female saints, four exquisite women, each wrapped in a different-colored mantle. In the middle of these, in a window taller and wider than the others, the Lady of

Whispers was enthroned, smiling a quiet benediction on the inhabitants of the room.

Those five women were Sophie's guardian angels. During the day they filled her room with sparkling colored light, always changing and moving, allowing her to gauge the time of the day by the color of the walls. Early morning was a pale blue, then came red, then gold in the middle of the day, then a light green that grew darker as evening approached, and finally finished in a dazzling purple. By day the women in the windows shared their colors with Sophie, but it was at night that they really did her a service. They drove away the darkness and kept her company so she was never alone, never unprotected, their pacific faces holding at bay the voice that haunted her perpetually. No one could hurt her, Sophie believed, as long as she was under their watch.

So often had Annie, the chambermaid, found her asleep on the floor beneath the windows that Octavia had finally had a divan made to fill the space, large and stuffed with the softest feathers. It was on this commodious piece of furniture that she now deposited Sophie and then disappeared. When she returned a quarter of an hour later, she was trailed by a servingwoman pushing a large tub on wheels filled with steaming water and another carrying a wooden box holding glass vials.

"Strip," Octavia commanded Sophie, and was surprised to see her friend cringe. "What is wrong?"

"I never," Sophie said, rising from the divan and pulling off the shirt Octavia had admired, "want," she continued, balling up the leggings and kicking them into the corner of the room, "to hear," she went on, stepping into the bath, "that word"—Sophie slid down into the tub—"again." She ducked her head down and let the hot water cover her completely.

Octavia stood at the edge, carefully adding drops of oil from one of the glass vials. The scent of jasmine soon filled the room, and as Sophie brought her head to the surface, she felt herself relax. With her eyes closed and the deliciously aromatic water lapping around her, her mind began to settle down. There were three things she had told herself to remember, she remembered, but she could not remember what they were. In the hope of reclaiming them, she began to slowly recall the events of the previous night.

She recollected the idiotic cat-and-mouse game through the streets of London and the horrible striptease and the wager, but after that everything got fuzzy. There had been a bird who was noisy, and a man who was silent, and...

"Ouch!" she hollered, sitting straight up in the water. Sophie reached a finger toward her upper lip, found it unadorned, and turned toward Octavia, who was dangling the sopping-wet false mustache in her hand. At that moment, Sophie remembered one of the things she had forgotten. "I am very upset with you," she told Octavia sternly.

"Because I took the mustache off? It did look rather fetching, but—"

Sophie interrupted. "If it was not for you I never would have ended up in his bed naked."

"I don't see—" Octavia began, but stopped herself. Certainly she had been encouraging Sophie for months to at least explore the caresses of the opposite sex as a way of getting over her discomfort with men, but she did not recall having recommended that she throw off her clothes and go to bed with them all at once. Nor had Sophie ever given the least sign of listening to her, other than making faces involving gnawing on her upper lip with her teeth and rolling her eyes, or grunting like a wild boar. This turn of events was very perplexing, even worrying, and Octavia thought for the first time that perhaps the bump on Sophie's head was more than superficial. "I am afraid I do not understand what you are talking about," she said gently. "Did you hit your head hard? Do you remember where you are?"

Sophie glared at her. "It was that mustache paste you made. I think I am allergic to it. It made me feel very strange and..." Sophie's voice trailed off.

"The mustache paste made you take your clothes off?" Octavia queried as if it were the most natural thing in the world, while she busied herself collecting the clothes Sophie had strewn around the chamber.

Sophie was somewhat appeased by her friend's tone. "No, he did that when he made me strip. But I probably would have been thinking more clearly and would have avoided it, if it weren't for the mustache paste making my insides feel like I had been drinking hot spiced wine, and my knees like they were made of cream pudding."

Octavia now understood Sophie's earlier reaction to the command "strip," but the words her friend was speaking were certainly not the words of Sophie Champion. Sophie Champion would rather have leapt off the top of Saint Paul's than take her clothes off in front of a man. The only thing that sounded like Sophie at all was the guileless gourmet description of what were clearly the symptoms of physical attraction. As Octavia's concern that she really had poisoned Sophie ebbed, her curiosity about what human male could possibly have induced such sensations in her friend increased. "Who was this man who ordered you to strip?" she asked nonchalantly.

"The Earl of Sandal," Sophie replied, avoiding her friend's eyes.

"I see." This was the delicate part, Octavia knew. She paused for a moment, twirling a lock of golden blonde hair around her finger as she tried to figure out the best way to phrase her question. "And after you took your clothes off, you decided to go to bed with him?"

"Are you mad?" Sophie was no longer avoiding Octavia's gaze. "With that disreputable caterpillar? That odious worm? That— that—" Sophie spluttered and decided to change tactics. "Go to bed with him? Never. And then, because of your mustache paste and his infernal hatefulness, I was compelled to make a wager with him. And the next thing I know I am lying in his bed, naked, and it is nearly midday and my clothes are gone." Sophie stopped for breath.

Emme entered the room then, carrying a silver cake platter, but she stopped abruptly when she saw the pained expression on Octavia's face. "What is wrong?"

"Oh, nothing," Octavia answered, obviously struggling to keep breathing and avoid either weeping or laughing, Emme could not be sure. "Sophie was just telling me about how the mustache paste made her sick and compelled her to strip off her clothes, make a wager, and then spend the night with the Earl of Sandal, and it is all my fault."

The silver platter fell to the floor with a bang, sending a round sugary confection flying across the floor. "You spent the night with the Earl of Sandal?" Emme stopped gaping long enough to ask.

Sophie rose from the tub, frowned at the round confection, and then turned her frown on Emme. "Where is the orange cake?"

Emme managed to unlock her jaw. "Richards says there is no need to make orange cake when you order a dozen meringues from Sweetson the baker to be delivered every week."

"Meringues are quite delicious," Octavia added in a slightly stilted tone.

"Maybe," Sophie said, waving the comment aside. "But they are not orange cakes and I did not order them. Why would I order anything from anyone else when I have Richards—Satan's knockers!" Sophie had just remembered the second thing she had forgotten to remember earlier, and it was all thanks to the meringue. Relieved, and feeling much better after her bath, she stepped out of the tub, scooped the fluffy confection from the floor, kissed it, and tossed it out the window. Then she danced toward Emme and gave her a kiss likewise. "Thank you. It would never have come back to me if not for you. Now, be wonderful and tell Richards that I don't know anything about ordering meringues and I am still begging for orange cake."

She watched the now doubly stunned Emme totter out of the room, and then swung toward Octavia. "I need clothes, women's clothes, but easy to move in," she explained.

Octavia and Emme had grown accustomed to Sophie's unusual behavior and no longer thought twice when she went from pensive to ebullient in the blink of an eye, but this business of sleeping with men and kissing desserts was out of the ordinary, even for her.

Beginning to wonder if indeed the mustache paste had made Sophie mad, Octavia opened the armoire that was stuffed with the gowns she had designed for her friend and selected a pale blue silk.

"No, not that one," Sophie said, shaking her head, and Octavia felt that her worst fears were confirmed. Sophie had never, in all their years together, expressed an opinion about her clothes.

"What about the green gown?" Sophie asked. "The new one, with the other green on the bottom and that stuff all over the front."

This description sounded more in character, but even so Octavia had to bite her tongue to keep from asking if Sophie would not rather lie down—say for two weeks, perhaps in a comfy apartment at Bedlam—as she extracted the requested gown from the armoire. It was one of her recent designs, light green silk the color of a young apple, over a darker green silk skirt. The "stuff" on the front was actually elaborate embroidery work depicting delicate vines that curved over the bodice, drawing the eye and emphasizing its low, square cut. Flowers of light pink, blue, and purple grew out of the vines, and just above the left breast there was a small bumble-bee. Octavia signed all of her gowns with a bee, causing that humble insect to become the most sought after object of adornment in London for the past two seasons. Women eyed one another with disdain if there was no bee visible and scrutinized each other's embroidery to learn if it was a real Octavia Apia or a sham. But Sophie paid attention to none of this as she flounced miserably in and out of balls, Octavia's best advertisement and London's most envied model, nor was she thinking about it now.

No, she was not thinking about the many compliments she had received on the gown before, or the fact that it made her eyes look remarkably green, or the hungry, desperate way every man had gazed at her the last time she wore it out, or that she had been described the next day, in public, as the most beautiful woman in London. She had chosen it, she knew, only because she remembered it was comfortable and not on the off chance that the man who lived in the palace across the street might look out his window as she departed. Or rather, exactly on that off chance, so that she could show the callow beetle that she did not care what he thought of her. Or something like that.

As she stepped out of the house, brushing from her riding cloak, crumbs of the orange cake she had inhaled, she suddenly remembered the third thing she had forgotten. She hesitated for a moment, about to go back in and ask Octavia about the pistol, but decided against it. She could ask her later, Sophie thought, mounting her dappled mare and taking the reins from the stable-girl, when she returned home to eat two dozen more cakes.

Setting out across London, she could hardly have known that there would be no later. Sophie Champion would not be going back to Hen House. Not later. Not ever.

This was no way for the Phoenix to be spending his day, Crispin thought to himself as he shifted uncomfortably on the unsteady stool-like torture apparatus and started on the final bundle of papers. He would rather have been out facing a group of Spanish brigands armed to the teeth desperately protecting their unlawfully collected treasure, or the French royal firing squad with pistols loaded, or even a Turkish merchant who had padded his body with gunpowder that would explode at the merest touch by another person and embarked upon a suicide mission to blow up the English ambassador's residence in Constantinople. He would rather have been dealing with any of these (as he had—the firing squad more than once, in fact) than sorting through other people's perfumed love letters in someone else's perfumed den of iniquity.

Indeed, if Crispin had known that Richard Tottle's personal apartments would be covered almost entirely in pink silk, he never would have come. The walls, the doors, the bed, the divan, the curtains, all were of pink silk, and what could not be covered in silk was at least made pink. The floor was topped with a carpet needle-pointed in a thousand pink roses, the mirror was framed with pink glass flowers, the fireplace was surrounded with pink tiles, portraits of pink women smiled out of pink frames ... not even the chamber pot, Crispin was appalled to see, had escaped the plague of pink-ness. Consulting his pocket watch, he saw that he had been there for less than an hour, even if it felt like five.

Having given up on finding the other half of the list Tottle had been clutching when he died, Crispin decided to render it mean-ingless by destroying the cipher that had been used to encode it, which anyone would need to decode it. He himself had the only other copy, and without it the list was completely illegible. But so far Crispin's searching had been in vain: he had been unable to find the cipher anywhere, and he did not know how much longer he could last in Tottle's salmon-pink sanctuary. He had just decided to take the love letters he was sorting through with him and look at them in the soothing space of his dark-wood-and-burgundy library, when he heard the footsteps on the stairs.

Noting that they did not stop at the floor below, where the offices were, but continued up toward the door to the pink paradise, he carefully replaced the letters in the top compartment of the (pink) desk and concealed himself among the (pink) drapes.

Whoever was on the other side of the door was no professional. Not only had they crept up the stairs noisily enough to alert the dead, but they were now struggling with the simple lock on the door. He was half inclined to slide across the room and undo the lock for them, if only to ease the tension of waiting, but suddenly the door opened and the footsteps entered the room.

Sophie was glad there was no one there to see her gaping. She had never been in a room like this before, had only vaguely imagined that such places existed. There could be no doubt that it was conse-crated entirely to pleasure, from the triple-wide bed to the paintings of women—Satan's knockers, what were they doing to that satyr in the one between the windows?—to the strange musky odor that per-meated the air. She moved around the room slowly, taking in the proliferation of pink furnishings, astutely studying the paintings (could her leg go in that direction? she wondered, extending one of them out slightly as she studied a woman who was ecstatically mak-ing love with a swan) and feeling completely overwhelmed.

And perhaps a bit ill, a sort of relapse of her feelings from the night before. She had just removed her riding cloak, having begun to feel a little warm, and started to wonder what could be causing the illness now, since the mustache was gone, when the pink curtains on her right stirred slightly and a figure emerged.

"Don Alfonso. What a pleasant surprise," Crispin said in a voice that left it unclear whether he meant it sincerely or as the saltiest sarcasm. "You have shaved."

Sophie should have known this would happen, she told herself, smoothing the skirt of her gown. She should have expected him to be there, she thought as she ensured her bodice was straight, making a mess of things, probably stealing things so that he would win their bet. That thought was immediately followed by another, and before she could stop herself she looked at him and said, "You bastard."

"Perhaps Miss Champion should take lessons from Don Alfonso about the basics of courtesy. Generally it is considered good form to wish someone good day before belittling their bloodlines."

"You drugged me," Sophie replied, ignoring his etiquette pointers. "You put something in the wine last night and drugged me so that you could get here before me and take away important evidence."

Crispin raised his eyebrows. "Ingenious. I had not even realized it myself. With your powers of deduction, evidence would just be a hindrance."

"Then you admit it?"

"Unfortunately, while I enjoy your company excessively, I did nothing to prolong your visit to my house last night. You yourself mentioned that your last meal had been days before, and I suspect that the wine you gulped like a sailor just went to your head." Noting that she was about to protest, Crispin went on. "Do not imagine that I enjoyed trying to sleep through your snores on my divan."

Sophie's eyes grew huge with indignation. "I do not snore."

"You most certainly do. At first I thought one of the wild bulls from the bullbaiting ring must have run away and invaded the room, but then I realized it was just you." Despite concentrating on not laughing uproariously, Crispin still had plenty of attention left over for watching Sophie's rising wrath. However, he now saw he had made a mistake, because he had not anticipated that once antagonized she would inhale and exhale quite so deeply, making it impossible not to look at the low-cut bodice of her dress, or that she would color quite so marvelously against its green silk. What had begun as an exercise to unsettle her, seemed to be unsettling him instead, and Crispin had to remind himself that he had a job to do, a very important job, no part of which involved throwing the woman before him on the pink bed and making love to her. Indeed, the sooner he got away from her, the better off he would be.

Sophie shared his opinion. She had just realized, with horror, that she had wronged Octavia. It was not the mustache paste that made her ill; it was the Earl of Sandal. He was not only obnoxious but noxious as well. She felt distinctly sick in his presence, and it was not helped any by the enormous bed just behind her, or the paintings covering the walls. The best thing to do was to get away from him as soon as possible.

"I humbly beg your pardon," Sophie said, her manner suggesting new meanings for the words "humbly beg," "and I assure you my snores will never bother you again."

"Good," Crispin said with finality.

"Good," Sophie echoed. "Now, if you will just show me what you have taken, I will leave here and not trouble you at all."

Crispin spread the fingers on his hands and turned them over so she could see both front and back. "Empty," he explained. "I have taken nothing. Of course, if you do not believe me, I would be happy to remove my clothes and let you inspect them yourself."

This was very bad. The thought of sharing the pink Parnassus with him, naked, occasioned a new wave of the spiced-wine warmness that made Sophie unsteady on her feet, and she stepped backward, until she felt the supporting structure of the bed behind her knees. "I would rather let you win the bet than have to see you unclad," she told him. "In fact, I would rather let you win the bet than have to see you at all. I will go down to Richard Tottle's office on the floor below and look around until you have finished here."

Crispin was disgustingly gallant. "I should hate to have it said that I chased a lady out of a chamber such as this. I will go downstairs and allow you to stay here, studying the paintings unfettered. With practice, I think, you could master that position with the swan."

The door closed on his back before Sophie could tell him that he was by far the most terrifically horrible millipede in all London, probably in all England, possibly in all the world. There were about a dozen other unflattering adjectives longing to push themselves out of her lips, but she bit them back and told herself to concentrate on the task at hand. She went first to the bundles of love letters that Crispin had been flipping through earlier, and untying them, she began to read. They appeared to be notes left by the two people who shared the room when one or the other was absent. Half the bundles, tied with a silver cord, were signed "Your forever loving, Dickie." That had to be the private nickname of Richard Tottle. The other packets, tied with gold cord, were all concluded with the words "Hundreds of kisses from your dearest Darling." Sophie read the salutation for the fourteenth time and groaned. If she had hoped to glean any information from Richard Tottle's lover, Sophie now saw, she was bound to be disappointed. How could she possibly figure out which of the hordes of darling women in London "Dickie" had been receiving hundreds of kisses from? And why couldn't she have used a real name like normal people? Sophie had begun pacing around the room, flapping one of the offending letters in each hand, when the door burst open and a man entered.

"Constable," he pronounced gruffly as he took her arm. "Come with me, miss. You are under arrest."

Chapter Six

The constable had to drag Sophie down the stairs. She was too stunned to speak, or even fight, which suited him just fine. When they reached the landing in front of the office, he ducked in and said, "I'll take the chambermaid back to Newgate for questioning."

A fat man detached himself from the group going through the stacks and stacks of paper in the office, and approached very close. "She's a tender morsel," he said, squinting at Sophie myopically. "Why not let us do the questioning here?"

Sophie began to stir a little, but the constable tightened his grip on her arm. "I got my orders," he told the other man. "Take any witnesses to the prison for questioning, those are my orders, and I'm going to follow them."

The fat man did not spare a glance for the speaker but kept his eyes on Sophie and periodically licked his lips. "Very well," he agreed finally, giving his belly a doleful pat. "But don't forget to save some for the rest of us. A fine dish like that, you eat too much and you'll be sorry later."

The constable grinned, and directed his charge down the remaining stairs. They had just shut the door of RICHARD TOTTLE, ESQ., PRINTER TO THE QUEEN's place of business, when Sophie hissed through closed teeth, "What the devil do you think you are doing?"

"Saving your life," Crispin hissed back from under the hat he was wearing as a disguise, his hand not leaving her arm. "The final entry in Richard Tottle's account book is for a payment of one thousand two hundred pounds from 'Sophie Champion' for 'Information.' And apparently, based on what those constables in there were saying, someone found the tattered remnants of a bill of credit for that amount signed by you in Richard Tottle's purse. Another group of them have already been dispatched to your house to arrest you. Unless for some reason you would relish being apprehended by that charming and hungry gentleman in there, I suggest you come along quietly."

"What do you mean," Sophie asked, stuck back in the first part of his statement, "that there is an entry in Richard Tottle's account book under my name?"

"I should think that even with your rudimentary mental capacity that easy statement should make sense," Crispin growled, dragging her onto his horse in front of him.

"And I should think that even with your glaring ignorance of the laws of civilized society, you would have learned that forcing women against their will onto your horse and insulting them is unacceptable. I demand that you let me down this moment. I have my own mount."

"Good." Crispin's grasp around her waist tightened. "By leaving your mount here, we guarantee that the constables will start their search for Sophie Champion in this neighborhood and give you time to get out of London." As he spoke, Crispin took off the ridiculous floppy hat of Tottle's that he had appropriated when he heard the footsteps on the stairs, stuffed it under his saddle, and signaled his horse into motion with a click of his tongue.

"What do you mean, 'get out of London'?" Sophie turned her neck around as far as it would go to face him. "How do I know there really is a warrant out for my arrest? Or that you did not put that entry in the ledger yourself while you were in the office, or leave that bill of credit on the body when you searched it, in order to frame me, so you could win our bet?"

"Because I am a gentleman," he told her, eliciting a snort that called into question the status of her own gentle blood. "And because I took the liberty of pouring ink over the last entry in the ledger, to complicate things a little."

Slowly, the expression on Sophie's face changed into one that he had not seen before. "Why?" she asked simply.

"I would never want you to say I won our bet unfairly," he evaded. "But you will have to leave London."

"I will do no such thing," Sophie said, still facing him.

Crispin sighed. "Would you at least agree not to go home? To go and stay somewhere that no one will know about?"

Sophie's eyes narrowed, and the thoughts that she had been having, thoughts that mitigated his odiousness from severe to manageable, instantly receded. "Do not for a moment suppose I would agree to move into your house."

"Do not for a moment suppose I was going to suggest it," Crispin returned in the same tone. "No, I was thinking of a friend of mine. He owns many houses in London and would undoubtedly be happy to host you."

"I have plenty of friends of my own with whom I can stay," she said indignantly.

"Friends you would be willing to send to the gallows for harboring a fugitive?" Crispin challenged.

"No," Sophie answered slowly. "Do you?"

Crispin nodded. "I saved Lawrence's life once, so he owes me a favor. Besides, he is quite skilled at staying out of official trouble."

Sophie took this information in for a moment, then asked, "Does he have a cook? A good cook?"

Not as good as yours is supposed to be, Crispin almost responded, but caught himself in time. He did not want her to know that he had been making inquiries about her. "Yes, one of the best."

Sophie brightened considerably. "Very well, I will go. But I will not be a prisoner."

Crispin should have been relieved, but instead he felt a strange dryness in his throat and tightness in his breast at the thought of leaving Sophie with Lawrence. It was not jealousy, Crispin told himself as he worked to quash it, because he had inured himself to that years before when he learned that such emotions make one weak. Not even if Sophie Champion was the most interesting woman he could ever remembering encountering. Not even if as boys he and Lawrence had made a game of seducing each other's female companions. Not even if Lord Pickering was considered one of the best-looking and most charming men in England. Crispin sifted through potential maladies in his mind, and then, with tremendous relief, realized the problem. It had nothing to do with Sophie or Lawrence at all. Dry throat, tight knot in his breast— clearly he was just thirsty. The fact that his thirst was redoubled when he happened to look at the back of Sophie's head and catch the sunlight turning her hair into a thousand dancing rubies meant nothing at all. He was sure he had read somewhere that rubies made men thirsty.

Thirst tied in well with the errand he needed to do, but the presence of Sophie did not. He had found several other entries in Tottle's ledger that surprised him, and one name in particular, but not having had time to spill ink over the record book's entirety, he worried that the constables would see it and eventually track it down. Before that happened, he wanted to interview Kipper Norton and find out why he had paid Richard Tottle a hundred pounds promptly on the first of every month.

Kipper, he knew, spent the better part of his days in one of London's more devious establishments, which pretended to be a patriotic association—even going so far as to supply entertainments in honor of the Queen's birthday and other festivals—so that those noblemen with vigilant wives might make repeated and lengthy visits without arousing their suspicion. In reality, the Worshipful Hall Of Righteous English Statesmen was an extremely expensive house of pleasure with very comfortable benches, chairs, and private rooms. The thought of taking Sophie there made Crispin even thirstier, but he worried about the delay that getting her settled with Lawrence would entail.

"Your friend cannot live here," Sophie said over her shoulder as they drew into the stable yard of the Worshipful Hall. "It is a house of pleasure and—" She broke off abruptly and turned to face him, her eyes filling with suspicion again. "Unless you plan—"

Crispin stopped her before the accusations could begin. "No. I have to see someone, someone I think will be here, and I have to do it before the constables find his name in Tottle's ledger as well. I thought it only fair to bring you along. If you object, you may stay here."

"Why should I object?" Sophie challenged, sliding off his horse. "I bought the building."

Crispin stared down at her, momentarily dumbfounded. "You what?"

"Well, not intentionally. Several years ago, Judith and Delilah—the Cruet Twins—came and asked me for five thousand pounds and I gave it to them. They were so eager for the money that I did not ask what it was for, and by the time I found out that I had funded a brothel, they had already paid me back. They wanted to pay me interest, but I would not accept it."

Crispin had climbed off the horse and relinquished the reins to the uniformed stableboy by then, but he continued to stare at her with a mixture of disbelief and, despite himself, admiration. He had never met a woman quite like Sophie Champion.

She leaned close to him to confide shyly, "I have to admit, I have never been inside a place of this type. I am excited to see what it is like."

" 'Excited,' " Crispin repeated, and followed her in.

She paused as she crossed the threshold to let her eyes adjust to the artificial darkness. "Isn't it wonderful?" she whispered as she surveyed the entrance hall. It was paneled in dark wood, and each wall was hung with paintings of English noblemen, which looked to have been done early in the century. "They told me when they paid me back that they made the entry look like a proper patriotic society so that if people strayed in by accident, they would never know otherwise. That painting against the far wall, the one of King Henry the Eighth, cost five hundred pounds."

Crispin nodded as she propounded the many merits of the entrance hall, only half listening, his mind completely absorbed with the idea that giving out interest-free loans was a very strange way for a woman, particularly a woman of questionable means, to employ her money. He was roused from this thought by the appearance of a somnambulant-looking steward. "I am looking for Kipper Norton," Crispin announced, extending a silver coin toward the man. "He told me to meet him here."

The steward nodded, then slowly moved his sleepy eyes to Sophie. "There is a charge for female nonmembers," he told Crispin, who reached into his purse and extracted another silver coin.

"They did that so that when men choose to bring their wives or mistresses here, the other girls do not lose out," Sophie explained as they followed the formal steward through a door. "I think it is a very wise idea."

Crispin was newly struck dumb by this statement, as well as her subsequent account of how Judith and Delilah had decided to cover everything in red velvet because it seemed people spent more money in such surroundings. He wondered briefly if red velvet had the same, parching effect on men as rubies, and decided it did when he noticed that passing through the main red-velvet chamber—with all those men leering at Sophie—was giving him a mammoth thirst. Fortunately, he had regained his power of speech enough to order a tankard of ale by the time the sleepwalking steward had shown them into the dark corner, plush in red velvet, where Kipper Norton was making a close study of the décolletage belonging to a brightly painted blonde.

The steward cleared his throat, and Kipper looked up, confused. He squinted at them for a moment, an act of near impossibility given the way his eyes bulged out of his head, then recognition flashed across his face and he smiled gaily at Crispin. "Sandal, what a pleasure to meet you here." His eyes moved to Sophie, and his smile broadened. "Glad to see you brought one of your own. I hate having to share."

Only Sophie's surprise at how much Kipper looked like a floun-der, despite his thin red hair, kept her from explaining that she was not there in the capacity he had assumed. Whatever the cause of her silence, Crispin was grateful for it as he slid onto the bench on the other side of the table from Kipper and the blond woman, and motioned to Sophie to slide in next to him.

When they were seated, Kipper took them in, a sly smile spreading across his face. "She's foreign, isn't she?" he asked Crispin. "One of the ones that you brought back from France with you, right?"

Crispin saw his chance to continue her blissful silence and seized it. Before Sophie could reply, he was saying, "Yes, French. She can't speak a word of English, or understand it either." He drained the tankard and leaned confidentially across the table toward Kipper, upsetting a dish of sugared almonds. "And you know what they say about Frenchwomen."

Sophie glowered at him. "Pompous caterpillar," she gritted out under her breath. She had been having such a nice time during her first visit to the Worshipful Hall, despite his presence, but now he had ruined it.

"What did she say?" Kipper asked immediately, his eyes bulging even more than usual with innuendo. "Did she propose one of those French things? You know, that 'Men Age a Troy'?"

Crispin was about to reply that she had actually requested a *tête-à-tête* with Kipper alone, when the murderous expression on Sophie's face caught his voice. "No, not a *ménage à trois*. She said simply that my friend seemed nice."

Kipper smiled fishily. "Tell her I am nice. Very nice. And very rich. My wife has pots of money." He pantomimed a pot of money, eliciting only a glare from Sophie, but increased interest from the blond woman next to him.

Crispin leaned over to whisper in Sophie's ear. "If you do not stop scowling this moment, I shall leave you alone with him. Is that clear? If it is, nod once, smile brightly, and coo something French sounding."

"*Vous êtes un bastard,*" Sophie cooed through clenched teeth with a nod and a sweet smile.

"She says she will remember that," Crispin translated. Then, noticing that the rekindled ministrations of the painted blonde upon hearing of Kipper's pots of wealth threatened to occupy Kipper's mind entirely, Crispin decided to proceed with his questions. "Kipper, I was wondering. Have you ever done any business with Dickie Tottle?"

Kipper rolled his fish eyes, trying to think. "Dickie Tottle? Never heard of him," he said, popping a sugared almond into his mouth. He extended the bowl toward Crispin. "Try one. They are very good. A specialty of the club."

"No thanks," Crispin declined, frowning slightly. "It's strange that you have never heard of him. He told me that you were one of his investors. Something about you giving him twelve hundred pounds for a new undertaking. That doesn't sound like a sum to forget about easily."

"Tottle told you that?" Kipper asked, his eyes popping. "The bastard. I was promis—" Kipper interrupted himself. His mouth opened and closed in the air, highlighting his resemblance to a fish, before he went on. "Now I remember. It was for a subscription. You know, so every time Old Bess gives a new proclamation or law, he'd print it up and send it over. Also any news from court. Very handy. Must stay on top of such things."

"I can imagine. What was the latest number about?" Crispin asked casually. "Was that the one about the war with Naples?"

Kipper nodded so furiously that Sophie feared his eyes might fall out. "Yes. Naples. He is ruthless you know. Very bad business, that Naples fellow. Sure you won't have some almonds?"

Crispin was relieved to see out of the corner of his eye that, despite exploding with the information that Naples was a place not a person, Sophie had her mouth clamped shut and appeared to be leaving the questions to him. "How did you find out about this patriotic service?" Crispin asked with interest.

"How did I find out?" Kipper repeated, beginning now to arrange the almonds in a star shape on the table. "Why, I don't remember. Must have been something the wife brought home." He raised his eyes from his artwork to look uneasily at Crispin. "Why are you asking about all this anyway? What business of yours is it, Sandal, if I choose to educate myself a bit? Become a bit knowledgeable about the affairs of state?" Kipper, warming to his topic now, seized on Crispin's earlier words. "It's an Englishman's duty, you know. It is patriotic, you said so yourself. What with this dangerous Naples fellow arrayed against us, we must all be ready to do our duty for England and for Bess, to take up arms, and shout together, 'Death to Naples, the Ruthless Enemy of Our Queen.'"

This was too much for Sophie. She had her mouth open to speak, unable to keep from bursting any longer, when Crispin's hand on her thigh stopped her. The sheer surprise of feeling it there was enough to silence her even before Crispin leaned close to whisper, "The next time you open your mouth, I will give you the longest, deepest, most devastating kiss you have ever experienced."

Sophie swallowed hard and set her lips. She was sorely tempted to tell him exactly what she thought of his threats, particularly about the chances of him giving her the longest, deepest, and most devastating kiss she had ever experienced, but another part of her reminded her that Sophie Champion had a policy of avoiding men's kisses with the same fervor with which she avoided death, and this was not the time to compromise.

Kipper had moved his attention from the nuts to his companion and was wiping his brow, wet with the blessed perspiration of the patriot, on her fevered bosom during this exchange. He clearly felt confident that his speech had been successful in deflecting Crispin's questions, and he smiled triumphantly as he raised his head from its cushion and faced Crispin again.

But triumph turned to tragedy when Crispin remarked in a voice tinged with wonder, "You are an inspiration, Kipper. You must tell me how I can subscribe."

Kipper's face darkened. "I tell you, I don't know. And I wish you would stop hounding me, Sandal. I come here to get away from the teasing of Lady Norton and enjoy some pleasant company, for once"—here he gestured toward the painted blonde—"and you are getting in my way. Pleasant English company," he added as an afterthought, leering at Sophie as if suspecting she was one of Naples's generals.

"You did not happen to see Dickie Tottle last night, did you?" Crispin asked, unimpeded by the leer.

"I told you, I haven't ever seen Dickie Tottle," Kipper replied, gulping a handful of almonds. He went on with his mouth full. "Why would I spend an evening with a man when I could spend it with Angel? Last night I was sitting right here, just as I am now."

The blonde leaned toward him to whisper, "Not exactly as you are now." She licked her lips slowly and moved her hand to the laces on his leggings. This potent reminder made Kipper's eyes bulge even more, and he gulped the almonds down as he set himself anew to the task of charting the peaks and valleys on the fine specimen of English womanhood beside him. He was so absorbed in this patriotic work that he did not bother to look up as Crispin dragged Sophie from the table.

Crispin could feel her seething next to him, but he ignored it as he guided her out of the building. Something that Kipper had said had given him an idea, and he needed a moment to assimilate it.

But Sophie's anger would not be contained. She did not even notice the decor of the Worshipful Hall as she and Crispin exited, too absorbed was she in resenting the disrespectful, hideous, and wholly unacceptable behavior of the Earthworm of Sandal. He had silenced her, insulted her, and threatened her, and she was not going to let him get away with it. They had barely crossed the threshold of the patriotic association and reentered the stable yard when she wrenched her elbow from Crispin's grasp and began, "You are the mo—"

Crispin pulled her toward him, cutting off the flow of words with his lips. "I warned you," he whispered, not lifting his mouth from hers. "I told you this would happen."

Sophie willed herself to push him away or pull away or run away or melt away or even simply turn away. She ordered herself to stop acting weak and foolish, to show him how strong she was, how she did not need him. Instead, she stood there and let his lips play over hers, first gently, then with more insistence.

As their mouths slid together with increasing pressure, Sophie felt a curl of heat begin in her stomach and spiral through her body, until she could no longer feel her legs, or arms, or hands, or nose. This was better than hot spiced wine, better even than orange cake, she thought sacrilegiously, and she wanted to taste more. Sophie lost herself in his kiss as she had not lost herself in anything for years, gave herself up to it completely, achingly, overwhelmingly. It was not frightening, not weakening, just devastatingly marvelous. Unable to stop herself, she let out a short moan as his tongue wrapped itself around hers.

Crispin was gone. He wanted to lap the moan off her lips, lips that moved deliciously under his, opening to let him explore them, parting so that he could run the tip of his tongue over them, trembling in response. Lips that moaned again into his, the sweetest sound he had ever heard, lips that parted more fully to let his tongue slip between them, circling slowly, tasting and licking and savoring the sweetness of her mouth, of her.

His tongue slid against hers, dancing around it delicately, gliding off its tip, embracing it in its warmth. Sophie was ravenous, for him, for his touch, for his flavor, starving for the feel of his tongue not only in her mouth and on her lips but everywhere, over all of her. Her body was filled with wave after wave of the intoxicating heat, washing over her, making her feel like she was spinning, like she was all powerful, and like she was going to collapse. She had never kissed anyone before, and she never wanted it to end. Pressing her body against his, she reached up and ran her hand through his soft, thick hair, urging his lips against hers, demanding them, begging them to cover her with their kisses.

Her hand moved from his hair, along his cheek, and toward his neck with a softness that contrasted with the heat of her kiss, a tentativeness that made Crispin gasp for breath. She really must have been some sort of Siren to have this effect on him, to take his well-governed body and make it completely ungovernable. His only thought was to get her out of the stable yard and her devilishly cut dress so he could feel her bare thighs against his, so he could touch her and taste her and lick her all over, so he could learn what it would take to get her eyes to open all the way, learn if they were blue or green, learn how she would react when she reached her climax, learn how his name would sound on her lips, learn how she would change his life.

Crispin pulled away, inhaling sharply. When he looked at her, she did not see the pain he was feeling, or the desire, or the awe, or the anger at himself, anger, bordering on fury, that he had allowed such a thing to happen, such thoughts to pass through his mind. He felt as though he had been a traitor to himself, as if he were undermining his own strength, his own power, his own survival. What if she had been sent by his enemies? What if her presence was a clever trap to weaken him, unhinge him, make him set aside the valiant, solitary strength that had served him so long, a devious weapon to make him vulnerable? Everything he knew about her, he reminded himself, made it seem possible. Everything he knew about her suggested he should put as much distance between them as he could if he was going to survive.

When he looked at her, she saw none of this, because he did not want her to. Instead, she saw what he planned for her to see, a look of triumph.

"I am glad *you* enjoyed that," he said condescendingly.

Sophie felt as though she had been kicked in the stomach. Her face burned with shame, and she had to grip her hands into fists, tense every muscle in her body, to keep from trembling, to keep from doubling over in pain. He had purposely humiliated her, purposely led her on, only to laugh at her. He had pretended to be enjoying it himself, pretended to be feeling the delicious heat and tension just as she was, pretended to like her, just to make her feel wretched.

She wanted to wash herself, wash his taste from her lips, wash his fingers from her hair, wash his smell and sound and feel from her forever. He made her feel foolish, and embarrassed, and unwanted, made her hear a voice in her head she had struggled for so long to banish. "*You are filthy, wicked, and lustful,*" the voice had whispered to her in the darkness, "*and you must be punished.*" Sophie felt chilled again, and vile, and hateful, as the voice came back, the voice that she had striven so hard to block out. She had walked away from everything she knew, turned away from her past, in order to flee the voice. But she had never been able to escape its message.

Sophie Champion, she knew, should have slapped the damned Earl of Sandal. Sophie Champion should have told him that she would rather have kissed a Chinese death-snake—twenty of them—than him, should have laughed in his face, should have stomped on his toe, should have stormed off and never spoken to him, or thought about him, again. But she—the woman who was not always as much like Sophie Champion as she wanted to be, the woman who feared she really was wicked and vile—she could not.

Instead, she just stood and looked at her hands and wondered at the horrible ragged feeling in her stomach. After a long interval had passed she asked, in a quiet voice, "Shouldn't we be going?"

All Crispin's triumph and condescension drained from him. Without thinking, he put a finger under her chin and gently raised her face to his. Like that, with all the fierceness gone, it was even more entrancing than he remembered. His eyes locked on hers, searching, apologizing, and for a moment they were completely silent. When he spoke, his words came without premeditation. "I enjoyed it too," he said, clearing his throat. "In fact, Miss Champion, I cannot remember when I have enjoyed anything more."

Sophie felt a new kind of chill then. She just looked at him for a moment, wariness warring with disbelief and joy, and feared she might cry. She swallowed hard and shook his finger from under her chin. Turning her face slightly, she used the sleeve of her gown to get something out of her eye that was causing it to tear down her cheek, then faced him. "I do not believe I have ever met a man more odious than you are, Lord Sandal. If you ever do that again, I swear that I will give you the longest, deepest, most devastating disembowelment you can imagine."

Crispin smiled broadly. "I can hardly wait." He took her arm, which he noticed was shaking, and helped her mount the horse. When he slid on behind her, and felt her lean into him, he noticed that his arm was shaking too.

Sophie wondered later if it was because of what he had just done or what he was about to do. Because before the horse had taken three steps, a shot rang out and a deep voice bellowed, "Stop in the name of Her Majesty Queen Elizabeth. We have a warrant for the arrest of Miss Sophie Champion."

Without the slightest flicker of surprise or hesitation, Crispin steered the horse toward the complement of heavily armed guards blocking the mouth of the stable yard. "Finally," he told them, his tone berating them for their tardiness. "It has certainly taken you long enough. You can't imagine what I have had to do to keep her occupied."

Chapter Seven

"You bastard," Sophie said, the numbness returning.

"You see what she is like." Crispin addressed the captain of the guards, conspiratorially. "I have already spoken to her once today about her language, but she is reprobate."

"Aye," the captain agreed, looking at Sophie in a way that suggested he hoped to use her to test the old adage about women with loose tongues having loose morals. "She looks like a feisty one."

"She is." Crispin tightened his hold around Sophie's waist. The gesture was unnecessary, because in her numbness Sophie was unable to flinch, let alone struggle. "If you and your men will clear the street, I'll take her to Newgate myself."

"Aye. But I got orders to manacle the prisoner and bring her surrounded by eight guards," the captain said, shaking his head slowly.

"As you wish," Crispin said, shrugging. "I can't guarantee what might happen if I let her off this horse. She is very wily." As he spoke, he squeezed Sophie tighter, wrenching her out of her numbness and causing her to struggle against him rather desperately for breath.

The captain saw this example of her unbounded wiliness and reconsidered his orders. "Aye," he said thoughtfully. "I suppose if

Your Lordship was to undertake to deliver her, no one could blame me for letting you. So long as my men are around, at least she'll have her eight guards."

Crispin gave him an encouraging smile. "It is the least I can do for my country," he said, causing Sophie to squirm again, this time unforced. "And I should be happy for the escort, in case she tries anything devious."

"Aye, aye," the captain said, apparently by way of agreement, and he ordered his men into formation around Crispin's horse. Only two of them had horses of their own, and they were to be the advance guard. The other six, including the captain, surrounded the horse on foot, ensuring that the prisoner could not escape from any side.

Sophie's numbness had subsided, leaving her with an awful sickening feeling, which was not ameliorated by the firm grip Crispin was keeping on her waist. Indeed, as they left the stable yard, his arm tightened even more, and she turned around to protest.

"There is no need to do more damage to me than you have already done," she hissed at him, seething. "You are a—"

"Be quiet." Crispin did not even look at her as he spoke, but kept his eyes directed on the group of three men to his right.

"You dare to silence me," Sophie growled. "After all—"

Crispin's arm squeezing the breath out of her would have been enough to halt her words, but the events that followed left her truly dumbfounded. One moment they were riding in the middle of an unassailable cortege of guardsmen, and the next, they were flying over the guards' heads diagonally. People along the street stopped to gawk as the aerial horse landed on the dirty surface of the road without missing a stride. Mud sprayed everywhere as they galloped forward, and the crowd parted hastily to let them pass rather than risk having their necks trampled by the Pegasean beast and its two riders.

When they had cleared the guards and were well ahead of the horsemen, Sophie felt Crispin lean forward slightly and pat their mount on the neck, whispering, "Good work, Fortuna."

"That was incredible," Sophie told him with breathless admiration, the words disappearing under the sound of Fortuna's hooves.

Crispin nodded but looked grim. "We are not done yet," he muttered with his jaw clenched, and as if on cue, the sound of hooves behind them grew louder.

Sophie leaned down along the horse's mane and tilted her head to see behind her. The two mounted guardsmen were in hot pursuit, the lighter burden of only one rider giving their horses an advantage. They gained steadily, and the hooves of the lead guard's horse were poised to trample Fortuna's, when all of a sudden she lurched sideways.

Crispin urged Fortuna into a narrow alley that ran between two wider streets. Only one of the guards had been quick enough to make the turn, and Crispin felt momentarily relieved to have evened the odds somewhat, but relief soon turned sour. They had nearly reached the far mouth of the alley, and Crispin was already preparing for a sharp turn into the next street, when the second mounted guard appeared before him. Crispin tightened his grip on Sophie and gave an imperative tug on the reins, and once again Fortuna treated a group of astonished spectators to an aerial display. This time the maneuver was not quite perfect, one of Fortuna's back hooves grazing the helmet of the guard blocking the alley. This had the happy effect of sending the guard flying from his horse, but also made Fortuna's landing unsteady.

Fortuna faltered once as she touched down, and Crispin feared they would have to dismount, but she resumed her pace before the other guardsman had time to follow them. They were in another alley, this one longer and apparently curved, because Sophie could not see where it ended. Or rather, she could see where it seemed to end, in a blank wall that was rushing to greet them, but she felt sure if that were the case, Crispin would not be spurring his horse ahead with such wild abandon.

She was wrong. The pounding of the guard's horse behind them echoed off the stone walls of the alley, growing louder as they reached what she was now sure was a dead end. She was about to turn around and ask Crispin if this was simply another one of his clever ways to make her arrest seem more exciting, when all the air left her body and she felt herself falling rapidly toward the ground.

Instead of hard-packed dirt, she fell on something yielding and was immediately dragged through a narrow opening. She barely had time to gain her feet before something was slid in front of the opening, and everything became dark. Very, very dark.

Sophie went completely cold, began to shake, and moved quickly toward the opening by means of which they entered and through which she could see a faint outline of light.

"What the devil are you doing?" Crispin demanded in a low and menacing whisper. "We are going the other way."

"No," Sophie shook her head. "No, I have to get out. I can't stay here."

"Nor can you go out," Crispin told her impatiently. "A dozen of the Queen's best guardsmen, not those boys we were tussling with earlier, will soon be making a thorough search of this area, and it is only a matter of moments before they find that trapdoor and follow us. Come on." He took her hand and pulled her forward.

But she would not move. She stood there, terror stricken. "I can't," she said in a voice that was unfamiliar to Crispin, but in a tone he completely understood.

For the second time in as many days, Crispin was taken by surprise. This woman, who was completely unmoved by anything except the most goading insults, whom even the threat of death or the gallows or a crew of the Queen's finest guards could not alarm, this woman whom men called a siren because she bewitched them, this woman who seemed not to know fear, she, Sophie Champion, was afraid of the dark. Acting on instinct rather than reason, he slid toward her and put his arms around her.

She flinched from his embrace and began to tremble violently. With harsh clarity Crispin understood that hers was no shapeless, childish fear, but a real, tangible fear based on something that had happened to her. He was surprised again, this time by the pang this realization brought with it.

"Sophie," he whispered to her, removing one of his gloves and trying to take her hand in his. "Sophie, I do not mean you any harm. Do you understand?"

She recoiled from his touch again. He could not see her, but he could hear her jagged breathing. "Maybe," she squeezed out finally. "But I cannot go in there."

"Close your eyes." His voice was low, soothing, not at all like the voice that haunted her. "Close your eyes and follow me."

"No." He felt her shaking her head. "I can't. I won't. I...I...I am—"

"I know." Crispin spared her the pain of admitting her fright. "But you must trust me. I will not lead you astray. And it is your only hope of escape."

Sophie was as mortified as she was terrified. She had never admitted to anyone that she was afraid of the dark. It was the one vestige of her childhood she had not been able to shed, the one link between Sophie Champion and the girl she had once been, and she hated herself for it. She knew Octavia had figured it out years earlier, because Octavia knew everything, but they had never discussed it, and Sophie had always felt it was her own secret. And her own, her only, weakness.

The sound of heavy footsteps circling around the entrance of the cavern lent urgency to Crispin's voice as he broke into her thoughts. "Sophie, please. Trust me," he admonished.

Maybe it was the sound of the footsteps. Or maybe it was the sound of her name on his lips. Whatever the cause, Sophie did then what she had sworn she would never do. She closed her eyes, extended her hand, and entrusted herself, her life, her body, to a man in the dark. At first she shuffled along behind him on the uneven surface of the cavern, barely responsive to his warnings to duck low or watch her step, breathing desperately in large, hungry gasps, but soon the floor beneath her feet grew more level, her fear began to ebb, and her breathing grew even.

His voice, smooth and low and kind and encouraging, kept her trembling at bay. The warm, unthreatening feel of his hand, leading her steadily and without innuendo, kept her moving forward almost without realizing it. Like that, with her eyes closed, the darkness seemed paradoxically to recede. She was somewhere outside of herself, cocooned in the safety of his words and his touch, impervious to the fears and voices that tormented her in the darkness. Instead of feeling weak and vulnerable, she felt safe. She did not know if they had been walking for minutes or hours or days when Crispin stopped, withdrew his hand, and told her to open her eyes.

She was standing in a narrow, wood-paneled hall, with no end in sight and a door on one wall. Crispin was holding a taper, which he had apparently taken from the large collection in a basket on the floor, and which he had lit as soon as she had relinquished his hand. The candlelight flickered unsteadily between them, and it took all of Sophie's courage to raise her eyes to his.

"Are you all right?" Crispin whispered.

Sophie nodded. "Thank you," she said, her voice still not quite her own.

Crispin put his finger to his lips. "*Shhh.* You are scarcely out of danger yet."

"I thought," she began, then stopped. "Out there, I thought..."

"That I was going to turn you over to the constables?"

Sophie nodded.

"I could hardly collect my winnings from you if you were in jail," Crispin pointed out sensibly. And with great difficulty. For he found, standing in this narrow space with her, that his senses were completely inundated, and not by logic. The trust she had put in him, following him into the darkness despite her fear, made him feel as though he had been given custody of a rich, and dangerous, treasure, the only fear of a woman without fear, the trust of a woman who did not trust easily. In the flickering candlelight she even looked like a precious gem, her eyes, her lips, her hair, all seemed to be begging to be lavished with attention, covered in kisses, sampled by his mouth and hands and eyes and...

"We had better keep moving," Crispin said, jolting himself to attention. "This way."

And none too soon. There was a great clatter in the direction from which they had come, and the sound of voices began to reverberate along the walls of the hallway. Without thought, Crispin reached out his free hand to Sophie and, also without thought, she took it.

The candle blew out as they made their way farther down the hall, but Sophie was too occupied with listening to the approaching footsteps to notice. She heard the guards divide up the various passages and doorways, heard the heavy breathing of those who were following them, heard the curse of a tall guard as he hit his head in the dark. Suddenly, she felt someone trample on the hem of her gown, and a voice that sounded like it was in her ear yelled out, "I've got her."

Crispin cursed himself for his earlier weakness, for the time he had lost in admiring her, as he felt desperately along the wall with his free hand. He hoped to heaven he remembered how the panel worked.

"I've got her," the guard yelled again, and this time Sophie felt a hand grab her arm. "Bring the light, she's right here."

That was the guard's last mission. One moment he was holding his prey, tight in his hand; the next, when his companions arrived with their lantern, he was holding nothing but an empty riding cloak. The shock of having a girl disappear into thin air, like some sort of apparition or demon, unsettled the guardsman completely, and from that day forward he was never right in the head.

His companions did not waste time pointing out to him the door in the wall ahead, but rather followed their hunch that the disappearing girl had merely left by that means and soon disappeared themselves.

The guards' lantern cast only a dim light, not enough to see in front of them. But they could hear the muffled footsteps of their quarry, hear them rushing just out of range, and they quickened their pace. The footsteps sounded closer now and the guards could tell they were drawing near.

Sophie and Crispin had not stopped to catch their breath when they were safely on the other side of the panel, but had kept going.

As if by premeditation, they developed a series of hand signals that allowed Crispin to warn Sophie of changes in direction or steps up and down without having to speak. Sophie's heart was pounding, and she could hear the sound of the guards' footsteps, but it was strangely distorted.

"I see something up there," the lead guard huffed to his followers as he raised his lantern. "I think we're gaining on them."

The words sent a chill down Sophie's spine, but it was nothing compared to the chill she felt when she heard the dogs begin to bark.

"Stop," Crispin whispered, but not early enough, and Sophie went careening into him.

"Why are we halting? They have dogs," Sophie insisted, now pulling blindly ahead into the darkness herself.

But Crispin was unyielding. "Those are Lawrence's dogs. The guards took the other tunnel, the one with the door. All the doors along that corridor are traps. Only the hidden panels go anywhere."

"Traps? Hidden panels?" Sophie repeated. "What is this place?"

Crispin relit the taper. "Pickering's Highway. It runs from Alsatia all the way to Whitehall, and even has an exit near my house. Lawrence found it advisable to connect all his properties with underground tunnels, so that the profits might be transported to his coffers without interference from his competitors. We should be fairly safe now."

Sophie spent a moment appreciating the cleverness of this ploy and the new security of their position, before the import of Crispin's words set in. "Your friend Lawrence is Lawrence *Pickering?*" Sophie spoke the name with a mixture of awe and horror. "You propose to leave me with the lord chancellor of the London underworld?"

"You make him sound like the ruler of Hades. He is not Pluto, merely a very good friend of mine. And I can hardly think of a better place for someone on the run from the Queen's guards than in his house. Despite his reputation, Lawrence has never once been to prison, or even been charged with a crime. Which is far more than you can say for yourself, Miss Champion."

Sophie blushed deeply, not, as Crispin supposed, at his gibe, but rather at the pang she felt when she heard him addressing her formally once again. A pang that was quickly squelched. She no more wanted to be on informal terms with the Earl of Scandal than she wanted him to kiss her again, she reminded herself convincingly. Certainly he had been kind to her, and had rescued her twice, but that was no reason for her to want to lift his hand to her lips and kiss it, and run her mouth over his palm, and lick the salty sweetness of his fingertips and let them roam down her neck, across her collarbone, let them drift along the bodice of her gown, let them dip down and gently—

No, kindness was certainly no reason for that. Lord Grosgrain had been a thousand times kinder to her, and she had never wanted to do those things to him. The thought of Lord Grosgrain brought her back to herself, and her investigation. Despite herself, she had to admit that Crispin was correct. There was probably no better place for her to hide in London than with the notorious Lord Pickering, probably no one better equipped to help her keep the authorities at bay.

"Very well," she conceded, as much to get Crispin to move away from her, and hopefully resuscitate her knees, as because she thought it was a good idea. "I will stay with Lord Pickering. But I will not be a prisoner."

"Of course not," Crispin agreed. "That would hardly be sporting of me. Now come on. I am thirsty." Thus saying, he set out abruptly down the corridor at a rapid clip. He still had Sophie's hand in his, and it was all she could do to keep up with him, what with her intoxicated knees and his burst of speed. He dragged her through two turns and up a short flight of stairs, and stopped finally in front of a fine wooden door with gilt gold moldings.

Sophie had the eerie feeling that she was being watched, but she did not hear anyone, nor could she make out any figures in the gloom of the corridor behind them. She was about to ask Crispin why they were just standing there, when the rasping of a large bolt being shot sounded and the door opened slightly.

"Who is she?" a harsh voice asked from the darkness.

"Sophie Champion," Crispin answered. "I guarantee her personally, Christopher."

The door opened a little farther, and a short, sleek man toddled out. He appeared, by Sophie's best guess, to be four hundred years old, but the black eye squinting at her through the monocle felt vigorous in its scrutiny. He circled her, tracing long lines with his eyeglass as he looked her up and down, surveying every inch of her being as if preparing to whip off her portrait later from memory. When he had memorized her to his satisfaction, he slid past her and nodded once to Crispin. "His Lordship is expecting you," he informed them, opening the door for them to pass. "Personal apartments."

"How would Lord Pickering have known we were coming?" Sophie asked as they started up a set of dimly lit wooden stairs.

"My guess is that Fortuna beat us here," Crispin said simply, as if a horse that could premeditate the actions of its master were a regular sort of beast. Sophie was tempted to press him about it, but something in his expression stopped her, and they ascended the rest of the stairs in silence.

Sophie watched her companion from the corner of her eye. The man next to her was cool and inscrutable, apparently without emotion, and certainly incapable of anything as human as compassion. Whatever motivated him to save her, twice, from the constables, was certainly pragmatic and not something messy like mere kindness. She repeated this to herself three times, until she had wrung away any suspicion that there might be something more, or that the heat emanating from where their hands were still clasped was indicative of anything other than their recent exertions. Indeed, given that he was only helping her for his own ends, she had better concentrate on finding out what those were and why he was so interested in the death of Richard Tottle, anyway.

The first landing brought them into a wide entrance hall with what Crispin knew was one of the best collections of modern Italian paintings in England. Seeing Sophie's awe at the sight of them raised his thirst to new heights, and he was tempted to tell her that Lawrence had not picked out a single one of them himself, but had been assisted by Crispin's cousin Tristan, whose collection was a hundred—no, four hundred—times better. Instead, he rushed her by them, pulling her up the remaining stairs so rapidly that Sophie looked behind her to see if they were again being pursued.

"Don't worry, the dogs are otherwise occupied," a voice tinted with amusement said from the top of the stairs. "Besides, I don't usually let them in the house when they are hungry."

Sophie was panting by the time they reached the speaker, and it was all she could do to perform a one-handed curtsy.

"Lawrence Pickering, this is Miss Sophie Champion," Crispin offered.

"I would have known without your introduction, my friend. The report of Miss Champion's beauty precedes her, and was by no means exaggerated."

"Nor, I see, was your reputation for wit, Lord Pickering," Sophie countered.

She now saw a glimmer of what made so many women describe Lawrence Pickering as "meltingly handsome." Indeed, had he not looked so much like Crispin, with his fair hair and bluish gray eyes, she might have thought Lawrence extremely good looking. But seeing the two together was like seeing a masterpiece and a copy side by side.

A masterpiece and a copy? Sophie repeated to herself with horror. What was happening to her? She resolved from that moment forward to find Lawrence Pickering the most handsome man alive.

"Touché, Miss Champion," the most handsome man alive said, bowing. "I can see that we will get along very well." Lawrence was about to reach for Sophie's right hand to kiss it, but he noticed the proprietary way it was grasped in Crispin's and raised an eyebrow in his friend's direction.

"Has Fortuna arrived?" Crispin asked, ignoring the eyebrow.

"Yes. Along with several members of the Queen's brigade babbling about the Earl of Scandal's latest caper, but I got rid of them.

Miss Champion, you are certainly a favorite of the Queen today. I feel honored to have you grace my humble home."

Crispin gave something between a snort and a snicker at Lawrence's words, so it was left to Sophie to reply, "The honor is ours, Lord Pickering."

"Please, call me Lawrence. All my friends do."

Sophie smiled at him, and Crispin felt suddenly parched. "Very well, Lawr—"

"I am thirsty," Crispin interjected, to keep things from degenerating further.

Lawrence smirked at Crispin. "I wish I could offer you a glass of the very special wine King Philip sent over to me last month—I'm sorry, what did you say?"

"Nothing," Crispin replied, narrowing his eyes and mouthing "braggart" to his friend.

"As I was saying, I wish I could have Kit bring you something from my modest cellar, but I'm afraid you'll have to go without. A messenger from Sandal Hall arrived an hour ago instructing me to dispatch you home at once if you should appear here. Apparently something to do with The Aunts." Lawrence's eyes were twinkling with merriment.

"Are you trying to be amusing?" Crispin asked, his throat an arid desert.

"If I were trying to be amusing, Crispin, you would be doubled over with laughter right now. I am simply telling the unadorned truth."

"You are not leaving?" Sophie turned to Crispin, and the note of alarm in her voice made his thirst disappear.

"I must," he told her graciously, but without a hint of emotion. "Do not worry, you will be safe here with Lawrence." Crispin's tone stayed level, but he gazed at his friend meaningfully. "You will see to it that she is well looked after, won't you?"

Lawrence returned Crispin's pointed glance and nodded almost imperceptibly. "I guarantee that she will have the best accommodations money can buy."

Sophie felt that some sort of negotiation had taken place between the two men, but before she had time to decipher their code of looks and gestures, her attention was distracted by Crispin.

"It has been a most memorable afternoon, Miss Champion. Thank you very much for your company."

Their eyes met as Crispin brought their joined hands to his lips, did not waver as he planted a soft, lingering kiss on her palm, did not move as their fingers slowly untwined, did not separate until Crispin turned to descend the stairs.

"Thank you," Sophie whispered softly after him.

After a decent interval, Lawrence cleared his throat. "Tell me, Miss Champion—"

"Please, call me Sophie." It was a poor substitute for hearing it from Crispin's lips, but it would have to do.

"You do me too much honor, Sophie. Tell me, why exactly does the Queen desire your presence in her prison so intensely?"

Sophie gave a feeble smile at his description. "I cannot say. I believe she thinks I murdered a man. But I assure you, I am not dangerous."

Lawrence remembered the way Crispin had clutched her hand and wanted to disagree, but he stopped himself. "There is a world of difference between actually *being* dangerous and seeming dangerous to the Queen. The first you can live with. The second will get you killed."

"Lord Sandal tells me that you are expert at avoiding the latter," Sophie said, taking the arm he proffered and allowing herself to be led toward a set of double doors. "Do you think you could give me any tips?"

Lawrence smiled thoughtfully. "It is really very basic, fundamentally a question of bartering. Everyone has their price, and the Queen is no exception. I learned long ago that if I can be of service to Her Majesty, she and her guards will leave me alone. In fact, I have just concluded a most interesting deal with her which will ensure my freedom from their interference for many months to come."

"What kind of deal?" Sophie asked with authentic interest.

"The simplest kind. A plain, unadorned exchange." As Lawrence spoke, he opened one of the double doors. "Her Majesty gets something she wants, and I get something I want."

Sophie followed Lawrence into his office and heard the door close behind her abruptly. She had been completely absorbed in what he was saying, and it took her a moment to realize that they were no longer alone. Indeed, the ample chamber was completely filled by soldiers clothed in the armor of the Queen's guard. Almost all of them were wearing helmets, but she recognized the fat constable from Richard Tottle's print shop.

"You'll not escape me this time, Miss Champion," he told her, licking his lips, and his beady eyes did not leave her as he issued his commands. "Tie her up, men. You heard what the Earl of Sandal said. We're to make sure that she is 'well looked after.'"

"The bastard," Sophie said, her numbness returning.

Chapter Eight

Crispin rode home slowly, in no great hurry to greet The Aunts. The last thing he needed, with all that had occurred since his return to London, was The Aunts, his father's sisters, taking up residence at Sandal Hall. He knew they had names, the names had been drilled into him relentlessly by his father, but to him they would always be, simply, The Aunts. It was enough.

Crispin and his brother, Ian, were convinced as children that The Aunts ate broken glass instead of food and routinely sacrificed small animals in the demonic rituals that gave them their strength. During Crispin's lifetime, The Aunts had between them run through twelve husbands, mainly by comparing them incessantly and unfavorably with their beloved younger brother, Hugo, Crispin's father. Since the death of the dozenth lord, The Aunts had undertaken the authorship of *A Compendium of Proper Behavior Every Man and Woman Ought to Know for the Improvement of Social Converse and the Strengthening of the English Nation*. It was, of course, dedicated to the memory of Hugo, the ideal picture of English manhood, decorum, and civility, and they had been kind enough to send excerpts of it to Hugo's heirs every year at Christmastide so they might measure themselves against their father and better feel their inferiority. Just thinking about the most recent selection, "On the Appropriate Vocabulary for a Gentleman (With an Appendix of Apparently Harmless Words from Which Great Harm May Come)," nearly made Crispin want to shout "Bottom" (a Strictly Forbidden Word) at the top of his lungs. Crispin would more willingly face the most sophisticated and best-trained imperial army than The Aunts.

And, indeed, he had. As well as cunning ministers, hired assassins, deadly courtesans, suicidal zealots, traitorous courtiers, two firing squads, and a host of strange beasts—from the sand snake of Turkey, which disposes of its prey by strangling, to the almost invisible Gaelic spider, whose venom makes its victim feel like its blood is on fire for hours before it finally kills—that had been variously introduced into his chambers to destroy him. The secret commission from Queen Elizabeth that Crispin had accepted two and a half years earlier had allowed him to prove to himself, if not to The Aunts, that he was at least the man his father, Hugo, had been. During his service as the Phoenix, Crispin had stemmed three invasions of England, disrupted five attempts to assassinate the Queen, prevented sixteen heavily laden English ships from being captured, and saved the Exchequer well over eight hundred thousand pounds. But now he had been abruptly recalled from his duties, recalled to London, to infamy. And possibly to death.

A fortnight, fourteen days, was hardly an infinity of time in which to do what needed to be done. Seven days had passed since his meeting with Queen Elizabeth and the dead ends had merely multiplied, until the night before when he found himself at the Unicorn staring down at the body of the late Richard Tottle and at half a piece of parchment clutched in his fingers. That piece had proved very useful to Crispin, and the other, missing half, very dangerous. At least until that afternoon in Tottle's office on the floor below the pink paradise when the ink that Crispin had accidentally spilled over Tottle's ledger also ran onto a detailed catalog of Queen Elizabeth's dinner menus for the past month. The menus were real, but the catalog was more than a culinary record—it was also the key needed to decipher the other half of Tottle's list. With it gone, the missing piece of parchment could do no harm, and Crispin could turn his full attention back to investigating why Tottle had been killed and, more important, why someone wanted to discredit the Phoenix.

He had toyed with the idea of pretending to have information about the Phoenix in a more direct attempt to find out who was behind the reward and why, but discarded it. Asking too many questions would only arouse suspicions he preferred to keep dormant, suspicions easily awakened if anyone bothered to note that the time of the Phoenix's operation on the continent corresponded exactly with the duration of Crispin's putative exile. The gossip that had been carefully spread through England about Crispin's exploits in Europe had thus far worked to prevent such an identification, the rumors of the Earl of Scandal's wayward, dissolute lifestyle making any relationship between him and the Phoenix seem absurd, but only thus far. Crispin had done his best to behave infamously in every major court in Europe, he and Thurston staying up well into the night many nights concocting better and more outrageous activities for him to perform the following day in order to flesh out his rakish persona. But all that hard work could be erased in the blink of an eye if he was not careful. Even if he could not directly protect his secret identity, he had to be scrupulous not to undermine it himself.

Which recollection brought with it the first comforting thought he had all day. As Fortuna steered herself into the stable yard of Sandal Hall, Crispin congratulated himself on the fact that he could be sure, absolutely sure, that at least The Aunts believed in his rakish persona. There was no doubt but that they had arrived with trunks full of pamphlets and lectures to administer to him about his misdeeds of the preceding two and a half years. At any other time this would have made him want to groan, but now he saw how he could put it to use. Given The Aunts' wide acquaintance and even wider circle of gossips, he decided to do his best to confirm them in their opinions of him. Once they got started commenting on his behavior to their friends, people would be hard-pressed to see the

Earl of Scandal as anything other than a luxury-loving wretch. He had just begun taking bets with himself as to what they would start in on first, the dishonor he was heaping on the Sandal name or his delinquency in getting married, when he crossed the threshold of his house.

"I am pleased to see you safely returned, sir," Thurston said, materializing before Crispin had taken more than two steps. "Your aunts are anxiously awaiting you in the Green Room."

"I will be very happy to see them," Crispin responded with feeling.

Thurston's eyes opened ever so slightly wider, a sign of intense surprise, at Crispin's enthusiasm. "Very good, sir. If I might take the liberty, sir, I have laid out your blue silk doublet in your apartment."

Crispin waved the suggestion aside. "I wouldn't dream of changing. All this dirt going to waste? Never."

"Very good, sir," Thurston replied, the eyes opening a hairbreadth more, but Crispin was already brushing by him on his way up the stairs.

He entered the room at a pace he knew The Aunts had treated in a chapter entitled "Unseemly Haste," and was moving toward them when he stopped abruptly.

"Who are you?" he asked, frowning, of the man seated in a chair alongside The Aunts. These two august ladies, still beautiful and blond despite their years, would hardly have appeared to the casual observer as women who would as soon bite the heads off of flowers and young children as dine upon a trout, but Crispin knew better. The taller and more lethal one, Lady Priscilla Snowden, spoke first.

"This is our nephew," Lady Priscilla told the seated man. "Please excuse his lack of manners. He was raised in Italy, you know." She turned her steely eyes on Crispin. "This, nephew, is Mister Jack. He has been waiting many hours for your return and is telling us the most fascinating tales of—" She turned back to the seated man. "What did you call it?"

"Coney catching," Mister Jack replied in a gruff voice. "Finding a gentleman as has come into London from out in the country and ridding him of his extra wealth."

"He is writing a book about it," Lady Eleanor Nearview, the Other Aunt, informed her nephew. "He is a very enterprising young man." Her tone made it clear that there were other young men in the room about whom the same could not be said. "Very much like your father, Hugo," she added, lest Crispin had missed the innuendo.

"'Work need fear no task,' that is what our beloved brother always said," Lady Priscilla told their guest.

"No, sister," Lady Eleanor corrected with a frown. "'Worth need wear no mask.' That is what our dear Hugo said, sister. I am quite sure."

"Are you, sister? Quite sure?"

"Quite, quite sure," Lady Eleanor confirmed. The two ladies regarded one another sharply, and for a moment it looked as though they might be headed for open conflict.

Then, sniffing, Lady Priscilla changed to a more amicable subject. "I say, do you smell something off, sister?"

"It's His there Lordship," Mister Jack volunteered. "Stinks like a sewer."

Lady Priscilla and Lady Eleanor both nodded. "So he does," Lady Eleanor agreed. "A fine turn of phrase."

Crispin had been standing, stunned and silent, during this exchange, but he now found his voice. "It is a pleasure to welcome my two dear aunts to Sandal Hall." He was drawing near to give each of them a kiss when Lady Priscilla's raised palm stopped him.

"Do not lie to us, nephew," she instructed in clipped tones. "We know your feelings. And we have a great deal to say on the subject."

"A great deal," Lady Eleanor reiterated.

"A very great deal," Lady Priscilla continued, nodding. "But we shall contain ourselves until after you have met with Mister Jack. You have kept him waiting long enough."

"Mighty fine of you two," Jack said amiably. "My business with His Lordship will be over quicker than a bug's eye, I promise you, provided he's willing. Not that I can stand the smell too long neither."

The Aunts each inclined a head to acknowledge Jack's kindness, and he and his odiferous companion made their way in silence to

Crispin's library. When they were both seated, Crispin behind his desk with the raven on its perch at his shoulder and his guest across from him, Mister Jack began the discussion.

"Damn fine ladies down there. It would be a pity if something happened to them."

Crispin said nothing, just watched his companion.

"So you see," Jack went on, "it would be best for you to mind your own business."

"Disgusting slug," the raven piped in, startling both men.

Crispin recovered first. "I am afraid I do not follow you."

Jack glared at the bird. "All I'm saying is that the death of Richard Tottle is not your concern." Jack reached into his tunic and extracted a paper that he carefully unfolded and pushed across the desk toward Crispin. "To prove it, I'm authorized to pay you one hundred pounds."

Crispin frowned down at the bill of credit before him, then at his enterprising companion. "Let me get this straight. You are offering to pay me one hundred pounds to stop looking into the death of Richard Tottle."

Jack gave his version of a smile. "That's the shape of it."

For a moment Crispin just stared at him. Then he tipped his head back and laughed. It was a luxury he had not allowed himself in a long time, not since before he had gone to Spain, and it felt wonderful to let it out. "A hundred pounds," he repeated, still laughing. When he had subsided into the occasional chuckle, he returned his gaze to Jack. "A hundred pounds would scarcely keep my household fed for a day. Why don't we do this? Why don't I give *you* a hundred pounds right now, and you can tell me who you are working for?"

Jack seemed to hesitate for a moment, the enterprising gleam flickering in his eye, but then shook his head. "Ain't no good. I got to get your promise that you will stop interfering in the death of Richard Tottle."

"Why? What business is it of yours?"

"None of mine, I'm only the errand boy. But I am empowered to assure you that justice will be done in the death of Richard Tottle."

Jack spoke the last phrase as if he had memorized it from a hornbook.

Jack's pronunciation made Crispin chuckle again. "What exactly do you mean that 'justice will be done'?"

"Only that we already know who to have arrested for the murder and your meddling won't help any."

"You refer, I take it, to Sophie Champion?" Crispin asked offhandedly.

Jack struck an apologetic tone. "I ain't empowered to say any names."

"This *is* a problem." Crispin sounded equally apologetic. "I couldn't really agree without knowing who your intended victim is."

"I can assure you it's someone who is deserving," Jack offered.

But Crispin only shook his head, a sad smile on his lips. "I am afraid your assurance is not enough. What if I refuse to stop investigating?"

"Then I am empowered to assure you that you will not like what happens."

Crispin stopped smiling abruptly and leaned across the desk. "Please tell your employer that no one threatens me."

"I ain't threatening *you*," Jack said with emphasis. "Only it would be a pity if them two ladies out there should happen to have an accident."

"Have an accident, have an accident," the raven chanted.

Crispin shook his head again. "No," he mused. "No, I do not think they will experience any accidents in the near future. Indeed, I am sure of it."

The look of enterprise returned to Jack's expression. "Does that mean you agree to our terms?"

"Certainly not. It means that I am confident that nothing will happen to my aunts, or to any other members of my household. And I can be confident because if anything does happen, I will perform such acts on you that you will beg, in vain, for your death." Crispin leaned back comfortably in his chair, adding conversationally, "If you care for a reference about what occurs when I am inclined to blame someone, ask Lord Grip how he came to be missing his left leg. Or, rather, don't. I cannot recall how much of his tongue I left behind." Crispin looked up to see his steward enter, as if on cue. "Ah, Thurston. Can you recollect in what state we left Lord Grip's tongue?"

"I believe we left it in a very good state, sir. In a lovely glass carafe on His Lordship's bedside table."

Crispin nodded, then trained his cold blue-gray eyes on his visitor. "I feel that our discussion is at an end. I wish you a good evening, Mister Jack. And I hope, for your sake, we shall not meet again."

Jack said nothing, but the lack of color in his face and his unsteadiness as he rose from the chair gave a fair index of his state of mind. His hand trembled as he took his walking stick from Thurston and turned to go. But he was not completely without his wits, for he turned back and made a grab for the bill of credit from the desk.

"Certainly not," Crispin said, retaining the paper. "This is my only link to you. How else will I know where to look if I need retribution?"

Crispin waited until he heard not only the door to his apartment but also the main door of the house close behind Jack before the chuckling resumed. Lord Grip joined in, hopping up and down and repeating, "Strip! Slug! Strip! Strip!" Crispin patted the bird fondly and decided he would have to give Thurston a raise for that comment about the carafe. Perhaps the bill of credit now lying on his desk.

Looking down at the paper, Crispin shook his head again. Only a fool would try to bribe the Earl of Sandal with a measly one hundred pounds, and the threats had been as pathetic as the offer. He mentally wished Enterprising Jack and his cronies good luck taking on The Aunts. But the offer did confirm what Crispin had concluded at the Worshipful Hall, that Richard Tottle's life, as well as his death, was more complicated than it seemed.

Crispin closed his eyes for a moment and pulled up the image he had stored there earlier in the day, the image of Tottle's register.

Crispin had trained himself to make a mental portrait of any face he came across in his undertakings as the Phoenix, and the same skill worked with documents. He could see Tottle's register in his mind as if it were lying on the desk before him. Scanning its pages mentally, he easily found what he was looking for. There were seven of them, seven names, all of them listed in the register as having paid either one hundred pounds a month or a lump sum of twelve hundred pounds. Perhaps one of them would be more eager to talk than Kipper had been. Crispin had just made up his mind to send each of them a message inviting them for an interview as soon as possible, when he moved his mental eye down the remembered page and saw the last name.

Sophie Champion.

She, too, was listed in Tottle's register, indeed, hers was the final entry. With a strange tightening in his chest, Crispin had to admit that every corner he turned in this investigation seemed to lead him right back to Sophie Champion.

Her name changed to her face in his mind, and Tottle's register melted away. Against his will he pictured her as she had been when he left her at Lawrence's, and against his will he felt an unfamiliar twinge that had to be jealousy. Damn her and her unnerving effect on him. He knew next to nothing about her, and what little he did know, from Elwood, suggested she was a dangerous siren capable of luring men—even possibly her own godfather—to their doom. Yet never before had he had such difficulty concentrating on anything, particularly not anything as crucial as saving his own neck in seven days. Sophie Champion was not even the type of woman he liked. For one thing, she was too smart, too independent, and too irksome. And for another, she was not small and delicate, she did not have hair the color of the finest butter, or breasts that recalled Spanish oranges. She made him feel things—anger, annoyance, and frustration primarily—that he had set aside years ago. Not to mention amusement. Or desire.

There was something completely wrong about his reaction to her, and he was delighted when he hit upon a way of quashing his disturbing impulses and investigating the real nature of her relationship with Lord Grosgrain, simultaneously. First thing the next morning, he would pay a visit to Lord Grosgrain's widow, the lovely Constantia, who, as the perfect embodiment of a shallow, sweet-tempered, light-haired, orange-breasted sylph, could answer his questions and reinforce his preferences simultaneously. Who knew but that he might not decide to propose to her after all? Then afterward, bolstered by Constantia's charms and information, Crispin would march back to Pickering Hall and make Sophie Champion answer his questions at last.

But first he needed something for his thirst. Before he could reach for the bellpull to summon Thurston, the man himself materialized, carrying a carafe of burgundy wine in one hand and a small packet in the other.

"Fine work with the tongue," Crispin commended him, reaching for the carafe and decanting its contents into a silver goblet. "I never would have thought of that myself."

"Thank you, sir," Thurston replied, unmoved. Then he extended the packet to Crispin. "This just arrived, sir, by special messenger."

Crispin swallowed the goblet's contents in one gulp and took the package. Using a magnifying lens, he closely examined the wax seal, and when he saw it was red and marked with a sundial over which the north star hovered at two o'clock, his thirst was entirely forgotten. "From North Hall," he announced to Thurston, then added, tapping the seal, "Red book, second volume."

North Hall was the house of Crispin's cousin L.N., Lucien North Howard, the Earl of Danford. L.N. was the most mysterious of the six men known throughout Europe as the Arboretti, and the most powerful. Not simply because he was the titular head of the Arboretti—the enormous shipping empire Crispin and his cousins had inherited from their grandfather—but because he was the actual head of Queen Elizabeth's secret service. Crispin alone of all the Arboretti knew this. Indeed, it was L.N. who had recruited Crispin into Queen Elizabeth's secret service two and a half years earlier, L.N. who oversaw his missions,

L.N. who, in fact, oversaw every branch of Elizabeth's vast spy network.

Crispin had written to L.N. asking for any information he might have about the Phoenix, and had heard nothing, until now. But when L.N. wrote to Crispin from North Hall it was always about Arboretti affairs, never Phoenix-related, so Crispin knew that this missive was unofficial. The color of the wax, however, indicated that the red cipher had been used, one of their most sophisticated business ciphers, reserved for highly confidential messages. To the naked eye, the message read:

> Welcome back. I should have written earlier, but I was at my house in the country. There was a faire in town, or rather half a dozen of them, some blonde, some dark, and two luscious redheads. Twins. I will leave the rest to your imagination, but suffice it to say that I, like Caesar veni, vidi, vici—came, saw, and conquered—although he might have had the order wrong. Remember Cecilia? She is married now, the mother of two brave blond boys. My, how the great are fallen. Best wishes, your cousin, L.N.

Crispin's study with the magnifying lens had revealed an almost imperceptible shadow of red around the seal, revealing that it had been broken and refastened by an expert before its delivery, and he hoped that whichever of his enemies happened to be skimming his correspondence had enjoyed L.N.'s commentary on conquering the fair sex. For his part, Crispin was much more interested in the punctuation of the seventh sentence and the spelling of the word "faire." Using these as guides, he consulted volume two of the red cipher and had the message translated in less than ten minutes.

"'Bill of Credit found on Richard Tottle's body signed by Sophie Champion was drawn on Loundes and Wainscot,'" Crispin read aloud, and then frowned. The bill of credit that Enterprising Jack had offered him in exchange for his silence was also drawn on that bank.

Crispin sat, glowering at the note for a space, then shrugged. It was probably just a coincidence.

"There is no such thing as coincidence," Lawrence had told his brother, Bull, over a decanter of wine earlier that evening. "Nor luck. Nor destiny. We plow our own paths, Bull. I have told you that a thousand times."

"Still, you have to admit it was lucky her coming here like that," Bull had stubbornly asserted for the eighth time.

That had been hours ago, just after the soldiers left, but even now, alone in his office, Lawrence had grudgingly to agree. Indeed, for him it had been a very lucky day. Not only had his cooperation with the Crown in the matter of Sophie Champion versus Regina Britannia earned him five new licenses for gaming houses in the suburbs of London, enabling him to turn his already booming properties there from quiet illegal clubs to bustling places of public resort—he had particularly high hopes for a new place called the Velvet Slipper, where the women overseeing the tables would wear nothing but, yes, velvet slippers—but it had also been more personally gratifying.

He smiled to himself as he thought about the message he had just sent. It was certainly going to make its recipient very, very happy. He was about to ring for another decanter of his best wine, to toast himself and the success of his enterprise, when the panel in the wall behind his chair slid open and a woman came out.

She approached slowly, seeming to float toward him rather than walk, until they were facing each other. She knew he liked to watch her move, liked to watch her compact, lithe figure glide up to him, liked to see her hair, so blond it looked like the finest spun gold, fall between their faces as she dipped down to kiss him. She let him rest the wide palm of his hand against her hip and use it to guide her into his lap.

"Darling, this is a marvelous surprise," Lawrence said when she was settled there.

"I only have a moment, but I was desperate to see you and find out how everything went this afternoon." She brought his lips down to cover hers for a moment, then, seductively but firmly, pushed his face away.

Lawrence smiled down at her, his treasure. "Perfectly, my love."

"You must be delighted." She took a sugared almond from the bowl on his desk and ran it suggestively down her neck to the embroidered bee at the center of her bodice, drawing his eyes to her flawless breasts.

"I am," Lawrence said in a voice newly husky, bending to retrieve the almond from its resting place with his tongue. "And I would be still more delighted if you would allow me to marry you right now. Tonight."

"You know that is impossible, Lawrence," she chided him as she kissed sugar from his lips.

"Darling, you torture me. May I at least carry you to my bed and make love to you for the next ten hours?"

She reached out her hand to stroke his cheek. "Soon, dearest. Very soon." She rose from his lap and moved toward the staircase hidden behind the panel. "I wish I could stay tonight, but I really must be off. You know how they will talk at home."

After a few more entreaties and denials, Lawrence lapped the last grains of sugar from her cleavage and walked her down the stairs to her waiting litter. Ensconced there among the rich velvet pillows, each embossed in gold with her personal emblem, she looked like a goddess of love, the embodiment of wealth and privilege and beauty. The embodiment of all that Lawrence wanted in the world.

Chapter Nine

"You fool," the golden-haired woman told Sophie. "You forsook my precepts, and look where it has gotten you."

"I am sorry," Sophie said, bowing her head. "I did not mean to, Your Excellence."

"Your intention does not interest me. It is your actions. You allowed a man to touch you. You kissed him. You enjoyed it. What of the chastity that you swore to me in exchange for your strength?"

"I do not know what happened," Sophie pled to the angry goddess. "It was out of my control."

"You mean," the goddess Diana went on from her golden throne, smirking, "you mean that you lost control. As I knew you would. As I always predicted."

The goddess's voice changed now, becoming deeper and thinner, and her face and her throne were covered in shadow. It was as if a large hand had closed over them, obliterating them, but the new voice rang out clearly. "You were wicked. You were wicked and evil, just as I told you, just as—"

"No," Sophie interrupted.

"We both know what happened that night, what you did," the thin voice whispered in Sophie's ear. "I will tell everyone."

"No," Sophie begged. "No, please. I didn't—"

"Save your pathetic protests," the voice went on. "No one will believe you. You are nothing, nothing at all. I hold your life in my hand." Sophie felt a hand at the waist of her gown, where Octavia had made the secret pocket, and then saw a small, gold disk flash before her eyes. "I have this," the voice went on. "It is all the proof I need. You cannot escape me. I love you."

"No," Sophie cried again, this time stridently. "NO!" she shouted, shouted with so much force, so much strength, that she jolted herself awake, jolted herself out of her nightmare.

It took her a moment to figure out where she was and what had happened. She shivered as she looked around her, the thin streak of dusty morning light that entered the cell barely adequate to illuminate its four rough walls and dirt floor. But it was enough to show that the space was empty, that Sophie was alone, that the voices had been part of a dream. Her breathing slowed as this thought seeped in, but her hand was unsteady as she reached for the small pocket in her gown.

Her fingers slipped in and her heart stopped. The pocket was empty. The medal was gone.

There had been someone in her cell with her after all. He had been there. The conversation was real. It was not a dream, not even a nightmare. It was much, much worse.

"No," she said aloud, her voice uneven. "No." She steadied herself against the stone wall as she rose to her feet, horror overtaking the numbness that had filled her since the previous night. Indeed, she was so overwrought that she did not hear the soft thud of the medal falling from her skirt to the dirt floor. But from the corner of her eye she saw the gleam of gold as it landed on its edge in the anemic beam of sunlight, and she had retrieved it with unsteady fingers before it could settle in the dust. It lay in her palm, the goddess Diana, goddess of the moon, of the hunt, and of chastity, seated on a throne, with a hawk seated next to her. It was the only memento she had left of her past, the only reminder of her former life, her former self.

She rarely let herself think about her life before the fire, before her parents died, before . . . before everything changed. She chose to blot out all memories of her past uniformly, in an effort to keep the horrible ones at bay. But as she stood in the dreary cell, feeling more alone than she had in years, recollections from her childhood came flooding back to her. Sophie recalled how her beautiful mother used to chastise—but not punish—her when, instead of paying attention to the details of household economy, she had buried herself in her brother Damon's mathematical texts. A shudder went through Sophie as she remembered the happy hours she spent with her brother, teaching him the rudiments of algebra or the latest mathematical theories out of Italy, providing him with easy translations of famous Greek texts and simple explanations of complicated proofs, so he had more time to indulge in his real love, making foul-smelling, goopy substances in a shed he called his laboratory.

But as interesting as the math texts were to Sophie, her father's ledgers were even more fascinating. She remembered poring over them, trying to understand why prices fluctuated and how you could invest in a crop that would not exist for ten months and turn an enormous profit in five. When she was thirteen, she secretly instructed her father's agent to use the hundred pounds she had been left by her grandmother for her dowry to buy shares in a mining company. The hundred turned to five hundred, then a thousand, and by the time of the fire, when she was fifteen, she had amassed a personal fortune of five thousand pounds, more than many a nobleman's entire holdings.

After the fire and the nightmare that followed it, the five thousand pounds in gold that Sophie had carefully buried in an iron box in the garden was all she had in the world, that and the medal of Diana. She opened her palm now to study it and was almost sure that Diana was smirking at her. *You are a fool,* the goddess seemed to be saying, as she had in the dream, and Sophie had to agree with her. Only a fool would have fallen for the Earl of Sandal. Only a fool would have trusted him.

Sophie jammed the medal into the small opening at her waist, cursing the smirking goddess, cursing the Earl of Sandal, cursing, above all, herself. As she began pacing her small, bare cell, she tried to decide which was more unpleasant, the physical pain of hunger or the equally gut-wrenching emotional pain of betrayal. Not betrayal by Sandal, that would have been no match for hunger. No, what was making her suffer so forcefully was her betrayal of herself.

In the dim light of her dismal cell, it was all so clear, the earl's mockery and contempt, his trickery and deceit. There was no question that he had saved her as a prank and had been planning to turn her over to the Queen's guards all along. They had said as much when they arrested her, quoting his words back to her, letting her hear them as if for the first time. It was then that she realized she had allowed herself, even willed herself, to be misled, then that she saw what she had resolutely overlooked, only then, when it was painfully clear that he had set her up.

And she had played right into it. She had been grateful, damn it, absolutely grateful. All that time she had looked at him with new respect he was laughing at her, and sending her to her death. With this realization, Sophie felt her embarrassment give way to anger. She may have behaved like an utter brainless aphid, but he had no right to toy with her. Only someone with the heart of a bristlebug would treat a fellow being like that. It was inhumane, and cruel, and undeserved.

"Bastard," she said aloud, half wishing the numbness would return. The comments of the guards the night before about readying herself for a speedy visit to the gallows suggested that she had little time, but she would use what little remained. Her opponents had been thorough, very thorough, in their attempt to frame her for Richard Tottle's murder, but there had to be some loose thread, someplace where their plan was likely to unravel. Something nagged at Sophie, and she cast her mind over the events at the Unicorn and at Sandal Hall afterward, until she found it.

The gun. Her gun. It was always kept in the library at Hen House, on a shelf with other gifts given to her in gratitude for her help. Surely it could not have been removed without someone—Octavia or Emme or Annie or Richards or one of the other servingwomen—noticing. With this thought, Sophie felt positively triumphant because she saw a way to foil her enemies. Whoever had stolen the gun either was, or knew who was, Tottle's murderer. All Sophie had to do to learn that person's identity was send a note to Hen House asking who had visited her library and what, if anything, they had taken.

Which, she realized with a renewal of the sinking feeling, was tantamount to saying that all she had to do was find a way to walk through the wall, fly over the city of London, and spot the murderer by dint of some funny glow given off by his guilt. Because her cell did not contain so much as a chamber pot (which she sorely needed), let alone a scrap of paper, a dab of ink, or a messenger to carry a note. She knew that money could buy her all those things, but she had none, her purse having been lost in the pointless scuffle with the guards on Pickering's Highway. Or, perhaps it had not been pointless. Perhaps that had been its point. In any event, she had nothing of value at all. Except the medal.

Sophie once again placed it on the palm of her hand to study it. She had scrupulously carried it with her for eleven years, the only piece of her past she possessed. And now, it was also her only link to the future. Sophie ran her thumb over it once, lovingly, then moved to the solid plank door of her cell, put her mouth close to the seam where it joined the wall, and yelled, "Guard!"

Sophie had some difficulty persuading the man to accept her commission. If he had known then what he discovered later that night when the tall man approached him at the tavern, that the strange medal with the naked woman and a bird was worth four hundred pounds in real gold, he would not have hesitated for a moment. As it was, he finally agreed, returning as the clock outside the prison chimed ten, with an ample basket of food, and a scrap of paper.

Sophie read the note first, and immediately lost her appetite. "Lord Grosgrain borrowed your pistol," the paper said. "There have been no other visitors to the library."

Crispin knew something was wrong long before he crossed the threshold of Pickering Hall at half past eleven that morning. His uneasiness had started much earlier, when he awoke after only three hours of troubled sleep. Sophie—what she knew, who she was—had taken over not only his waking thoughts but also his dreams. His mind kept revolving around Sophie, Sophie cheating at dice, Sophie smiling, Sophie frowning, Sophie arguing, Sophie speaking French, Sophie speaking Spanish, Sophie kissing him, Sophie in a mustache, Sophie with Lawrence, Sophie blackmailing her godfather. He wanted to go to her immediately, but he knew the longer he stayed away from her, the better off they would both be. Right now he could not think clearly about her at all, and clarity was what he required most. Constantia would provide the perfect antidote to all this, he knew, but somehow, despite his decision the previous night, he could not bring himself to go and see her.

In his uneasiness he had resolved to skip his visit to Grosgrain Place, but before he had passed by its polished doors, he heard a heart-stopping shriek from inside and a sound like breaking glass. Dismounting in a hurry, he had rushed into the entrance hall, then mounted the stairs until he found the source of the screaming.

Constantia, beautiful in a sapphire blue silk robe, was standing stiffly beside a fiery-orange divan, staring with horror at a collection of pastries scattered at her feet. A plate lay in shatters on the floor around the divan, and as Crispin reached the open door of the room, he saw Constantia stomp on one of the pastries, reducing it to crumbs.

"I told you I never wanted to see these again, Nan," she wailed at a trembling serving girl standing on her right.

Nan bowed her head. "But cook says, ma'am, as how he don't want to make any new cakes, since it would be a pity to waste all these beautiful meringues—"

Constantia gave a kick and sent a meringue skidding across the floor into the far wall. "Tell the cook his opinion is of no interest to me. I instructed him to destroy these and I demand that it is done at once. At once!"

"Yes, ma'am," Nan replied, bending to collect the offending pastries in her apron. "Yes, ma'am," she repeated, brushing past Crispin and hurrying out the door.

Having discovered that no one was being murdered, Crispin had decided to sneak away before he was recognized and proceed to Sophie, but he was too late. Constantia saw him standing in the doorway and appealed to him with outstretched arms.

"Crispin, darling, when did you come in?" she said, her voice soft now, her face no longer a mask of fury.

"I heard shouts from the street, and I feared for your life," he explained, not moving from the threshold. "But now that I see you are all right—"

Constantia ran to him and threw herself into his arms. "Crispin, I am nothing like all right. Milton's death has completely destroyed me." She pressed her face into the silver lining of his doublet, so that her golden hair tickled his chin. "Oh, Crispin, hold me, hold me like you used to. Let me lose myself, my grief, in your arms like I did before."

Crispin kept his eyes glued to the table clock behind Constantia, which said a quarter past ten, as she sobbed into his doublet. They were still standing like that, her pressed against him, him monitoring the hands of the clock, when a tall, fair young man burst into the room.

"Tia," he said with alarm. "Tia, what is it? What is wrong?"

Constantia withdrew herself from Crispin and turned to the newcomer. "Basil, they did it again. They brought meringues again. And you know how they remind me of your father, of everything I have lost, of..." Constantia swallowed hard to keep back the tears that glittered in the corner of her sapphire eyes. Then, noticing the way Basil was eyeing her companion, she stepped forward to make introductions. "Basil, this is my dear friend and our neighbor, the Earl of Sandal." She turned to Crispin. "Crispin, this is Basil, my stepson, now Lord Grosgrain."

The young man clearly did not like Crispin, but Crispin was delighted to see him, because it meant he could leave the comforting to someone else and get on with his business. Before he could take his leave, however, Constantia pled with him to stay "just a little longer" and steered him onto the orange divan next to her.

Crispin's eyes flickered in a continual relay between Constantia's beautiful face and the face of the clock, ticking off the time, time he was not spending with Sophie. He did not initially notice how tightly Constantia was gripping his hand, or how closely she was pressed up against him, or how often she directed her comments, and her lovely smile, in his direction. When a constable was shown in at just before eleven, he tried to rise and leave, but almost instantly sank back down into the chaise. This was due not, as Constantia thought, to a certain pressure she was exerting on his thigh but rather to the constable's announcement that he was there to ask questions about Miss Sophie Champion.

Crispin's preoccupation vanished. He listened with deep attention as the constable asked Constantia and Basil if they had been at home to see Sophie go out the night of Richard Tottle's murder, an attention that was piqued by Basil's reaction to the question, which included a complete loss of color and a series of strange choking noises. Basil appeared to be so overcome that it was Constantia who answered the constable, Constantia who explained that she and her stepson had been at home together that night, trying to select a new painting by Lyle, the famous artist, and had been too busy to notice anything going on outside. Basil was quite a connoisseur with a wonderful eye for beauty, Constantia leaned forward to confide—giving both the constable and Crispin a lovely view of her connoisseur-worthy décolletage—and she would not dare make a decision without him.

The constable, whose eyes had grown huge, said, "If you would like, ma'am, I can stay here with you and protect Your Ladyships." He rushed to correct himself, "I mean, Ladyship."

Constantia smiled warmly at him. "You are too kind, Constable—"

"Call me Ralph, ma'am," the constable put in, blushing.

"You are too kind, Ralph," Constantia said charmingly, "but I am sure I need no special protection."

Using all the ingenuity at his disposal, Ralph tried to argue but lost, and, with great reluctance, left. Crispin had just risen to do likewise, despite the protesting grip on his hand that suggested his company was not as dispensable as Ralph's, when Basil caught his attention outright.

"I think you should have accepted his offer of protection, Tia. I am the justice of the peace of this parish, you know, and I am far more knowledgeable about crime than you are. If Miss Champion killed once, she very well might come after you. You know I suspected all along that she had something to do with Father's death."

"Basil, do not say such things!" Constantia commanded him. "Miss Champion is not a murderer."

"Anyone could become a murderer for an estate the size of Father's," Basil said, his cheeks flushed with indignation.

"But, Basil, she gave it all back," Constantia told him.

Crispin, standing, was watching this exchange as if it were a championship game of tennis.

"Hardly. She only gave us what was ours by right." Basil now looked up at Crispin. "You see, my father left this house, his estate in Newcastle, and his entire company, Leverage Holdings, to Sophie Champion. And he left us nothing."

"And then," Constantia picked up, "Miss Champion gave me Grosgrain Place and Basil the Newcastle property, Peacock Hall. What is more, she settled an annuity on each of us that far exceeds our wants."

"Bosh," Basil put in, throwing his hands in the air and becoming pinker. "I am telling you, Tia, it was a cover. She used her generosity to keep us from asking questions about the will. She was blackmailing father, there is no doubt in my mind. How else would you explain the thousand pounds a month he paid her while he was alive? I think she learned of the terms of his will, learned that she would get everything, and killed him off."

"Basil, you are being wretched," Constantia sobbed. "I am sure Miss Champion did nothing of the kind."

Crispin had momentarily lost interest in the clock. "Tell me, Basil, do you have any grounds for thinking that she murdered your father? Were you here the day he died? Did you hear Sophie quarrel with him? Or did you see her go out?"

Basil's face slowly turned from pink to white. "No," he answered haltingly. "No, I didn't. I couldn't have. I—"

"—was right here, with me," Constantia explained, turning to Crispin. "Basil and I almost always have breakfast together, and we were still at table when the constables arrived with the—the—" she faltered, "dreadful news. It is all right, Basil, you can tell Crispin. He is not one to believe that a stepmother and stepson breakfasting together is scandalous."

Basil sighed with relief and addressed Crispin. "What Tia says is true. We were here, in her dressing room, taking breakfast together. And, as you can see," he went on, clearly in the pink again, "there are no windows that look out over the stables or Hen House. We could not possibly have seen anything."

"I, for one, am sure that there was nothing to see," Constantia announced, leaning forward and letting her dressing gown slip open again as if to remedy the lack of visual stimuli.

The display was wasted on Crispin, whose attention had returned to the hands of the clock, but found an appreciative audience in Ralph, who chose that moment to reenter the chamber.

"I beg your pardon, Your Ladyships," he said, performing a series of bows made awkward by the fixed direction of his gaze. "I just wanted to tell you that you need not fear any longer."

"Fear what?" Basil demanded, not overpleased by Ralph's attentions to his stepmother.

"Fear the murderer, ma'am," Ralph told Constantia's cleavage. "Sophie Champion. We got her locked up in Newgate. No cause for alarm anymore."

The sound of Crispin's pocket watch snapping closed jolted Ralph's eyes from the appreciation of female form.

"I beg your pardon, Constantia," Crispin said with one of his enchanting smiles, "but I really must be off. An appointment in the city," he elaborated vaguely. One promise to spend an entire evening with Constantia sometime soon, three professions of reluctance, and two apologies later, Crispin finally managed to take his leave. He was charming. He was witty. He was seething with a cold rage whose equal he had never experienced.

No one observing him would have guessed that he was bothered by anything more weighty than whether to have his new breeches cut tight or lose over the knee, but Fortuna knew her master well, and he had barely lifted her reins when she took off at a dangerous gallop. He urged her on as fast as she could go toward Pickering Hall, narrowly spinning around corners, his sense of malaise more intense with each hoof-fall, his jaw more tightly clenched. His pocket watch showed eleven-thirty when he arrived in the stable yard and leapt to the ground. He took the stairs to Lawrence's office two at a time, burst through the door without knocking, and stood defiantly in front of his friend.

"Where is she?" he demanded.

Lawrence leaned around him to address the four other men in the room. "Gentlemen, if you will excuse us. Sandal seems to be having a fit."

"Damn you, Lawrence." Crispin pounded on his desk as the other men tripped over themselves fleeing. "Where is she? I must see her right away." Something in his friend's face struck Crispin then, and he drew back as if he had been punched. "What have you done with her, Lawrence?"

"Nothing. Nothing at all. She is perfectly safe," Lawrence assured him with a strange smile.

Before Lawrence could take another breath, Crispin was around the desk, pinning him to his chair. "Where is she, Lawrence?"

Lawrence hesitated for a moment before replying, simply, "Newgate."

Crispin shook his head. "You bloody bastard," he muttered. Then, without another word, he released his friend and began moving toward the door.

"Crispin," Lawrence called imperatively after him, rising from behind his desk. "I had no choice. I could not refuse."

Crispin swung around just before reaching the door and snorted. "I never could have believed that our friendship was nothing more to you than another asset to be bartered with. What you meant to say is, you could not refuse their offer. What did they give you? Scotland?"

Lawrence came toward him. "What they gave me does not matter. The point is that they got here an hour before you did. They
must have suspected you would come this way, and they were ready.
As soon as you entered my house, you were trapped. There was
nothing I could do to stop it."

"You could have warned us when we arrived," Crispin pointed
out with deceptive calm. "You could have had Christopher tell us
before we came in."

"Don't you understand, Crispin? They were watching me as closely
as they were watching you. I did not have a chance to tell Christopher
or Kit or anyone anything. There was even a guard with a pistol
pointed at us the entire time we were talking on the landing, and they
told me that if I made any sign to you at all, they would shoot."

Crispin regarded his friend through narrowed eyes and said sarcastically, "After all we have been through together, I certainly
would not expect you to risk being grazed by a bullet for me."

"Not me, you idiot. They said if I made any sign, they would
shoot Sophie."

For a moment Crispin's face went completely rigid, and Lawrence
could imagine the deadly scene his friend was picturing. But there
was no point in dwelling on that, and no time.

"Disguises," Lawrence said finally, deliberately puncturing Crispin's train of thought.

"Disguises?"

"We are going to have to wear disguises when we break her
out," Lawrence explained, then rushed to add, "assuming you will
let me help you. Disguises so that they do not know who rescued
Sophie. After all, we, or you, don't want anyone to know where
Sophie is hiding this time."

"No," Crispin confirmed, "we certainly don't."

The table clock in Lawrence's office began to chime twelve as
two bearded sailors rode out of the Pickering Hall stable yard,
much more comfortable on their mounts than seafaring men usually were. Heedless of this or the fact that they were being watched,
they spurred their horses on and galloped furiously toward Newgate.

Chapter Ten

"It is Sophie Champion," a slender young woman with dark eyes and auburn hair who had a faint perfume of cloves stated unequivocally. "I never forget a smell, and it smells like her."

"But Sophie Champion is no criminal," a small, rosy-cheeked lady put in. "She'd never be in prison because she'd never do anything wrong. Ask her about it, Helena."

The young woman nodded at the rosy-cheeked one and then looked pointedly at Sophie. "What do you have to say to this charge, Miss Champion?"

For a moment, Sophie could only blink. She had been so devastated by Octavia's note that she had not paid attention when the guards moved her from one cell to another, had not even noticed the six other women crowded into the small space. But now they were arrayed around her, staring at her, waiting for her answer. "I do not know," she said finally. "I did not do anything wrong, I swear to that, but I have been a fool. Someone is trying to make it look as if I murdered a man, and I am letting him do it."

"Why?" Helena, who appeared to be the leader of the group, asked. "Everyone knows you are as smart as ten men. Why are you letting him get away with it? Why not just turn the tables on him, like you did when Sir Argyle tried to seduce you and instead found himself in bed with a porcupine and unable to walk for a month after?"

"Or like you did when you rescued Emme Butterich from being kidnapped by marking the coins with powder so you knew who'd got it and where they went?" contributed the rosy-cheeked lady.

"Or even when you gave sweet Letitia Roth a dowry so she could marry that handsome Edgar Gordon despite her father's gambling all the family's money away," a woman with a deep voice put in.

"I heard that they are expecting a baby," rosy cheeks told Sophie. "Isn't that delightful?"

Sophie nodded, completely overcome by what she was hearing. She had no idea that anyone outside of the residents of Hen House and those whom she had helped knew about her work, or even cared. But the women continued to talk around her, this one recollecting the young girl Sophie had saved from being sold by her brothers, this other the woman to whom Sophie had given a plow horse so that she could salvage the farm that her drunken husband had allowed to go fallow. The cell had begun to sound like an aviary of chirping birds as each woman competed to tell the story of the friend, relative, or neighbor who had been helped by Sophie Champion, until suddenly the hinges on the metal door squealed and two guards pushed in. They were both tall, and they were both wearing the black cloth masks reserved for the hangman's assistants.

"Sophie Champion," one of the guards rumbled, and the women fell silent. "Sophie Champion, please step forward."

"I am Sophie Champion," Helena announced with a toss of her head, before Sophie could say anything.

"No," Sophie said, first to Helena, with gratitude, then, in a different tone, to the guards. "No, I am Sophie Champion."

"Which is it?" the guard asked, turning to his companion, who did not speak but merely pointed at Sophie.

Taking his cue, the first guard moved toward her, but was stopped by a wall of women. "What do you want?" Helena asked protectively. "What are you going to do to her?"

"Aw, don't be jealous," the guard said, moving one hand toward his crotch. "There's plenty for all of you, once we get Miss Champion out."

"She's not going anywhere with you," the rosy-cheeked lady announced. "She's staying here with us."

"Ain't that sweet," the guard addressed his colleague. "They want to watch. It's too bad we can't oblige them."

As he spoke, he moved closer to the female cordon. "You got until the count of three to get out of my way, you hags," he announced.

"Do not worry, ladies," Sophie said, gently pushing herself to the front of their ranks. "I doubt this oaf can count beyond two."

"You didn't tell me she was a witty one," the guard said to his taciturn companion. "I never had much use for the witty ones."

"Just get on with it," the other guard barked, speaking for the first time. "The sooner we leave here the better."

Sophie could not see the face beneath the black mask, but she heard the voice, and her blood ran cold. She knew it was impossible for him to have found her, knew her memory had to be playing tricks on her, and yet, it sounded exactly like the voice. His voice. The voice of her nightmares. Her stomach curled, her head began to pound, and her throat closed up, clogged with a thousand gagged screams. She could not breathe, could not see, could not think.

Sophie had almost no recollection of what came next. She remembered shouting and clawing and punching, but in the end it did no good. He got her anyway, got her despite her most valiant efforts, just as he said he would. That was her last clear thought upon hearing the voice, and her first thought upon waking, hours later, in an unfamiliar bed, aching, alone, and naked.

What woke Sophie were the echoes of footsteps endlessly pacing a marble floor. Judging by the sound, they were not in the room with her, but even so, she dared not open her eyes. She was scared, more scared than she could ever recall being. Her only hope, she knew, was to escape from him, and as soon as possible. But she felt paralyzed, unable to move, barely able to breathe.

She was willing herself to open her eyes and at least survey her new prison when she heard the pacing cease and footsteps enter her chamber. By the time he reached the bed, she was lying on her side, to all appearances in a deep slumber.

"I know you're not sleeping," an unexpected voice said. "I can tell by your breathing. You are really a wretched dissembler."

Sophie's eyes flew open, and when they confirmed what her ears had told her, that she was, somehow, being addressed by the Earl of Sandal, her first emotions were a mixture of relief and a strange kind of joy that he cared enough about her to rescue her. But these gave way, almost instantly, to confusion, and then, to anger.

"You bastard," she said, sitting up and pulling the wine-colored coverlet up with her.

Crispin concealed his immense satisfaction at seeing her alert and apparently unchanged under an abbreviated shake of his head. "I really wish you would come up with a more original line. Even 'you slug' was better."

Sophie ignored his sally at wit. "Where is he?"

"That is hardly an improvement," Crispin said with resignation.

"Satan's knockers, answer me. Where is he?"

"Who?"

"Your boss. Your colleague. Whatever he is to you. The man who dragged me from the prison."

"That was me," Crispin said, pointing a finger at his chest as he seated himself on the edge of the bed. "Although I would not say 'dragged.' I more carried you."

"You are lying," Sophie said without equivocation.

"Ask any of the other women we freed with you," Crispin challenged, trying to subdue the strange emotion within him. "Helena is still at Hen House, and I can send for her if you persist in thinking me a liar."

Sophie ignored his offer. "You expect me to believe that you rescued all those women, and me, single-handedly?"

"No. Lawrence was there too."

"Lawrence?" Sophie asked with a mixture of disbelief and outrage. "You and Lawrence dressed as the hangman's assistants and—"

"No," Crispin interrupted, "those were the other men. Lawrence and I were dressed as sailors."

"Who were they? The others, the ones dressed as hangmen?"

Crispin looked at her with puzzlement. "I'm afraid I did not wait for them to regain consciousness to learn their names. One of them was bald under his hood, and the other one had dark brown hair."

"Are you sure?" Sophie queried. "Brown hair?"

Crispin was unsettled by the intensity of her interest. "Why? Were you expecting someone in particular?" When Sophie did not answer, he went on. "Next time I will pay more attention to the men I have to knock down in order to get you out of prison."

"There will not be a next time," Sophie said positively.

"How can you be sure?"

"Because I will not make the mistake of trusting you or your friends again, Lord Sandal. Is this what you consider fun? Luring women into your clutches by having them arrested and then playing dress-up to free them?"

Crispin did not like it, but he understood her anger. Although he could not imagine what she must have endured in the dark prison cell the night before, he had been seized by the same rage when he had learned of Sophie's imprisonment. "Lawrence had no choice yesterday. The Queen's guards arrived an hour before we did. They must have guessed we would go there. As soon as we went to Pickering Hall, we were trapped. They threatened to shoot you if Lawrence tried to warn us."

Sophie began to have doubts. The man from her nightmares was neither bald nor dark-haired. It was possible, entirely possible, that she had mistaken the voice, that she had only thought she heard it because she had been dreaming about it. Possible, she repeated, but not likely.

She decided to cling to her disbelief. "That is a very clever story you and your colleagues have concocted. I suppose you think I should thank you. Very convenient, you being there to save me again. But I will not fall for it this time."

"Miss Champion, I promise that no one has concocted anything."

"Why should I believe you?" she demanded, her eyes flashing.

"Because it is true," he said simply. Because I almost exploded with anger when I saw you in prison—Crispin continued in his head—and admiration when I saw you fighting the guards. Because you did not need me to save you. Because I wish you had. Because I—

Crispin cleared his throat, clearing away these thoughts. "I understand that you must be upset, but you are safe now."

"You do not understand anything," Sophie nearly spat at him. How could he know the terror she had experienced? How could he comprehend the effect that voice had on her, even if she had only imagined its presence? How could he understand the terrible hollowness inside of her when she thought that he had betrayed her? *You* understand. You who harry me, you who toy with me, you who rescue me one minute and summon the constables for me the next. What do you understand?" she demanded, punching her fists into the coverlet. "And why do you keep helping me and then dumping me in trouble?"

Damn she was stubborn.

And beautiful.

And dangerous.

Crispin's tone was studiously cool as he said, "My intent is only the first part. The trouble is your own contribution."

"Really?" Sophie sat forward, bringing their faces close together. "Did I suggest going to Lawrence's house?" She was disappointed to see that the cankerworm did not even flinch.

"No," Crispin replied slowly, reminding himself, in their proximity, that she was not to be trusted. Or admired. Or thrown onto the bed and made love to. "But you would have been arrested earlier if not for me."

"Maybe," Sophie sneered at him. "Or maybe I would not have been arrested at all. I certainly am not going to let myself be arrested again. Tell me where my clothes are so I can leave."

"We had to dispose of your clothes. They had been overtaken by a family of fleas. Not to mention the way they looked."

"How would you have looked if you'd spent the night in prison?" Sophie demanded fiercely, poking Crispin in the chest.

Crispin caught her finger. "I do not know. I would never find myself in prison."

"You ought to." Sophie leaned in closer. "It is cowardly to send me somewhere you would not go yourself."

Crispin redoubled his efforts to stay cool and formal as their noses almost touched. "Your powers of reason overwhelm me. I did not send you to prison, Miss Champion, I freed you. At the possible expense of my life. And my reputation."

At the word reputation Sophie growled and brought her face so close to his that he could feel her breath on his cheek. "Why? Why did you bother? Was it so you could see me naked one last time?"

Her tone lashed Crispin, and he pulled away from her abruptly, letting go of her finger at the same time. "I promise you, Miss Champion, your naked body has not once crossed my mind."

Sophie did not notice the tension in Crispin's voice when he replied. She felt only the sting of his words, a sting underscored by his drawing away from her. She had not realized that they were so close, but when he moved, she felt his absence. "Good," she affirmed forcefully, at the same time rising from the bed and taking the wine-colored coverlet with her. "I am glad. And you will be glad to know that my naked body, while not crossing your mind, is crossing your threshold. This is the last you will see of me, or it, forever. I neither need nor desire your help. I'll not wait around for the constables to arrive this time." Having delivered this speech, she passed into his library and through the first door she saw, slamming it behind her.

Crispin made no move to follow her. It was not because, as a fugitive from justice completely nude but for a burgundy silk bedcover, he knew she had nowhere else to go. It was because he did not give a damn what happened to her. Because she was at the very least a liar and a threat to his sanity, and he would be better off with her gone.

And also because she had stalked right into his privy. He hoped she was enjoying it.

Bastard, Sophie repeated to herself as she paced the diagonals of the small room. Bastard slug cricket mealyworm stinkbug. She was furious, furious at fate for landing her in this situation, and furious at herself for not being smart enough to escape it. It was not fair to make a dramatic exit and end up in the privy closet. It was a very nice privy, with a velvet-covered privy stool and an empty silver chamber pot and herbs on the floor to mask the odor and instructive paintings on the walls, but it was still a privy, it still smelled like a privy. And the only way out was the way she had come in, right past the no doubt gloating face of its owner.

She could just picture him out there, smirking, waiting for her to emerge so he could make some crack about how he could see that she neither needed nor desired his help, that she could get herself out of trouble on her own. He would taunt her until the constables came, then feign surprise when they clapped her in irons and took her away. She kicked the chamber pot across the room, wishing it were his head. Or hers. Clearly, she no longer needed hers, since it was not working. The women in the prison had been right, Sophie Champion would never have ended up in this situation. Sophie Champion would have been smarter than that.

Was smarter than that. And she would not let herself be held prisoner again just because she wanted to avoid the taunts of a detestable snout beetle.

Pulling the coverlet around her body more tightly, Sophie turned toward the door to go, but found that it was already open.

"May I come in?" Crispin asked from the threshold.

It took Sophie a moment to respond, because he did not look anything like a snout beetle. Or anything like detestable. He had removed his doublet and was wearing only breeches and a thin linen shirt. Like that, in his most casual clothes, his broad shoulders and strong, sculpted legs were even more impressive, even more stunning. "Do as you please," she said finally.

Something flickered behind Crispin's eyes at the offer, but Sophie did not catch it. "I merely came to tell you that your bath is ready, Miss Champion."

Sophie, who found that her fingertips had begun to tingle with the desire to touch the golden hairs visible at the neck of his shirt, at first did not hear his words. When they finally entered her mind, she could only stammer, "I do not want a bath." Then, in a stronger voice she added, "Besides, I am leaving."

"I would really suggest you bathe, if only to reawaken your mind for your escape. It will make you feel better. And I assure you, you will enjoy it."

There was something in Crispin's tone as he spoke the last words, something suggestive and alluring that dissolved Sophie's opposition. He had entered the small room, filling it with his presence, and with his scent, and now with innuendo. *I assure you, you will enjoy it,* Sophie heard over again in her mind, and simultaneously felt her allergy returning, its symptoms worse than ever. Now, instead of just making her feel odd, it coalesced into real, particular desires. The desire for his mouth to cover her mouth. The desire for his fingers, all ten of them, to trace circles over her breasts, her stomach, her thighs, her bottom. The desire for his arms to pull her close, for his tongue to seek out her tongue, for his body to slide against her body, for his lips to say her name. Wicked desires, a voice inside her head told her. The desires of a wicked, wicked girl.

"I could not," she said abruptly, her tone cold with self-loathing. "I could not take a bath with you."

Crispin misunderstood the strain in her voice. "With me? Of course not. You need have no fear of me. I would not touch you with a bamboo cane, Miss Champion."

His words stung Sophie. She did not know that Crispin was only repeating the exact phrasing of an oath he had taken while she slept, an oath that said he would not touch her or go nearer than necessary to her, for any reason. He had rescued her from prison exclusively because he needed to extract information from her, quickly. And for him to accomplish this purpose, he would have to keep his head unclouded, which meant keeping himself away from her.

It had seemed like a better idea in her absence than it did now in her presence, particularly as she passed close to him on her way out of the privy.

"I take it that you are accepting my offer of a bath," he asked when they were both safely out of the small room.

"Yes." Sophie's voice was taut with the strain of keeping it level. She would show him, show herself, show the voice, that she was not wicked. And his point about waking herself up had been just. "Only for the sake of my escape."

"Good. Follow me." Crispin led her back into and then across his bedchamber, slid open the latch on one of the immense windows that made up the wall nearest to the bed, and gestured her to pass through. Together they crossed the perfectly manicured carpet of grass which covered the entire expanse of his second-floor hanging garden, following a flagstone path that led away from the bedroom and curved behind a thick hedge of lavender. The plant was in full bloom, covered in small purple flowers, and filling the air with its marvelous scent.

Crispin motioned for Sophie to precede him, but as she rounded the hedge she froze.

Everything in Crispin's private garden was extraordinary, but what she saw now took Sophie's breath away. She found herself in front of a crystal blue pond, from which steam was rising. It was surrounded on all sides by delicious-smelling flowers—roses, snapdragons, gardenias, orange blossoms, sweet peas—and the steamy vapors rising from the surface of the water were filled with the heady scent of their mingled perfumes. A statue of the goddess Venus seemed to float above the far end of the pond, water trickling melodiously from her pedestal, the white marble of the figure turning purplish pink in the gathering twilight.

As she took in the fountain before her, Sophie thought that she had never seen anything, never even dreamed of anything so beautiful in her life. The mist rose up to greet her, wrapping its sweet smell around her, beckoning her in, but she could not move. Self-disgust was lost in the beauty of the place, and she could only stand on the edge, filled with awe and wonder.

"Is there something wrong, Miss Champion?" Crispin asked when some time had passed.

His voice was as cold and sharp as a cake-slice, cutting through Sophie's awe and wonder and reminding her where she was, what she was. She shook her head, keeping her face averted from his. "No," she answered quickly. But then, unable to stop herself, went on. "Or rather, yes." She turned to face him now. "What is not wrong? Here I am, accused of murder, a fugitive from the Queen's justice," *the captive of my wicked desires,* she thought to herself, but said instead, "the captive of a man who hates me, with no—"

A crease appeared in Crispin's forehead. "How do you know I hate you?"

"You have done nothing to hide it, my lord."

"True," Crispin observed, nodding. "Carry on."

"Why?" Sophie was outraged, outraged by his callousness and by the tears that were creeping down her cheeks. She was confused and miserable. She hated him for bringing her to such a place, for making her feel the way she did, and she hated herself for not being able to stop it.

When she spoke, she did not know what she was saying, and she felt like the words were coming not from her lips, but from somewhere deep inside her. "Why should I go on? So you can mock me further? So you can gather more evidence of what a fool I am? So you can stare at me with your passionless eyes? So you can let me know with even your smallest gesture how undesirable you find me?" Sophie was shaking now, despite herself, and her words spilled out in a torrent of pain. "So you can make me want you more, make me wonder more about what it would be like to have you hold me, what it would be like to wake up just once in your arms? So you can tell me how vile I am, how wicked—"

Crispin took two steps toward her, wrapped her in his arms, and stopped her mouth with his lips.

Chapter Eleven

He kissed her with a force that surprised both of them, pressing his lips hungrily against hers, pulling her toward him, enveloping her in his embrace, in the heat of a desire that burned through his restraints, his self-control.

Later Crispin told himself he had done it in order to win her trust, to make it easier for her to confide in him, to make her more willing to answer his questions. Later he assured himself that he had done it to expedite his investigation, that he had been acting on professional instinct. But at the time he was conscious only of the overwhelming desire that overtook his body in her presence, the desire to stop the words she was saying, erase them from her lips, to melt the pain and the fear and the shame he heard in her voice, to grow stronger by being strong for her. The desire to hold and kiss and touch and nibble and bite and love and caress her everywhere, to know this woman completely.

In his kiss, Sophie forgot herself. She felt as if a spark passed between their lips, scorching away her self-loathing, scorching away her past, and igniting a ribbon of flame that unfurled throughout her body with amazing rapidity. The voice in her head was drowned out by the sensations of her body, by the heat that ran from where their lips touched down through her breasts, down to her toes, winding into a tight knot between her legs.

She pushed her body harder against his, pressing herself against his chest through the coverlet, and felt his warmth on the points of her breasts. Their mouths opened to each other, and she felt his tongue caressing hers, wrapping itself around her, fanning the flames of her growing desire. She willed him to touch her and, as if by magic, his hands were there, sliding over the silky fabric of the coverlet, his palms moving slowly over the sides of her breasts until his thumbs came to rest on her nipples. He stroked them gently, making small wide circles over the fabric and then smaller ones. She cried out as he touched them, softly, cried out in pleasure, and in surprise as his touch echoed from there to between her legs, setting her completely on fire.

Without thought, without taking her lips from his, she dropped the coverlet to the ground and stood before him completely naked.

Crispin could not stop himself. His desire for Sophie became almost excruciating when her naked body pressed against his chest. Tracing the outline of her lips with his tongue, his hands passed down from the marvelous globes of her breasts, sliding down the curve of her waist, reveling in the suppleness of her skin. He had never felt anything so silky, so deliciously soft yet firm, anything he craved so much before in his life. His shaft pressed desperately against the fabric of his breeches, straining the stays, begging to be freed, and bucked even harder as her hand moved down his chest and rested there.

Sophie was thrilled by the feel of his arousal, thrilled by the long, hard bulge that moved under her fingers. He liked her, liked to have her touch him. The thought of him responding to her that way intensified the flames within her, increasing the ache between her legs to a feverish pitch. As if he were reading her mind, she felt Crispin let his hands slip from her waist down to her bottom to trace slow circles there, and then move to the front of her thighs.

Crispin's thumbs traced the outline of the triangle of red curls between her legs, then dipped lower, into her wet heat, running up and down the length of her, grazing over the small pearl of flesh hidden there, now hot and swollen.

Sophie gasped as he touched her, and Crispin took his mouth from hers.

"Is something wrong?" he asked with real concern, but without moving his thumbs from their plaything.

Sophie could not answer. The feeling of him touching her, touching her like that, touching her there, the feel of his thumbs gently massaging her tender bud, as he looked at her, deprived her of all speech. She gulped and opened her mouth. "No," she managed to whisper. "It is only that, no one..." Her whisper trailed off.

"Do you want me to stop?" Crispin searched her face.

"Please no," Sophie answered with feeling. "Oh, my lord, no do not stop." She did not know what she was saying, she knew only that he had to touch her more, stroke her more deeply, soothe the ache that was threatening to take her body over. She had never felt anything more exquisite than his fingers there, anything more exalting, except now, when, together, they slid over her, first down, then back up, pulling her tight between them, one sliding over the top, the other pressing up from below.

Just when Sophie thought that nothing could ever feel better, Crispin added the rest of his fingers. All five fingertips of Crispin's left hand now played over her body, drawing her toward him, playing over her hot, slick wetness. He toyed with her bud, tickling it with his fingertips, then crushing it against the wide palm of his hand. He let it slip along the length of his fingers, pulling it between them, between his thumb and index finger, then between his index finger and middle finger, all the way down to his pinky, which he allowed to rest directly on her, making tight little circles. A tremor ran through Sophie's body as Crispin increased the pressure, and he knew she was close. Without taking his pinky from her nub, he lifted his mouth from hers and began to move it down her body, first dusting her neck with soft kisses, then her breasts, then flicking his lips across her stomach, until he was kneeling before her, with his head between her legs. He brushed his cheek back and forth against the soft, sweet-smelling curls beneath her stomach, then turned his lips to the little pearl nestled there and gently wrapped them around it.

When he took her into his mouth, Sophie knew she had died. Nothing earthly could feel the way this felt, nothing real could fill her with this fire, this mixture of extraordinary heat and warmth, this tightness that spiraled and became more and more taut. His tongue, slick but slightly rough, dabbed at her cautiously as his lips closed around her, one of his hands holding her open to him, spreading the petals that surrounded her bud so he could suckle it completely. The fingers of his other hand rested between her legs, and she felt one of them slide gently, slowly, slowly, inside her.

Crispin slipped the tip of his middle finger in and out of her, letting it rub against the sensitive place just inside her passage. He spread her wider and when she looked down, she could see the pink tip of his tongue flicking back and forth over her pink nub, first lightly, then harder. Faster, then slower.

Watching him, watching his mouth on her body and feeling his hands holding her open and his finger slipping inside her, Sophie felt like she was dangling at the edge of a precipice or being slowly driven mad. Instead of soothing the fire inside her, Crispin was fanning it, making its flames increase until it raged unchecked. Each time Sophie thought she was going to explode, he stopped, withdrew his fingers, lifted his mouth, just blowing on her, letting her feel his hot breath on her but nothing else. And then, when he decided that her boil had calmed to a simmer, only then did he resume, starting slowly, lightly. Each time he began again the feeling was more intense, the fire burned hotter. He tickled her, teased her, tormented her with his light touch, making her body rage for him.

With his lips he touched her gently, chastely, brushing her pearl against his stubbly cheek, and Sophie lost the battle she had been waging for control. She pressed herself against him, begging, insisting. "Please," she cried out. "Please, Crispin. Please do something."

She did not know she had spoken, but the next moment she gasped with pleasure as Crispin slid his finger firmly into her tight passage and at the same time opened his lips wide and drank her in deeply, entirely.

Pleasure built between her legs at his touch, unchecked this time, flooding over her as he licked at her. His teeth grazed over her, his fingers skidded across her, and pushed into her and pressed against her and Sophie knew her knees were going to give way. The fire he had been kindling inside of her burst into the whitest hot flames, which swirled over her, engulfing her, flames that surrounded her and lapped at her ankles and thighs and breasts and lips, burning through her reserve and fear and tension until they reached her most sensitive place, and as he sucked her in one last time, she exploded.

Sophie bucked against Crispin, pushing into him and pulling away from him simultaneously, stopping his hand and insisting that it keep going, moaning aloud, first quietly, then louder, until her moans turned to joyful laughter and, still laughing, she collapsed on the ground.

Crispin lay down next to her and took her in his arms. Her generous response to him, her laughter, was unlike anything he had ever experienced, filling him with a sense of power and joy he could not recall having felt before. Not to mention arousal. Which only grew worse as Sophie, recovered slightly, slipped her hand tentatively into the neck of his shirt and rested her palm on his chest.

"Thank you," she whispered. "That was extraordinary."

"Yes, it was," Crispin agreed. "But now I think you should take your bath."

"Mmmm," Sophie said, moving her hand from his chest down to the stays on his breeches. She fumbled with them, brushing her hand accidentally across the bulge there, and it was Crispin's turn to moan. Her fingers slipped into his breeches, the tips brushing at the tip of his shaft, and then she rolled him into her hand.

"What are you doing?" he managed to ask through clenched teeth.

"I want to give you pleasure too." Sophie moved her hand up his length, and then down, enchanted with the strange texture of his organ. "I want to touch you like you touched me."

Her caresses made him feel like he was soaring. Without wings, without supports, over an unknown land without borders but with countless dangers. This woman, he knew then, had the power to destroy him. He was not prepared for this, prepared for what she was doing to him, something that went far beyond physical pleasure. Using every ounce of restraint he possessed, he brought his hand down and stopped her caresses.

"What is wrong?" Sophie asked, alarmed.

"Bath," Crispin said in a tight voice. "You have not taken your bath."

"But—" Sophie began, and he silenced her.

"Bath first. Then"—he waved his free hand, waving good-bye to that uncharted territory—"then we will see."

Without waiting for her to protest, Crispin rose and lifted her in his arms. He carried her the few steps to the pond and set her down gently. "Get in."

Sophie shook her head. "Did I do something wrong?" Suddenly the voice came flooding back, overwhelming her. "I apologize, Lord Sandal. I could not stop myself. I should go."

Crispin, who was having trouble thinking clearly, could not understand these words. "Apologize?" he repeated lamely. "Go?" She was never going anywhere. Or at least, not until he got answers to his questions.

Sophie nodded, not meeting his eyes. "I shouldn't have acted that way. So, so wickedly."

Crispin used a finger to raise her face to his and sought her eyes. "You were not wicked. You were wonderful. Do you understand?"

Sophie shook her head. "It is kind of you to say so, but I know what you must think of me."

"I doubt that," he said in a tone she could not read, but it was not one of disgust. "I doubt that very much." Crispin was not sure he himself knew what he thought of her. "Sophie, what happened just now was not wrong. Did it feel wrong to you?"

"But you pulled away. You were disgusted by me."

Crispin was having trouble understanding the words again. "Disgusted? Is that what you think?"

Sophie gave a small nod.

Crispin moved so he was standing right next to her and put her hand on his shaft. It danced under her touch. "I assure you I am anything but disgusted by you." His voice, low and smooth, made Sophie feel strange and excited all over again. "I was merely suggesting we try something else. In the bath."

"You will come in with me?"

"I will be back in a moment. You get in first." Sophie was about to protest, but Crispin gave her a soft kiss on the forehead. "I promise I will be right back."

As she slid into the bath and settled herself on the underwater ledge which served as a bench, Crispin turned and made his way back to his room. He needed a moment to think, to organize his defenses, before he proceeded with his plan. There was no question that women were more pliant, more willing to answer questions, when they were amorously inclined. That, of course, was the reason for this seduction. But he would scarcely be able to ask any questions if he did not keep better control over himself. He raked a hand through his hair. Only six days stood between him and an accusation of treason, he reminded himself. Six days during which Sophie would be sharing his bed. Six days during which Sophie would be sharing his life. He needed to assure himself he did not lose track of what was important. And besides, night was falling and he wanted to light the garden torches so she would not have to be afraid in the dark.

When Crispin returned, he found Sophie shoulder deep in the warm water, her eyes closed, her lips slightly parted. She looked like something out of an antique myth, a true Siren or one of the nymphs that were always such a temptation to the gods, the kind of magical creature who could lure even the most stalwart man from his duty. In the light of the torch that Crispin lit near the pond, the drops of water on her hair shined like a net of diamonds interspersed with rubies. Crispin shed the robe he was wearing and slipped into the water next to her, kissing her gently on the lips.

Her eyes opened, to look into his, but she did not speak. Crispin moved over her and their kiss deepened, its origin not in their lips but somewhere outside their bodies. Sophie's hands moved over Crispin's back, studying, memorizing the feel of his muscles under her fingers, the way they moved and flexed as he adjusted himself over her. She twined them in the golden hair of his chest, then let her flat palms glide down his stomach to his hard organ.

Crispin's preparations, his plans, the words "*six days,*" none of them were force against the experience of her touch. Instead of lessening, it seemed to have become more powerful, to have grown more tantalizing, more overwhelming, in the intervening minutes. He moaned as she used both hands to move up and then down his shaft, moaned as her thumbs massaged the indentation at its tip.

"Make love to me, Crispin," she breathed into his ear. "I want to have you inside of me."

It was the sound of his name on her lips even more than her words that unraveled him. That and the feel of her against him. Crispin could no more reason than breathe, but he was sure that if she kept touching him like that his vital powers would evaporate. He caught her hand, brought it to his lips, and turned so he was sitting next to her.

Despite the proddings of his body, he felt suddenly cautious. "Are you sure?"

"I know what I want," Sophie told him in a voice without hesitation. "I want you."

Crispin pulled her so she was sitting astride him. Her silky thighs wrapped around his waist and her curls moving ticklishly over his member made him pray for control. He willed himself to go slow, not to hurt her, but he wanted her with a fierceness that threatened to overwhelm his restraint.

Sophie gasped in delight as she came into contact with his shaft, and gasped again as Crispin moved himself so she could slide up and down his length. Holding her with one hand, he reached down with the other and let his fingers ride over her whole length until his palm came to rest on her swollen nub. Sophie gave a little yelp and then another as he gently moved his palm in a circle, using its full breadth to massage her. He started softly, barely touching her, and with each circle he pressed slightly harder.

Crispin began to move his hand up and down again, rather than around, so his fingers and his palm were alternately gliding over her. He stroked her lightly at first, just skating over her wetness, and then pressed harder, so that his other fingers plunged into the folds surrounding her nub, massaging it from the sides, slipping in even deeper, even more completely. Her yelps gave way to moans, and she pressed herself against his hand, directing his fingers around and into her, furious for his touch, close to finding her release.

Keeping his index finger on her nub, tracing small circles with it, Crispin slid first one, then a second finger into her. She moaned, and he added a third, stretching her tight passage in anticipation of him. Then he moved his hand away and let it rest on her thigh, still holding her gaze.

"Are you certain you want this?"

Sophie nodded, unable to speak but completely sure she wanted more of him.

Crispin went on. "Absolutely certain? You are very taut. It might hurt. It might—"

Sophie reached out for him and pulled him to her. "I want to hold you inside me, Crispin, like I have never wanted anything else."

Crispin reached between her legs again and touched her with both hands, but this time he did not stop there. Carefully, he used his fingers to spread the petals that surrounded her, opening her to him. He lifted her hips to rest the tip of his shaft against her and rubbed her little nub with his finger. When she bucked against him in pleasure, he slid into her, lowering her onto his member, stopping once for her to adjust herself, and then pushing himself completely into her narrow, warm, yielding passage. Crispin gasped with wonder. Sophie was smiling at him, arching to meet him, crying out to him. She made a present of her body to him, a present more precious than any other Crispin had ever received.

Sophie felt no pain, just pure, powerful pleasure as he moved into her. "Crispin," she moaned, "this is heaven. You must never

ever stop." She pressed her chest against his to reach his mouth for a kiss. The sensation of him sliding into her while his finger stayed on her most sensitive place was driving her wild. She could not control herself, did not want to control herself, as the divine fullness between her legs brought her closer and closer to her climax.

Crispin was in agony. He was determined to delay his release until she had found hers, but sliding in and out of her firm passage as she pressed against him and demanded him was almost more than he could endure. He had planned to go slowly, be reasonable, not get lost in her, in the pleasure of being inside her. But planning and reason had no place in this new land she sent him flying over. He could not think, could not ponder, could almost not breathe as he soared on wave after wave of pleasure, savoring and glorifying in every long vibration of her body.

Crispin reached up and brought her mouth to his powerfully, parting her lips with his tongue. His kiss undid Sophie. She flew against him, clutching him, and he heard her laugh and felt her climax throbbing around him. She kept laughing, laughing and pushing herself against him, wanting to make the feeling go on forever, stretching it through one climax, then another, until Crispin could wait no longer and with a final deep thrust and a moan he had never heard himself make before he exploded into her, as she exploded around him for the last time.

Their bodies were still sending secret, pulsating messages to each other, Crispin was still inside her, beneath her, when Sophie's laughter subsided. She kissed the side of his neck and his shoulder, and laid her head on his chest as he wrapped his arms tight around her.

"Can we do that again? Just exactly like that?" she asked when she had caught her breath.

"No," Crispin replied definitively. He felt strange. It had been a long time since his last amorous excursion, but not so long that he had forgotten what it was supposed to feel like. And he knew it was not supposed to feel like he had woken from a boring dream into a fantasy world of light, color, taste, and smell that he had never known existed before. Was not supposed to make him feel like he was only now, for the first time in his life, home.

Sophie raise her head from his chest in alarm at his answer and his long silence. "No?" she repeated

"No. Not like that, anyway." Crispin kissed her tenderly on the forehead. She was delicious. "There are too many other things to try."

"Let's do them all. Right now."

Crispin groaned. Then lied. "There will be plenty of time for that." He lifted her off him, shuddering slightly, and cradled her in his arm. "Now, *tesoro*, I think we should go to bed."

Sophie, who was playing with the hairs on his chest, stopped. "What did you say? What did you call me?"

The word had slipped out without Crispin's realizing it, completely inadvertently, as if it had spoken itself. "I said *tesoro*. It means treasure."

"*Tesoro*," Sophie repeated to herself as he carried her from the bath and settled her in his large, silk-covered bed. When he got in next to her, she reached out to him and led his hand between her legs.

"Thank you," she said, pressing her curls against him, wanting him to know how grateful, how marvelous he had made her feel. "Thank you for..." The rest of her words were lost in the regular breathing of peaceful sleep.

Crispin watched her as she fell asleep, wound around him, watched the moonlight play over her bewitching features, watched her hair spread itself over her shoulder like a magical net, watched her enchanting breasts rise and fall with her breathing, and felt the base of his spine begin to tingle.

Dawn had only begun to part the clouds with her pinky fingers when the servant soundlessly closed the door to the Sandal Hall stable yard. Clutching a grimy notebook to his chest, he checked the windows to make sure he was not being watched and darted out into the Strand. He hesitated for a moment, looking up and down the deserted street, then rushed into a nearby alley.

The old beggar woman crouched outside Sandal Hall rose and followed him. She moved quickly toward the alley, showing herself far more energetic and taller than one would have imagined, and just as quickly stopped. The alley was empty. The servant and his carefully recorded notes of all that had transpired that night in Lord Sandal's private second-floor garden had vanished.

Chapter Twelve

The rock flew through the window of the bedchamber, bouncing off Crispin's shoulder and landing on the pillow next to Sophie's head. Crispin reached around Sophie, who was still sleeping curled up next to his body, and felt for the means of his rude awakening. As his fingers closed around it, Sophie's eyelids fluttered, and she tilted her head upward to look at him with drowsy eyes.

"Is it time?" she asked, yawning.

"Time?" Crispin repeated.

"Time for you to show me the things we did not do last night. You said there were some."

Crispin smiled and gently stroked her head. "There are, *tesoro*, but I think we had better wait. There is no reason to rush."

Sophie nodded sleepily, then stretched and resettled herself next to him. "Very well. Wake me when it is time."

For a few moments Crispin was so preoccupied with looking down at her and the feeling of her body along his that he forgot the object in his hand. His malaise from the night before had disappeared with the arrival of day, and he was overcome once again by her extraordinary appeal. Indeed, he was just thinking that perhaps it *was* time, when the reassertion of his professional duty brought him back to himself. He shifted gently, so as not to wake her, while bringing the object in his hands to his eyes.

From the feel and heft of it, there had been no question that it was a rock, but Crispin could also tell it was wrapped in something. That something now revealed itself to be a large, heavily inked piece of paper. Crispin had once narrowly averted being killed by lethal dust—a single whiff was enough to execute a man in five minutes— that had been sent to him within the folds of an apparently inno- cent-looking letter, and had, on another occasion, almost been blown to a thousand pieces by a seemingly innocuous-looking stone that was actually filled with gunpowder. He was therefore very care- ful now as he unwrapped the rock, but he might have spared his efforts. The rock was just a rock, the paper simply a piece of paper.

Or rather, a very particular piece of paper. As he smoothed it out on the bedcovers before him, he found the source of its menace. Across the top, in large roman type, he read, "*News From the Court of Her Royal Highness the Queen*" and across the bottom, in slightly smaller type, "*Printed by Richard Tottle, Esq. By Order of Her Majesty.*" The story in the middle was rendered almost completely illegible, however, by the large letters scrawled over it. These read:

YER LORDSHIP MIND YER BUSYNESS OR YE WONT LIKE IT

Crispin chuckled aloud, waking Sophie again.

"Is it time now?" she asked with her eyes still closed.

He leaned down and kissed her gently on the forehead. "No, *tesoro*, not just yet. But I fear it is time for me to arise."

"And get food?" she asked, opening one eye. "I am glad you are hungry too. I could eat two dozen orange cakes."

No sooner had she spoken than a knock sounded on the door of the bedchamber. Both of Sophie's eyes snapped open now, register- ing fear.

"Don't worry," Crispin soothed her. "It can only be Thurston." He slid out of the bed and moved toward the door, opening it just enough to speak through.

"Good morning, Your Lordship." There was nothing in Thurston's tone to indicate that it was the least bit unusual to be speaking to his master, naked and with lavender flowers caught in his hair, through a crack in the door of his bedchamber. "Their Ladyships send their greetings and request that you visit them at your earliest convenience. I also thought you might need this before your appointments begin."

The door opened slightly wider and then, after a brief whispered exchange, closed. Crispin returned to the bed bearing a heavily laden silver tray, which he set in the middle of the coverlet.

Sophie was sitting up by then, studying the paper and rock with great attention. "What is this?" she asked, waving the paper in front of his face.

"I would say it is a joke," Crispin replied, taking a large bite from a biscuit and offering one to Sophie.

"It doesn't look like a joke to me," she mumbled with her mouth full. "Did it come with the rock?"

Crispin nodded. "Through the window. Schoolboy stuff. No one would send a real threat like that. My god, you were not jesting about being hungry."

Sophie smiled at him with her mouth full of her third biscuit, then frowned as she looked down at the paper. "What are you going to do?" she asked finally, between chews.

"First, I am going to wipe the crumbs of my breakfast from your face. Then I am going to ignore the note."

Sophie's frown deepened. "I would not recommend that. You cannot be sure they are not serious. I think you should cease your investigation."

Crispin, who was trying to erect a barricade between Sophie and the biscuits before his breakfast was demolished, stopped suddenly and raised one eyebrow at her. "Is that what you would counsel? An end to my investigation?"

Sophie nodded, reaching around the pillow that had mysteriously appeared in front of the tray. "Absolutely."

Crispin's expression grew grave. "Miss Champion, I little expected this of you. Underhanded tactics like these." He shook his head sadly.

Sophie ceased the contortions she was engaged in to reach the biscuits without falling off the bed long enough to demand, "What do you mean?"

"Do not bother to deny it. Clearly you hoped to win the bet by scaring me off."

"You think I had this note, this rock sent?" Sophie was outraged. "You accuse me of cheating? Of—"

Crispin broke into a wide grin, and Sophie saw that he was joking. And that he was handsome. Very handsome. And very troublesome. "You—you—" she said, struggling for the right word.

"Bastard?" Crispin offered.

"Bedbug," Sophie countered, poking him with her finger. "You were making fun of me."

"It was the only way to keep you from eating all the biscuits," Crispin replied, putting the last one, dripping deliciously with raspberry preserves, into his mouth entire.

Sophie had to look away from him as he chewed, not because she was upset at the loss of the biscuit, but because the small dab of jam on his chin was making her think about what it would feel like to lick it off, which made her think about kissing him, which made her think about having him touch her, which made her think about the previous night, which made it impossible to think about anything else. And she had something else to think about.

Crispin had only just swallowed when she addressed him, checking first from the corner of her eye to ensure that he had rid his chin of the distraction. "What did Thurston mean about 'your appointments'?" she asked, apparently nonchalant.

"Nothing," Crispin replied, licking jam from his fingertips. "Just a few things I must see to today."

It almost worked. Sophie was almost too overwhelmed by watching his mouth on his fingers and imagining it on her fingers to notice the slight pause before he answered. But not quite. Her expression was grave as she said, "Lord Sandal, I little expected this of you. Underhanded tactics." She waved a hand in disgust. Crispin appeared ready to speak, but she went on over him. "Do not bother to deny it. Clearly you are trying to win our bet by lying to me."

Crispin rolled his eyes, then gave a resigned sigh. "You are correct. My appointments are part of the investigation. I sent letters to a handful of Richard Tottle's subscribers informing them that I was considering taking over his printing business and wanted to discuss the terms of their subscription with them before I made my final decision."

Sophie's expression had changed entirely. "My lord, that is a marvelous plan. I thought all along there was something suspicious about the subscriptions, and now we will know for certain."

"*I* will know for certain. You will not be there."

Sophie's expression changed again, this time to a glower. "Why not? What will stop me?"

"A warrant from the Queen's constables and a bounty of two hundred pounds on your head as an escaped prisoner, for starters," Crispin replied, unruffled. "Do not forget that you are a wanted criminal, with the hangman's rope practically around your neck. If I were you, I would not be so eager to show myself in public."

Sophie screwed up her eyes and scrunched her nose at him, and Crispin was glad to note that he had her stymied. He ignored the faces she was making as he brushed crumbs from the coverlet. Had he not turned to deposit the tray on a nearby table, he would have seen the dangerous smile spreading slowly across her face and would have been alerted to what was coming. As it was, he was completely unprepared and almost dropped the tray when he heard himself addressed in a thick Spanish accent.

"Don Alfonso, who fortunately abandoned his clothes here the other night, thanks His Lordship for his concern, but assures him his identity will trouble no one."

Crispin was already shaking his head vehemently before he turned around. "Absolutely not. No," he said, moving back toward the bed and cursing himself for underestimating her.

"Why not? Or was the threat of being taken by the constables merely a cover for your real fear that I will solve the murder before you do?"

Crispin was determined not to let himself be goaded. "Your disguise is wretched. Anyone could recognize you from across the county of Kent."

Sophie sneered at him. "Nobody at the Unicorn recognized me."

"I did," Crispin pointed out sensibly.

"Perhaps, but you are uniquely pernicious. Besides," she added, kicking off the covers, "what have you got to lose by letting me try? If I am identified, then I will be sent back to prison and you will win the bet. The only possible reason for your reluctance is that you recognize my superior wit and fear to lose."

At that moment, as she lay stretched out naked on his sheets. Crispin recognized only her superior annoyingness. His professional instinct was once again aroused, and it pointed out to him that letting her sit in on the appointments would only solidify the trust he was hoping to breed in her and provide an opening for the questions he meant to ask. Not to mention that it would give him an opportunity to observe her, closely, in breeches.

"Very well, Miss Champion, you win your point. Don Alfonso can attend the meetings. On two conditions." Sophie looked skeptical, but Crispin pressed on. "First, you will sit quietly and say nothing. And second, you must let me choose your mustache."

Four hours later, Crispin Foscari, the Earl of Sandal, and his Spanish secretary, Don Alfonso, closed their second-to-last interview. They had learned several interesting things, among them that Sir Ichibald Riff thought the only thing worth talking about was his new wife, forty-six years his junior and feisty as a jaybird; that Lady Elery never went anywhere without her pet terrier, Carlyle, or her pet nephew, Gordon; that Carlyle was not partial to ravens, and that Gordon was partial to his aunt's money and thought that spending any of it on "that Richard Tottle trash" was nonsense; and that the Duke of Groat was partial to Crispin's French brandy. Sophie, in her capacity as secretary, dutifully recorded all of these pieces of information, and two dozen others, none of which gave the faintest glimpse into the mechanics of Richard Tottle's subscription service. All three of the interviewees insisted that they had subscribed to Richard Tottle's news service because they wanted to stay informed of Queen Elizabeth's doings, although Sir Ichibald eventually admitted he had done it at the urging of his wife, who wanted to improve herself for him. "Not that I married her for her brains," he leered, and Crispin had been forced to laugh in order to cover Sophie's growl.

The interviews had taken place in Crispin's library, and it was there that Sophie and Crispin awaited their final caller. None of the interviewees had cast so much as a suspicious glance in Sophie's direction, a fact she was careful to mention to Crispin after each of the appointments, to which he retaliated that it was all because of the mustache.

Sophie had not batted an eye earlier when Thurston appeared with an enormous case filled with fake hairpieces, from which Crispin had selected a discreet mustache for her, thin and curling at the ends, which he hoped would be unflattering and therefore undistracting. Crispin had fobbed off her questions about why an earl would need such a number of disguises with an excuse about boyhood theatricals, and she little realized that she was now wearing a piece of the Phoenix's elaborate collection of costumes, the collection that allowed him to move among European capitals without ever being recognized. She was, however, rather smitten with the hairpiece, and in particular with the fact that, unlike its predecessor, it did not itch at all.

"You will have to tell Octavia what is in this mustache glue," she commented to Crispin when the door had closed behind a slightly unsteady Duke of Groat. "Her recipe was not nearly as good, and it gave me an allergy."

Crispin, who had risen and passed through the door that led to the privy, groaned. "Please do not make me imagine that you intend to spend much more of your time traipsing around London bemustached. The city can hardly stand the gallants that swarm the streets now," he said over his shoulder, shutting the door behind him.

Sophie's retort was canceled by the arrival of a fashionably short, fashionably coiffed, fashionably painted, voluptuously endowed woman of middle age, swathed in dark green silk.

"Lady Dolores Artly," Thurston announced, then bowed himself out of the room.

Lady Artly ran her heavily lined eyes around the large library until they came to rest on Sophie, who was contentedly twirling her mustache in a chair against the far wall. A small, seductive smile played over Lady Artly's tinted lips as she approached Sophie's chair and then curtsied. When she arose, one of her layers of green silk slipped deliberately to reveal a large expanse of powdered bosom. "It is *such* a pleasure to make your acquaintance, Lord Sandal," she purred.

It took Sophie only a fraction of a second to decide on a course of action. "The pleasure, Lady Artly, is all mine," she said, pitching her voice low, and manfully gesturing the lady into a seat next to hers.

"The pleasure is all mine," Grip the raven squawked, making Lady Artly jump in her chair and throw herself into Sophie's arms.

"Do not fear, Lady Artly, it is just a bird," Sophie murmured in a deep voice, trying to extricate her arm from her companion's grasp while sending a warning glance in the direction of the raven, which, she could have sworn, winked at her.

"Please, please call me Dolores," Lady Artly begged, once she was sufficiently recovered. "I have long been *such* an admirer of yours, Lord Sandal." If there had been any question of the direction of Lady Artly's interest in the Earl of Sandal, it was resolved as she leaned close to Sophie, led her hand toward the ample bosom, and whispered in her ear, "I have often thought we could find *such* enjoyment in one another's company. Two people of the world such as you and I."

Sophie, who wondered if this sort of thing happened to the Earl of Sandal every day, was spared having to respond by Crispin's return to the room, eliciting another chorus of "The pleasure is mine" from Grip. Lady Artly withdrew quickly, dropping Sophie's hand and pulling the green silk back over some small part of her bosom. "Who is that man?" she asked sharply.

Sophie smiled reassuringly, as she imagined Crispin would. "There is nothing to worry about, Dolores," she said in her low voice. "That is only my secretary, Don Alfonso." Crispin had opened his mouth, but Sophie shot him a look that silenced him. "He is here merely to record our conversation and will not speak."

Lady Artly looked Crispin up and down, with an expression that made it clear he did not meet her idea of a fashionable secretary. "I would rather we were alone, Lord Sandal," she said finally, the sharpness gone from her voice and the purr back in place. "I have *such* a lot to confide in you, and Spaniards make me nervous. Could you not dismiss him? For me?"

Crispin blinked twice to make sure he was seeing what he was seeing, since he could not possibly be hearing what he was hearing, but lost all capacity for blinking as Sophie turned to him and said sternly, "Go, Don Alfonso. I will ring for you when I need you."

"Go, Don Alfonso," Grip piped in, hopping on one foot. "Get the girl."

"Listen," Crispin began, moving toward the two women. "I—"

Thurston's entrance cut him off midsentence, to Sophie's great relief. "I beg your pardon, my lord," the steward said, addressing the room generally, "but there is a personage below who desires to see you."

Sophie seized the opportunity. Turning her head completely from Lady Artly, she gave Crispin a huge grin. "Don Alfonso, I would be much obliged if you would attend to that matter and leave me to see to our charming guest."

Sophie, who did not know that there was a peephole into the library through which everything that passed in there could be seen and heard, was surprised and pleased by Crispin's acquiescence. Indeed, taking his cue from Thurston, he did not even bat an eyelid as he bowed and said, "Very good, my lord," then followed his steward from the room.

When they were alone together again, Lady Artly resumed her leaning position. "You handled that man with *such* mastery, my lord," she praised Sophie. "You are frightfully powerful."

"Frightfully powerful," Grip chirped. "Frightfully, frightfully, frightfully."

Sophie rose from her seat abruptly in order to avoid the pair of lips that had somehow wended their way toward her. "Yes, well," she said in an offhanded baritone as she moved toward the raven's cage to give the bird a stern look, "someone has to be." She began to pace the library twirling her mustache, trying to remember now how Crispin had begun the earlier interviews, and relieved that the raven seemed to have gotten her hint and was now dozing with its head under its wing. "Tell me, Dolores, did you enjoy your subscription to Richard Tottle's *News at Court*?"

"No, I most certainly did not."

Sophie stopped her pacing and mustache twirling. This was the first less than positive reaction they had gotten to their questions about Richard Tottle's broadside, and possibly the first clue as to its strange machinations. Sophie tried not to seem too excited, lest she scare the clue away. "I am sorry to hear that. Was it the content you objected to?"

Lady Artly's face assumed a pained expression. "It is *such* a painful subject for me to talk about. Won't you come sit down next to me again?"

Sophie returned to the seat she had left and submitted to having her hand raised to Lady Artly's cheek.

"I only tell you this because I know you will understand," Lady Artly began, fluttering her false eyelashes. "It is *such* a terrible thing to have to admit. You can imagine how I feel."

Sophie, whose hand was now being pressed to Lady Artly's breast, did not have to leave much to her imagination to know exactly how Lady Artly, or at least her skin, felt. She nodded sympathetically.

"Oh, Lord Sandal, it is awful. It was not I, but my husband, Harry, who subscribed to those wretched papers. I knew when it started, when the meringues began to come, that something was amiss. You see, Harry hates sweets, yet he was paying that baker, Sweetson, a hundred pounds a month for those dreadful French confections. And whenever I asked him about it, he told me to mind my own business."

Sophie, who had little experience with how a married couple negotiated the ordering of pastries, was having trouble comprehending the problem, but she tried to look as though she understood. "I can imagine how hard that was for you."

"Can you?" Lady Artly brought her face very close to Sophie's. "Yes, I suppose, Lord Sandal, you can. You are *such* an understander of women. You can see how difficult it would be for a woman like me."

Lady Artly made a move to caress Sophie's cheek, but Sophie pulled away slightly, pretending to cough. She did not know how stalwart the mustache paste was and was not about to put it to the test of being caressed.

"Oh, dear, are you ill, my lord?" Lady Artly asked with great solicitude. "Let me cradle your head—"

Sophie stopped coughing abruptly. "No, no, it is just a cold I got from being out in the rain. Nothing to worry about. Tell me, what did you do when the meringues began to arrive?"

Lady Artly looked despondent. "Nothing. What could I do? Besides, the meringues stopped coming for a few months, and I thought perhaps Harry had seen his error. But then, then those dreadful papers started."

Sophie had not been able to read much of the broadside printed by Richard Tottle that had arrived through the window that morning, but nothing about it appeared to warrant the description "dreadful." "You mean Richard Tottle's papers?"

"No, no, those came later. No, I mean"—Lady Artly took a deep breath—"*The Lady's Guide to Italian Fashion*. Harry, reading a fashion broadside. It was all so clear then."

Lady Artly's voice had begun to quiver, and Sophie understood that while nothing was clear to her, something was clearly wrong.

"Lady Artly—Dolores," Sophie said in a low voice, but the woman stopped her with a hand.

"Please. Save your condolences, your excuses. I know when my husband is having an affair. There is no other explanation. First the French sweets, then the Italian fashions. He has a mistress stashed somewhere, I am sure of it. And I think she must be one of the Queen's ladies-in-waiting. Why else would he take Richard Tottle's paper, but to look for the name of his mistress in its pages?"

Sophie opened her mouth to speak and was again stopped. "No, I know what you would say. You would say that no man who was married to a woman with *such* looks, *such* style as I myself possess, would have a mistress. That I am all the woman he, or any man, would ever want. And you would not be the first to say so. But Harry is ungrateful and unrefined. He does not know what a prize he has in me. He is not like you. He does not appreciate me as you do. That is why I came to you today."

Sophie was growing more confused with every word, and in particular, Lady Artly's final words. Could Lady Artly be proposing that they have an affair to get back at her husband? Sophie hesitated for a moment before asking, as neutrally as possible, "Is there a service I can render you?"

Lady Artly pulled a kerchief from her waist and dabbed at her eyes. "I want you to find Harry's mistress and lure her away from him. You can do it, Lord Sandal. No woman can resist you." She put the kerchief away and turned her eyes back to Sophie. "Even I, a married woman, am not immune to charms such as yours. I must admit, your portrait in the broadside never moved me, but now that I see you in person, and see your mustache…" She lowered and then raised her eyes slowly.

"You do me too much honor." Sophie spoke as formally as she could, sitting up rigidly in her seat.

"Lord Sandal, you need not be modest." Lady Artly leaned close to Sophie. "You are worthy of far more than mere praise from me. I am a woman who could really cherish your finer points." A finger crept across the arm of the chair and drew a long, suggestive line up Sophie's thigh.

Sophie suffered a second coughing fit then, which caused her face to turn red and again nearly resulted in her having her head cradled on Lady Artly's bosom. But she could not keep coughing forever, and she was at a loss as to how to end the bizarre interview, when the great clock in the downstairs hall began to chime.

"Oh, dear," Lady Artly said with alarm, "I must be going. I hate to leave you in the throes of such a bad cold, all alone, with no one to look after you, no one to comfort you."

"I shall be fine," Sophie assured her, with a few precautionary coughs just to keep Lady Artly's hands at bay. "It is better if you go. We would not want anyone to suspect us."

"Of course. You are right, Harry should not know I have been here. He is *such* a jealous tyrant, and I should hate for you to have to fight a duel on my behalf."

Sophie's recovery was almost complete now. "I certainly would not shrink from it," she answered, not hesitating to risk Crispin's neck, then stood quickly and strode toward the bell rope in the corner of the room. "But, just to be cautious, I shall have Thurston show you out."

Lady Artly rose majestically, gathering her green silk swathing about her. "I know we shall meet again soon," she told Sophie. "You will do what I asked, won't you? You will do that for me, for your sweet Dolores?" Sophie, who had been rendered rather short of breath by the coughing fit, did not have time to respond before Lady Artly rushed on. "Thank you, Lord Sandal. I knew I could count on you."

Lady Artly edged toward Sophie, apparently expecting something in the way of an embrace, but Sophie bent down to avoid the red-tinted lips and instead, taking the lady's hand, gave it a chaste kiss.

"*So* gallant," Lady Artly sighed. "*So* divine." And with that, and the appearance of Thurston, she disappeared in a swirl of green silk.

Lady Artly passed Crispin at the bottom of the stairs as she went out. "Good day, Don Alfonso," she told him. "Be sure to assist your master well in his undertaking for me. He is *such* a wonderful man."

Crispin, nodded, rendered mute as much by the sheer quantity of green silk as by the fact that Sophie had apparently agreed to do something for the creature wearing it, then returned his attention to the task at hand. He did not want to lose any time giving Sophie hell. He set his jaw slightly more with each step he climbed toward his apartment, concentrating on the lecture he was going to inflict on her for her behavior. She had violated their agreement entirely, had done nothing like sit meekly in the corner, and she was going to be sorry for it. First, he was going to lock her in his bedchamber. And then, he resolved, she would answer his questions. All of them. Truthfully. He had only five days to save his neck, and he was going to start by making her talk. Today he would find out what she had been doing at the Unicorn, what had passed between her and Tottle, and what exactly was her interest in the Phoenix. And, he added, what exactly was the nature of her relationship with her godfather. His spine began to tingle ever so moderately with this thought, but he ignored it. As he reentered the library and saw her sitting at his desk, kicking it with her foot and twirling one end of her mustache around her finger, his resolve jiggled but the words "*five days*" soon restored it.

Something about her interview with Lady Artly was nagging at Sophie, something about what the fashionable woman had said, and she was momentarily too distracted trying to figure out what it was to note Crispin's return. "Oh, there you are," she said, coming out of her reverie. "I am starving. What are we having for supper? And who was waiting for you downstairs?"

"That's none of your business," Crispin replied coldly, then demanded, "What the devil were you thinking, impersonating me to that woman like that?"

"Did you say we were having roasted loin of pork sautéed with apples?" Sophie went on, heedless of his displeasure. "And spinach soufflé? Oh, there is no spinach? Yes, then Lisbon sprouts will do fine."

"Answer my question. Why did you impersonate me, against my direct orders?"

Seeing she was not going to get anywhere on their menu until this was dealt with, Sophie sighed. "You never told me I could not impersonate you. Besides, I did nothing of the kind. *She* mistook *me* for you. I merely failed to correct her. You will be interested to know that she thinks I, or rather, the Earl of Sandal, is handsomer in person than in your engraved portraits. And she liked my mustache."

"I can't begin to tell you how you arouse my jealousy. What service did you promise to do for her, Your Lordship?"

Sophie began to look a bit grim. "She wants me, or actually you, to find out if her husband is having an affair and, if he is, to seduce his mistress. Easy stuff for you apparently. She made it sound like the Earl of Sandal did such things every day, before breakfast." Sophie wanted to kick herself for the petulant note she heard in her voice, so she kicked the desk instead.

"Before breakfast?" Crispin replied with mock alarm, forgetting for a moment that he was very angry at her in his pleasure at her obvious jealousy. "Never. Before supper perhaps."

"Supper?" Sophie brightened considerably. "Squabs stuffed with spinach, onions, raisins, and breadcrumbs, and basted every twenty minutes with a mixture of white wine and butter?"

Crispin ignored her. "What else did you learn from her?"

The brightness dimmed. "Nothing. That was all, just a request. I hope she is pretty."

"Who?"

"The mistress." Sophie was impatient. "The mistress you are supposed to seduce."

"Unfortunately, I am trying to limit myself to one seduction a week, and I do not think yours is finished." When he found himself on the way toward the desk to expand on that theme, Crispin stopped himself. "Nor is our work. There is still one person who was a subscriber that we have not consulted."

Sophie, wondering if perhaps they could not do it after they made love, or after they had supper, or both, asked distractedly, "Who?"

"You."

Sophie's distraction evaporated. "But I did not subscribe."

"Your name was in his ledger for the precise amount of the subscription."

"Perhaps," Sophie said, shaking her head in a futile effort to make sense of what was happening. "But that does not mean I subscribed. I never met Richard Tottle. Or gave him any money."

"Really?" Crispin asked with undisguised incredulity.

"Yes." Sophie paused for a moment, trying to decide, then blurted, "I admit I went to the Unicorn to meet Tottle, and I received word that he was in the smoking room, but when I got there..." Her words dried up abruptly.

"What happened?" Crispin coaxed. "Was he already dead?"

Sophie shook her head slowly, looking miserable. "I do not know if he was alive. It was dark in the smoking room. Very dark. Completely dark." She shuddered. "I was... I did not go in. I just left."

As she spoke Crispin remembered, remembered having to light the tapers when he entered, and realized that he should have understood immediately, as soon as he saw her reaction to the dark in Pickering's Highway. She had been afraid to enter, and too embarrassed to admit it.

"I see," Crispin said finally, kicking himself for not having caught on sooner. "But your bill of credit was found on Tottle's dead body. If you did not give it to him, who did?"

"I do not know," Sophie said with such clear relief that Crispin was immediately put on his guard.

"Let me ask the question another way," he said carefully, circling around the desk toward her. "To whom did you give that bill of credit?"

The relief drained from her expression. "I don't remember," she replied, more a question than a statement.

Crispin was leaning over her now, his hands on either arm of her chair, his eyes looking into hers. "Do not lie to me, Sophie. I want to help you, but I can do that only if you are honest with me."

Under other circumstances, circumstances that had his lips hovering something more than two inches from hers, Sophie would have told him that she did not need his help, did not even want it, but now she could not form the words, let alone think them. It was as if his very proximity hypnotized her. Before she realized what was happening, she heard a voice, her voice, answering his questions.

"The bill of credit that they found on Tottle's body was mine," the voice explained. "I mean, I wrote it. But I did not give it to Richard Tottle. I gave it to my godfather, Lord Grosgrain, the morning he died, just before he left his house. He told me he was going to see Richard Tottle that morning, but there is no way he could have given it to Tottle because he was killed only minutes later at the end of the street—more than a mile from Tottle's print shop. Whoever killed him must have found the bill of credit on his body and kept it, then planted it on Tottle to implicate me. Just like they did with my pistol."

Crispin did not move. "Your pistol?"

"Yes, the one that was used to kill Richard Tottle. According to Octavia, Lord Grosgrain borrowed it the day before he was killed. He hated firearms, hated violence of any kind, so he must have been terrified for his life when he took it." She looked at him intently. "Don't you see? Lord Grosgrain must have suspected someone was going to try to kill him and took my pistol to defend himself."

"From whom?" Crispin queried.

"I don't know," Sophie said, but so oddly that Crispin eyed her sharply. She melted under his scrutiny. "I do not know, but I have a suspicion. I think it was someone called the Phoenix."

Crispin abruptly removed his hands from the arms of her chair and began to pace the library, trying to ignore the prickly sensation at the base of his spine. "Why?"

Sophie told herself she was not disappointed that he had not kissed her. "Because Lord Grosgrain said he would pay me back

'unless the Phoenix gets me first.' Those were his exact words."
Crispin stopped pacing and looked steadfastly at the wall. "Does
that mean anything to you, my lord?"

"I am not sure," Crispin said aloud, more to the wall than to her.
Realizing he had spoken, he turned toward her and watched her
closely as he went on. "The other day, Lawrence mentioned that
there was a reward out for someone named Phoenix. He is supposed to be some sort of secret spy of Queen Elizabeth's." Noting
that Sophie's face showed only confusion and that, given the way
her lips had just opened, she was preparing to ask him about nine
hundred Phoenix-oriented questions, he decided to change the
subject. "Let's return to what you were saying earlier. It sounds like
you surmise that your godfather did not die in an accident, but was
murdered?"

"Yes," Sophie confirmed "I am sure of it. But about—"

Crispin put up a hand to stop her from interrupting. "And that
whoever killed Lord Grosgrain found the pistol and your bill of
credit on his body and then planted them both on Richard Tottle to
implicate you?"

"Exactly. But the Phoen—"

"Which means," Crispin went on, resuming his pacing, "that
whoever killed Lord Grosgrain also killed Richard Tottle. And has
it in for you." He was explicating this as much for her as for himself, testing it for strength, probing it for weak spots. It all seemed
to make sense, but none of it explained her initial unwillingness to
admit to him that she had written the bill of credit for Lord Grosgrain.

"Tell me," he said finally in a deceptively light tone, stopping
directly in front of the desk and leaning toward her. "Why did Lord
Grosgrain ask you for twelve hundred pounds?"

Sophie spread her hands. "He said he needed to give that sum
to Richard Tottle and he did not want his name to appear on a bill
of credit and he did not have that amount in gold."

"Doesn't it strike you as strange that he would ask you, of all
people, for money?"

Sophie tilted her head back. "Why strange? He was my godfather. My very good friend. Why wouldn't he ask me, of all people?"

Crispin felt a spark of something it took him a moment to identify as disappointment. Why couldn't she just tell him the truth? Why couldn't she just trust him? "Because he was paying you a thousand pounds a month," he said finally.

Blood stopped circulating in Sophie's body, or so she felt. "I beg your pardon?"

"Let me rephrase that." The tingling in Crispin's spine was unignorable now. "Why would Lord Grosgrain ask you for twelve hundred pounds when he was the one supplying you with money to begin with? Or do you deny that?"

"No. It was my allowance," Sophie said, giving the excuse she and her godfather had made up years earlier. "Only—" She stopped, struggling to master the quaver in her voice. Her secret, Lord Grosgrain's secret, the secret they had together protected for so long, was in jeopardy. When she resumed, her tone was cold and distant. "Only I do not see how this could possibly have any bearing on your investigation of his death. My money and its source are none of your business."

Crispin's spine was on fire. Damn her and her lies. Disappointment veered dangerously into anger, and he moved with an eerie calmness around the desk. He again leaned over her chair, but this time his tone was not seductive. "I do not think you understand, Miss Champion. You are not safe from the law until the real murderer of Richard Tottle is found, and, since everyone thinks it is you, no one but me is seeking him. I am the only person who can help you, the only one who can solve the murder, and you would do well to give me any assistance you can."

Sophie sought desperately for some way to change the topic, and finally hit upon it. "This is a rather elaborate ruse to win a bet, my lord," she countered hoping her tone was as chilling as his. "What makes you think I cannot solve the murder myself?"

"Many things. Principally the fact that I am locking you in this room when I leave this afternoon, and you will not be able to get out of it until you answer all my questions truthfully," Crispin explained with icy precision.

Sophie rose abruptly from her seat, pulling away from him, outraged. "You would not dare."

"That is where you are wrong, Miss Champion. I would, and I shall."

Sophie's outrage turned to burning scorn. "I thought you were a man of your word, a man of honor, Lord Sandal, but I see I was mistaken. You are a cringing coward. You think nothing of cheating on our bet in the lowest, most craven way imaginable." As she spoke, she watched Crispin's eyes turn dark, his face leaden, but she plunged ahead anyway, astonished by the words she heard herself speaking and by their frightening ring of truth. "You would do anything to win our wager. Indeed, I am willing to bet that everything that happened last night between us, everything you did and said, was only done to make me trust you, so you could learn what I know and win more easily."

"Anything is fair in sport," Crispin said condescendingly, his tone borrowed from a Nordic wind.

"Not locking me up." Sophie found that she was almost trembling, trembling with rage and something else. She did not speak but rather hurled her words at him, wanting to hurt him badly. "Not treating me like a prisoner. Not acting like a spineless coward who will stoop to anything—even trapping an innocent woman and holding her captive—to get his way."

"Very true, Miss Champion." Crispin's eyes were the color of iron, and his voice was completely devoid of anything human. "I thought I was helping you, but you show me that I was wrong. Do whatever you please. For my part, I do not give a damn what becomes of you."

The final, killing words hung in the air of the library even after he stalked out of it, slamming the door behind him. They bounced around, repeating themselves in Sophie's head, reminding her, berating her. *I do not give a damn what becomes of you,* the voice in her head chorused gleefully over and over again. *I do not give a damn what becomes of you.*

Day turned to night, and Sophie sat completely still, completely silent, completely numb. She neither blinked nor breathed, did not flinch or tremble, but simply sat, a stone-cold statue.

The tears that streamed down her cheeks unchecked, unstoppable, were the only sign of life.

Chapter Thirteen

Poverty kills Beauty, and wealth exalts it. The pursuit of Beauty, there-
fore, is the pursuit of wealth, of gold, which is the highest pursuit. Gold,
the rarest and most splendid of the metals, is the symbol of Beauty.
    ~~Gold is the way to Beauty.~~
    ~~Gold is the road to Beauty.~~
    ~~The road of Beauty is paved in gold.~~
    Gold. Gold gold gold. I must have gold.
    Beauty must have gold. More gold, more, more, more.

As he staggered toward the door of the workshop, clumsily retracing
the steps he had used to enter minutes earlier, the blindfolded
man heard the scratching of the pen resume where he had interrupted it.

The pathway to Beauty is through gold, it wrote.

The man was nearly unaware of the hand Kit placed on his
elbow to guide him, nearly unaware of the steps he descended,
nearly unaware of anything but the echo of the soft words he had
just heard. "My sources within Sandal Hall tell me that the earl and
your Sophie Champion are quite intimate," the whispered voice
repeated, over and over again in his head, always in the same half-
amused, half-menacing tone.

The path to gold is through blood, the pen inscribed.

The man could barely contain his rage. Crossing the threshold of the workshop, he pulled off his blindfold so forcefully that it almost ripped the fake scar from his forehead, but he noticed this as little as he had noticed Kit's assistance.

~~Gold must be paid for with blood~~

The man's eyes were glued to the formidable walls of Sandal Hall, staring at them defiantly, as if straining to see through them. As he stared, his hands curled into two powerful and menacing fists.

~~Gold must be paid for with death.~~

Sophie Champion was within those walls. The woman he had spent his whole adult life looking for.

Gold must be paid for with sacrifice.

The woman he had to have, no matter the cost.

Chapter Fourteen

The streets of London had turned to rivers of mud by the time Crispin tried to negotiate his way homeward. The thunderstorm that began in the afternoon had covered the city in sheet after sheet of rain, immense, swollen drops that fell in torrents from the sky.

He was soaking wet when he entered Sandal Hall from the stable yard. Before he had time to track mud through the main hall, Thurston appeared to take his wet cloak and boots.

"Good evening, Your Lordship," he said as Crispin stripped off his sodden cape. "I trust you had a pleasant afternoon."

"Dreadful," Crispin growled at him. Which was not strictly true. For while the weather had been abominable, and his mood worse, he had, in fact, learned something very important.

Following the instructions he had received that afternoon by messenger while Sophie was engaged with Lady Artly, he had gone to a house in the suburbs of London and been greeted at the back door by a young, frightened woman, who thanked him profusely for coming.

"I am sorry to make you go so far out of your way," she had apologized, "but I could not come myself to the interview you proposed and I did not dare entrust this information to someone else."

Leading him down a narrow corridor, she explained that the house belonged to her uncle, Matthew Grey, once a well-to-do merchant, but now an invalid, who might ring for her at any time and to whom her absence was inexcusable. She had asked Crispin to come in the afternoon, she went on, because it was when their housemaid did the shopping and therefore no one would know he was there.

She said all this in whispers as they wound around the lowest level of the house, until they arrived in the kitchen. There was an air of lost grandeur about everything Crispin saw, particularly about the large, jeweled box in the middle of the planked table.

"I keep them in here," the young woman explained, opening the box with a small key and taking out a collection of papers. She flipped through them, then chose one and handed it to Crispin. "This is what most of them are like."

"*'How well does Matthew Grey know his niece? Some say too well,'*" Crispin read aloud, then looked up at the girl. "Where did you get this?"

"It was sent to my uncle, inside this cover," she handed Crispin another piece of paper.

"*'If you do not want Sir Edgar to see this, accept the subscription that will be offered to you within a fortnight,'*" Crispin read this time. "Who is Sir Edgar?"

"My betrothed," the young woman answered, blushing. "Sir Edgar Wellit. His family is very proper, and if he or they ever saw anything like that note, the betrothal would be over in a flash. I do not know what I would do."

Crispin looked sympathetic. "What happened next? Did you subscribe to Richard Tottle's paper?"

"No, that was second. First my uncle took a subscription to *The Lady's Guide to Italian Fashion*, for six months, at one hundred pounds a month, and we heard nothing. But then, more letters came, just like those, and that was when Richard Tottle's paper began to arrive."

Blackmail. A very sophisticated, even ingenious, form of blackmail, Crispin thought to himself. The content of the letters need not even be true, and he hoped in this case was not, but the threat of disclosure was enough to make people empty their purses. And by doing it through the subscription service, the identity of the black-mailer remained unknown, and therefore untouchable. The publish-ers had only to forward a lump sum each month to the benefactor who brought them so many new subscriptions. Crispin wondered if Richard Tottle or the publisher of *The Lady's Guide to Italian Fashion* even knew that they were part of a blackmail scheme.

"Do you know who printed *The Lady's Guide to Italian Fashion*?" Crispin asked.

The girl shook her head. "I destroyed the papers without even reading them, lest someone see and somehow know. But yesterday a man from a bakery came and told us that, instead of Richard Tot-tle, we should pay our hundred pound a month to his master."

"Did he give you a name?"

"Sweetson, in Milk Street," the young woman said unhappily. "I decided to tell you this, Lord Sandal, because Edgar, that is my betrothed, he reads all about your adventures and thinks very highly of you. My uncle cannot afford to pay the hundred pounds a month much longer, and I am afraid that when he stops, if he stops before the wedding, well..." She shuddered. "Yesterday, Uncle Matthew was asleep when your message arrived, so I read it first, and when I saw it, I knew, I knew then that it was the answer I had been pray-ing for. I was, well, hoping that if I explained it to you, and then, if later they do send a letter to Edgar, you could talk to him and make him understand, so he won't throw me over. He will believe any-thing you say. I know this is an enormous favor to ask of a stranger, but I have nowhere else to turn."

Crispin had agreed to talk to Edgar, should it come to that, and had left, brooding over the scheme he had just unearthed. Instead of making his investigation easier, however, it made it suddenly harder or at least less likely to yield a useful result. It increased the number of possible suspects in the murder of Richard Tottle, for any one of the people who were forced to subscribe under this sys-tem might have thought that killing him would end their vexation.

This larger pool of potential murderers dimmed the likelihood that Tottle's death had any direct tie to the people trying to destroy the Phoenix, in search of whom Crispin had undertaken the investigation into the printer's demise.

And yet, Crispin did not feel overly bothered by this apparent hiccup in his inquiry. That rainy afternoon, as he remounted Fortuna and steered her toward home, his mind was occupied once more with Sophie Champion. This preoccupation, not any concern over finding Tottle's murderer or the Phoenix's enemy, was what led him to describe his day as dreadful, particularly his reflection on his own behavior toward Sophie earlier that afternoon.

He had to admit that he had behaved badly and unfairly, not to mention clumsily. True, she was hiding something from him, hiding something about her relationship with her godfather, but that was no excuse for him to speak to her so harshly. Besides, deep down he knew that he had lied to her himself. He had said that he did not give a damn about her.

Thousands of people had lied to him as the Phoenix, and he had never lost his temper with them, in fact, had done just the opposite. Lies, he had learned, were most easily unraveled when the liar thought they were being believed. Throwing Sophie's words back in her face was perhaps the least effective way to learn the truth. But he had not been thinking rationally that afternoon, and that was what disturbed him most. His upset about Sophie's relationship with her godfather, about the care with which she protected it, about his own inability to either confirm or debunk the rumors he had been hearing about them, had impeded his judgment. But Sophie was right; none of that had any bearing on his investigation. Nothing could be less important to the interests of the Phoenix than knowing the exact nature of Sophie Champion's relationship to Milton Grosgrain. Nothing could be less important to the Phoenix, Crispin repeated, and the Phoenix's concerns—not the Earl of Sandal's—were what mattered.

Crispin had just set out toward Sweetson the baker's to continue his inquiry—reminding himself forcefully that it was the Phoenix that mattered right now and not himself—when he hit upon the happy thought that it would be in the best interest of both himself and the Phoenix to apologize to Sophie. That way he could re-earn her trust and get her to answer the rest of their collective questions. And it would make him feel less like a cad. It was this sole interest and not any desire just to hear Sophie's voice that had led him to redirect Fortuna's steps and spur her into a record-setting gallop, and this plan of action that he was determined to undertake immediately when he ran into Thurston in his own entrance hall.

Thurston cleared his throat as Crispin leaned over to strip off his soggy boots. "I have a message for Your Lordship from Their Ladyships, your aunts."

"Are The Aunts now sending you to give their lectures?" Crispin asked morosely.

"No, my lord, they merely asked me to inquire about the nature of the laughter they heard last night. They thought it sounded rather maniacal, and they wanted to be sure you were not keeping a madman, or madwoman, anywhere on the premises. Your father, the late lamented Hugo, would never have kept a mad person in the house, they asked me to inform you."

The reminder of Sophie's ecstatic laugher the night before, coupled with the idea that The Aunts mistook it for that of a bedlamite, brought a smile to Crispin's lips despite himself. "I hope you told them that *I am* keeping a madwoman in my apartments."

"I did, my lord, but they did not seem to believe me."

"Too bad." Crispin shrugged. "By the way, how is the madwoman?"

"I cannot say, my lord, I have not seen her these several hours. She did not touch her supper, or her dinner."

"She did not eat? Strange." She must have been quite upset, Crispin realized with a pang.

Thurston cleared his throat again. "She did ask me to have a message delivered to Hen House for her. I have prepared a copy of it, as well as a transcript of the discussion she held with Lady Artly."

"Anything interesting?"

"I do not believe so, my lord. Nor was there a reply. But Mister Pickering passed to give Miss Champion his regards."

"Sly, Lawrence, very sly." Crispin shook his head. "How did she receive him?"

"He did not come in, my lord. I had the impression that he was not eager to see Their Ladyships. Perhaps you can tell Miss Champion that he called? She was not in the library when I looked in."

"Of course." Crispin started up the stairs, then turned back to his steward. "Are you wearing cologne, Thurston?" he asked, sniffing.

"Oil of clove, sir," Thurston replied, and for the first time in their history together Crispin could have sworn he saw his steward blush. "The scent is said to be pleasing and inspiring, sir."

"Of course. Well, good night, Thurston."

Crispin spoke his last words over his shoulder as he began to ascend the stairs to his apartment. It had never once crossed his mind that Sophie would leave—she had no place to go and could not possibly get by Thurston unnoticed—but now, taking the steps two at a time, he wondered if he had been too sanguine.

He had been. Not only had Sophie found a way to get out of Sandal Hall unobserved, she had used it several hours earlier. Indeed, she had slipped out of it and had already reached the outer wall of the house before she stopped and retraced her steps back to Crispin's apartment.

It was Grip the raven who had roused her from her corpselike state, when, hours before, he suddenly sprang to life and, hopping up and down, begun squawking, "meringues, meringues, meringues," over and over. Initially, Sophie had assumed he was just hungry, but when he refused any part of her untouched supper, she realized that he was repeating a word he had heard during her discussion with Lady Artly. And not merely a word, but the word Sophie had been looking for. *Meringues.*

She had wasted no time composing a note to Octavia and dispatching it via Thurston to Hen House. It was a nuisance not being able to go herself, but the cordon of constables around her former home made that impossible. Even Don Alfonso could not be sure of passing by them. Her plan had therefore been to await Octavia's answer in Crispin's apartment and then leave before he returned.

But when the answer had not arrived after the first hour, or the second, she realized she would have to go without it. Making sure that her mustache was still in place, she had stuffed several candles and a tinderbox into the doublet she was wearing and lowered herself down into the secret passage from the library she had discovered earlier that day. The passage, while not well maintained, was ample, and within minutes she found herself standing within hailing distance of the Strand.

That was where she had made her decision. Crispin's words from the afternoon, not the horrible words but those spoken just before, came back to her. *I am the only person who can help you, the only one who can solve the murder,* she heard him saying in her head, and she knew he was partially right. She was not, by any means, willing to cede the entire investigation to him, as he seemed to desire. But she could use his help, or better, his knowledge, to find her godfather's killer on her own. For all his hateful dung-beetle-like qualities, there was no denying that Crispin had information she could use. She would wait for him, she decided, coolly force him to disclose what he knew, and then leave.

The decision to return was a logical decision, based purely on the need to ensure that justice was served. It had nothing at all to do with a desire to see the Earl of Sandal again. Why would she want to see a man who was so beastly to her? Certainly he had the power to make her feel the most extraordinary things, to make her feel wonderful about herself, desirable, good, but then the next minute he made her feel wretched. She was still confused about what had happened between them the previous night, confused by her feelings and her willingness and his openness and kindness, confused even more by the cruel coldness of his words that afternoon. *I do not give a damn what becomes of you* echoed again in her head, and she had realized then why the words stung so much. It was because she could not say them back.

The Earl of Sandal would be fine, probably better, without her. She would not burden him with the fact that she did give a damn, several damns. She would not explain to him that she had never felt so free, so alive, as she did with him, even more that morning when they were just quietly having breakfast together than the night before. She would not admit that she felt exalted when she was in his arms, like a princess when he responded to her, like something precious and worthy, worthy of affection, worthy of respect. He had made her feel strong during the few hours they had shared and made her feel, for the first time in her life, glad to be a woman. To be Sophie Champion. She would not tell him that it had been eleven years since she cried as she had that afternoon. She would not share any of that with him, would stay only long enough to find out what she needed to know, and then go. That was her decision, the decision that turned her steps back to Sandal Hall, the decision that she reaffirmed as she climbed out of the hidden passageway and back into the library, the decision that had left her playing with Don Alfonso's dice on a bench shaded from the rain next to the pond where they had first made love, the decision that she now repeated to herself as Crispin, wet clothes clinging to every sinew of his body and making him look like a soaked mythic god, stood staring at her from the threshold of his chamber.

"I am glad you are still here," he said, his heart racing faster than he would have liked at the sight of her.

Sophie's hand stopped mid-roll. "What?"

"I said, I am glad you stayed." Crispin crossed the lawn of his private garden and seated himself on the bench opposite her. "I wanted to apologize for my behavior this afternoon."

This was not going at all as Sophie had planned. She was expecting cold hostility, glares, perhaps a sarcastic smirk. These she was prepared for. But there was nothing in her emotional arsenal to prepare her for an apology. "You can't do that," she announced, furiously tossing her dice at him.

"Can't do what?"

Sophie glowered at him. "You cannot treat someone cruelly and then march back and apologize without any warning."

This was not going at all as Crispin had planned. "I am sorry. I am not accustomed to working with other people." *To needing other people,* a voice in his head amplified. "What I did was wrong."

"You are damn right it was wrong." Sophie's eyes were flaming now. "Is this how you treat everyone? You seduce them by bringing them here"—she gestured harshly toward the pond and the statue of Venus—"and then you tell them you don't give a damn about them?"

It took Crispin a moment to reply, and when he did, his voice was low. "I have never brought anyone here before."

Sophie gulped. "Good. You shouldn't. Not if you are going to treat them that way." She became very interested in the dice cradled in the palm of her hand. "You can't just boss people around and expect them to obey, treat them like they are your prisoner and be mean to them and—"

"I only did it because I was afraid you would leave."

Crispin's words cut through Sophie's anger. For a moment she sat completely still, stiller than she had ever been in her life. Then she raised her eyes to his, eyes shining with held back tears, and asked, "Don't you understand that when you treat me like that, I want to leave?"

Crispin nodded. "I do now. But you didn't go. Why did you stay?" He gave her a lopsided smile. "Was it to berate me?"

Sophie ripped her eyes from his, from his smile, in a desperate effort to recall why she had not left. She tossed the dice and the cubes clicked over the smooth surface of the bench, but she paid no attention to how they landed. She was torn, torn between wanting to trust these new words, between wanting to let "*I am glad you stayed*" erase "*I do not give a damn what becomes of you,*" but she knew she should not. They were just words, words the Earl of Sandal seemed particularly adept at tossing around, just as some people tossed dice. She should leave, should stand up, cross the perfect lawn, and leave, should just go—

"You win," Crispin announced, breaking into her thoughts. Judging from the confused expression on her face that she did not know what he was talking about, he held up the dice. "You rolled six and I rolled nine. You win. Now I have to answer any question you ask."

"What are you talking about?"

"It's a game I used to play with Lawrence. Whoever rolled the number closest to seven that was not seven won. The winner got to ask the loser a question, any question he wanted, and the loser had to answer. Honestly. You won, so you get to ask the first question."

Sophie had been practically on her feet, her leg muscles tensed, ready to stand, to walk away. That, she knew, was the right thing to do. But she had won. How could she pass up the opportunity to ask Crispin anything? *Anything.* After all, she had stayed only because he had information she wanted. And here he was, practically offering it to her. Her leg muscles relaxed.

"Very well, my lord, I shall ask a question. Why did you want to see Richard Tottle?"

This time Crispin recognized the odd feeling he was having as one of disappointment immediately. Did she care about him only because of the investigation? asked a voice inside his head.

So what if she did, another voice countered. The investigation was all that was important.

Perhaps to you, the first voice put in, but—

"Need I remind you how this game is played, Lord Sandal?" Sophie chided. "Lest you are trying to come up with an evasion, I remind you that the rules, as you stated them, required an honest answer."

Crispin shook his head, shook the voices back down into whatever dark cavern they occupied. "Nothing of the sort. I resent your accusation, Miss Champion," he said with a soft smile. Then he cleared his throat. "I wanted to see Richard Tottle because he was the best source of gossip from the Palace in London and I wanted some information."

"What kind of information?" Sophie asked, interested now.

"Need I remind you how this game is played, Miss Champion? One question per roll."

Sophie reached out for the dice and rolled a five. But her triumphant smile turned to a scowl when Crispin rolled an eight.

"My turn," he announced, and saw that she was nervous. This was the time, this was the moment to ask her about her godfather, when she could not, would not, lie. Here, at last, was his, the Phoenix's, chance to find out everything he wanted to know about her.

Crispin slid closer to her on the bench, touched her hand with his pinkie, and asked, "What is your happiest memory?"

The question took Sophie completely by surprise. "My happiest memory?" she repeated vaguely, her eyes fixed on the pool in front of her. She decided to lie. "My happiest memory is of swimming in the pond outside of Peacock Hall, Lord Grosgrain's countryseat, in the moonlight."

Crispin frowned. "Wasn't it cold?"

Sophie shook her head. "The water was heated by the huge furnace that always burned in Lord Grosgrain's laboratory in the cellar of the hall. People came from all around to bathe in the waters there. They were said to have healing properties."

"What did Lord Grosgrain do in his laboratory with the furnace?" Crispin ventured.

Sophie looked at him pertly. "I believe that is another question, my lord, requiring another roll of the dice."

Crispin greedily threw the dice. He tossed a four, and thought he was doomed, until Sophie tossed eleven. She glared at the dice, then turned her glare on Crispin. "Lord Grosgrain did alchemical experiments in his laboratory," she explained, answering his question before he had posed it. "He believed he could turn lead into gold, and he worked at it day and night. Until he met Constantia," she added, then stopped.

"Why, what did Constantia do?"

Sophie waved her hand. "She made him happy. And he wanted to make her happy, which meant moving back to London. And moving his laboratory to a rented space in Saint Martin's Fields, in the suburbs."

Crispin, surprised at Sophie's willingness to talk, decided to push. "Were you jealous of his relationship with Constantia?"

"Jealous?" Sophie repeated as if the thought, the word, were completely alien. "Not at all. I was thrilled. I had never seen my godfather as happy as he was with her. Constantia gave him more joy than you can imagine. The way his eyes lit up when he looked at her, or even talked about her—" Sophie stopped midsentence. She really had not been jealous, not even slightly. But she realized with a start that she was now. Now she wished she could make someone feel that way and look at her that way. Someone that was glad she had stayed. Someone that did give a damn what became of her.

All at once, she saw that she had been a fool to remain at Sandal Hall. No information was worth the peril of Crispin's proximity. "I believe, my lord, that was three questions rather than one," she told him when she felt she could trust her voice again. "And I believe that it is time for me to go. Good night, Lord Sandal."

She made to rise, but Crispin pulled her back down, keeping hold of her wrist. "Where are you going? You cannot go."

"Why not?" Sophie asked in a voice that was half challenging him to stop her, half pleading with him to do so.

"Because," Crispin began, then paused, looking for reasons. Because it is dark, and raining, and following you will be a challenge. Because I do not want you to go. Because I never want you to go. Because you are the best hope for my investigation, and for my happiness . . . "Because I owe you one question," he answered finally. "After all, I did sneak some in on my last turn, and it is only sporting to let you ask one in recompense."

Crispin's tone was light, but he was holding his breath as he waited to hear her question. She hesitated for a moment, knowing that she should leave, but once again the opportunity to learn what information Crispin possessed was too tantalizing to pass up. Besides, it was just one question. A single question. The last question she would ever get to ask him. It had better be good.

With her investigation hanging in the balance, Sophie asked, "What is *your* happiest memory, my lord?"

Crispin exhaled sharply, then replied with a candor that shocked them both. "Hearing you call me Crispin."

Neither of them moved, Sophie because she was afraid she would burst into tears, or song, and Crispin because he was afraid if he let go of her wrist, she would leave.

Sophie broke the silence first. "Are you mocking me, my lord?" she whispered.

"Crispin," he corrected gently. Then he shook his head. "And no. I mean it."

"What about earlier today?" she asked, forcing herself to look straight at him. "You said that you did not care what happened to me. And now—"

"No, I said I did not give a *damn* what happened to you," he interrupted to correct. "Surely you can see the difference." Very tenderly, he stroked her cheek with his thumb and looked deep into her eyes. "Besides I think, perhaps, I was wrong."

"Perhaps?" Sophie's heart sounded like a badly rehearsed drum corps in her ears.

"Perhaps," Crispin repeated huskily. He was suddenly overwhelmed with a need to hold her in his arms, to feel her soft hair on his neck, to brush the tip of her nose with his lips. Lifting her from the bench so they were both standing, he gingerly peeled off her mustache and pulled her to him. He leaned down, intending to place a shallow kiss on her lips, but instead found himself crushing her mouth against his deeply, passionately, unreservedly, whisked forward on a tide of something more potent than desire.

Sophie kissed him back, pressing her lips hard against his to convey her gratitude, her joy. There was no "perhaps" in their kissing, nothing held back, just pure passion that coursed between their bodies. Crispin kissed the path her tears had taken earlier that day, surprised by the saltiness of her cheeks, kissed down her neck, along the open front of her tunic, kissed her ear, her temple, the tip of her nose. He pulled her tunic over her head and kissed her breasts, kissed their round, pink tips until they became firm, then ran his hands down to the laces of her leggings.

He stripped off his shirt and moved closer to her and Sophie felt the warmth of his chest against hers. His fingers adeptly undid the ties on her breeches and her fingers unsteadily unknotted his, until both pairs fell away. Naked now and laughing nervously, they stepped out of the tangle of their clothes, and into each other's arms.

"*Tesoro*," Crispin whispered in her ear, holding her close to him. "I missed you today, *tesoro*. Did you miss me?"

The tears in Sophie's eyes were tears of happiness now. "Perhaps," she whispered back smiling into his shoulder. They stayed like that, quietly embracing, reveling in the feel of their bodies together, the feel of skin on skin, cool tears against unshaven cheeks, hard muscular planes on soft, yielding breasts, the feel of their growing intimacy, their growing arousal.

And then Sophie's stomach grumbled. Crispin pulled away from her slightly and saw her blushing.

"I am famished," he announced.

Sophie looked up at him. "You are? Not me. Would you like some beef stew?"

He wrinkled his nose. "I am not sure. I was half thinking of a roasted goose. With some braised carrots."

Sophie shook her head. "No. You do not like carrots. You want beef stew. With little onions in it. And beans swimming in butter. And peaches."

"You are right. I do not like carrots. What I want is beef stew with little onions in it," Crispin repeated.

"And beans—"

"—swimming in butter. And peaches," Crispin confirmed.

Two hours later, after an extended picnic in the center of Crispin's bed where the required attire was a silk robe, the beef stew had been pronounced superb and the beans delicious. "Crispin, that was marvelous," Sophie murmured when she had licked the last of the gravy up. "I could not eat another bite."

"You cannot miss dessert," Crispin admonished. "It is the most important part." As he spoke, he cleared their dishes from the bed and returned with a glass plate filled with sliced peaches and a chilled pot of sweet cream.

"I don't think—"

Sophie's powers of speech left her as Crispin dipped a slice of peach into the cream and then brought it to his lips. She saw his tongue reach out to lick the cream from its tip, using long, unhurried strokes, and she felt as if he was licking her instead. As she watched, he slid the slice of peach into his mouth, dragged his teeth along the top, and then, with agonizing slowness, bit down.

Sophie sank into the bed. The sight of his teeth raking over the peach and then sinking into its soft, orangy-pink flesh, staggered her senses. She had to feel him do that to her, had to feel him lick and nibble at her the same way, right then, right that instant. She pulled herself across the bed toward his reclining figure, possessed with the need to taste the peach on his lips, to touch him and be touched by him, to have him inside her, but when she tried to bring her mouth to his, she was stopped by his finger between them.

"Not yet," Crispin murmured. "Tonight we are going to do everything slowly."

It required all of Crispin's physical restraint, all the skills learned during years of constraining his urges, to keep from turning her onto the bed and plunging himself into her body. His member ached with desire for her, to know more of her, but he held himself back, putting his hard-learned control to work for her pleasure.

"Lie down," he instructed, reaching out at the same time to slide her robe from her shoulders.

Sophie was in a trance, a trance in which every fiber of her body came to life, tingling. Everything her body touched had a marvelous new texture, everything it came into contact with aroused her more. The smooth, silky fabric of the coverlet sliding under her felt like lover's hands gently massaging the globes of her backside, the lightest brush of Crispin's robe against her breast became the most amorous of caresses, Crispin's breath on her neck as he moved close to her was a forceful, passionate kiss that made the place between her legs ache uncontrollably for his touch.

Sophie watched, her eyes opened wide, as Crispin dipped another slice of peach into the cream. He brought it toward her, toward her lips, and her mouth opened for him, but he did not stop there. Instead, he moved it over her, not touching her, tracing lines in the air that echoed like veins of molten gold in her body, until one drop of cream fell into the valley between her breasts. He dipped his head down to lick it with his tongue, and his soft golden hair brushed against Sophie's breast, tickling the tip, making her arch toward him.

"Be still or I will stop," Crispin commanded, and she relaxed immediately.

He dipped the peach into the cream again and this time brought it to rest lightly on her lips. Her tongue darted out, hungry to taste it, but Crispin dragged the slice away, dragged it down over her chin, down her neck, leaving a line of cool cream and boiling desire. He drew a circle around her left breast, then smaller circles, until the peach rested on her nipple. The cold fruit playing over her warm body drove Sophie wild, and she had to clutch her hands into fists to keep from moving.

Her fingernails dug into her palms as Crispin began to lick the cream from her body with his tongue, flicking it over her lips, down her chin, across her chest, spiraling around her breast to her nipple. He used his whole tongue now in long, slow strokes as he lapped the cream from there, wrapped his tongue around her nipple and felt it grow hard in his warm mouth, then turned his attention to the other one. He took a bite of the slice of peach and, holding it between his lips, used it to stroke her right nipple, its cool, uneven texture winding Sophie into a fever pitch of excitement. Small rivulets of juice ran down the sides of her breasts, rivers that made Sophie's body tingle, made her want to cry out, cry out louder as he took her nipple between his lips and touched it lightly with his teeth.

Crispin recorded ever tremor of her body, every swallowed moan, memorized the places that he could tell drove her wild, lost completely in the act of pleasuring her. The ache in his member grew with each touch of his mouth to her skin, suffusing his entire body, straining his restraint almost beyond bearing. Without taking his mouth from her breast he reached a hand toward the silver tray and managed to cover another slice of peach with the cream. This time he brought it to her thighs, running it up from her knees, along the sensitive skin between her legs, using it to coax them apart, until it rested on the pearl of flesh nestled between her curls.

His mouth still danced on her nipple, doing wondrous things there, sending out pulses of sensation, which were doubled, tripled, quadrupled as Crispin increased the creamy cold pressure of the peach against her. He pushed its curved surface down over her nub and into the petals that surrounded it, and Sophie could no longer contain herself. Her hips arched up to meet him, and he pressed into her harder. She felt the soft, lissome flesh of the peach gliding over her, then inside her, felt it between the lips of her passage, felt its coolness even through the glaze of her arousal that covered it, felt its creamy tip massaging her bud.

Crispin turned it then, so the wide part of the slice rested directly on her most sensitive place, and slid it back and forth over her, pulling her left, then right, as his tongue traced the same path on her nipple. Something burst into life inside of Sophie, swelling from a tight seed of sensation into a full-grown plant, tendrils spreading from her nub, swollen, aching, down into her legs, up into her arms, wrapping around her breasts, being fed by Crispin's kisses, by his caresses. It spread through her body until she tingled from head to toe, more alive than she had ever felt before, and more desperate, desperate to explode, to let the vines blossom into a thousand flowers. She pushed her hips more insistently against the peach, moving up and down as Crispin moved it back and forth, spreading her burning, aching bud, the pressure inside her mounting uncontrollably. The slick fruit moved over her, dousing her in its sweetness, its juices mingling with her own, running down her petals in tingling rivers. Crispin's fingers around the peach delved into her creaminess, massaging at her along with the fruit, sliding the peach into her, letting it stroke the sensitive place just inside her passage as his fingers gently pressured her swollen nub in a wide circle, until she began to cry out, until she was at the very edge of exploding.

Simultaneously, Crispin lifted his mouth from her breast and slid the peach from between her legs. Trembling from head to foot, it took Sophie a moment to understand what had happened.

"No," she cried, plaintively. "No, Crispin, please, do not stop. I am so close—"

"I know," Crispin replied. He settled himself along her body, stretched out to his full length, and slipped his arm under her head. "So am I. That is why we must stop."

Instead of replying, he held her eyes with his as he brought the slice of peach up to his lips. He breathed in deeply, breathed in the mingled scent of her arousal and the peach, a perfume so powerful, so sensual that Crispin was almost undone. The slice of peach was wet with Sophie's moisture, and he brought it to his tongue to sample.

Sophie's mouth met him there, and together they ate the ambrosial fruit, licking it from one another's lips, savoring it on one another's tongue. Their eyes continued meeting, even as Sophie rubbed against him, even as she reached around Crispin and plunged one of the slices of peach almost entirely into the cream.

"Now it is my turn," she told him. "Lie down."

Crispin knew this was not a good idea, that he was near bursting merely from looking at her, but he could not stop her, did not want to stop her. He lay still while she unfastened the ties on his robe and pushed it from his shoulders. All his muscles were tight as she straddled his waist, letting her spectacular breasts hang just above his lips and then, with the dripping peach in her mouth, traced a cold line down his body.

She did not stop at his chest, but dragged the fruit all the way to his navel, leaving a small pool there, and then continued down, to his tormented member. It rose to greet her, and she ran the peach along it, leaving long creamy lines, and Crispin gasping. When he realized what was happening, when he felt first the peach and then, dear god, her mouth on his member, Crispin groaned and prayed for control. She rubbed her lips lightly along his shaft, rubbing them in the cream, tickling him with the lightest touches of her tongue, then opened her mouth and drank him in, surrounding him with warmth, her lips massaging him and sucking at him. He looked down at her, watched her full lips move over him, watched the creamy line of her mouth glide over his tip and then fall to suckle the base of his organ, felt her tongue lap over him, and could not stop himself from raising his body and pressing deeper into her mouth.

Sophie was completely consumed with the joy of pleasing him, lit by his noises of pleasure, kindled by his groans. She drank his shaft in deeper to feel it throb, let her fingers follow her mouth up and down its length, exploring its surface, tickling over the tip. His body, his reactions to her touch, thrilled and excited her. She wanted to make this last, to go slowly, but she could not wait to hear him call out to her in climax. She moved her lips up his length faster, following them with her fingers, stroking him and sucking on him from tip to base, pushing him into her mouth as deeply as he would go, until Crispin jerked powerfully and pulled himself from her.

"I want to be inside of you," he gasped, dragging her up, over his chest. "I want to feel you around me."

Crispin did not know what he was saying, only that it was true, that he wanted to lose himself entirely in this woman, to feel her body pressing against him, challenging him, wrapped around him, when he climaxed. He rolled her onto her back and mounted her, using his hand to open her for him, sliding into her wet passage.

The vines that had been growing inside of Sophie erupted into life, into blossom, and Sophie felt as though she were expanding, bursting out of the bounds of her body. Crispin immersed himself in her, riding her forcefully, plunging his shaft between the hot, firm walls of her body, letting the curve of his member roll over her nub as he pushed in and out of her. The golden hair that surrounded his organ brushed over her arousal, teasing it with each dive he made into her, pulling it down with him and then pressing it back up. He withdrew himself to run his full length over her until she called out to him, and then he immersed himself in her again. Sophie wrapped her legs around Crispin's waist, burning to take him into her more, to have him drown completely, unreservedly into her. He set her on fire, she was alight for him, she could hear the flames lapping at her, feel the heat between them, smell the smoke of the fire kindled by their lovemaking, taste—

Sophie's eyes snapped open, and at the same moment Crispin stopped moving. The room was filled with black, acrid smoke that burned their eyes and their throats. And the bed, the bed on which they were lying, was completely engulfed in flames.

Chapter Fifteen

The hangings of the bed were a wall of fire, and flames crept along the edges of the coverlet toward Crispin and Sophie at its center. Crispin sat bolt upright, rolling off Sophie and pushing away the smoldering coverlet beneath them simultaneously. The black smoke stung his eyes, his throat, as he turned from side to side, seeking a way out of the scorching inferno. The fire and smoke blocked the rest of the chamber from his view, and he did not know if it, too, was alight, but it had to be their destination, because their only hope was to get off the raft of fast-moving flames that drew ever closer. He saw a small gap in the flames to his left and was pulling Sophie toward it when one of the beams from the canopy of the bed came crashing down in front of them, flaming, blocking their way, and setting fire to the sheets. The only way out now was through the fire. Crispin, coughing, dragged an only slightly smoldering blanket over his shoulders, covered Sophie with the rest of it, gathered her into his arms, and pushed backward through the flames.

His skin screamed in protest as it passed through the sheet of fire. He felt like he was being boiled, scorched alive, like he was being peeled, jabbed by a thousand hot pokers, and then, abruptly, it was all over. They were through the wall of flames.

The rest of the room was mercifully untouched, but as he stood looking at the bed, another piece of the canopy broke off with an awful noise and slid to the ground near where they were standing, sending out sparks and streams of flame in two directions. Crispin was too furious, too filled with wrath at whoever had done this, to notice that Sophie was not moving at all, that she was staring transfixed at the flames, a haunted, glazed expression in her eyes. She neither clung to him nor looked at him but lay, tense and terrified, in his arms.

Even if he had noticed, there would not have been any time to think about the strangeness of her behavior. He had to summon the household to help him put out the fire before the entirety of Sandal Hall was a pile of ash. But first he had to conceal Sophie.

The privy, just through the library, was the best place to hide her, he concluded—no one would have cause to enter it—and he hauled her there, depositing her gently in the middle of the room.

"Stay here, make no noise," he commanded.

She did not nod, gave no indication of having heard him, but just stared into space, standing where he left her as he quickly shut the door behind him.

In the hours that followed, the entire household, the entire neighborhood, went to work dousing the blaze. Even the old beggar woman who lounged on the Strand came to help, looking furtively around as she passed pails of water in a long relay from the well in the kitchen yard up to the bedchamber. When the fire was out, nothing remained of the bed and not much was left of the rest of the furnishings of the chamber. Miraculously, the library was untouched, but the flames had been so fierce in the bedroom, their heat so powerful, that the wooden moldings of the room had turned to ash, and several of the panes of glass in the windows that led to Crispin's private garden had melted. Surveying the destruction, Crispin could not believe that he, they, had survived. It was clear they were not meant to.

The night sky was already growing light when he finished thanking and shaking hands with each of the people who had come to his aid. He gave the hunched beggar woman a gold piece, and as he bent to look into her face, mostly concealed by her hood, he felt a flash of recognition, of something familiar. But it was gone as quickly as it had come. By the time she had lowered her odd, gold-colored eyes and shuffled off in the direction of the door, he had forgotten all about it, thinking now only of Sophie.

His fury, which had galvanized as he stood in the middle of his destroyed bedchamber, changed when he opened the door of the privy and saw her. She was curled into a ball in the corner, her arms wrapped around her legs, the same fearful, half-wild expression in her eyes as when he had left her. She looked like a hunted animal, tense and terrified and ready to strike if attacked. Anger gave way to concern as he looked at her, concern and also confusion.

"Everything is fine now," Crispin said gently, moving toward her. "The fire is over. You can come out."

She did not speak, just shook her head and pressed herself farther into the corner.

"Sophie, can you hear me?" He kneeled down to her. "You are safe. There is nothing to be afraid of."

Her voice was toneless when she spoke. "He was here. He found me. He said I could never escape him, and he was right."

Crispin sat down next to her and wrapped an arm around her shoulder. She tensed for a moment, but then relaxed. "Who?"

Sophie closed her eyes now and leaned into Crispin. "I am so sorry, my lord."

"Why?" Crispin leaned back against the wall and rested her head on his chest.

"This is all my fault. I should have left. Your beautiful chamber was completely destroyed because of me."

"I will acknowledge that your touch sets me afire, but I don't think it does the same to my bedclothes," Crispin said lightly.

She looked up at him. "This is not a joke, my lord."

"I was not joking. How else could you be at fault for this fire?"

"He set it because I was here. Because he knew I was here and he wanted to punish me, to remind me that I am wicked. To remind me that I am his."

This caught Crispin's attention. "Whose? Who do you belong to? Who is this man? Are you married?"

"No, nothing like that." She sat quietly, trying to decide how much to tell him. The beating of his heart echoed in her head, and the smell of him—sweaty and sooty and Crispin-y—soothed her slightly, and she began speaking. "When I was fifteen, my mother and father died in a house fire."

Crispin pulled her closer. "I am so sorry, Sophie. I had no idea."

"Very few people know. But that is not why I am upset. It is what happened afterward." She stopped for a moment, and then decided to go forward. "There was a man. A man who said he loved me. He is the one who rescued me from the fire, and he took me someplace, he said, to help me."

Sophie took a deep breath. "The man locked me in a room with no windows, more like a closet, a small, completely dark box." She shuddered at the recollection. "For three weeks, until I escaped, he kept me there, alone, in the dark. Long, terrible days of darkness, of nothingness. I tried pounding on the door and screaming, begging, pleading with anyone to help me, but no one ever came. Except him. Every day he would come to the closet and sit for hours, whispering to me through the door." There were tears running down Sophie's face, but she ignored them. "I tried to cover my ears, to hide my head, cowering in the farthest corner of the closet, but his words kept coming, filling the darkness, until I could no longer tell whether they were in my mind or in the air, whether they were his or mine. He told me that I was wicked, that I used my body to tempt him, that I was trying to make him vile, to lure him to unnatural acts. He said I was trying to charm him into succumbing to me, but it would not work, he would not fall for my wiles. He said I was filthy, that my body and mind were corrupt, that I was possessed with villainous urges." Her voice cracked. "He told me..." Sophie could not go on.

Crispin hugged her close, letting her tears spill down his chest. When her sobs had somewhat subsided, he asked, gently, "What else did he say?"

Sophie still had tears coming down her face as she continued. "He said he knew I had to be punished, that I had to be shown the danger of my wantonness, of my unnatural desires. So he had set fire to the house. He said that our parents' deaths were my fault, that I killed them with my lustfulness." Sophie squeezed her eyes shut, tightly, to stop the tears, and the pain. She was trembling against Crispin's chest. "He said that as long as I obeyed him, he would tell no one of my wickedness. He told me that no one would ever want me when they heard what I was, how I was. That I was his, that I would always be his, only he knew how to love me and I could never escape from him. And then tonight—"

"But you did escape from him," Crispin interrupted her. "You got away. And you are safe. He cannot get you now."

"He has, don't you see? He burned your house just like he burned my parents. To get me. To remind me. To show you. What I am." She pulled away from Crispin but could not bring herself to look at him, to see the disgust in his face.

Sophie heard his breathing change and instinctively felt his muscles tighten in his chest, tighten in horror at what he had been harboring in his house. She had been afraid to tell him even that much of the story, afraid that he would now see her for what she really was, afraid that he would confirm what the man said, but hoping he would deny it, deny every word.

He had not. Instead, he stiffened beneath her, obviously cringing away from her, obviously corroborating that everything was true. She was wanton, she was responsible for so much pain, for death, for the mess his apartment, his life, was in. Sensing that he was about to speak, Sophie stopped him, careful not to touch his mouth with her upraised hand. "Please, do not say anything. I understand. I will go."

"Why do you persist in saying that? And what do you understand?" Crispin spoke harshly. His fury about the fire had been transformed, instantaneously, into a different kind of rage. Rage against anyone who could treat Sophie, his divine, wonderful, sensuous Sophie, that way. Anyone who would dare to abuse her, abuse her desire, abuse her person. "Who was the man?" he asked finally, planning to kill him before another hour was out.

Sophie hesitated. The face she knew so well danced before her eyes, mocking her, laughing as she struggled not to lie and yet not reveal the shameful truth. "I cannot tell you who he was," she whispered. "I hardly saw his face the night of the fire, and afterward," she fumbled, "afterward it was dark. I wish I could tell you, if only so you could thank him for warning you about me, but I really cannot."

Overwhelmed by incredulity, Crispin missed the double meaning in her words. "You think I wish to thank him?"

"No," Sophie rushed on, "I guess not, after what he did to your lovely bed." She rose to her feet. "I am sorry. I should go. I can only imagine how you are feeling, how you must see me now."

"Really?" Crispin asked, quite sure she did not know how she looked to him at that moment as she stood over him, naked in the moonlight. "How do I see you?"

"There is no need to be cruel, my lord," she said flatly, but he saw that she was trembling. "I do not blame you. I can tell you find me distasteful. Even disgusting. That you wish I were gone. That my presence makes you"—Sophie sought for the right word—"uncomfortable."

There was a moment of silence, a moment during which Sophie dared to hope for a denial, but her hopes were crushed.

"Uncomfortable," Crispin repeated finally. "Yes, you do make me uncomfortable."

She could not have asked for more unequivocal corroboration of her worst fears. "Good-bye, my lord," she said, turning quickly so that he could not see her tears, and moving toward the door.

"Wait," Crispin called, and she stopped with her fingers on the handle. "You did not let me finish." He rose and walked toward her.

"I have heard it all before. I do not need to hear it again. Especially not from you." Her voice broke on the last two words.

"Yes, you do. You especially need to hear what I have to say." Putting his hands on her shoulders Crispin turned her so that she was facing him, then raised her eyes to his. "In your presence, Sophie Champion, I feel pleasure unlike any other I have ever felt. In your smile I see beauty I could not have imagined. With you, I laugh like I cannot remember laughing. Around you, my body behaves uncontrollably, my mind is not my own, and I cannot convince my mouth that anything tastes as good as your lips." His expression as he looked at her was serious. "All of that makes me damned uncomfortable. But also happy."

It took a moment before the words settled in and Sophie echoed, "Happy?"

Crispin nodded. "Very happy." He caught one of her tears on his fingertip and brought it to his lips. "Please do not go, *tesoro*. I like being uncomfortable with you."

Sophie stood trembling, unable to believe what she was hearing, what she was seeing. He was standing in front of her, one long dimple now framing a crooked, irresistible smile. And he was saying that he liked her. Her. Sophie Champion.

"I like being uncomfortable with you too," she just managed to whisper through her tears before his lips closed over hers.

Their lovemaking that late night was gentle and sweet, and astonishing to them both. It began slowly, Crispin languishing inside of Sophie, and built, minute by minute, hour after hour, into a frenzied race. It was long past dawn when they clutched each other desperately, unwilling to let their lovemaking end, unable to prolong it, long past dawn when they reached their crescendo together, riding the long, sinuous waves of their pleasure until they ebbed completely.

It was long past dawn when Sophie, checking to be sure that Crispin was asleep, pressed her lips to his chest and whispered, "I love you."

The man looked up angrily from the document he was writing. "I asked not to be interrupted," Lawrence growled at the serving boy hovering on his threshold.

"I know, sir. I am very sorry, sir. But it is Lord Sandal, sir. To see you, sir. He says it is urgent."

Frowning, Lawrence set aside his pen. "Send him in."

By the time Crispin entered the office, no trace remained of either the document or Lawrence's frown.

"I hope I am not interrupting something, Lawrence, but I had to see you," Crispin said as he seated himself on the opposite side of Lawrence's desk.

"You know you are always welcome," Lawrence told him with the beginnings of a wide smile. Then he stopped abruptly and looked skeptically at his friend. "You seem very chipper."

Crispin was feeling wonderful. His bed had been destroyed, his house had almost burned to the ground, his life had almost been taken from him—and might yet be in four days—but he could still hear Sophie's laughter in his ears and still taste her on his tongue from their kiss good-bye. "Being in England agrees with me," he responded evasively as he sat down. "Or at least some aspects of it."

"Aspects such as Sophie Champion?" Lawrence asked with real interest, and then burst into laughter when he saw the expression on Crispin's face. "My god, you are in love, aren't you?"

"Are you trying to get me to commit so you can start taking bets in your red book?" Crispin asked with a raised eyebrow, narrowly avoiding the question.

Lawrence ignored this distraction. "It figures that you would fall in love with one of the only interesting women in England and not even bother to admit it. But I want you to know that I am not jealous. And I approve entirely."

"I cannot tell you how relieved I am," Crispin said sarcastically. "However, what I—"

Lawrence interrupted him. "I know it is not in your nature to recognize such things, but Sophie Champion really is marvelous, Crispin. She almost took my breath away when I saw her here for the first time, when I saw that little crinkle in her left cheek when she smiles—"

"It's her right cheek," Crispin corrected.

Lawrence raised his eyebrow. "Right cheek. Anyway, I thought she was lovely, but it was only at Newgate, watching her reduce those guards to quivering masses of fear, that I saw how really remarkable she is."

"She was pretty spectacular at the prison, wasn't she?" Crispin mused with a smile, despite himself. "Did you see how that guard cowered when she just looked at him? I don't think he would have followed us even if I hadn't knocked him unconscious."

Lawrence nodded. "And what about when she refused to leave unless we brought all the other women with us? I don't think my arms have recovered from the pummeling I took before I could convince that one called Helena that I was trying to help Sophie, not hurt her. According to Elwood, your Miss Champion was already quite a hero to some people, but that prison break was the cream on the pudding. She is practically immortal in their eyes."

"Would that she were," Crispin replied, recollecting his errand. "Someone tried to kill us both in bed the other night, and damn near succeeded."

"What?"

"Someone shot flaming arrows into the canopy of my bed last night and set the entire thing on fire. Clearly their idea was to kill me. And Sophie. I want to know who did it, and I was hoping you could tell me."

A frown passed over Lawrence's brow. "Someone used arrows to light a fire in your room?"

"Yes. Ingenious devices, they must have been specially made for it. Somehow they managed to keep the fire burning even as they were shot through the air. I suspect gunpowder, but I have never seen anything like them before. I saved one to send to my brother, Ian. Anyway," Crispin went on, "I thought you might know who had developed such a weapon. Or might have heard something about someone trying to kill me."

Lawrence shook his head thoughtfully. "I don't know anything about either the arrows or a contract on your life. Do you have anything else to go on?"

"Just the name of a bank. Loundes and Wainscot. Have you ever heard of them?"

"Damn stodgy bunch of toads," was Lawrence's reply. "They once told me, in not so many words, that they would not touch my money. Something about having principles. Bastards," Lawrence muttered.

"Where are these paragons based?"

"North counties somewhere." Lawrence waved a hand vaguely in the direction of the rest of England. "Newcastle maybe? I have blocked it from my mind. Why do you ask?"

"Something someone said made me think they might be mixed up with this."

Lawrence's head was shaking back and forth violently. "Not a chance. There is not a man among them who would have the imagination to set fire to a bed." His tone changed, becoming more jovial. "Are you quite sure it wasn't you and Miss Champion?"

"Your mind, Lord Pickering, is wanton."

"You are the first person to say so, Lord Sandal," Lawrence said smarmily. "Most people consider me a paragon of propriety. You are just sore because I saw through your little secret before you even knew it yourself. But you can't hold it against me. I am quite an expert on love these days."

Now it was Crispin's turn to look hard at his friend. "An expert on love? Are you in love? Lawrence Pickering in love?" Crispin asked incredulously. "I don't believe it."

"It's true," Lawrence said, smiling so radiantly that Crispin could no longer doubt.

"Who is she? How did it happen? When did it happen? Why am I the last to know?" Crispin demanded in a torrent.

Lawrence was almost blushing. "She is someone I have known for a long time, and long admired, but it is only very recently that we have considered a more permanent arrangement."

"A permanent arrangement?" Crispin repeated with disbelief. "Does this mean you are getting married?"

Lawrence nodded. "If eve—"

The door of the office bursting open stopped Lawrence's confession. Before he could resume, his deputy, Grimley, strode to the middle of the floor. "My lord, I must speak to you," he said breathlessly. "I need your advice, my lord, badly. It's—"

Lawrence interrupted him, nodding toward Crispin. "As you can see, Grimley, I am already engaged."

Grimley's eyes settled on Crispin for the first time, and he made an awkward bow. "I beg pardon, my lords, but this is most important. Lord Pickering, I really must speak to you. In private."

Crispin, unwilling as he was to part from Lawrence in the middle of their interesting conversation, understood the none-too-subtle hint and rose from his seat. "I'll leave you two to your important and private business," he said with a grin. "But I promise you, Lawrence, I'll be back to hear the rest of your tale."

Lawrence smiled broadly at his friend as Crispin crossed the threshold, but as soon as the door shut, his face wore a deep, troubled frown.

The message was delivered shortly after Crispin left, not by a footman, but by Octavia, in person. She was ushered up a secret back passage by Thurston so that her visit would not be known to anyone. Sophie, seated at a wide desk in the library carefully tossing dice, did not hear the concealed door open, and only looked up when Octavia's feet echoed on the wooden floor. At the sight of her friend, a warm, welcoming smile spread across Sophie's face and she rushed forward.

"It is wonderful to see you, Octavia," she said, coming around the desk to embrace her. "Did you get my message?"

It took Octavia a moment to reply. She was not sure what she had expected, but after receiving one cryptic message from Sophie delivered by a prison guard, and another by the Sandal Hall footman, and having heard about the fire in Sandal Hall the night before, she had assumed that her friend would at least be careworn, if not entirely haggard. Instead, she looked radiant. "Sophie, are you all right?"

"Yes," Sophie answered positively. "I feel wonderful."

"And the Earl of Sandal?" Octavia asked. "He is treating you well?"

Sophie blushed. "Very well. His cook is very good. Don't tell Richards, though."

Octavia nodded with astonishment. When a discreet messenger had delivered a note to Hen House telling her that Sophie was safe and hiding with the Earl of Sandal, she and Emme had been worried. For two years, one of Sophie's principal amusements had been to read aloud the stories about the Earl of Sandal, pointing out, with minute precision, all the ways in which he was a mealworm or a caterpillar or, on particularly bad days, a tick. They had concluded, therefore, that finding herself in his clutches would be worse than boiling in oil to Sophie, worse than being stung by a hundred bees, worse than a life without orange cake. They imagined Sophie pacing impatiently, cursing Satan's knockers a thousand times as she bashed a toe or knee into a piece of furniture, railing against the louse and his house at the top of her lungs.

But Octavia found Sophie wearing one of his robes, naked beneath it, happily playing dice games at his desk. If the errand that brought her had not been such a painful one, Octavia would have been inclined to laugh.

Instead, she said, "I think we should sit down."

The broad smile on Sophie's face vanished as they moved toward a silver-and-burgundy-striped divan. "What is it? What is wrong? Did something happen at Hen House?"

Octavia shook her head, pushing a lock of light blond hair behind her ear with an unsteady hand. "Everything is fine at Hen House. You will be glad to know that Helena has settled in nicely."

"Helena?"

"You know, the young woman who escaped from prison with you."

Sophie nodded, remembering now.

"The others all had places to go," Octavia explained, "but Helena asked if she could stay. Richards has begun letting her do the roasts. She says Helena has an extraordinary sense of smell, which makes her indispensable with seasonings."

"Richards lets her in the kitchen?" Sophie asked with a mixture of surprise and envy.

"Yes. But that is not what I came to tell you about." Octavia hesitated for a moment, gnawing on her lower lip. She kept her eyes aimed at her lap as she went on. "Sophie, this is very difficult for me to tell you. I did not respond to your message yesterday, because I did not know what to say. Finally, Emme told me I owed you the truth."

"My message about the meringues?" Sophie was puzzled. She had only asked where they came from and when they had begun arriving.

Octavia took a deep breath. "You see, I ordered the meringues. From Sweetson, the baker."

"Good," Sophie said, trying to be encouraging.

But Octavia only looked more miserable. "It is not good. I did not want to. I—" She paused, then raised her eyes and rushed on. "I am being blackmailed. A letter came, hinting about something in my past, and with it was a billet which explained that if I did not want duplicates of the letter sent to my friends and clients, I would accept the subscription which would be offered to me within the week. And then Sweetson's man came and offered me a subscription for meringues at a hundred pounds a month."

"A hundred pounds a month?" Sophie repeated with surprise.

"I did not take all of it from the household funds," Octavia assured her quickly, but she had misunderstood.

Sophie's surprise was not at the size of the sum, but at the fact that, multiplied times twelve months, it was the exact amount of the bill Lord Grosgrain had asked of her. For a subscription. Was Lord Grosgrain being blackmailed before his death?

"But that makes no sense," Sophie said aloud without realizing it.

Octavia looked at her. "That I used my dress money to pay the blackmail?"

"No, no, I was thinking about something else," Sophie apologized. "You could have used the household funds. You could have used any of my money. Why didn't you tell me about this?"

"I was afraid." Octavia looked miserable.

"Afraid?"

"Afraid that if you found out, if I told you and Emme what the note said, you would make me leave."

Sophie was aghast. "Nothing anyone could tell me about you would do that."

"Not even if they told you I murdered a man?"

Sophie did not miss a moment. "No. Not even that." She leaned forward and asked with excited interest, "Did you?"

Almost sorry to have to disappoint Sophie, Octavia shook her head. "I did not murder anyone. But it certainly could have looked like it. It was while I was with Lawrence Pickering, and—"

"You know Lawrence too?" Sophie interrupted.

"Have you met him?" Sophie nodded, and Octavia went on. "Yes. For a time"—here Octavia's eyes left her friend's—"for a time when I was very young, he and I were lovers."

Octavia could not help but smile when, raising her eyes, she saw the expression on Sophie's face. It was one of pure, unmitigated shock.

"You were Lawrence Pickering's mistress," Sophie paraphrased.

"If you prefer to put it that way," Octavia agreed, and pressed on. "While we were together, a man was killed, a man whom I was known not to like, and the evidence pointed at me. Lawrence found the real murderer, but with all the tension, things between us soured then and I left for the country. Where I met Emme. And then you."

"Have you told Emme this? About Lawrence?" Sophie asked with concern.

"Yes. She was not happy, but she understands. It was fourteen years ago. He was eighteen and I was only sixteen."

"Were you in love with him?" Sophie asked.

"In love?" Octavia echoed. "I suppose I thought I was, at the time. Now, in retrospect..."

Sophie did not press her, putting aside the thousand other questions she wanted to ask about intimate relations, in the interest of finding out more about the blackmail. "Why did you decide to accept the subscription? Why not tell them that you were innocent and refuse to pay?"

"Can you really imagine the Duchess of Ivry having her dresses designed by someone who might have been a murderer? Or even someone associated with Lawrence Pickering? It would have ruined my dress business."

"I would have supported you," Sophie put in, almost hurt. "I would have given you as much money as you needed."

"More, probably, knowing you, but it was not about money. I design dresses because I love to, not for the money."

Sophie nodded absently, her mind back on the knotty question of what Lord Grosgrain could possibly have been blackmailed for. From what Octavia had said, she realized that the reason for the blackmail need not be a real crime or indiscretion, but she still had a hard time imagining what damaging information anyone could have had about her godfather. She had not yet stopped thinking about it when their interview ended and Octavia disappeared back down the secret passage.

It was this question that compelled her to go and see Sweetson, the baker. She needed to better understand how the blackmail worked, needed to learn if the people issuing the subscriptions had the injurious information themselves, or if they were just agents for someone else. And, if the latter was true, who that someone was.

Donning Don Alfonso's outfit and, with Thurston's assistance, a new mustache, she had set out for Sweetson's to get her questions answered. In order to avoid being seen by too many people on the streets, she used smaller byways to traverse the city, until she found herself behind the baker's shop. She knocked and got no answer, but the door gave under her hand and opened of its own accord.

There was no one in the back storehouse, unless they were well concealed as a bag of flour, nor in the adjacent kitchen. It was when she reached the front room that she saw him, seated in a chair in front of a large table with his face lying in a pile of flour.

Her initial surmise that he was asleep was quickly put to rest by the blood, now dried brown, which had drizzled out of the corner of his mouth and stained the flour.

Sophie was staring at the corpse, unable to move, when a voice spoke from behind her.

Chapter Sixteen

"I should have known I would find you here, Don Alfonso," Crispin said dryly. "You have a way with corpses."

"You are a fine one to talk." Sophie swung around to face him. "I only seem to find them when I am with you. What are you doing here, anyway? Are you following me?"

"Following you, in those breeches, is something I would very much enjoy, but I came here on my own. And you? Aren't there enough baked goods for you at Sandal Hall?"

"How can you joke in front of him?" Sophie gestured toward the dead man.

"I assure you he is well beyond hearing. I am assuming that you had nothing to do with his death, but I would like to hear it from your lips."

"Are you accusing me of murder, again?" Sophie was appalled.

"No." Crispin shook his head. "Merely pointing out the strange coincidence of finding you here and him dead. You did not kill him, then?"

"I arrived only a few minutes before you did," Sophie answered distractedly.

Crispin, noting her failure to answer his question directly, circled around to look at the corpse without moving it. "If that is the case, then you are certainly not guilty. This blood has been dry for hours, if not a full day."

Sophie nodded, not really paying attention to this absolution. The bet was weighing heavily on her mind. If Crispin did not know about the blackmail then she did not want to tell him, but if he did, perhaps he had information that could be useful to her. In the interest of finding Lord Grosgrain's murderer, she decided to take a risk. "How did you find out about the blackmail?"

Crispin spread his hands. "Informers," he replied vaguely. "And you?"

"Octavia. She was forced to subscribe for meringues." Sophie leaned toward him. "Did you know that she and Lawrence Pickering were lovers?"

"Octavia your friend and Lawrence my friend?" Crispin asked with real surprise.

"Yes. Years ago. That is what she was being blackmailed about."

"Octavia," Crispin mused to himself. "Really."

Sophie nodded. "Yes. I guess there was something about a murder. You see, the blackmailers send a letter—"

"I know all about it. Very neat scheme. Did she have to subscribe to Tottle's paper too?"

"No, just the meringues. But I figured that Tottle's *News* must have worked the same way. Any of the people we interviewed would have been good candidates for blackmailing."

Crispin agreed. "Have you looked at the body yet? We should be sure that there are no more handy pieces of paper lying about with your name on them."

Sophie watched with dismay as Crispin lifted the baker's head from the pile of flour on the table. His eyes were still open, his face a mask of shock, just as Richard Tottle's had been. Whoever had killed them both had certainly taken them by surprise, suggesting it was not someone from whom they felt they had anything to fear. Sophie thought this over as Crispin frisked the corpse, delving into the waist of his breeches and feeling among the folds of his tunic, careful to avoid the long, unmarked knife that protruded from the man's stomach.

"Nothing," he announced, slumping the baker's head back onto the table. "They must have assumed—"

Crispin stopped midsentence. For the first time, he noticed the man's hand, dangling down along the side of the seat. It looked strange, and lifting it, Crispin discovered why. Something was clasped between the man's fingers, something shiny. With great difficulty Crispin pried first one finger, then another open and extracted the object. It was a piece of shimmering light blue fabric with a bumblebee embroidered on it.

He held it up for Sophie to see.

"That is one of Octavia's bees," she exclaimed. "You know, from her dresses. She is famous for them."

"Do you have any gowns with bees on them?" Crispin asked slowly. "Any, for example, in light blue taffeta like this?"

Sophie's face fell. "I have one exactly like that. She made me wear it to several balls recently so people could see her new design."

Crispin could only imagine how spectacular Sophie looked in that color blue, and how memorable. Anyone seeing the bee against the blue background would undoubtedly connect it with the beautiful renegade already wanted for one murder. Even in his brief foray from Lawrence's house to the bakery, Crispin had heard talk of little else besides Sophie Champion, divided fairly evenly between condemnations of her as a murderess and applause for her wondrous escape. He had also heard, in passing, several women comparing stories of friends of theirs who had been given funds by Sophie Champion for enterprises they wanted to undertake, and several others who had been rescued from bad fathers, brothers, or husbands with Sophie Champion's aid. Even allowing for exaggeration, Crispin calculated that Sophie had given away the better part of three fortunes, and found himself struggling not to confront the question of where all that money had come from. But unlimited resources—no matter how they were procured—would not save her from the gallows. Whoever was trying to frame her had to be found. Soon.

The sound of a key turning in the lock of the front door interrupted Crispin's thoughts abruptly and underscored their importance. Jamming the piece of fabric into his doublet, he moved toward Sophie and pushed her into what appeared to be a closet at the back of the chamber, following behind her. They had only just closed the door when they heard footsteps enter the room they had left, and stop in front of the corpse.

Sophie and Crispin found themselves standing on a shallow, cold landing, completely dark but for the thin line of light dribbling in from under the door. Crispin reached out a hand toward Sophie and she took it, grasping it tight. Behind them, the darkness was absolute, and Crispin concluded that there must be a set of stairs, descending into the cellar of the building.

Those stairs, and the pitch-blackness at their base, were their only hope, Crispin knew, and probably the incarnation of Sophie's worst fears. But they could not stay on the landing—the constables who were examining the corpse were sure to open the closet door looking for clues—and their sole chance of escaping from detection was to hide themselves in the darkness below. Crispin squeezed Sophie's hand and felt her squeeze it back, if not firmly, at least without hesitation.

The sounds of the corpse being moved in the outer room muffled their footsteps as they descended the stone stairs into the cellar. Crispin went first, slowly, pausing whenever Sophie needed to pause. At one point, when the darkness had become complete, she stopped and pressed herself into the wall.

"Go without me," she whispered breathlessly. "I can't. Please, just go."

Crispin could tell by the way her palm had grown cold and stiff that she was gripped by fear. "Close your eyes, Sophie," he whispered. "It will be fine. Remember last time? Remember how nothing happened? I will not hurt you. Close your eyes and trust me, *tesoro.*"

The sound of his voice when he said that word soothed Sophie as it always did, as he knew it would. She obeyed him, shutting her eyes, and felt the warm safety of Crispin's arms closing around her, then lifting her to his chest. Her breathing became more even as he descended the last ten steps, taking them sideways to ensure that Sophie's head did not hit the stone wall.

The floor at the bottom was covered in rushes, which crunched with a crazy echo each time he moved. It was even colder down here, and over the wheaty smell of the rushes, Crispin caught a rich, milky scent.

"Mmmm," Sophie murmured into his chest. "Butter."

She was right. They must be in Sweetson's buttery, or at least his cold storage. And if that was the case, there must be another way out, a way that opened directly into the court at the back of the house so that deliveries need not be carried down the narrow, rickety stairs.

"Sophie, if I set you down, will you be able to stand?" Crispin whispered to the bundle in his arms.

"Do not leave me alone," she answered, desperation tingeing her words again.

"I have no intention of leaving you alone. I will be right here in this room with you. But I must look around for a way out, and if we both look, we will make more noise."

Sophie pressed herself against him. "You won't leave me alone? You won't leave me here?"

"No, *tesoro*. Never." Crispin felt her release her grip on him slightly and he lowered her to the ground. Feeling with his foot, he found a large, hay-covered block and steered her toward it. "Sit down here, and don't move."

Sophie did as she was told, keeping her eyes closed, and listened attentively to the noises around her. She could make out the clamor of voices, at least two, in the room upstairs, and the shuffling of feet. A heavy thud told her that the body was being moved again, but the sound of dragging stopped before it could have reached the outer door.

At that point, footsteps approached the door of the closet. Sophie felt the block, definitely of butter, beginning to melt beneath her as the hinges of the door above squeaked open. She opened her eyes to see light flooding in from upstairs, illuminating the top two thirds of the staircase, but leaving the bottom dark. Sophie leaned forward slightly on her slippery perch and looked up.

She saw two men at the door. One of them was so wide that he blocked most of the light, but in the little that remained she was able to see enough of his features to know that she recognized him. He had been at Lawrence's the night she was taken to prison. As had the shorter one standing next to him, she now realized. Yes, even though she only had him in profile, she was sure that he was another of the men who had hauled her from Pickering Hall.

"Come on. There ain't no one down there. Let's go." The shorter man addressed the wide one strenuously.

"I smell something," the wide one said. "Something suspicious."

"It's butter, you idiot," the shorter one told his companion. "Haven't you ever thought of a baker having butter? We want to get him out of this place before the others come. We don't have time to be looking for anyone in a buttery."

The wide man took one step down the stairs and, bending slightly, squinted into the darkness. For a moment Sophie could have sworn he had seen her, was looking right at her, but then he straightened up. "Very well. We will move the body. But I am going to lock the door and come back later. I still say there is something suspicious down there."

The two men left the landing and shut the door behind them, plunging Sophie once again into darkness. Worse, this time she heard what had to be a heavy chain being dragged through the door handles and a lock being clicked into place.

The noises upstairs died down and at last faded away entirely. It was completely dark, completely silent. A chill ran up Sophie's back, and then another as she heard a rustling in the straw in front of her and felt someone's breath on her face.

"Crispin," she whispered.

There was no reply.

"Crispin," she whispered again, now more desperately. "Crispin, is that you?"

The rustling ceased for a moment, but there was still no reply. Then Sophie felt something brush against her, and then a hand, grabbing her, first her arm, then her thigh.

She opened her mouth to scream, but nothing came out. And then, just when she thought she could, someone put a hand over her mouth, gagging her. She whimpered in terror, flailing in the darkness, tears streaming down her face, too scared to hear the voice whispering in her ear.

"*Shhh,* Sophie, I am right here," Crispin repeated. "It is okay, it is just me," he went on, soothingly.

Sophie stopped moving.

"If I take away my hand, *tesoro,*" he asked, "will you shout?"

Sophie, numb with fright, shook her head, and Crispin removed his hand.

"What scared you?" he asked, pulling her close to him.

"Why didn't you answer me?" Sophie panted. "When I said your name, why didn't you tell me it was you?"

"I did not hear you say my name. I was in another part of the chamber."

Sophie clutched his arm. "There is someone else in here with us. He touched me. He breathed on me. And now he is locked in here with us."

Even in the pitch blackness, even without seeing her face, Crispin could tell that she was petrified with fear. There was no chance that he could convince her to move through the darkness toward the other side of the buttery in this state, he knew.

With Sophie still hanging on to his arm, he fumbled in his tunic until he found a tinderbox and a scrap of candle. Having heard the lock click into place on the door above, he judged that they were, for the time being, safe from intrusion, and so he lit the candle stub. The wick flickered to life, confirming that they were indeed in a buttery, surrounded by large blocks of butter, with several metal tubs containing cool water lining the walls. Sophie exhaled slowly as she looked around her, seeing that her fears had been groundless, that there were only the two of them there.

She had never thought she would be so relieved that she had been locked alone in a pitch-black room with a man. Her heartbeat had almost returned to normal, when a shadow moved on the wall beside her. Sophie leapt toward Crispin, bumping into him and sending both him and the stump of candle spluttering to the floor. The flame blew out as it fell, leaving them once again in complete, heart-wrenching darkness.

"Who is there?" Crispin demanded, rising quickly. He held Sophie to his chest with one hand and rested his other on the hilt of his rapier. "Identify yourself, or I shall strike."

The only reply was a muted shuffling.

Crispin drew his sword. The sound of the steel blade sliding from its sheath and cutting through the air echoed terrifically in the stone chamber. He flourished it once, slicing the air with a succinct whistle, and heard a whimper from just in front of them.

"Please," a small, female voice begged through the whimpering. "Please don't hurt me. I ain't meant no harm."

"Who are you?" Crispin asked, directing the point of his rapier downward.

"Just the chamber girl. Just the girl who works for Sweetson. I ain't no one."

Crispin's tone softened. "What are you doing down here, in the buttery?"

"They told me to hide until they come for me, and not show myself or talk to no one, and then when they say, to tell what I seen."

"What did you see?" Crispin asked with interest.

"I saw her kill him. The woman in blue. I saw her stab my master."

Sophie drew a sharp breath as the girl spoke, but Crispin pressed her to his chest to keep her quiet.

"A lady in blue," Crispin repeated. "You saw her kill your master."

"Yes, sir. Lady in blue."

"What color hair did she have?" Crispin queried.

"I ain't supposed to tell anything about her hair. Just that I seen a lady in blue. Blue taffeta."

"I see." Crispin seemed to take this in for a moment, then his tone changed. "How much did they pay you to say that?"

"They didn't pay me nothing to say it, it's true," the girl answered defiantly, but her voice had become higher pitched, and the faint noise of coins being fondled in a purse reached Crispin's ears.

"I bet," Crispin mused aloud, "that they said that if you told anyone about them paying you, they would take the money away. Isn't that right?"

"No." The girl shook her head so intently back and forth that Sophie and Crispin could hear it. "They said if I told anyone, the money would turn to ashes. Imagine, all them pretty gold pieces turning to ashes. So I said I'd not tell who paid me. Only about the lady."

"That was wise. Say, how many pieces did they give you?" Crispin asked conversationally. "I once had two gold pieces."

The girl almost snorted with disdain. "I got four. Four o' the shiniest you ever laid eyes upon. Do you want to see them?"

"Very much," Crispin answered enthusiastically. "But first we have got to get out of here. I don't suppose you know where the door to the kitchen courtyard is?"

The serving girl, in her element now, begged to differ. "If you give me your hand, I'll lead you there," she offered.

After only two collisions with yielding cubes of butter, Crispin, Sophie, and the serving girl found themselves standing in the courtyard behind the baker's house. Sophie was taking huge gasps of air, drinking it in, while the other two stood off to the side.

The serving girl looked to be about ten, with huge eyes and filthy pieces of brown hair clinging to her head. She smiled shyly at Crispin once they had emerged into the light.

"Let's see those gold pieces," Crispin said, winking at her and extending his hand.

"I'll show 'em to you. But I don't like him," the serving girl pointed to Sophie. "I don't like men with mustaches."

"Neither do I," Crispin confided in her, motioning to Sophie to stay behind them. "We won't let him see the coins."

The girl nodded, then reached into her petticoat and extracted a purse. It was blue, made of the same fabric that Crispin had found clutched in the dead man's fingers. The serving girl emptied it into her hand, revealing four gleaming gold coins.

"Aren't they beautiful?" she preened as they caught the evening light. "Aren't they the goldest you ever seen?"

"Yes, they are," Crispin agreed enthusiastically. "What would you say to making a trade with me?"

"A trade?" The serving girl was wary.

"Yes. I will give you five of my gold pieces, in exchange for four of yours." Crispin reached into his purse and laid the five pieces of gold enticingly in his palm.

"Yours are dirty," she replied. "Mine are clean."

"Yes, but mine won't turn to ashes if you tell who gave them to you. And you will have five instead of four."

The girl seemed to consider this. "Five," she repeated, nodding. She handed over the four glittering disks and then clutched the five dull gold pieces Crispin laid in her palm. When she had examined her new coins to her satisfaction, she raised her eyes to Crispin's to ask, "You won't tell them I traded their gold pieces, will you? I wouldn't want them to think that I didn't like their pretty ones."

"I promise," Crispin swore. "But you'll have to tell me who it was so I know who not to tell."

"I saw a lady in a blue dress," the girl repeated firmly. "Blue taffeta. She killed my master."

"I know. But who paid you?" Crispin asked patiently.

The girl crossed her arms over her chest and shook her head. "I don't know nothing but a beautiful lady in a blue dress."

"I told you, these gold pieces that I gave you won't turn to ashes if you tell who paid. Now who was it?"

The girl grinned widely, like a student who knows they have the right answer. "You did. You paid 'em to me."

Sophie, who had been listening to their exchange at a distance, let out a chuckle. "It looks like she has you routed, my lord."

Crispin ignored her. "I know I gave you those old ones," he said, smiling through his clenched teeth. "But who gave you the ones before? The shiny ones?"

The girl shook her head. "I wouldn't want to tell you and have them turn to ashes. I wouldn't do that to you. Him maybe"—the girl jammed a thumb in Sophie's direction—"but not you. I like you too well."

"It would seem," Sophie started in on him as they made their way back to Sandal Hall on foot, "that you are entirely too likable to the fair sex. If I might give you some advice, my lord—"

"I don't want any of Don Alfonso's advice about women," Crispin growled.

"Very well." Sophie shrugged. "But it is only fair to point out that Don Alfonso has never been duped out of a gold piece by a girl one third his age. Never."

"Fascinating," Crispin replied in a tone that suggested the conversation was over.

"No, not once," Sophie went on over Crispin's protests, warming to her theme. "Not only that, but Don Alfonso always gets his money's worth."

Crispin did not reply this time, merely smiled quietly to himself and ran his fingers over the four coins in his palm. He *had* gotten his money's worth. More than his money's worth.

The warm air coming through the window ruffled the pages of the book Sophie was studying. She was afraid to light a candle and attract attention to her presence in Lord Grosgrain's study at the top of Grosgrain Place, so she was sitting next to the window, trying to see as much as she could from the light of the half-moon.

After their return to Sandal Hall that afternoon, Crispin had announced that he had a delicate errand to attend to, on which Don Alfonso was not invited. Instead of voicing the protest he had prepared himself for, Sophie acquiesced quietly.

In part, it was because she had errands of her own to do. As soon as Crispin was gone, she had dashed from the house, crossed the street, and scaled the side wall of Grosgrain Place, the wall facing away from Hen House, entering Lord Grosgrain's study by the window. The purpose of her visit, she told herself, was to glean what he had been blackmailed for. The study was where he had kept his most important papers and was also the only room of the house that had ever really felt like his. It was here that they had met, at first weekly, then less often, to discuss the management of Leverage Holdings. It was here that they had been together for the last time, here that he had asked her for that fateful bill of credit, here that he had alluded to the Phoenix.

More than six weeks had passed between meetings when Lord Grosgrain had summoned her to Grosgrain Place that final time. In the months before his death he had grown moody and distant. And profligate. Going over his books, Sophie saw that he had been forced to ask her for the twelve hundred pounds not only so his name would not be recognized but, more crucially, because he did not have it immediately at hand. Somehow, he had managed to spend through an enormous chunk of money in a very short time.

But Sophie had noticed this before, puzzled over it the first time she read through his ledgers. She and Emme and Octavia had tried to guess what improvements to Grosgrain Place could possibly have cost one hundred thousand pounds when the Queen's own palaces ran on one tenth that amount. Sophie had come tonight supposedly to look over those books again, to wonder once more where the money went, to seek, in vain, for a clue to the mystery of her godfather's death.

She knew now she had also come with another objective: she had come for guidance, her godfather's guidance. She had come for a sane place to think about Crispin, a place to put her thoughts in order, a place permeated by the wisdom and stability that her godfather had always provided. This was the real reason she had acquiesced so easily when Crispin said he had errands to do. She needed time away from him, time to sort out the strange, amazing, feelings she was experiencing.

She bit her lower lip as she remembered what she had done that morning, how she had told him she loved him, whispered it to him, and she wondered where the words had come from. She never thought she would say such words to anyone. It had happened without her realizing it, without passing through her mind. But she was not sorry. Indeed, she found she was rather glad. Excited even. But also a little scared.

There could be no question of him loving her back, she knew. The Earl of Sandal was the most notorious bachelor in Europe, let alone England. And if he had returned with the express purpose of marrying a well-bred English lady, he certainly would not be considering her. Nor was she sure she would want him to. After all, marrying was something she had sworn never to do. People only married for financial gain, she reminded herself, and she wanted for nothing financially. She would rather, much rather, be the Earl of Sandal's mistress and preserve her independence than be married to him, she told herself.

And knew instantly that it was a lie. It was not that she wanted to marry him, exactly. What she wanted was simultaneously so much more and so much less than that. What she wanted, what she craved deep within her, was for him to love her back. The times he told her that he enjoyed being with her, those, even more than the incredible climaxes he showed her, were the high points of her life. It was as if a new world had been opened up to her, one of pleasure without shame, of desire and passion without dread, companionship without wickedness.

She was no longer sure who Sophie Champion was, what she stood for. Everything she had ever known, everything she believed in, had been thrown into turmoil by Crispin. The axioms that had governed her behavior for so many years now rang false. Instead of feeling weakened by her feelings for Crispin, she felt stronger; instead of lessened, she felt expanded. She wanted to share all of herself with him, tell him everything, the whole truth about her life. Yet something held her back, stopping her mouth each time she began. And sitting surrounded by the comforting spines of her godfather's library, she knew what it was. She was not sure if she could trust him.

Or rather, if she should. She cast her eyes over Lord Grosgrain's study, desperately searching for a sign, a hint, anything that would guide her.

But there were no hints, no signs for her. She was completely on her own, as she had been ten years earlier before she went to live with Lord Grosgrain. He had spent the next decade preparing her, helping her grow strong, teaching her to trust herself, her instincts. No one could make this decision but her, she knew. Only she would be able to say.

Disappointed but strangely tranquil, she decided to go. She had already been there for several hours, it was well past midnight, and who knew but that Crispin might be back. Looking trustworthy. She carefully restored Lord Grosgrain's books to their various shelves, touching each one lovingly, and then backed out of the window. Paying especial attention not to make any noise, she slid along the windowsill and reached out for the trellis she had used to climb up. It was covered in thick clinging jasmine vines, which muffled the sounds of her footsteps and cushioned her grip. As soon as she had a good hold on the trellis, she began her descent, moving quickly lest anyone notice her against the gray granite of the building. One set of windows that had not been lit before now showed a faint light, and as she passed, Sophie leaned toward it to glance in.

Constantia, completely nude, was facing the window, her golden hair spread across an orange cushion, her perfect little body stretched across her chaise longue. A man knelt before her with his back to Sophie, and as Sophie watched, he moved his head from her mouth, down her breasts, until, at Constantia's insistence, he buried his face between her legs. Constantia arched up to meet his mouth, and Sophie knew exactly how she must be feeling. Exactly. Because the man was Crispin.

Chapter Seventeen

Sophie had received her sign. She almost fell from the trellis as she watched Constantia's eyes close and her lips part in ecstasy. Sophie forced herself to move then, forced her stiff limbs to continue the climb down, and she had just reached the bottom when Constantia's climactic cries spilled through the window.

There was nothing surprising about it, really, Sophie told herself. The Earl of Sandal was entitled to have as many lovers as he wanted, she reminded herself. He was known for his conquests, she advised herself. On more than one continent. It was what she should have expected, what she did expect, what she had every right to expect.

Forgetting all about her plan to try to peep into Hen House and check on the location of her blue taffeta dress, Sophie crossed the Strand and went directly back to Sandal Hall. She knocked and was admitted by the sleepy night porter at the main door, but did not ascend the stairs to what was left of Crispin's apartment. Instead, she continued straight through the hall, straight out, out into the night, into the main garden. She did not pause to look at the rare Dutch flowers Crispin had just planted or to admire his knot garden, but strode past them all until she stood on the water steps, looking out at the Thames.

She peered intently at the water, trying to lose the sight of Constantia, of Crispin, in its glassy surface, but it did not work. She felt vile, and foolish. Very, very foolish. The thoughts she had been harboring in Lord Grosgrain's apartment now flooded back to her, mocking her. She stripped off Don Alfonso's doublet, stripped off his breeches, pulled off his mustache, and dove, naked, into the water.

When Crispin got home, half an hour later, she was still there. Unlike Sophie, he had taken the stairs to his apartment, taken them two at a time in his excitement to see her, but had found it empty. She was not in the library, where a bed had been set up for them. Or in the charred bedroom. Or the hanging garden. Or the privy. Or the armoire. Or under the desk. Or behind the clock. His labors that night had piqued his desire to see her to such an extent that he was about to rouse the household to tell them that Sophie had been stolen, when he glanced out the back windows of his chambers. From there he could see out over the Sandal Hall garden, and, beyond that, the Thames.

What he saw that night, however, was neither garden nor river. It was something supernatural, something incredible. A thousand white stars danced on the surface of the water, swirling first in one direction, then in the other. They twisted over the river in complex patterns, eddies of magical light, curling tendrils of stars radiating out from a single dark space, at their center. As Crispin watched, the luminous points converged over the dark space, and then, from their midst, a creature emerged. The stars spilled over her as she rose from the water, dancing around her, glistening on her hair, her skin. Stars twinkled on her eyelashes, on the tip of her nose, over her nipples, along her knees as she emerged inch by inch. She was perfect, too perfect to be real, her skin glowing like marble in the dwindling moonlight, her hair streaming down her back, curving around her bottom, hugging her waist. Crispin was transfixed watching her, wondering where she had come from, at the same time knowing that there was only one person, one woman, it could be.

He descended the stairs three at a time. He did not spare a glance for his flowers, for the new watering system he had installed, did not pause to run his fingers over the fresh green growth on his hedges, or to notice the holes being dug even at that moment by devious moles. He did not think about the fact noblemen simply did not cavort with naked nymphs in public, even on their own river steps, or that The Aunts' windows overlooked the garden. No such mundane concerns could draw his attention from the shimmering magical being at the end of the garden. Standing on the river steps, her back toward him, with droplets of water clinging to her body like jewels, she seemed to be more dream than real.

Indeed, Crispin felt as if he were in a dream, a wonderful dream, as he slid his arms under her breasts from behind and pulled her against him. "Sophie," he breathed into her hair. "*Tesoro.*"

He had approached soundlessly, and his chest was already pressing against her back, his arms already hugging her to him, before Sophie realized what had happened. She wanted to protest and pull away, but she could not bring herself to at first, the feel of him behind her was so wonderful, so natural, and when she caught what she thought was a whiff of Constantia's perfume on Crispin's clothes it was too late. At least, Sophie decided, she could show that she was not a fool, that she was as sophisticated and mature as the abhorrent centipede behind her. "Did you have a pleasant evening, my lord?" she squeezed out suavely.

"Adequate," Crispin answered lightly, too distracted by the silky tendrils of hair tickling his nose to give it much thought. "More than adequate, actually."

Sophie matched his urbane lilt. "You know, you and Constantia Grosgrain make a very handsome couple."

"Mmmm," Crispin replied, following one curl around and under her chin with his lips.

"I am being serious, my lord," Sophie explained in the most blasé of voices. "You should marry her."

Something in her tone caught Crispin's attention. "Marry who?"

"Constantia," Sophie said impatiently.

"Marry Constantia?" This was not the turn of conversation Crispin had expected. "Have you been talking to The Aunts?"

"No." Sophie tried to ignore his arms around her, the heat of his body against her back as she looked out into the night. "You would be good together."

"Mmmmm." Crispin went back to studying her curls, not seeing any reason at all to continue in this vein.

But Sophie, setting a new standard for worldliness, went on. "And it would make so many people happy. Not the least of which would be you, my lord."

Crispin dragged himself away from the contemplation of the sweep of Sophie's neck to seize on one of her words. "Happy. Right now what would make me happy would be to strip off my clothes, dive into the water, make love to you looking at the stars, and then fall asleep with you in my arms. I am sweaty, amorous, and exhausted."

Sophie stayed worldly. "I can imagine. It must have been hard work."

"Backbreaking," Crispin confirmed. "My shoulders and knees are completely worn out."

The picture of him kneeling in front of Constantia, bending down toward her, flashed before Sophie's eyes, and she shivered. But she could not keep herself from asking, sophisticatedly, "Why didn't you lie down?"

"Lie down?" Crispin was incredulous. "There was too much to do, and not much time. I wanted to get back to you."

"To me?" Sophie repeated hollowly. "You wanted to get back to me?"

"Yes, to tell you all about it. I knew how excited it would make you."

"That will not be necessary," Sophie said coolly. "I don't need to hear any more than I already have."

Sophie's lack of interest surprised Crispin. "But I have not gotten to the good part yet. There was a lot of resistance to overcome—"

"It certainly did not look like it to me," Sophie murmured under her breath, pulling her back away from his chest slightly.

"What?"

"Nothing."

"Anyway," Crispin continued, "I finally managed to pick the lock and slide into the main chamber, and you will never believe what I found inside."

"A paradise unlike any you have ever known?" Sophie asked flatly.

"Paradise? No, I would hardly say that. Inside it was more—"

"It?" Sophie was outraged. "You call her 'it'?"

"What would you have me call it?"

"At least use her name," Sophie said, pulling away from him completely now but not facing him.

"What name? I didn't know it, or, if you prefer, *she*, had a name. Anyway, *she* was immense and ready—"

"How can you say that? How can you talk about her that way, as if she were just some sort of gaping empty space waiting for you to fill her up?"

"Isn't it—" Crispin corrected himself, "Isn't she? Isn't that what a warehouse is, an empty space to be filled up?"

Sophie swung around to face him for the first time. "A warehouse? You call her a warehouse? Is that all women are to you, a place to stash your, your, your *merchandise*?"

"My *merchandise*?" Crispin repeated, his eyes wide. "What the devil are you talking about, Sophie?"

"The same thing you are. Although I did not expect a man of the world like you, Lord Scandal, to have recourse to quite so many euphemisms."

"Euphemisms? What euphemisms?"

"'Lock.' 'Entrance chamber.' 'Warehouse,'" Sophie listed them on her fingers. "Why didn't you just say you were making love to Constantia Grosgrain in her dressing room?"

"I was what?"

"I saw you. Saw you with your head between her legs. 'Trying to break into her warehouse,' I suppose you would say."

Crispin just stared at her for a moment. Then, as it all sank slowly in, he opened his mouth. And began to laugh uncontrollably.

"My god, Sophie. My *merchandise*," he spluttered to himself through his laughter. "You thought that I—"

"This is not funny, my lord," Sophie insisted, struggling to maintain her worldly veneer. "Were you or were you not picking Constantia Grosgrain's lock tonight?"

Sophie's phrasing elicited new peals of laughter from Crispin. "It is strange that you should ask the question that way," he said, struggling to smother a chuckle. "Because, in a manner of speaking, I was. But not the manner you are thinking of."

"What are you talking about?" Sophie demanded.

"I was picking a lock that belonged to Constantia's late husband. Your godfather. A real lock," Crispin hastened to explain, still laughing. "The lock on his laboratory."

"Was that before or after you made love to Constantia in her dressing room?" Sophie asked, disposing once and for all of the euphemisms.

Crispin, sensing that she was really upset, suppressed his merriment. "Sophie, I did not make love to Constantia Grosgrain in her dressing room tonight."

"There is no need to deny it," Sophie told him, glowering. "I saw you."

"You saw me? Tonight? In the dressing room? With Constantia?" Crispin rearranged the words, hoping they would make more sense. "But I was not anywhere near her dressing room tonight."

"Then where were you?"

"In Saint Martin's Fields. At the counterfeiter's warehouse."

"I thought you said you were at Lord Grosgrain's laboratory," Sophie snapped. "Or was that just another metaphor for Constantia's nether parts?"

"I beg you, Sophie, to leave Constantia and her—her lock"— Crispin threatened to burst into laughter again—"to leave them out of our discussion. I went to Lord Grosgrain's laboratory. What

I found was a counterfeiter's paradise." Noting the disbelieving expression on her face, Crispin continued, "It was a warehouse full of coin presses fitted out with dies to make the gold pieces of a dozen kingdoms. And in sacks along the walls was over a million pounds worth of false currency, ready to be shipped out."

"Are you saying," Sophie spoke slowly, "that my godfather was a counterfeiter?"

"I am afraid that I am," Crispin conceded. "Or at least that he was part of one of the largest counterfeiting operations ever undertaken in England."

"But that is impossible. He knew nothing about organization, about planning. About money."

"He did not seem to have any trouble amassing a sizable fortune in coal mines," Crispin pointed out.

Sophie waved his comment away. "I cannot believe it. I cannot believe that he was a counterfeiter."

"Actually, the operation I uncovered tonight is massive, and unless he was a criminal mastermind, there is no way he could have run it on his own. I suspect he was only in charge of one part. The chemical part, for example."

"But how did he—" Sophie started, then stopped, finding a far more interesting question. "How did you think to look in the warehouse?"

"It was simple, really. The coins that I bought from the girl at Sweetson's today were fakes. Good fakes. Fakes that only someone very adept at sublimating different metals could have made."

"Someone like an alchemist," Sophie put in. "Is that why you thought of Lord Grosgrain?"

"In part, but there was also the nagging question of what he was being blackmailed for." He looked at her sharply, then looked away. "It was merely a hunch that took me to his laboratory tonight." She did not need to know that he had recognized the coins instantly, as soon as he saw them in the girl's hand that afternoon, recognized them not only as counterfeits, but very special counterfeits, counterfeits identical to those he had confiscated during his first operation as the Phoenix two and a half years earlier. That time he had foiled the counterfeiter's ability to get the money into circulation, but he had been forced to leave the country before he could find the leaders of the organization and destroy it entirely. This time he intended to stop them for good.

"So Lord Grosgrain was being blackmailed because he was a counterfeiter, and that is why that spy, that Phoenix, killed him?" Sophie asked.

"The Phoenix did not kill him," Crispin said positively, and was on the verge of saying more, but Sophie, lost in her own thoughts, interrupted him.

"It does not make any sense," she mused. "What would possess Lord Grosgrain to become a counterfeiter? Why would he do it?" She was speaking more to herself than to him, but Crispin answered.

"Perhaps he needed the money. He was paying you a thousand pounds a month, after all."

Sophie shook her head. "No. He had access to plenty of money."

"Are you certain?" Crispin asked. "He may have owned coal mines, but the price of coal has slipped recently. Are you sure he was financially solvent?"

"Quite, quite sure. I—" Sophie started to say something, changed her mind, then changed her mind again. She hesitated for a bit longer before demanding abruptly, "Are you sure you were not with Constantia tonight?"

Crispin frowned at the change of topic. "I thought we were not going to mention her again," he began, but was stopped by the expression on Sophie's face. "Yes, I am quite, quite sure I was not at Constantia's tonight."

"If it was not you, who was it?" she demanded.

"How much of the man did you see?"

"Just his back." Sophie went rigid. "It was enough."

"Ah. That explains it then. For while I flatter myself that my good-looking face is unique, the fact is that there are hundreds of men in England who look like me from the back."

Sophie disagreed entirely, but did not say anything. Instead, she studied him in what was left of the moonlight. "Can I trust you, Crispin?"

"Of course."

Sophie closed her eyes for several seconds, then opened them slowly. "I have guarded what I am about to tell you as an inviolable secret for ten years. It is not my secret, not really, but it is mine to protect. If I share it with you, will you keep it?"

The dreamy nymph of earlier had become a powerful, mesmerizing goddess. Crispin nodded reverently, completely awed by her solemnity.

"I know exactly how much money Lord Grosgrain had," Sophie began, "because I gave it to him."

Crispin snapped out of his trance. "What do you mean you 'gave it to him'? I thought he owned coal mines all over the country."

"No." Sophie shook her head. "He did not own coal mines. I did. I do."

"You own coal mines?"

"Yes. And waterworks. And windmills. And four shipping canals. And half a dozen sheep farms. I started buying them just before I turned sixteen, but I needed a man to act as the titular head. That was why I hired Lord Grosgrain."

"You *hired* him? Your godfather?"

Sophie realized she had misspoken, had almost revealed too much. "Sort of. No one would deal with a sixteen-year-old girl, you see," she explained, rushing past her mistake, "but they were more than happy to work with Lord Grosgrain, even though he did not have a single notion of how to run a business."

What she had said was completely incredible, Crispin thought. And yet, given what he knew of Sophie Champion, entirely possible. "The thousand pounds a month Lord Grosgrain paid you," Crispin interjected. "You said it was an allowance, but clearly, if you held all his money, you did not need one. Why was he paying you?"

"He claimed he was trying to reimburse me." Sophie looked wistful as she remembered. "When we bought our first coal mine, he was destitute. He had spent his entire fortune on his alchemical experiments until there was literally nothing left. He was so poor that he had been forced to send Basil to live with relatives just to make sure the boy got enough to eat. I knew a bit about alchemy, enough to enable him to make a name for himself at it and earn some of his money back, and I had some money of my own. We pooled what we had and invested it, and later, when our enterprises were doing well and Lord Grosgrain was rich again, he wanted to pay me back for the prosperity I brought him. But I never accepted it. I always found a way to return it to him without his knowing."

"Of course." Crispin nodded as if this were all perfectly normal, as if sixteen-year-old girls with the price of a coal mine in their purse and a little knowledge of alchemy joined forces with penniless elderly noblemen to orchestrate large-scale business transactions every day of the week. He went on slowly, as though he was explaining something to himself. "Then Lord Grosgrain left you the business and all his property in his will not because you were blackmailing him but because you actually owned it already."

"Yes," Sophie confirmed. "We never wanted it to get out that he was not the real owner, it would have been a crushing blow to his reputation. That was why we kept it a secret. Indeed, I purposely circulated rumors suggesting I might be blackmailing him whenever anyone started asking us about our relationship. As a result, Lord Grosgrain was always afraid that if he died without directly addressing the question of ownership in his will, someone would challenge me, challenge my authority over the business."

"Your authority," Crispin went on. "So you made the business decisions behind the scenes and then he executed them up front?"

"Something like that," Sophie agreed. "Of course, now everything has changed."

"I can imagine," Crispin said positively. He could guess just how she felt, because everything had changed for him as well. He had, at long last, gotten all his questions answered. He did not have to wonder what Sophie's relationship with her godfather was. Nor whether she was a blackmailer. Nor where she got the piles of money she gave away.

Nor whether he was harboring any feelings for her. He reached out his hand to catch her cheek.

"You will not tell anyone, will you, my lord?" She asked nervously, rubbing her face against his palm. "His reputation was the most important thing to Lord Grosgrain, and if anyone ever found out that he had accepted money from me, if Constantia ever found out—" Sophie just shook her head.

"I won't tell anyone." Crispin moved forward, cupping her cheek in his hand, and bent to kiss her.

"Good," Sophie whispered just before their lips touched, "because if you do, I shall have to disembowel you."

"I believe," Crispin said as he kissed her mouth, "you threatened me"—he kissed her chin—"the same way"—he kissed the line of her jaw—"once before." His lips trailed along her neck until he reached her ear. "I would not want to call you a braggart, but..." He left the sentence unfinished, using his tongue rather than words to make his point.

"You will not be so lucky twice," Sophie assured him breathlessly. "This time—oh, my lord—I—oh, Crispin—will not be—" The sentence ended in a series of moans.

Crispin had turned her around and was kissing her back, his hands resting lightly on her breasts, his thumbs on her nipples. His lips coasted over each of her vertebrae, then skimmed along the sides of the delicious valley between the globes of her bottom. When she began moaning, he had just coaxed her legs apart and settled himself between them. He moved his hands down from her breasts, and all at once Sophie felt his cheek on her thigh from below and his hands on her now tingling nub, from above. Crispin used his fingers to caress her as his tongue slipped between her wet folds, plunging into her passage. When Sophie's legs began to tremble, he slowed his fingers and pulled slightly away. He held his mouth under her, letting the liquor of her arousal drip onto his lips, then used the flat of his tongue to lick her full length, lapping from underneath up to where his fingers were teasing her.

"Oh, Crispin," she moaned and sighed simultaneously. She gripped his shoulders to support herself as the pressure built within her until, with a seemingly endless kiss on her tender bud, Crispin sent her over the edge. Wave after wave of intoxicating pleasure flooded Sophie's body, crashing over her, leaving her gasping, panting, and moaning, "Crispin, I love you."

It took them both a moment to realize what she had said.

"I mean," she rushed to correct as Crispin pulled himself up between her legs. "I mean, I love being uncomfortable with you."

Crispin stood before her looking serious. "I love being uncomfortable with you too."

"You do?" Sophie was genuinely surprised. "You, you *love* it?"

"Well, I find I am quite partial to it, yes."

"Crispin?"

"Yes, Sophie."

"Crispin, there is something I must tell you."

"First there is something I must tell—What is it, Thurston?"

"Good morning, my lord," Thurston said, as if there were nothing the least bit unusual about finding his master and a naked goddess chatting intimately on the river steps at dawn. "I did not like to interrupt, my lord, but there are men here."

"Men?"

"Men with a warrant, my lord. To search Sandal Hall and all properties pertaining thereunto."

"A warrant to search Sandal Hall?" Crispin glared at him in disbelief. "What the devil are they looking for?"

"I believe, my lord, that their object is Miss Champion."

Chapter Eighteen

Crispin strode into the main reception hall, glared at the men assembled there, and demanded, "What do you think you are doing?"

In his outrage, Crispin did not notice Basil Grosgrain standing behind two of the others, but his blond head came into view now.

"As justice of the peace for this parish, it is my regrettable duty to serve this to you." Basil held a piece of paper toward Crispin, but kept his distance. The expression on his face made clear what he thought of Crispin's rumpled and dirty clothes. As Crispin looked over the warrant, Basil went on smarmily, "I apologize for the early hour, Lord Sandal. I hope we have not taken you from any important labors."

Crispin tilted his head up, briefly, to glare at Basil with one eye. "I was working in my garden," he said, then returned to the paper. It was a warrant, a completely legitimate looking warrant, authorized by the Queen's secretary, for Lord Basil Grosgrain, Justice of the Peace and Knight of the Garter, to search the premises of Sandal Hall, including all corridors, storehouses, outbuildings, secret passages, priest holes, and byways, for the person or effects of one Sophie Champion, wanted for the murder of Richard Tottle and a notoriously dangerous criminal destined for the gallows. During the search, no one would be allowed to enter or leave the building without permission, and the grounds would be encircled with guards.

"On what basis was this issued?" Crispin asked when he finally looked up.

"Anonymous tip. Several of them." Basil got a gleam in his eye. "Sorry to do this to you, Lord Sandal, but I could not shirk my duty."

"Duty, the finest alibi of all," Crispin agreed, laying particular emphasis on the word "alibi." He did not allow himself time to grin over the way Basil flinched, but went on. "I cannot imagine why you think this"—Crispin looked down at the paper—"this 'Sophie Champion' woman is hiding here. Why would she take refuge in my house?"

"You can't guess, can you?" Basil asked, smiling sickly.

"No," Crispin confirmed. "I imagine you have a better idea. After all, I learned most of what I know about her from you the day the constable came to question you about your—I mean Miss Champion's—whereabouts at the time of the murder. By the way, what was the name of that painter whose picture you helped your stepmother select the night Richard Tottle was killed? Liar? Lies?"

"Lyle." Basil's lips, indeed his whole face, had gone very white. "Why?"

"I just thought I would ask him a few questions," Crispin replied idly. "About paintings, of course. What do you think of his work? Is he any good at *trompe l'oeil*? You know, those paintings that present a false picture?"

"I would not know, Lord Sandal. I have only seen his figurative compositions."

"Ah, well. All painting is a deceit, an illusion really, if you think about it. Painters are our best dissemblers. Lucky for you, isn't it?" Crispin's expression was open, candid, even friendly as he regarded Basil.

"I do not understand your meaning, my lord."

"I did not mean anything, really. Just that there is so much ugliness in the world and if you really are a connoisseur of beauty, you must be grateful for the deceitful hand of the painter. At any rate, I am sure this Liar of yours will be able to give me just what I am looking for." Crispin patted his companion's back amiably.

Basil disentangled himself from Crispin's friendly embrace. "I believe, my lord, that we should begin our search."

"Of course. I nearly forgot what you were here for. You'll want to get it done quickly, I imagine, so you can be in time to take breakfast with your stepmother. You do that most every day, do you not?"

"Yes, but I hardly—"

Crispin put up a hand. "There is no need to explain. I apologize. I should have been more sensitive to the pain it must cause you to hear it mentioned. After all, that is where you were, breakfasting with Constantia in her dressing room, the morning your father was killed, isn't it? I apologize for being so unfeeling."

"You have nothing to reproach yourself for, Lord Sandal," Basil said through clenched teeth.

"Very kind of you," Crispin lauded. "But you do."

"I do what?"

"Have something to reproach yourself, or rather"—Crispin smiled at his mistake—"have something to reproach *me*, for. I should not have taken up so much of your time with my banter. But it is so important to get to know one's neighbors."

Basil was glaring at Crispin, a vein in his throat vibrating, when The Aunts swept into the room.

"Lord Grosgrain the younger, how delightful of you to call," Lady Priscilla said with a noticeable edge in her voice.

"And to bring all these men with you," Lady Eleanor added. "We were wondering when you would present yourself to us."

"Yes, I was just telling Basil about the importance of getting to know his neighbors," Crispin put in.

"Do not judge us all by our nephew's standard," Lady Priscilla begged Basil, having cast a cold eye on Crispin's attire. "As my dear brother, Hugo, always said, 'When the fruit falls far from the tree, it gets badly bruised.'"

"No, sister," Lady Eleanor objected. "'When a foal has legs like a V, it is destined to lose.' That is what Hugo said, I am sure of it."

"Quite sure?" was on the tip of Lady Priscilla's tongue when she was rudely interrupted by Basil.

"I beg your pardon, ladies, but I am afraid I must get my search under way."

Basil had made a mistake of the first water. Two sets of Aunt eyes, finely tuned to rebuke any sort of social breach, bored into him.

"Do you really mean to search this house, young man?" Lady Eleanor asked in a tone that had sent at least two husbands to the grave.

Basil hesitated for a moment, giving Lady Priscilla a chance to address Crispin. "Nephew, what is all this drivel I hear? Have you got a woman hidden in the house?"

"Of course not." Crispin was astonished by the suggestion. "I cannot imagine what makes Basil think that I would harbor fugitive criminals on my premises. Indeed I, my name, my house, the memory of my father, and the spirit of neighborliness are insulted. Gravely insulted."

The Aunts, having found a new enemy in Basil, nodded at Crispin in commendation for his fine performance. "You see, Lord Grosgrain the younger," Lady Priscilla spoke to Basil, "our nephew may not be the gentleman his father was, but he is not so uncultivated as to offer his home as a sanctuary for the criminal classes. Criminals are flouters of the standards of Proper Behavior and destroyers of the English Nation."

Lady Eleanor picked up the thread of her sister's comment. "Surely you know we would never share a roof with such people. Therefore it must be clear that you need not send your men prying into the house."

"It would be most disruptive," Lady Priscilla pointed out.

"And most impolite," Lady Eleanor sharpened the argument.

"'A deed done in haste is a waste,' as our brother, Hugo, always said," Lady Priscilla added.

"No, sister." Lady Eleanor frowned slightly. " 'Food with no taste is a waste.' That is wha—"

A raised eyebrow from Lady Priscilla stopped her sister in mid-sentence. Not to waste it, Lady Priscilla then turned the raised eyebrow on Basil. "We would view a search as an insult to ourselves."

Basil had only just recovered his composure. "I assure you, I mean no insult to Your Ladyships, but I must execute this warrant. I do so by order of Her Majesty."

"Lizzie sent you?" Lady Eleanor asked with incredulity. "Lizzie knows you are here?"

Basil seemed to shrink four sizes when confronted by two women who referred to the Queen of England as "Lizzie." "I am Her Majesty's representative in this parish, yes," he explained haltingly.

"So she did not send you. I knew it. Lizzie would never let us be insulted like this. Nephew," Lady Priscilla commanded, "bring me quill and paper. I will write to her immediately."

Crispin, who was greatly enjoying himself, was about to oblige The Aunt when he heard Thurston clearing his throat at his elbow.

"You sent for me, my lord?" Thurston asked, clearing his throat two more times.

"Yes." Crispin acknowledged the signal Thurston had just given him, then bowed to address The Aunts. "I apologize for the upset this may cause Your Ladyships, but after careful consideration, I have decided, in the interests of duty and neighborliness, to allow Basil to execute his warrant."

"But, nephew. This is an outrage," Lady Eleanor began.

"I know it will be an inconvenience to you," Crispin went on, "but it really does seem the best course of action. I would not like there to be any doubt about the sort of thing that goes on under the illustrious roof of Sandal Hall. If I am to find a virtuous wife, my name, my house, must be unblemished."

This was logic that The Aunts could not refute. Fearing lest their nephew change his mind and begin dancing a jig naked in the street, they lost no time retreating from the group, calling anew for ink and paper, and retiring to their sitting room to begin drawing up a list of likely betrothal prospects.

Basil stayed silent through the flurry of The Aunts' departure, then turned to Crispin and said, with real gratitude, "Thank you, my lord."

"It is my duty as an Englishman to serve Justice and her sister, Truth," Crispin replied loftily. "Now I suppose you will want to start in the servants' chambers. It is the most likely place for a criminal to hide, wouldn't you say? By the way, I forgot to ask. I was hoping you would allow my steward and me to accompany your troops and ensure that no damage is done to my property."

The gratitude was gone from Basil's face. "That is most irregular, my lord."

"Very well. But if you do not consent, I shall hold you responsible for any item which is broken or missing. Many of them belonged to my dear father, Hugo, and I would really feel that if I allowed a single dent, a single scratch, I would be committing a form of patricide. And patricide is a wretched crime. Don't you agree?" Crispin paused to look inquiringly at his companion.

Basil muttered something that might have been "you bloody bastard," but Crispin took to be "Yes, quite."

"I am speaking metaphorically, of course," Crispin continued, "just to make a point about how I value my possessions. Are you prepared to ante your father's, or rather, *your* fortune against the carelessness of your searchers?"

Basil's answer was pronounced in a far less pleasant tone than Crispin's. "Do as you like, Lord Sandal," he said through lips so tightly pressed together that they looked like two lines. "But if you interfere in any way with the execution of this warrant, I shall have you removed by the sheriff. Is that clear?" Without waiting for an answer, he turned to the short man on his right and spoke. "Come, Sheriff. Bring your agents. We will begin our search in His Lordship's chambers."

"You think to find a criminal in my apartment? I suppose we can only judge others as we would be judged." Crispin said this jauntily as he followed Basil into the library and was pleased to see the vein on the man's neck begin to bulge again. With any luck, he would have Basil in apoplectic fits before the day was out.

Thinking about that was far more pleasant than thinking about what would happen if by some awful mischance Basil's minions managed to uncover Sophie's hiding place. In addition to the twelve men surrounding every entrance to and exit from the house, Basil had ten with him to conduct the search. Under other circumstances, Crispin would have been fascinated to watch them poking through the charred remains of his bedroom, removing all the books on the shelves of his library to try for secret compartments, and unscrewing the legs of his chairs to ensure there were no hidden levers there, but his mind kept returning to Sophie, to what she had said next to the Thames.

Fifteen times in thirty minutes he was about to pull Thurston aside and demand to know where Sophie was hidden, and fifteen times he stopped himself. He could not, however, keep himself from asking if she had enough candles so it would not be dark wherever it was, and all eight times he got the same affirmative response. Crispin was about to inquire for the ninth, just to be sure, when one of the men, a fat one with beady eyes whom Crispin had already decided looked too intelligent, began flapping his hands.

"I think I found something here," he called to his companions. "Come on the quick, and bring the ax."

"Bring the ax," Grip the raven echoed as Crispin interposed himself before their rushing forms.

"Gentlemen, would you like some wine?" he asked, ever the suave host. "Why not pause for a moment and refresh yourselves before taking an ax to my walls?"

"Lord Sandal," Basil came and stood in front of Crispin. "If you interrupt my men's work again, I will have you escorted out."

"Interrupt?" Crispin looked incredulous. "I was merely trying to aid them, revive their flagging spirits. They look a bit haggard already. And there are still forty-two rooms to search."

"Forty-two, forty-two, bring the ax," the raven called.

This double reminder found fertile soil with the sheriff. "Forty-two more after this one? I believe he is right, sir. A little wine would be good for the men."

Crispin smiled at him. "Thurston, go and bring several decanters of that choice vintage we brought from France."

"Does His Lordship mean the wine from the cellar of the King of France?" Thurston inquired.

"King of France," Grip repeated, hopping up and down. "King of France, forty-two, pull the daisy."

"Of course. Nothing is too good for our neighbor and his friends."

Basil blocked the threshold, stopping Thurston's departure. "Sheriff, I urge you to reconsider," he said vehemently. "It has not even gone half six in the morning. Besides, the wine may be drugged. It could be poisoned. And I am certain that we will not be forced to inspect the whole house. We shall find the girl shortly. If we were not close, why would he offer such a diversion?"

The sheriff hesitated, and Crispin stepped in. "I offered only because I was going to have some wine myself."

"Aw, sir, I am feeling a bit parched o' the throat," a stocky member of the search party told the sheriff. "An' I always like a bit o' something before I work."

"Have some wine, pull the daisy," Grip rasped in support.

But this encouragement was gratuitous, for Crispin could read his victory on the sheriff's face. "Thurston, the Burgundy," he repeated, and this time Thurston's departure went unhindered.

To Crispin's disappointment, however, his interruption did not lure the searchers from their work. Before his eyes, they carefully unhooked the clasps around one of the panels below his bookshelves and used the ax to pry the panel off. Crispin was wishing that Thurston were back with the wine already as the panel pulled away to reveal an opening. He was not even swallowing, let alone breathing, when the beady-eyed man took a lit candle and inserted both it and his head into the opening.

He exclaimed something that sounded to Crispin like, "I'm an asses mother," and pulled his head out of the opening. His face was white and his eyes, though still beady, were opened so far they looked almost normal.

"What is it?" Basil was there, beside him. "Did you find her?"

The beady-eyed man moved his head first right, then left, and Crispin wanted to kiss him. The man gulped, reached his hand in, and brought it out. "I found this." The light of the candle sent prisms of color around the room as it was caught in the facets of the ruby bracelet the man was holding up. "And that's not all." He reached in again and pulled out a gold cord with eight thumbnail-sized emeralds dangling from it, a choker set with two dozen diamonds, and a pair of matching earrings.

Basil shot a look of sheer malice at Crispin, who had thrown himself into a chair and was chortling audibly next to the raven, who was dancing a jig and repeating, "Get the ax, forty-two, pull the daisy," over and over again.

"Do you think to toy with us, Lord Sandal?" Basil's bulging eyes flashed. "Do you think we are playing at something here?"

"No, my friend." Crispin felt cordial. "Nothing of the kind. It is merely that I have been looking all over for the family jewels and could not think where I had left them. They must have slipped back behind a book."

Crispin had never before seen the objects being displayed, was certain that they did not number among the famed Foscari family jewels, nor had he known of the secret compartment under his bookshelves. He was laughing for each of those reasons, as well as the expression on Basil's face, but they were not what made his laugh so resonant. Although all of that was amusing, what was more than amusing was the relief that swept over him when he saw that while they had uncovered a treasure trove, his *tesoro* was still safely hidden.

He played the unconcerned, jovial host. "I cannot thank you enough for recovering my precious objects. This really does call for some wine."

Thurston appeared then and began pouring and distributing beakers of the King of France's finest vintage to the searchers, even giving a small sip to the raven. Basil would not let them bring the cups to their lips until Crispin and his bird had each taken a swallow, but soon the sound of containers being greedily emptied could be heard. Crispin gestured to Thurston to refill the glasses, but Basil intervened, earning him little gratitude from Crispin and even less from his men.

Crispin's wine caper had bought him a moment's respite, but in the end the search continued unimpeded. He tried again to intoxicate the men when it was discovered that his armoire had a false floor, but a sign from Thurston told him he need not waste any more of his remaining barrel of France's finest, and nothing but an old shoe buckle was found.

They had just finished probing the last of the crevices of Crispin's half-ruined apartment—including, at Basil's order, a thorough dismantling of the burnt-out hulk of Crispin's bed—and were making ready to extend the search to the other forty-odd chambers of Sandal Hall, when one of the searchers whistled out. He was in the privy off the library, studiously studying something on the floor.

Crispin rushed over to him, breathing down his neck, straining to see, but there was nothing there. Or so he thought until he looked at the man's hand.

One ruby red hair shimmered between the man's stubby fingers. One glorious, precious hair, a jewel in an unsuitable setting. Crispin's first impulse was to eat it, thus disposing of the evidence, but Thurston's voice intervened.

"This is an embarrassment, Your Lordship," the steward said, hanging his head. "I should be checking on the staff more closely. Clearly that redheaded chambermaid lost it when she was cleaning the privy. I am very sorry, my lord."

"You say this belongs to one of the staff?" The sheriff was asking Thurston, but he looked at Crispin.

"Yes." Crispin coughed. "That is quite right."

"I would very much like to see this maid." Basil used the same tone he might have used if a child had told him there were three pink unicorns in his garden. He smiled his oily smile. "Please have her sent up. Unless she is mysteriously unavailable."

"Certainly." Crispin nodded heartily. "Thurston, bring the girl who cleaned the privy. The one with the red hair. And do not dawdle."

Crispin had no idea if he had any servants with red hair, could scarcely remember if he had any servants at all, so tightly was his mind gripped with anxiety. He knew that according to the Queen's law, if they did not find any evidence of Sophie's presence, they could merely search his house, but then would have to leave. If they found out that the hair belonged to Sophie, however, if they found any evidence at all of her presence at Sandal Hall, they could occupy his house for days, weeks even, dismantle it brick by brick, to find her. Sophie's only hope, his only hope, was to convince them that it was not her hair, that it belonged to someone else.

As the minutes mounted into almost half an hour, Crispin grew more anxious and Basil more smug. The searchers had ample time to complete their reinspection of Crispin's privy closet, without finding another telltale red hair, as well as finish with Crispin's apartment entirely, and had set about removing all forty paintings of famous Sandal ancestors from the walls of the long gallery, before Thurston reappeared accompanied by a tall, dark-eyed woman. Crispin recognized her at once as one of the women he had helped free from prison three days earlier. What Crispin had not noticed then, had been too preoccupied to pay attention to, was that she had long reddish brown hair.

"Here is the maid." Thurston led the woman forward. "She is called Helena."

Basil took one look at her and blanched. "But—" he began and cut himself off.

"Is something wrong, Basil?" Crispin was all solicitousness. "You look peaked."

Basil was not meeting his eyes because he was staring at Helena, who was staring back at him impassively.

"Do you two know each other?" Crispin asked upon observing this.

"No." Basil's answer was positive. "But I see that she does indeed have red hair. It must be hers that was found in the privy. Men, continue your search."

"Don't you want to compare the hairs, sir?" the sheriff asked.

"That will not be necessary. Back to work, all of you." Basil waved his arms around. "Sound the walls to make sure there are no hidden compartments. Leave nothing untried. I know she is here. I can feel her."

Crispin, who had learned years earlier not to be astonished by anything his steward did, was astonished. When the men had returned to work and Helena had disappeared through one of the serving doors, he led Thurston to a corner and demanded, "How did you do that?"

Thurston cleared his throat. "I happened to know that Miss Helena had the misfortune to come upon Lord Grosgrain the younger in the arbor that connects Hen House and Grosgrain Place yesterday."

"He did not harm her in any way, did he?" Crispin asked, his face becoming dark.

"No, my lord. But he was naked. And reading odes to beauty, sir. Of his own composition."

"Basil? Naked? Reciting poetry?"

"Yes, sir. To a cat, sir. Wearing the sapphire tiara you gave his stepmother two and a half years ago." Thurston sounded as if he were apologizing for having to mention such things. "As you can imagine, Basil was not overcome with delight to have been so discovered. And I merely surmised that presented with a choice between having his unfortunate behavior revealed to the sheriff and yourself or dismissing the evidence of the hair, he would select the latter."

Crispin, who was trying simultaneously to picture a cat in a tiara while avoiding picturing Basil naked, took a moment to respond. "Absolutely marvelous," he said finally. "That was utterly, simply, incredibly marvelous. Comple—"

Crispin would have continued his torrent of laudatory adverbs if a whoop from the other end of the long gallery had not stopped him. It had been emitted by the stout searcher, the one who would never get another opportunity to quaff the King of France's wine if Crispin had anything to say about it.

"I think we have it this time!" The stout searcher called out to his colleagues. "I found a secret door!"

Crispin wheeled to look at Thurston, to take solace in his always calm, always reassuring presence, but instead of being by his side, his steward was rushing toward the yelling man, with Unseemly Haste and a frown crinkling his brow.

Chapter Nineteen

It was a false alarm.

The door in the long gallery turned out to lead to a forgotten storehouse, filled with the toys and games that had been confiscated from Crispin and his brother, Ian, by The Aunts when they misbehaved. He saw their set of bones, and tennis rackets, a shovelboard stick, and, best of all, the checkers that Crispin had received from his grandfather Benton Walsingham for his tenth birthday.

Crispin had still had energy, at that point, to run his hands over the games and smile at the memories they evoked, smile at the prospect of teaching his niece, Tullia, to play with them when she was old enough, smile at the unnecessary perturbation the discovery of a heretofore unknown room had caused the imperturbable Thurston. He had still had time and room in his mind to think such idle thoughts, because he had not yet begun to worry about Sophie, worry first about her running out of candles if the search went on much longer, then about her starving, then about her being found.

Two other false alarms revealed more compartments with jewels—more emeralds, rubies, sapphires, and diamonds than Crispin had ever dreamt of possessing, not to mention the pearl tiara or the aquamarine doublet clasps. Even then he had still had enough energy to indulge in the savory image of Sophie draped in the gems, outshining their luster with her own. But by the time the last door had been found, the one that led to a long tunnel with four cells off it, ending in a large, round, chamber beneath his garden, Crispin had to admit that he was tired. And anxious.

At the beginning of the search, Crispin had not actually been concerned that it would uncover its object. Sophie was well hidden, Thurston had seen to that. But as the time wore on, as minutes turned to hours and hours to half a day, as the thoroughness of the searchers continued to turn up hidden compartments and rooms, his concern grew. Could she possibly be *that* well hidden?

When the nagging of this thought managed to suck the pleasure even out of tormenting Basil about his lousy alibi, Crispin knew he had to do something. Part of him thought it would be better to get away from Sandal Hall, to take a walk, to pay another visit to Lawrence, to do anything but pace back and forth as the walls, floors, moldings, and furnishings of his house were dismantled. But he could not bring himself to leave. If Sophie was going to be found, if she was going to go back to prison, he wanted to be there.

It was not her going back to prison that concerned him the most, although that would be unpleasant. It was what could be waiting for her there. The warrant that Basil had shown him was authentic, but it was also suspicious. To begin with, it was not the normal warrant that would be issued to find an escaped criminal. In addition, Crispin knew that it was no easy task to get a warrant to search a nobleman's house, particularly one as wealthy as he was. It certainly would have taken more than the anonymous tips Basil alluded to. It would have required influence, significant influence inside the Queen's Privy Council. And perseverance.

Whoever was the real impetus behind the warrant had to be both powerful and powerfully taken with the idea of finding Sophie Champion. Not in the interest of justice, but for some other reason. And Crispin did not like that thought at all.

Nor, if he was being especially honest, did he like the thought of not spending the night with her that night. Or of not hearing what it was she was going to say before Thurston had interrupted them on the bank of the Thames.

Crispin was startled when a shout from the adjacent room signaled the discovery of some new hollow panel or other, but his heart stopped racing as soon as he saw that it was just more jewels. He decided to forgo the extraordinary thrill of watching the rest of the search for the much more mundane pleasure of digging in his garden and was just heading to his apartment to change when a brisk voice called out to him.

"Nephew," Lady Priscilla chirped, beckoning him into The Aunt's sitting room. "We have drawn up a list of candidates to be your wife, and we want to go over them with you. Now."

"I cannot thank you enough, but just at the moment I have an appointment," Crispin improvised.

"No appointment is as important as settling this question of your marriage," Lady Eleanor informed him, pointing him into a stern-looking straight-backed chair. "Now, sit down and we shall describe the girls to you, and you will pick one. Who is first, sister?"

"Althea Bordine," Lady Priscilla read out from a pile of papers in front of her as soon as Crispin was seated. "A very good family, the Bordines, from Hertfordshire. Althea eats only cabbage."

"Eats only cabbage?" Crispin repeated, shifting in the narrow seat.

"Yes. She says that our modern diet, with so many ingredients, ruins the palate and corrupts the digestion," Lady Priscilla explained. "Think how salubrious that will be for your children."

"Not to mention economical," Lady Eleanor added. "Your father, our brother, dear Hugo, was a great one for economy." She paused to sigh in the great man's memory. "Who is next, sister?"

"Anconia Rasher-Rasher, of the Rasher-Rasher's of Norfolk. Your father, dear Hugo, went to school with her father," Lady Priscilla told Crispin.

Crispin looked grim. "What does she eat?"

"Oh, Anconia eats everything. But she will live only in a gray house. That is, a house in which all the furnishings are gray. She believes color dulls the senses and blocks the path to spiritual salvation."

"She is a terribly spiritual person," Lady Eleanor went on before Crispin could express his dismay. "It is said that she regularly communes with Archangel Michael. That sort of spiritual upbringing would be wonderful for your children."

"Wonderful," Crispin muttered. He could have sworn his chair was getting more narrow.

"Do you like her, nephew?" Lady Priscilla asked enthusiastically. "Shall we stop, then? Is she your selection?"

"No." Crispin was surprised to note that he almost shouted the word. He tried to shift in his seat but found that he was stuck. "No, pray go on," he said, gesturing awkwardly. "You went to such effort, I should really hear them all."

"Very well." Lady Priscilla consulted the list for the next name. "Appollonia Saint Alderghiest."

"Saint Alderghiest." Crispin experimented with crossing one ankle over the other and decided against it. "Is she another spiritualist?"

Lady Eleanor shook her head indulgently. "No, no. If anything, she is a bit of a rebel."

"Yes," Lady Priscilla picked up. "She will not touch water."

"Do you mean she does not know how to swim?" Crispin asked.

"No," Lady Priscilla went on. "She won't take a drop of water. Not to drink. Or to bathe in. She does not believe in it. She has not bathed in, oh, how long would you say, sister?"

"I believe she said twelve years. Ever since she was out of swaddling."

Crispin's genuine interest in this incomprehensible behavior, as well as his very real fear that The Aunts had contrived to hold him hostage by pinning him to his chair, were both suddenly overtaken by a chilling realization.

"How have you organized this list?" Crispin asked, trying to sound casual.

"Alphabetically, of course," Lady Priscilla replied. "Your father, our brother, dear Hugo, always said that was the only way to organize a list."

"Alphabetically by first name," Lady Eleanor expanded.

"Alphabetically by first name," Crispin repeated, thinking that those were the four most terrifying words in the English language. "And we have reached 'Appollonia.' How many names are on the list, would you say, dearest aunt?"

Lady Priscilla did not answer right away. Instead, she shuffled through a tall sheaf of papers on the table in front of her, her lips moving as she counted the names down. This had gone on for a long time, an ominously long time, when she looked up. "I lost count for a moment, but I should say not more than one hundred."

"One hundred." Crispin pronounced each syllable carefully.

"Shall we continue?" Lady Eleanor asked, then frowned. "Nephew, why are you sitting like that?"

Lady Priscilla, not wanting to miss an opportunity to improve Crispin, joined in. "Yes, why are you slouching? Your father, our brother, dear Hugo, never slouched. 'Posture makes the man,' he always used to say. Now, going on to Arianne Corner-Bludstone—"

Crispin did not wait to hear more. He rose abruptly from the chair, almost taking one of its arms with him, executed a quick bow to both Aunts, spluttered something about not feeling well, and was out of the room before they could comment or even realize what had happened.

He stalked down the hallway like a madman, greedily drinking in the air of freedom, and almost ran over Basil and the sheriff as he rounded the corner to his apartment.

"There you are," Basil pronounced, pulling back as if from a venomous snake.

Basil's discomfort restored a large part of Crispin's good humor in a flash. "What can I do for you gentlemen?" he asked convivially.

"I have just come to say, Lord Sandal, that we have finished."

"Must you go so soon?" Crispin shook his head. "Pity, it is nearly time for dinner and my cook really is superb. Tell me, did you find her?"

"Not this time." Basil tried to make the words sound threatening.

"Does that mean I can count on a return visit from you tomorrow?" Crispin asked hopefully. "If this is to be a regular thing, I will have to restock my cellar."

"Where have you hidden her?" Basil demanded.

"My dear neighbor," Crispin said, jocularly, "I assure you that I have not hidden Sophie Champion anywhere. I have no more secrets from you than you do from me."

Basil tried to look menacing and ignore Crispin's last comment simultaneously. "I will be back," he said, clenching a fist. "I will be back with another warrant, I promise you that."

"And I shall look forward to it. It is a joy to see a gentleman take such undisguised—one might even say naked—pride in his patriotic duty," Crispin commended him. "Indeed, if you were any more eager to get Sophie Champion arrested, I would think you had murdered Richard Tottle yourself and were trying desperately to pin it on her."

Crispin had spoken his parting words to the man's back, but Basil now swung around to face him. "What did you say, my lord?"

"Nothing." Crispin smiled widely. "Just a little banter between neighbors. Good day, Lord Grosgrain."

Basil stood, quivering for a moment, then turned and stomped down the stairs and out of Sandal Hall in the company of the sheriff. The searchers followed, and Crispin had a broad, fake smile for each of them, especially the beady-eyed one. When they had all gone, when the front door was closed and bolted, Crispin turned and hollered, "Thurston!"

There was no answer.

"Thurston," he called again.

Nothing.

This was bad. "Thurston, man, where the devil are you?"

"I believe he said he was going for a walk with a lady, my lord," a timid serving boy told Crispin.

"A walk?" Thurston never went for a walk. "Why? Where? When?"

"I do not know, my lord. Not long ago, my lord. I am very sorry, my lord."

Crispin prided himself on being terrifying to his enemies, but not to fifteen-year-old serving boys. "Thank you," he said politely, taking himself in hand. "You have done very well, and you need not apologize."

"Thank you, my lord. I am sorry, my lord," the boy repeated, simultaneously bowing and running down the hall.

Crispin cursed under his breath as he crossed the threshold into his library. Thurston was the only person who knew where Sophie was hidden, the only person who knew how to bring her back, and now he had disappeared. Gone for a walk? Idiocy! What if something happened to him? Crispin wondered with alarm. What if he got run over by a carriage, or trampled by a horse, and never came back, and Sophie wasted away from hunger? It probably would not take her long, she was most likely wasting away already, and if Thurston delayed any longer...

Crispin's mind spun round and round ridiculous hypotheses of the terrible harm that might at that very moment be befalling Thurston, while Grip chattered by his side. "King of France," the bird called out. "Get the ax, King of France, forty-two, pull the daisy, King of France, get the girl."

Still devising terrible ends for Thurston, Crispin toyed idly with the items on his desk. There were quills, papers, a statue, a book about plants, and a short dagger some aged relative had given him when he was ten, which he now used to open correspondence. The desk had been his father's, along with the statue, and he had not bothered to change or move either of them when he inherited the library. It was not that he was sentimental in any way about his father's possessions, or even about his father. "Dear Hugo" had always been much more of a mythic construction propagated by The Aunts than a real figure in Crispin's life. Not only did he seem so perfect as to be unapproachable, but he had also been too busy to pay any attention to his sons. Crispin's most frequent memories of his father were of discovering him in one of the pavilions on the family estate in the country, completely lost in the buxom embraces of a wildly moaning chambermaid.

"Get the girl, King of France, pull the daisy," the raven chirped.

When he had inherited that estate, Crispin had picked up where his father had left off with the chambermaids, proud that at least he could emulate the great man in something. But his father must have heard something in those moans, found something in those buxom embraces, that Crispin did not. Those affairs, those years of affairs, had left him unfulfilled. Crispin had wondered about "dear Hugo" after that, about the man who could be content with such passing pleasures, and had even asked himself if perhaps it was not a deficiency on his part that he could not be.

Grip hopped up and down. "Bring the ax, King of France, forty-two," he chorused.

Crispin had sold that estate before leaving England two and a half years earlier and had sold off most of his father's furnishings at Sandal Hall, but he had kept the library desk because it was commodious. And the statue that stood on the corner, because it was there. He looked at the statue now, almost as if he were seeing it for the first time, and was struck by how very ugly it was.

What could his father possibly have seen in the bronze casting of a lass, naked but for a ridiculous bonnet, standing in the midst of three very unrealistic looking sheep? The whole menagerie was mounted on a hillock, at the base of which was a garland of flowers. Crispin could not imagine what his father was doing with such an item and was on the verge of removing it once and for all from the library when a voice behind him said, "Pull the daisy get the girl."

Crispin turned slowly to look at the raven and could have sworn it winked at him. Then he turned slowly back, pulled the only flower that matched the description "daisy" on the base of the statue, and watched without surprise as a panel in the side of his father's desk slid open.

"Hello?" he called into the darkness behind the panel. "Hello, is there someone down there?"

The sound of absolute silence greeted him. Followed by more silence. Followed by a distant flickering of light. Followed by the emergence of four fingertips from the hole. And then another four.

And then two thumbs. And then, after a bit of grunting, the face he most wanted to see in the world.

"Are they gone?" Crispin only had time to nod before Sophie went on. "So nice of you to ask. No, nothing big, just a snack. Let's see, perhaps two pheasants? Oh, and a whole cow. And a pig. And a lamb. And six sticky puddings."

"Are you sure that will be enough?"

"For me. You should bring some for yourself, as well. And then come down here. I have a marvel to show you."

Crispin was backing up to execute her orders when she called out to him, "Wait. There is something I forgot."

"What?" He bent down to hear better.

Sophie stood on her toes to kiss him. "Oh, Crispin," she breathed against his lips, "I missed you so much."

"I missed you too, *tesoro.*"

She brushed her mouth over his lightly. "I love you, Crispin," she told him. And then, not waiting to hear the words she knew would not come, she rushed on. "Now go, hurry, get the food before I die of hunger and wanting you."

Crispin ransacked the kitchen, taking every mobile piece of food he could find until the cook threatened to chase him out. It was a motley feast he assembled, but he had neither the time nor the inclination to wait while the whole pig, lamb, goat, goose, sheep, and whatever else Sophie had requested were prepared. He nearly ran into The Aunts, who seemed to be in search of him, but a well-timed duck into a service corridor he had not known was there before saved him. He peeped out to ensure that the way was clear, then emerged stealthily.

Before he had taken more than three steps, a discreet clearing of the throat echoed behind him.

"Good afternoon, my lord," Thurston said, as if there were nothing in the least bit unusual about his master creeping around with all the food and half the plates in the house. "I know you were looking for me while I was walking Miss Helena back to Hen House, my lord, and I wanted to tell you that I am returned and that this arriv—"

"Not now, Thurston," Crispin said urgently. "I have an appointment."

"I can see that, my lord. But—"

"No," Crispin said positively, continuing down the corridor. "I am busy."

"I understand, my lord, however—"

Using his elbow, Crispin shut the door of his library in his steward's face. He had never before been so rude to Thurston, and he would pay for not stopping to listen, pay for it dearly, later. But at the time no message could have been nearly as important, no missive as urgent, as his need to be with Sophie.

He set the tray on the floor under the desk and whispered her name. At first nothing happened, but soon a candle flickered into view and her smile floated above it. "Food?" she asked.

"Food," Crispin confirmed. A decanter of wine was handed through the panel, followed by a braised leg of lamb, a plate of sautéed sorrel, half a steak pie, a tureen of something green, six pork chops topped with walnut sauce, two capons roasted until golden, rice with almonds and cinnamon, three oddly shaped melons, a plate of cold asparagus, cherries, trout in brine, six candles, two spoons, a knife made out of sugar left over from last Easter, a loaf of bread, a tray to carry it all on, and Crispin. His legs went first, guided by Sophie's hands, which not accidentally strayed over his thighs when he was only halfway through. He wanted to protest as he felt her fingers unhooking the lacings of his breeches, but he could not find the breath. He should stop her, he thought to himself, he should not allow her to do this. He opened his mouth, but his cry of "halt" turned into something closer to "*Alaaahhhh*" when her lips touched his shaft. All thoughts of opposition, along with all thoughts of breathing, left him then, and he gave himself up to the sheer pleasure of her touch.

He could feel her, her hands moving up and down his length, her mouth encasing him with its warmth and then pulling away, but with his head still outside the desk he could not see her. He had never had an experience like this, never had half his body suspended in a sensual dream, and it sharpened his senses. He closed his eyes and let his form fill with the feeling of her caresses, not separating them into mouths and tongues and teeth and fingers and hands, just letting them wash into him and around him. He felt himself sliding between her lips, into the marvelously smooth and tight passage of her mouth, her cheeks sucked in around him as she pulled him into her. She swallowed, pressing him against the roof of her mouth with her tongue, then let him slide in and out as her hands caressed the length of his shaft.

The tension of the day turned to a different sort of tension within Crispin as her hands, both hands, moved over his slick, wet member. She sucked hard at his tip as she pushed her mouth over him, and then let her fingers reach out and stroke the base of his shaft. That touch tingled over him, sending all his emotion, all his tension, exploding and shimmering into her. Not knowing what she was doing, what he was doing, he panted and moaned and trembled and tightened his muscles and poured himself into her mouth. She pressed her lips against him and savored his climax, imbibing every glorious drop, every sweet shudder of his release, every sign of his response to her.

When she moved her mouth away, the remainder of Crispin's limp body slid through the opening under the desk. He staggered as his feet hit the floor, and would have fallen if Sophie's smile had not helped him stand. She was wearing nothing but the red-and-gold silk dressing gown he had given her the first night he made her strip, and was standing in a small puddle of light being given off by a lantern.

"I am sorry, my lord," she said, with even less contrition than Basil had shown that morning when issuing the warrant. "I could not stop myself."

"And I certainly could not stop you." Crispin move toward her and bent to kiss her red lips, then her eyelids. "I had no idea my father's old desk could be so exciting."

"You have not yet seen the half of it." Sophie pulled away to show him but was distracted by the sight of Crispin's lower torso in

the half-light. She sighed, then dragged her mind back to the exciting news she had for him. "If you put your bottoms back on so I
can think straight, I will show you something amazing." When he
hesitated, her voice became plaintive. "Please, Crispin, it is a wonderful surprise."

"If you are sure." Following her orders, Crispin pulled his breeches
up. When he had securely retied each lace and retrieved the tray of
food, Sophie reached for his arm. She lifted the lantern from the
table next to her and held it above her head.

They and the table were standing on a small wooden platform,
Crispin saw, with wooden stairs leading off one side and down into
the darkness.

"I found the opening under the desk the other morning and told
Thurston how to open it by pulling the daisy," Sophie explained to
Crispin as she led him down the stairs. "It seemed the perfect place
to hide because the desk did not look big enough to conceal a person and the panels underneath would be expected to sound hollow
if they were tried."

"Do you think this hiding place was made on purpose?" Crispin
felt a strange sense of foreboding as he descended and thought he
heard his father's voice telling him to go back.

"Oh, yes," Sophie assured him, stopping their descent. "Just wait."

Sophie had used the secret door under the desk the day she
undertook her escape and return to Sandal Hall, and had that day
noticed the door cut into the wall of the passage, but she had been
too preoccupied with trying to come up with reasons not to leave
that did not involve wanting to see the Earl of Sandal again to
bother exploring it. Today, however, in the long hours that followed
Thurston's closing the secret panel in the desk, she had returned to
the mysterious door and been well rewarded for her curiosity.

She now knew every horizontal, every diagonal, every dimen-
sion of the secret chamber, having traversed them all a hundred
times as she waited for the search to be over. Her feet had barely
kept pace with her thoughts, but they both seemed to come across
immobile obstacles with some regularity. The most insurmountable

of these, besides the walls of the chamber, was Sophie's inability to believe that her godfather had been a counterfeiter. And yet, she had to admit that it made so many things—the blackmail, Lord Grosgrain's recent battery of huge expenditures, his fear of the Phoenix—clear. But if he were being blackmailed because of the counterfeiting, why was he killed? Did it not make more sense to kill the blackmailer?

As indeed, she reminded herself, someone had or at least had killed the blackmailer's agent in the person of Richard Tottle. And if the evidence of the bill of credit and the pistol planted on the dead man's body was to be believed, the same person committed both murders. Sophie had bashed her toe into a wall then, hard, and her thoughts had come crashing to a halt. When they resumed, she had the glimmer of an idea, the idea that perhaps it was not Lord Grosgrain who was being blackmailed but someone close to him, someone for whom he would pay the blackmail willingly, someone who wanted to stop the blackmail by killing Richard Tottle and was forced to kill Lord Grosgrain as well or risk raising his suspicions. Sophie recalled the morning she had gone to deliver the bill of credit to Lord Grosgrain, remembered the raised voices she had heard from his study, and the red face of Basil as he stomped by her out of the house, clearly unhappy after a meeting with his father. Could it have been Basil who was being blackmailed, Basil who—?

Sophie hit another wall then, both literally with her toe and figuratively with the idea of Basil as a killer. She just could not see it—neither Basil as a murderer nor the wall. She realized then, with some shock, that her candle had burned out long before and she had spent the better part of two hours alone, in the dark. Without being afraid.

Crispin. Crispin had done this. Crispin had freed her from the fears of her past. Crispin had given her back herself. She realized with a start that she was no longer scared at all. Not of the dark. Or of the voice.

She felt liberated and strong. And very, very grateful. Try as she might to redirect her thoughts toward Lord Grosgrain's murder, they kept spinning back to Crispin and the magic he worked on her. Mercifully, Crispin's voice calling to her had penetrated the darkness of the chamber then, because her longing to see him and tell him and thank him was hard to contain. She was filled with miraculous feelings that warmed even her much battered toes, and with a wonderful sense of expectation. She, too, could teach him something about himself he did not know.

Her excited anticipation of the surprise she had for him had been building and came to a peak now as, hand in hand, she and Crispin arrived at the bottom of the stairs. Sophie led the way across the narrow corridor and through a door, holding her lantern low, so that Crispin could at first see nothing of the chamber around them.

He had never been here, never even suspected the existence of a secret room under his father's desk. But his surprise at finding it was nothing compared to the surprise he received when Sophie raised the lantern above her head.

"Blasted Aunts!" he said, his eyes agog. It was a small, square room with its walls completely covered in mirrors. Each mirrored surface was lined with six velvet-covered shelves. And each shelf was empty but for the eight or ten enormous pieces of jewelry arrayed on them. The jewels were arranged by color, rubies with rubies, emeralds with emeralds, sapphires together with sapphires, pearls with pearls, all carefully displayed. There were earrings and rings, scepters and sword hilts, bracelets and belts and buckles and broaches, crowns and chokers, clasps and collars—every conceivable shape and size and kind of ornament so long as it was encrusted with gems.

"You are rich," Sophie trilled relieving him of the tray of food. "You are also the son of a jewel thief."

Crispin's eyes became more agog. "No." He was shaking his head in disbelief. "It is not possible."

"Look." Sophie held up a sheaf of manuscript pages. "I found these down here. A meticulous catalog of the 'collection' of Hugo, Earl of Sandal, stating the date and manner of each acquisition,

though keeping its provenance vague. Many of them are quite ingenious. My favorite is June thirteenth, fifteen hundred and sixty seven,
when he made love to Countess V—— while prying her rings out
from under the floorboards."

Crispin took the pages from her and moved into the light of the
lamp. He passed his eyes over them quickly, skimming the out-
landish exploits, matching the objects described there to those along
the walls, noting in passing that it was not organized alphabetically.

"There are some missing," Sophie informed him as he got near
the end. "Some that he describes are not here. I think you should
demand their recovery. I for one would love to see the ruby bracelet
he removed from the arm of Queen E—— herself while pleasuring
her under the table at a state dinner."

"I'll show it to you when we go back out," Crispin said nonchalantly.

"You mean you knew about this?"

"No." Crispin shook his head. "And I can still hardly believe it.
But among the dozen or so secrets that my house has been keeping
from me which were revealed today, were four caches of jewels.
Nothing like this"—Crispin gestured around—"but each containing a few, worthy pieces, including that bracelet."

Crispin put the manuscript down and cast his eyes around again.
Then he began to laugh. No wonder he had begun hearing his
father's voice as they descended. The man was probably haunting
the place desperate to ensure that his secret not be found out. Dear
Hugo, perfect, polite Hugo, Hugo to whom no door had been closed,
nor any pair of soft peachy thighs, Hugo whom everyone adored,
Hugo that spouter of wise adages, Hugo that model of gentlemanly
comportment, Hugo—his father, the man he would never be—had
been a jewel thief. What could possibly be better?

And what would The Aunts say? As Crispin had that thought,
the voices in his head began to jangle more loudly, warning Crispin
to leave, berating him for probing secrets that were not his, for risking the family honor. In a flash Crispin saw that his father had
been as subjugated by The Aunts as he was, that "your father, our

brother, dear Hugo," had been routed just as much, if not more than, his son. The horrible statue on Hugo's desk had been the means of his escape, his relief.

His fulfillment. Feeling a new affection for his father, and also a new pity, Crispin opened his arms wide and addressed the room.

"Do not worry, Father," he said aloud. "I won't tell The Aunts." And as if by magic, his thoughts fell silent.

At peace again, Crispin turned to look at Sophie, but her back was to him. After inhaling half the asparagus and all the cherries, she had blown the dust off a ruby tiara and was settling it atop her red mane. As Crispin watched, she hooked a pair of dangling ruby earrings through her ears and clasped a matching choker behind her neck. Then she let the red-and-gold silk robe slip from her shoulders and turned to face him, completely naked.

She was a goddess, an empress, a divinity come to earth, a siren, a sorceress, she was incredible and inexplicably beautiful. Crispin wanted to touch her, just let his fingers move near her skin, to assure himself that she was real, that she was there. She defied Crispin's imagination, defied his capacity to understand or believe. Awash with rubies, she glittered and shone from every angle, stirring his deepest depths.

Crispin's eyes glowed as he approached her, glowed with awe and wonder. They touched, still at a distance, then moved closer to one another, then closer. With each step Crispin shed another layer of his clothing, so that finally there was nothing between them but their skin. They pressed against the length of one another, pressing together, their eyes locked. Food was completely forgotten.

Crispin spread the silk robe over the wooden floor, and they lay atop it, Sophie on her back, Crispin alongside her. Reaching out a hand he found a ruby necklace, two large stones on a fine gold chain, and dangled it over Sophie's body. He moved the rubies like a pendulum over her breasts, then down her stomach, into the cleft between her legs.

The red stones rested amid the red curls there until he gently pushed them down further. Sophie arched up as her aroused nub was deliciously sandwiched between the gems, and moaned as the gold chain followed them. Crispin carefully made the chain taut and pulled it back and forth on either side of her nub and below, rubbing it over the soft petals there, letting the rubies press into her, framing her tender place like a jewel in a golden setting. He shifted slightly so she could see into the mirrors alongside and behind them, so she could watch his fingers, watch the gems, watch herself in her pleasure.

The feel of the gemstone between her legs, inside her, while the chain played over her nub made Sophie begin to tremble, but it was when she saw and felt Crispin add the pressure of his finger to the chain that she neared her threshold. She called out his name as he moved his fingers faster, moaned it out as he pressed the gemstones into her, and breathed it out as he followed the stones with a finger, slipping it smoothly between her wet folds. In the mirror Sophie could see his fingers working over her, dancing over her, the rubies appearing and disappearing between the wet folds of her body. She saw him push her nub with his thumb while sliding his middle finger into her, saw him lower his head over her slowly, saw his tongue, pointed, teasing her, watched it dart between the folds, following the rubies, looked at his golden head between her legs as he suckled her, then watched him rub her with four fingertips, and she exploded. Her climax crashed over his fingers, pulsing and throbbing around him, around the rubies, and her laughter whistled in his ears.

It had not died down when she reached her hand out for his shaft. She needed to feel him inside of her, feel their bodies together. "Crispin, make love to me."

The words sounded different, tasted different, as Crispin kissed them off her lips, ambrosial words. He slid the ruby necklace from between their bodies, from between her legs, and felt Sophie shudder. Her cherry-flavored lips trembled under his as they kissed lightly, once, twice, once again. Their mouths parted then, gone exploring, moving across smooth skin, over soft hair, along necks, finding each other briefly and then separating to go on their individual expeditions joined by tongues, teeth, hands, feet. They drank each other in, savoring tastes and textures and smells, lapping at one another's delicacies. Soon their bodies were pressuring them for more, to deepen the kiss, complete it.

Crispin rolled onto his back and bent his knees to make a throne for Sophie as she raised herself and guided him inside her passage, still tight and wet from her climax. She leaned back against his legs, aware of every place his thighs touched her back, of the way her bottom pressed into them, while his member pressed into her. For a time neither of them moved or spoke or breathed, too busy memorizing the feel of their bodies together, of this new kiss, too busy looking into one another's eyes. Never letting Crispin slip from inside her, Sophie lay down on top of him.

Their mouths touched, lips pressed against lips, and Sophie felt Crispin bucking within her of his own accord. It was then that the kiss changed, became more insistent, more fiery. Sophie began to rotate her hips in slow wide circles, letting him slide in and out of her as she danced around him. She straightened her arms and pushed her body up over him, lifting her mouth from his so her breasts could caress his chest with her movements, and her eyes could whisper her desires to him.

His eyes stayed on hers as he raised his head and took one soft pink nipple between his lips. He just barely touched it, then moved to the other, letting his lips, chapped from kissing, taste each first, fleetingly. Chapped lips parted then, sucking the softest, supplest skin on her body into his mouth, letting her nipples feel the warm wetness of his tongue. He rolled first one and then the other around in his mouth until they became firm and erect, until she moaned once, then again, louder.

Sophie felt his lips on her nipples everywhere. Every pull of his mouth, every skim of his teeth, spiraled through her body, bouncing off first one place then another, leaving points of heat and tenderness in its wake. When she moved to let him slide out of her, her bottom was caressed by his thighs. When she arched to take him back in, her hips grazed his, her breasts skimmed over his chest. Her feet touched his feet, wrapped around their ankles, were raised by them so she could take him in farther. Soon every part of her skin was alight, sensitive to the merest caress of his lips, responding to every thrust, every glide, every motion of their bodies.

Crispin reached his arms up and pulled her back to his chest, rubbing himself into her, covering her lips with his again. Her legs were bent on either side of him so that she could lift herself off of him, pull him far out of her and then slide back down over him, all the way to the base, pressing him into her as hard as he would go. He reached his hands down to stroke her, having learned that her climaxes were even more resonant that way, and she responded instantly, quickening her pace, breathing faster, deeper. The way the tips of Crispin's fingers brushed over her most sensitive place, the way that place felt when it was rubbed against him, when he thrust himself up to meet her, grinding himself and his hips against her, touching her with his entire body, immersing within her his entire length, made Sophie feel dizzy, alight, alive.

The light of the lantern shimmered in the thousands of gemstones that surrounded them, refracting their color and fire off the mirrors, filling the room with shards of color that moved and flickered each time they breathed. A hundred small rainbows danced over Crispin's chest, across Sophie's cheeks, along his arms, around her neck, and spilled down her back. The light slid over them, slid inside them, bathing them in its rainbow prisms, filling them with its hot power, melding them together.

Their lovemaking shined that night, rainbows danced from the places their bodies met, exploded from their fingertips, flashed from their lips, wrapped around them, and held them in their warmth. The glittering gems tumbled over them, falling from the shelves to join them, to sanctify them with their brilliant light, to give them their blessing, the blessing of a jewel thief. The stones wrapped their colors around the lovers, binding them together, glowing and ecstatic.

Sophie grasped Crispin's hand, holding on to him as tightly as she could, and Crispin felt himself soaring. She took him places he had never been, never even imagined. His body trembled with happiness at her proximity, with wonder at the immense joy she inspired within him, with ecstasy, and with a deep, overwhelming contentment that he had never experienced before. He gripped her hand and knew that he was holding on to the only thing he needed in the world to be happy.

Crispin felt limitless, superhuman, extraordinarily happy, and extraordinarily grateful. The woman next to him had given him more than he ever dared ask, more than he had known how to ask, had given him himself.

"Thank you, Sophie," he whispered, pressing their joined hands to his lips and looking directly into her eyes as together they climbed toward their release. Crispin had never felt so free, so vulnerable, so completely alive. He plunged into her and felt like he was tumbling off a cliff, floating and spinning and falling and flying at once, until he could contain himself no longer, and shouting her name and laughing and clutching her hand, he exploded into a pounding climax unlike anything he had dreamt of. Sophie's laughter mingled with his, shaking the foundation of Sandal Hall, shooting out of the chimneys, bouncing off the roof tiles, rising up to soar past the sun, past the moon, into the stars, and up and up and up.

Afterward, when their laughter had died down, they held each other solemnly, religiously, and so tenderly. Although they could not both have known that the unravelable knot they had just tied was about to be ripped crudely apart, they held each other as if they sensed its peril.

They lay together quietly, half dozing, their bodies always touching, their hands clasped, their hearts still pounding. After a time, Crispin raised his head and balanced it on one hand to watch Sophie. He dipped down, kissing her lightly on the nose, and was disappointed when she did not stir. There was something that he needed to do, and soon. But first there was something he had to ask her.

He dipped down again, this time kissing her eyelid. Still nothing.

"Sophie," he whispered. "Sophie, are you sleeping?"

Nothing.

"Sophie." He nudged at her with his body, then ran his toes up the back of her calf. "Sophie, can you hear me?"

Getting no response, he sat up.

"Sophie." He stared down at her, his face only an inch from hers. "Sophie?" He reached out a finger and poked her arm. "Sophie, are you awake?" Not even a twitch.

He drew back from her and said in his normal voice, "I know you are not sleeping. I can tell. Open your eyes. This minute. Before I count to three. One. Two. Th—"

"What happens if I don't?" Sophie asked, her eyes still closed.

"Bad things. You won't like them. Open your eyes."

Sophie wrinkled her nose, took a long, long stretch, planted a kiss on the back of Crispin's hand, then slowly raised her eyelids. "Lord Sandal, you really are a most charming companion. First you starve me. Then you will not let me sleep. Then you threaten me. I feel like I am in training to go to war against the Spanish fleet."

"I have to ask you something," Crispin said without remorse for his army-camp tactics.

"Oh, good. Now there will be an interrogation." Sophie slithered slightly to prop her head on Crispin's knee and wrapped his arm around her. She looked up at him, trying to be serious but unable to repress a smile. "I am ready, Admiral."

All at once, Crispin found that he was not. It had seemed so simple, so easy, just a few moments before when he had settled on it. But now the words seemed to have grown large and furry and terribly difficult to speak. He decided to change tactics.

"Sophie," he began. "Sophie, before—after—when at first—"

Sophie, a bemused expression on her face, sat up to face him. "Is this a riddle? Because if it is one of those complicated ones, I might need paper."

"It is not a riddle," Crispin said seriously. "And it is not a joke."

"It sounded like a joke."

"Sophie, do you mean it?"

"Not if you don't want me to. If you don't want it to be a joke, it doesn't have to be."

"That is not what I am talking about, and you know it." Crispin looked stern. "Sophie—" he began again, awkwardly.

"Yes, Crispin?"

"Did you mean it? When you said it? That—" He looked simultaneously so much like a little boy of ten and so much like a deeply pained man of eighty that Sophie took pity on him.

"Did I mean it when I said that I loved you?" she asked.

"Yes. Exactly. That is my question." Crispin spoke quickly because he was holding his breath.

Sophie reached out her free hand for his cheek. "I meant it. I mean it. Against all my better judgment, I love you, Crispin Foscari."

Crispin inhaled deeply, three times, then frowned, withdrawing his hand from her grasp. "Against your better judgment? Why? What is wrong with me?"

"Please, Crispin, it is better to leave it."

"Leave it?" The frown deepened. "I want to know."

"I really do not think—"

"Tell me," Crispin demanded with mock fierceness. "I want to know all my flaws. As *you* see them."

Sophie rolled her eyes and held up a finger. "Very well, my lord, but remember, you insisted. One. You are obstinate. Very obstinate."

"I am not."

"You are."

"Am not," Crispin maintained stubbornly.

"Two." Sophie held up a second finger. "You are bossy. Three—"

"I am not bossy. Don't say that." Crispin found he was enjoying this. "And I am not obstinate."

"Three." Sophie raised a third finger, undaunted. "You interrupt. Four. You—"

"I do not interrupt as much as you do. You interrupt much more than I do. You are always interr—"

"Four. You look better in breeches than I do. Five. You are always thinking about food. Six—"

"Will you marry me, Sophie?"

Sophie sat frozen, with both hands in the air, six fingers extended. "What?" she whispered hoarsely.

"I asked if you would marry me." It was much easier the second time.

"Marry you?" The hands fell to her lap. "Me? Be your wife?"

This was not going exactly as Crispin had hoped. "Yes," he answered slowly.

Sophie shook her head. "No. I cannot marry you."

"Oh. I see. Very well." He was cool about it.

"Don't you want to know why?"

It was Crispin's turn to shake his head. "No. No need. I understand." Crispin felt more naked than he ever had in his life. He reached out for his breeches, but Sophie's hand on his arm stopped him.

"I cannot marry you *now*. But I can, I will, after the bet."

Crispin's hand hovered over his pile of clothes. "After the bet? The bet we made?"

"Yes. Once that is settled, once I have won, then I can marry you. But not before."

"And what if you lose?" Crispin asked, his heart beating again.

"That will not happen, so you need not worry." Sophie smiled at him. But then a concerned crease appeared in her forehead. "Are you sure this is what you want, Crispin? Marriage? To me?"

"You are what I want, Sophie Champion. You are all I want."

The rumble of his voice and the look in his eyes as he spoke washed over Sophie like a magical potion, suffusing her with warmth, intoxicating her with love.

Only later did she understand what he was really doing. Only later did she see him for the bastard he really was.

Chapter Twenty

~~I killed my first woman~~ I consecrated my first sacrifice to Beauty when I was fifteen. The woman's filthy desires dishonored the gifts Beauty had given her, dishonored her comeliness and her wealth, making them wretched. She was unworthy, a blot, a cloud which cast a shadow over Beauty. I killed her for Beauty, and Beauty rewarded me, showered me in the woman's gold, more gold than I had ever seen.

But not more gold than I wanted. ~~Not enough gold. Never enough gold.~~ Not until now.

The pen stopped its progress across the parchment as the blindfolded man was led into the room. "I have been expecting you," he heard in his ear when he was seated.

He smiled, showing the gaps between his teeth. "I figured you would be when you got my note."

"Is it true? Have you identified the Phoenix?" The whisper tingled with excitement.

"It is true," the blindfolded man confirmed. "But I must have the girl. Where is she? Sandal Hall was searched and she was not found."

"Sandal Hall has many hiding places, many more than the Queen's constables would ever unearth. I am sure she is still there.

Safely ensconced between Crispin's arms. Or at least between his legs."

"Between the Phoenix's legs, you mean," the man said dryly.

The man heard a sharp intake of breath, and then, "Do you mean to say that the Earl of Sandal is the Phoenix?" When the man nodded, he received a whispered challenge. "Prove it."

The man swiveled in his chair to drop a piece of paper from his bound hands. "I intercepted this outside Sandal Hall this morning."

He heard his companion bend down, then the sound of the paper being unfolded. After a few seconds, a hand grabbed his ear and dragged it painfully forward. "I thought you understood that I was not to be toyed with. I shall have your Sophie Champion killed for this."

"I am not toying with you." The blindfolded man twisted his head away and sat back in the chair. "It is a cipher. Translated, it reads, '*To the Phoenix: counterfeiters will be moving their supplies three days hence.*' The footman had orders to deliver it directly to Lord Sandal."

Air stirred beside him as Kit, presumably in response to some signal, rounded the desk and leaned down to receive a set of hasty orders. Straining his ears, the man made out the words, "Move operations... couriers... warehouse tomorrow morning."

The blindfolded man felt air move against his cheek again and heard the door to the chamber close with a click. "I thought you might find that paper provocative," he said.

"Your thoughts interest me only so far as they concern the death of the Phoenix," he was told in a snappish whisper.

"And yours interest me only so far as they concern Sophie Champion."

"When you have destroyed the Phoenix, you shall have the girl. I give you my word."

The blindfolded man rose clumsily from the chair. "And I give you mine. The Phoenix will be dead by midday tomorrow."

Leaving the workshop, eyes uncovered again, the man did not meander lazily down the Strand as was his custom after the meetings, but rather turned into the first well-appointed tavern he came upon. He ordered a tankard of ale, took a sip, then moved toward the back of the establishment to relieve himself. Usually he stopped in six or seven taverns to make sure that the fellow who followed him from the workshop was good and drunk before giving him the slip, but today time was limited. Ensuring that his tail was absorbed in a lusty game of darts, the man leaned into an apparently solid piece of wood paneling that gave way noiselessly to reveal a flight of stairs. When he had descended these and was sure he was safely inside of Pickering's Highway, he scratched the blackening from his teeth, pulled the scar off his forehead, and shrugged out of the too-small doublet he always wore to the meetings. Only after he had completely changed his clothes and had concealed all the elements of his disguise in the basket of candles at his feet, did Crispin allow himself to sigh with relief. The masquerade had been exhausting and had taxed all his self-control, but at last it was almost over.

As he wound through one secret passage after another, he even found himself grinning. He had done what he set out to do, learned who was trying to harm Sophie and undermine the Phoenix, and why. What was more, he was forcing the counterfeiters to play their hand earlier than expected, play it on his schedule, play it so he would be waiting for them. Emerging from Pickering's Highway in the stable yard of a completely different tavern, he mounted Fortuna and turned her toward Sandal Hall. All that remained, he reflected lightheartedly, as he rode home, was to move Sophie to secure quarters and then spring his trap.

In the end, it was not quite that simple.

Chapter Twenty-One

Fortuna and her rider were only a few steps from Sandal Hall, just passing the alley in front of which Lord Grosgrain had been thrown from his horse, when a dingy man stepped into the street and grabbed Fortuna's bridle.

"You the Earl of Sandal?" he asked, shielding his eyes from the late evening sun with his free hand as he looked up at Crispin.

"Who is inquiring?"

"There's a gen'lman down here says as how he wants to speak to you," the dingy man explained, pointing down the alley. "Says how I'm to watch your horse and you're to go down there."

"What is his name?"

"Didn't tell me no name. Just told me to deliver my message."

"What did he say to do if I refused to dismount and go down the alley?"

"He didn't really say, but he gave me this to use." The man took his hand from his eyes to extract a dagger from his sleeve, letting its blade flash in the sunlight.

"Would you be using that on me or my horse?" Crispin inquired politely.

"Horse," the man answered without hesitation.

Crispin admired the man's sense of purpose, and his return home could wait. So instead of spurring Fortuna over the dingy man's head and careening down the alley, he dismounted gracefully, whistled something in Fortuna's ear, and strode past the man.

"You need not watch her. She'll go home on her own from here," Crispin explained, and then disappeared down the alley.

It was an extremely narrow passage, so narrow in spots that Crispin had to turn sideways to keep his shoulders from getting stuck, and extremely dark. The air, thick with humidity, hung heavily in the constricted space, clinging to the shadows along the walls, giving the whole place a murky feeling. Crispin moved slowly, his hand on the hilt of his rapier, but none of his instinctual reactions to danger were triggered. Indeed, despite the strange atmosphere and even stranger way the invitation was issued, Crispin did not feel that he was in any physical peril at all.

Nor was he wrong. He was halfway down what he could see of the alley when a voice on his right announced, "Over here."

Turning, Crispin saw what had to be the world's smallest court. And standing in the middle of it, which was also the front, back, and sides, was Basil Grosgrain. "Stay where you are," Basil told Crispin, moving his cloak slightly to reveal a massive broadsword at his waist.

Crispin was tempted to laugh. In the time it would have taken for Basil to unsheathe the clumsy instrument, organize both of his hands correctly on the hilt, and swing, Crispin could have had him dead six different ways. But he refrained from pointing this out. Instead, leaving his hands in plain view, he bowed politely. "You sent for me, Lord Grosgrain?"

"Yes. We need to talk."

"There are more comfortable places to talk than this." Crispin gestured around. "My library, for example."

"We needed to talk where we could not be overheard," Basil elaborated. "And I don't give a damn about your comfort."

"It was not my comfort I was thinking of," Crispin assured him.

"Oh, certainly. Of course. My comfort is of the utmost concern to you." Basil sneered unappetizingly at Crispin. "That is why you did your level best to upset me this morning at your house."

"I do not know what you are talking about, Basil, but if I did anything—"

"Shut up." One of Basil's hands curled over the hilt of the broadsword. "You are wrong to think that I killed my father."

"I do not think anything of the kind."

"Don't lie to me. You said as much today. You said that my alibi was false."

"Isn't it?"

"Shut up." Basil had begun to look a little wild-eyed, so Crispin complied. "You thought you were so clever. So funny. But will you think it is so funny when I slit your throat?"

"No." Crispin was unequivocal. "Absolutely not."

"Good. Now shut up and listen. Just you wait until you hear what I have to say to you, Lord Sandal. You won't be laughing then."

Crispin, who was beginning to be slightly alarmed by the expression on Basil's face, did not mention to him that slitting a man's throat at two paces with a sword that was four paces long was a near impossibility. "Back to this question of the alibi—"

"You were right," Basil admitted without hesitation, gripping the hilt of the weapon. "My alibi is false. I was not with my step-mother."

"Either time? Either the morning your father was killed or the night Richard Tottle was killed?"

"Either time. But that does not make me guilty. I did not kill either of them. And it is not my alibi you should be worried about."

"I will leave that worrying to you," Crispin said nobly. "And I thank you for this lovely talk."

"You are not going," Basil said. Crispin decided to take it as a question.

"Yes, I am Lord Grosgrain. Good day."

"Going back to that murderous hussy Sophie Champion, are you?" Basil's voice was mean. "What about *her* alibi? Why are you protecting her? She is a murderess, I tell you, and I—"

Basil was forced to stop speaking by the rapid constriction of his throat when Crispin grabbed him by it and slammed him against one of the handy walls. "That is no way to talk about a lady," Crispin advised Basil with their noses less than an inch apart.

"She is no lady. She is a murderess. And I can prove it to you."

Crispin had not imagined that Basil was so cruel, or so desperate. "Tell me. Prove it," he challenged, releasing his grip on Basil's throat. "What makes you so sure?"

Basil massaged his neck. "She has done it before. Murdered."

"What are you talking about?"

"Last week, after my father died, I hired a man to investigate your Sophie Champion. And I learned some very interesting things. To begin with, she was not my father's goddaughter at all. He did not even meet her until she was almost sixteen. And already running from the site of her first murder."

Crispin ignored the latter part of the statement. "How did they meet?"

"Does that matter? What is important is that my father, the fool, took her under his wing. And somehow she managed to ingratiate herself so much that he left her the entire business."

Crispin was tempted to tell Basil what he had learned the night before from Sophie's own lips, tempted to tell Basil that it was only by the kindness of the woman he was slandering that he even possessed an allowance, but he respected the secret. Instead he asked, "Did you ever hear your father say anything about Sophie's involvement in the business?"

"Sophie? In business?" Basil sniggered. "The only business she is in is spending money and entangling men."

"Entangling men?" Crispin raised an eyebrow. He could not deny that Sophie was alluring and enticing, but he doubted very much that she went out of her way to execute entanglements. "I see. Setting snares and such. Is that how she caught her first murder victim?"

"Keep laughing, Sandal. Just you wait. She did not have to set any traps for her first victims. She killed them in their beds. Her mother and father."

"Her mother and father died in a house fire," Crispin said before he realized how much he was admitting.

"Ah, so she has told you about this. Did she also tell you that she set that fire? That she lit it herself? On purpose? To murder them? No, I can tell by your face that she did not."

If Crispin's face showed anything, it was incredulity at the depths to which Basil was sinking. "I have to say, Basil, this is not very convincing. Do you have anything like proof?"

"You do not believe me? Then explain why she would need to change her name if she had nothing to hide."

"She changed her name?" Crispin asked with only the barest interest. He was now quite sure that Basil was making things up.

"Yes. Sophie Champion does not exist. Her real name is Diana Goldhawk. Look." He held up a small gold medal depicting the goddess Diana seated next to a hawk. "She used this to bribe one of the guards at the prison, and my man got it."

"Diana Goldhawk," Crispin repeated, in a voice that made it clear he thought Basil had fabricated the whole thing. "Not terribly original, using the name of an Olympian goddess. I suppose she has a raft of siblings with names like Venus and Minerva and Zeus and Apollo?"

Basil tried to sneer at Crispin. "Not Apollo. But she does have a brother named Damon."

"Has?" Crispin asked. "Didn't she burn him to a crisp as well?"

"Apparently he was not at home the night of the fire."

"How convenient." Crispin's tone was dry but light. "I don't suppose I could meet with him, you know, just to get the particulars from his own lips."

"I do not know where he is. But you can accept this as true. You have my word on it."

"Your word," Crispin exclaimed admiringly. "That is a handsome guarantee. I thank you for it and for your generous explanation of your alibi. Or lack thereof. Now, if you do not mind, I should like to be going."

"You are a fool if you don't believe me. That woman is dangerous. She will entangle you in her snares and not let you go. She is a murderess—" was the last thing Crispin heard as he came upon the mouth of the alley.

He turned from the passage into the Strand, his eyes not ready for the brightness of the street after the dim shadows of the alley. No one watching him as he moved toward Sandal Hall would have been able to perceive any difference in his face or bearing. He looked exactly as he had when he entered the alley, unperturbed and imperturbable.

But the base of his spine had begun to tingle.

With two words, Basil had demolished the foundations upon which Crispin had built all of his plans, had based all of his ideas. "Diana Goldhawk" was not just a name; it was the name of the sister of a man Crispin had killed. A man who was one of the primary parties to the counterfeiting enterprise he had demolished during his first mission as the Phoenix.

Crispin had recognized the gold disk Basil showed him as the one he had found in Sophie's shoe the first night they met. It certainly seemed to suggest that she was Diana Goldhawk. And if Sophie Champion was actually Diana Goldhawk, wasn't it possible, completely possible, that she had been using him all along? That she was out for revenge, to revenge her brother's death. Or, worse, that she was the actual head of the counterfeiting operation, the person angling for the Phoenix's destruction.

Crispin's mind balked. It could not be true, he told himself. He would have sensed it. After all, there was no way for her to know he was the Phoenix. And even if she suspected it, she would have had to make some effort to find out, would have attempted to question him or devise some test to make him reveal his identity. Which Crispin knew had not happened—his suspicions would have been aroused the first moment she tried to cadge information from him. Indeed, if anything, what was notable was the small amount of information she had tried to gather from him during their investigation. Even the night they played the dice game in his private garden, when she could have asked anything without risking suspicion. Of course, she had not had much of a chance, with the way she kept losing—

The half smile that had begun to form on the edges of Crispin's mouth at the memory vanished. Suddenly, he saw that he *had* been tested, completely and brilliantly. That night by the pond had casually fed him information about her godfather and alchemical lab, information that would only have been provocative to someone already interested in counterfeiting. Someone like the Phoenix. All she had to do afterward was wait to see how he would react to having his identity confirmed. By letting the information seem to come out naturally, in the course of her losses during their dice game, she avoided arousing his suspicions. Only there was nothing natural about their game, or rather, about the dice with which they were playing. Because they were Don Alfonso's dice. The dice Sophie had been playing with at the Unicorn the first night they met. The dice she had weighted to lose when she rolled them a certain way.

But *only* when she rolled them a certain way, Crispin rushed to put in. How did he know that she had not rolled them normally that night in his garden? How did he know that Diana Goldhawk was not simply a figment of Basil's imagination? How did he even know—

Without realizing it, Crispin had broken into a run. He had to ask her, had to learn the truth, right then. He entered Sandal Hall through the stable door, stomped up the stairs, and jerked the door to his library open so hard that it left a dent when it struck the wall.

He glowered fiercely around the room until his eyes fell on Thurston, hovering on the threshold. "Where is she?" he demanded.

"I assume Your Lordship is referring to Miss Champion. She left half an hour ago in response to your summons."

"My what?"

"Your message requiring her presence at the offices of Richard Tottle. It arrived just after you left. Miss Champion seemed rather excited when I helped her with the mustache."

"But that is impossible. Let me see it," Crispin demanded, extending his hand.

Thurston looked pained. "I am afraid Miss Champion took it with her. I made a copy of the note—"

That won't help," Crispin said, running a hand through his air. "It is not the words but the paper, the writing that I need. Did it look like it came from me?"

"Yes, sir. I did not suspect anything amiss."

"Odious slugs," Crispin muttered. He was at an impasse. If she was really just Sophie Champion, if she was really the woman she seemed to be, the woman who said, "I love you," the woman he had asked to marry him that morning, then she was walking into a trap and he should mount Fortuna and ride to Richard Tottle's as quickly as possible. But if she was Diana Goldhawk, if she was Damon Goldhawk's sister, ruthlessly cunning and out for blood, or out for the Phoenix, then he would be rushing right into a trap himself. He might have wasted four seconds before deciding to go and rescue Sophie, come what may, if Thurston had not cleared his throat.

"There was another message, sir. Earlier today. From Pickering Hall. The boy who delivered it said it was important. It is the message I was trying to deliver to you just after the search."

Crispin scowled at Thurston, then at the packet that Thurston was holding out to him. He took it unenthusiastically and ripped it open. It was brief, but in the face of its evidence he was left no choice about what to believe, or what to do.

> My Lord—
> Elwood just brought me this, and I thought you should know. The reward for identifying the Phoenix is being handed out by those prude bastards you were asking about, Loundes and Wainscot. And it is being paid from the account of one Sophie Champion.
> Are you sure she is worthy of your trust?
>
> LP

The tingling at the base of Crispin's spine became an ache.

Sophie's heart was racing as she ascended the stairs. When the note from Crispin arrived, telling her that he had an important clue and she should meet him at Richard Tottle's, she had wasted no time setting out. "*I have found what we were looking for,*" the note said tantalizingly, and Sophie knew the end of the investigation was near. Her enthusiasm stemmed as much from that as from the thrill of working with Crispin, working together with him not against him, the thrill of collaborating.

She had been so excited by the note and its implications that she did not notice the various men who followed her through the convoluted byways and twisted streets to her destination. She did not pay attention to the old woman settling herself outside of Tottle's shop as, following the directions, Sophie pried open a side window and entered through the ink room. She was not aware of the tall young man who lurked in a window opposite, counting how many steps she had to be taking, calculating how long she should need to ascend, and holding his breath until he saw her head framed in the window of the pink chamber.

He could not see her expression as she entered, but he could imagine it. It had to be one of shock.

She stood at the threshold, her hand glued to the door pull for a few moments before she found words. "Constantia. What are you doing here?" she finally managed to stammer.

Constantia patted a place on the pink silk bed next to her. "Sit down, Sophie. I have been waiting for you."

Sophie was suddenly on her guard. "Waiting for me? How did you know I would be here? Where is Crispin?"

"There is nothing to be afraid of. I did not bring the constables. I was sent by a friend of yours. A friend of ours."

"Who?" Sophie was still cautious.

"Please, just trust me." Constantia smiled her lovely, guileless smile, and Sophie finally sat down. "I do not know how long we shall be left unmolested, so I will not waste time. Sophie, dearest, we have always been friends, haven't we?"

"Of course."

"May I talk to you like a friend? Like a sister?" When Sophie nodded, Constantia went on. "Sophie, I did not love your godfather."

Sophie tried to sound soothing. "That does not matter. You were kind and good to him. And many people do not love their spouses."

"Of course. And I do not reproach myself for that. But I did not love him because I was in love with someone else. With Crispin."

Sophie called upon the worldliness she had learned the previous night. "Congratulations. He is a fine choice. Then it was Crispin in your dressing room with you the other night."

"The other night?" Constantia looked confused. "Crispin was in my dressing room, yes. But how did you know?"

"It does not matter. I am very happy for you. I take it, then, that he loves you back?"

"Yes. And that is just the problem."

Sophie smiled suavely. "There is no problem. He is yours, of course. I want nothing from him."

"You do not understand. It is not like that. It is much, much worse."

Sophie could not imagine anything worse than what she was hearing, but she soon found that Constantia had not exaggerated.

"Crispin proposed to me first when I was sixteen," Constantia began. "Although I loved him, I had to turn him down. My mother forced me to marry someone else, someone older, a wealthy older nobleman who had recently been widowed."

Sophie nodded, completely numb.

"Almost three years ago he died. Mysteriously. At the time I thought nothing of it, nor did I find it suspicious that Crispin had arrived in the countryside just days before he passed away. I lost myself in the joy of being with Crispin, being in his arms, listening as he called me *tesoro*." Tears glistened in Constantia's sapphire eyes, but Sophie was too numb with horror to cry.

Constantia swallowed hard, her graceful white throat quivering, and then resumed. "Crispin and I were about to become betrothed when he was sent away by the Queen. I loved him and I longed to go with him, but I had my reputation, my future to consider. Then every broadside printed seemed to speak of his exploits on the continent, and finally I decided I could wait for him no longer. When Milton, your godfather, offered for me, I accepted."

Sophie did not know why she was being made to listen to this, but she found that she could not leave. She felt as though someone was dragging her stomach out of her living body, someone was beating a tattoo in her head, like someone was grinding her up inside.

"Two days after Crispin returned to London, Milton died. Again, I thought nothing of it, just thought of the pleasure I would feel to be once again in my lover's arms, once again having him make love to me in his private garden. But he did not come right away. Indeed, he did not come for over a week. And I soon discovered why."

Constantia had been looking at her slim hands as she spoke, but she now turned her eyes on Sophie.

"Me," Sophie whispered. "Was it because of me? Oh, Constantia, I am so sorry—"

"There is no need for an apology, Sophie my love. We are not to blame. The blame lies entirely with Crispin. With the murderer."

"Crispin?" Sophie's incredulity transcended her numbness. "Are you saying that Crispin killed Lord Grosgrain?" Lord Grosgrain's words, "*unless the Phoenix gets me first,*" flooded back to her. "But what about the Phoenix?"

"Crispin is the Phoenix," Constantia told her succinctly. "And yes, he did. He took Milton from me. And he killed two others."

"Tottle and Sweetson," Sophie faltered. "Then Crispin is the one who tried to make me look guilty."

"Yes." Constantia took her friend's hand. "I am terribly sorry to be the person to tell you this. I did not know myself, until this afternoon when our friend told me, did not know that the man I loved, the man we both loved was a—a—a monster." Unable to contain her emotion any longer, Constantia burst into tears.

Sophie hugged her to her chest. As the other woman sobbed uncontrollably, Sophie lost herself in her own deadening misery. The way she felt was worse than anything she could have imagined, anything she ever experienced in a nightmare. Fear was nothing compared to the utter horror of knowing that she had been duped, completely and utterly taken in, had fallen for Crispin's charm, his beauty, his stock words. What Sophie had seen in Constantia's dressing room rose up before her eyes again now, and she wondered how she could have believed his denials so easily. It was because she had wanted to believe him, she knew. "*Tesoro,*" he had called her, and she had melted for him then, banished all further thoughts of resistance. "*Tesoro,*" he had said, and she had said back, "I love you."

A tremor went over Sophie's body, and Constantia sat up, sniffing into her light blue handkerchief. "Sophie, I apologize again. It is just so dreadful to think that he killed Milton to revenge himself on me."

"I understand why he would kill your husband, Lord Grosgrain, but why did he kill Tottle and Sweetson?"

"Oh, dear. I almost forgot." Constantia reached into her bodice and brought out two carefully folded notes. "These started coming to the house," she explained, holding them out to Sophie.

"'*How did Constantia Grosgrain's first husband die? Was it really just an accident?*'" Sophie read aloud from the first one.

"The other says approximately the same thing, only referring to Milton's death. And I was not the only one to receive these. It would seem that Crispin was being blackmailed."

"But instead of paying his blackmailers, he killed them," Sophie said slowly.

"Yes. And then, like a—a coward, he tried to have you arrested for his crimes."

Sophie saw a crack and seized on it. "But, Constantia, he saved me. He saved me from being arrested. And he asked me to marry him."

Constantia shook her head sadly. "Dear Sophie, you must not let yourself be blinded by your love. Don't you see, saving you and keeping you with him was part of his game? Part of the way he won your trust. He just wanted to keep you free long enough to finish his killing spree and ensure you got all the blame. Just like making love. For him it is simply a routine, simply a tool. He lied to you and seduced you so you would trust him. So he could manipulate you."

"No," Sophie said, shaking her head. "That is not true."

"Sophie, dearest, you have to believe me. He did it to me as well. He would smile at me, that smile with the long dimple, and say the loveliest things. He told me that with me he felt pleasure unlike any he had ever felt. That in my smile he saw beauty that he could not have imagined. That I made him laugh like he had never laughed before. That his lips—"

"Stop!" Sophie cried now, cried from the deepest part of her. She realized that she had been clinging to a belief that none of this was true, but she could cling no longer. To hear the words she had cherished, the words that had changed her life, the most special, unique words, words she thought were spoken just for her, repeated like that, broke her. There was no mistaking that anything he had said was a lie, everything he had done an act. "Stop!" she yelled, covering her ears. "Stop, please, please stop. I don't want to hear any more. Please."

"I am so sorry, Sophie. I do not want to hurt you. But you must know or you won't understand what he is. And that you should not blame yourself. Crispin is a master at this. He fooled me for ten years. Ten years." Constantia's voice grew quieter. "You should feel grateful that you are finding out when you are."

Sophie nodded, trying to imagine what "grateful" or what anything, for that matter, would feel like.

"I do not know how I will face him after this," Sophie said quietly.

"But you cannot. You must not. Sophie, don't you see? It is only a matter of time before he gives you up to the constables. You must not go back to Sandal Hall under any circumstances."

Of course. Constantia was right. Everything she said made so much sense. Looking back on it, Sophie wondered how she had not seen it earlier, how she had failed to remark on the coincidence of his appearing wherever there was a dead body, a dead body with some identifying mark to tie it to Sophie. How had she failed to note that he urged her to stay most forcefully the night that Sweetson was murdered? Or that he hadn't bothered to contradict her when she suggested that he was just making love to her in order to get her to talk? Or the ring of authenticity in his voice when he said, "*I don't give a damn what becomes of you*"? How could she have thought that his kisses were real, that his caresses were true, that she gave him the same pleasure he gave her? Or even that he enjoyed her company?

Constantia's soothing voice broke into Sophie's disquiet. "Listen to me, Sophie, dearest. I have a friend with a house nearby where you can stay. It is a lovely house, and I am sure it will not be a problem. And I will visit you there later. Together we will figure out what to do."

Not having the strength to protest that she would rather be left alone to die on the pink silk bed, Sophie acquiesced stoically.

As did Crispin, later that night, when five large constables presented themselves in his library to arrest him for the murders of Lord Milton Grosgrain, Richard Tottle, and Sweetson, the baker of Milk Street.

Chapter Twenty-Two

"Quiet in the court!" The chief justice banged the gavel three times and glared at the gallery from under his extraordinarily bushy eyebrows. "Quiet, I say. I will have quiet!"

When the spectators had reduced their loud exclamations to whispers, the chief justice returned his eyebrows to the prisoner. "I must warn you, Lord Sandal, the evidence against you is weighty. Are you sure you would not like to change your plea?"

"No, Your Lordship. I am not guilty of these crimes."

The courtroom threatened to erupt again, but this time a single glance from the chief justice sufficed to restore order.

"Very well," the justice sighed. "You must remain silent as the witnesses testify. You will have your turn to speak later. Bailiff, call the first witness."

"Miss Lucinda Flipps," the bailiff announced.

Crispin frowned. He knew the charges against him were false and concocted to detain him, but he little expected that the court would have to resort to dragging in people he had never met to defame him. He was still frowning when a rather gaudily dressed and gaudily endowed blond woman sashayed into the courtroom, waggled her fingers at him, and allowed herself to be seated on the witness chair.

The Queen's advocate, a wiry man with bright red whiskers named Fox, approached the witness. "Miss Lucinda Flipps, please state your occupation for the court."

Lucinda smiled coyly. "I'm a goddess of pleasure, my lord."

This time it took two fierce waggles from the eyebrows of the chief justice and several bouts with the gavel to quiet the gallery.

"This is no place for lewd jokes, madam," the chief justice told her ferociously. "Now answer the question."

"But I meant no joke, Your Excellencyness. It is what all us girls are called at Mount Olympus, where I work. You see, Mount Olympus is where the gods went to—"

"I am well aware of Mount Olympus and its history," the justice cut her off. "Very well. Advocate Fox, continue with your questions."

"Please tell the court what happened to you on the night of May the tenth of this year."

Lucinda looked very serious now. "I was standing on Fleet Street, talking to some of the other goddesses, when a man comes up and asks me if I like silver."

"Do you see that man here today?" Advocate Fox asked.

She waved her fingers at Crispin. "It was him. And since he is so handsome, I said, yes, I like silver as much as the next girl, but I prefer gold, and he says I shall have some if I do what he says, and I laughed and said with that smile, I'd do it for free, and he laughed and said what would I do? and I—"

A voice from the bench silenced her. "I tell you again, madam, this is a court, not a stage for your—your antics. Please confine yourself to the relevant portion of your interaction with Lord Sandal."

Lucinda looked confused until Advocate Fox, whose face had turned a rich vermilion that matched his whiskers, explained, "The part about the note."

"Oh. Yes. Well, then he wrote a note and told me to wait half an hour and then send someone to deliver it to Lawrence Pickering."

"Thank you." Advocate Fox breathed a sigh of relief. "Did you read the note?"

"He said I could. He said it was in code."

"Did he?" The advocate tugged at his whiskers and turned to look at Crispin with what the latter supposed was a withering stare. "And what did the note say?"

"Well, I could not read the code, of course, but what I could read said that there was a body in the smoking room at that fancy club up the Fleet. It didn't make much sense to me."

"And did you have any more conversation with Lord Sandal after that?"

"Conversation." Lucinda smiled. "That is funny. I am going to remember that. No, we had no *conversation*. None at all. I offered, seeing as how he gave me two gold pieces, offered to have as many *conversations* with him as he wanted, but he said he did not have time." She looked directly at Crispin now. "Your credit will still be good with me when you get out of Newgate, my lord. I'll never forget that smile of yours."

Advocate Fox was a rosy shade of scarlet as he dismissed his witness and turned to address the jury box. Crispin barely listened as the advocate pulled on his whiskers and drew the obvious conclusion for the jurors that Crispin had put himself in contact with Lawrence Pickering, the most notorious criminal in London, for the express purpose of having the body disposed of and his crime concealed. Why would an innocent man send such a letter, Advocate Fox asked rhetorically, and Crispin now found himself wondering the same thing.

At the time, however, it had seemed like a very good, indeed the best of ideas. He had chosen that method of informing his friend as the most anonymous. It would be nearly impossible to trace the original source of the note, or even the girl who had acted as an intermediary. Unless, of course, you happened to have been standing outside when Crispin chose her. Unless, of course, you had been following him, with his full knowledge. Unless, of course, you were Sophie Champion.

The sinking feeling that had gripped Crispin's stomach since his meeting with Basil was now redoubled. Everything he had believed to make sense, everything he believed he understood, everything he believed in as truth, had suddenly dissolved before his eyes. He was furious at himself for being such a fool. He remembered that his first thought on seeing Sophie Champion at the Unicorn was that—despite the ridiculous mustache—she was a dangerous professional, and he wondered why he had been so quick to discard it. He saw now, could not help seeing, that not only was she a pro but with regard to danger she was in a class of her own.

The bailiff's voice, announcing, "The Court calls Bert Noggin next," broke into Crispin's thoughts. The name meant as little to Crispin as Lucinda's had, but the fat constable from Richard Tottle's was easy to recognize when he waddled into the courtroom. He and several of his colleagues were called upon to give testimony that Crispin had been caught on Richard Tottle's premises searching Richard Tottle's papers the day after the murder, and had only escaped by taking an innocent young woman hostage and threatening to kill her if she objected. This was interesting news to Crispin, and he was just mentally commending those who had stage-managed his trial for their creativity when their *coup de grâce* swooped into the room in the person of Lady Dolores Artly.

As she passed near the balustrade behind which Crispin was seated, she whispered, "Don Alfonso, I think what you are doing, standing trial like this for your master, is *such* a wonderful gesture. Do not worry, your secret is safe with me," and winked.

Crispin could not think what answer to make to this wonderfully generous assurance, but fortunately none seemed required.

"Lady Artly," Advocate Fox said when that enchantress had been seated in the witness chair, "please tell the court what you observed during your meeting with Lord Sandal three days ago."

"To begin with, I noticed that His Lordship has *such* lovely manners. And—"

"Please constrain your comments to the interesting point about which we spoke last night," the advocate whined.

Lady Artly looked disgusted at having been cut off in such a brusque manner. "Very well. I just wanted to give the jury a picture of the type of man Lord Sandal *really* is. So they would not judge him by how he seems here." She winked at Crispin again.

"What you saw?" Advocate Fox reminded her with an impatient tug on his whiskers.

"Yes. At several points during the meeting, Lord Sandal began to cough rather violently. Becoming concerned, I asked him for the cause of his malady, and he explained that he had a head cold. Which he had gotten from being out in the rain."

"And do you know when the most recent rainstorm had been?"

"I most certainly do. It was the night of Lady Quinsy's concert, and my gown, *such* a lovely gown, was drenched. Ruined."

"Yes, but how many days was that before your meeting with Lord Sandal?" the advocate asked impatiently.

"Three. Three days before."

"Exactly. The exact night on which Richard Tottle was killed. This proves"—Advocate Fox turned to explain to the jury—"that Lord Sandal was out in the rain the night of the murder. I let you draw your own conclusions."

Crispin was interested in Fox's use of the word "*proves*." As far as Crispin could make out, the point was either that no innocent man would stand outside in the rain long enough to get a cold or that all men with colds were guilty. He found that he was growing somewhat interested in how any of this was going to be used to convict him of murder, and this interest was piqued when he saw the next witness being led in.

"Miss Sally Tunks," the bailiff announced as he seated Sweetson the baker's ten-year-old maid in the witness chair.

This, Crispin thought to himself, should be good.

Advocate Fox addressed the girl. "Please tell the court how you came to have five gold pieces, Miss Tunks."

"He gave 'em to me," Sally said without hesitating, pointing in Crispin's direction.

"For what, exactly," Fox probed.

But Sally did not answer immediately. "Don't worry, sir. I'll not let your gold turn to ashes," she assured Crispin before turning to the advocate. "He gave 'em to me," she told the advocate. "And I am to say the truth, that it was the lady in blue who killed my master. The lady in blue taffeta." Sally smiled broadly at Crispin, conscious of having done him an enormous favor.

"Did you see the actual murderer of your employer?" Advocate Fox asked.

"Oh, yes, sir. I saw it all."

"Can you tell the court who it was?"

"The lady in blue taffeta, sir," Sally said positively. "That is what the gentleman told me to say."

"Yes, but leaving the gentleman aside, who did you really see?"

Sally crossed her arms across her chest defiantly. "The lady in blue. And I'll not say different, no matter what. I would not do that to the gentleman."

At that moment, Crispin decided he would never have anything to do with another woman, ever, no matter what age, as long as he lived. Which, if the triumphant expression on Advocate Fox's face was anything to go by, would not be very long at all.

Sophie awoke as the bells of Saint Paul's tolled eleven. Her head was heavy, her eyelids felt swollen from crying, and her throat was sore from the litany of self-rebukes she had run through the previous night. She did not want to open her eyes, did not want to have to wake up and realize that it had been true, that Constantia had really appeared to her, that Crispin had really tried to frame her, that the short, ebullient interlude at Sandal Hall had itself been no more than a dream.

More than anything, Sophie wished she did not know. If it had merely been a question of learning that Crispin loved someone else, she could have lived, albeit with a hole where her heart and lungs should have been. But listening to Constantia talk, hearing her describe the things that Crispin had said in the heat of passion, exactly the same things he had said to her, that was too painful. How could she believe otherwise than that they had all been lies?

Sophie wished she could peel off her skin, reach inside herself, and take out the part of her that was hurting so desperately. It was his fault she ached so much. His fault she felt anything at all. Not because he had made her love him. But because he had made her trust him, and in trusting him, she had learned to feel again, had learned to experience all the emotions she had so carefully bolted away eleven years earlier after the fire, after the nightmare. What was worse, in falling for Crispin, she had traduced not only herself, but also the one person to whom she owed everything, Lord Grosgrain.

The easy and comfortable life she had led before the death of her parents was no preparation for the battle of survival that faced Sophie after the house fire, once she had finally managed to escape from the attic where she was held prisoner. Ragged and hungry and scared and half mad, she took to hiding in the countryside, traveling at night in order to be seen by as few people as possible, to leave as few traces as possible to follow when the man came after her. She was so lonely for company that she had adopted a caterpillar, who lived in her pocket and with whom she held long discourses. It was during her fourteenth night on the run—three days since her last meal and almost a week since she had said more than two words to anyone but her caterpillar—her fourteenth night of fear and desolation, when the loneliness and despair had begun to wend themselves into her very core, it was then, just when she was about to lose hope, that she heard the shouts from the river she was walking along.

She was his salvation, his champion, Lord Grosgrain had always said, but really he was hers. That night Sophie may have saved him from drowning—he had lost his footing trying to collect "moon pebbles" which he was convinced would bring his alchemical experiments to perfection—but he saved her from herself. He had been about to be battered to death by the churning blades of a water mill when she jammed the gears with a carefully aimed branch and dragged him to safety on the river's bank.

After he had coughed half the river from his lungs, he turned to examine the tall, skinny girl who had saved him. "That was quick thinking," he told her appreciatively. "And fine use of leverage."

The girl waved the compliment away. "Anyone could have done it."

"Possibly, but only someone who had studied Archimedes would have known the exact angle," he said with admiration. "What is your name?"

For a moment Lord Grosgrain thought she had not heard, but when he looked at her more closely, he saw that she was biting her lower lip and that there were tears running down her face. "I do not have a name," she said finally. "I am no one. I belong to no one."

"You belong to yourself, young lady," Lord Grosgrain had told her, wiping her face with his wet sleeve, "and there is no one finer to belong to." That was the first of many wise lessons she learned from him, although Lord Grosgrain always claimed he had learned more from her. He called her Sophie, after the ancient goddess of wisdom, and gave her the surname Champion because she had saved his life. From then on, Sophie had striven to live up to both her names.

When Lord Grosgrain was recovered enough from his near drowning to walk, he led her to the ramshackle cottage he used as both home and laboratory, and watched with a mixture of amusement and concern as she devoured every edible item in the place. He had tried to refuse the gold coins she offered him in recompense, but she would not let him. Finally, they hit upon a bargain: he would accept her money, so long as she agreed to stay and help him eat whatever he bought with it.

"Leverage," Sophie had proclaimed to him with a smile and her mouth full of burnt sugar pudding as she scattered the coins on the table. "I am forcing you to keep your door propped open for me."

They were both so satisfied by this bargain that they never terminated it. Those were the terms of her relationship with Lord Grosgrain when it began, and those were the terms they maintained. Sophie felt that she owed everything to Milton Grosgrain, who she was, what she was. He had taken her in when she had no one, given her a home and a name even when he had nothing to share, had nurtured her and taught her and been kind—so kind—to her. He had believed in her and made her believe in herself.

Together, they had built an empire of coal mines and water-works, with a mill here and there to remind them of how they had met, consolidating all of these in their company, Leverage Hold-ings. During his life, Lord Grosgrain's happiness had been Sophie's foremost concern, the foremost source of her own joy. She could still remember the day he proposed to Constantia and was accepted, the way he had danced into her apartments at Peacock Hall. She had never seen him happier, had never felt happier her-self. He had thanked her for making the marriage possible, know-ing full well that Constantia would not have been interested in him without his money, but not caring at all, and Sophie had loved him even more for that, for his unflinching honesty.

Thinking about Lord Grosgrain made Sophie feel both better and worse. Better because those were happy memories. But worse because he was gone, she was more alone than ever, and instead of turning in his killer, she had fallen into bed with him.

Just the thought of it made Sophie feel hot, hot with rage at herself and him and everyone, and queasy. Air. Air was what she needed. She rose from the bed and crossed the room toward the two large windows that looked down into the garden of the house, tripping over a large volume that appeared to be a journal. Bees buzzed around a flowering tree just outside the window and a breeze toyed with its leaves, but Sophie could neither smell the flowers nor feel the breeze because the window would not open. She moved and tried the other window but found it bolted shut as well.

She felt a moment of apprehension but realized that this was probably just a chamber that did not get much use and the owners of the house feared that it could be broken into. Indeed, the branches of the tree outside, she had to admit, would give very easy access to the room, even though it was on the third floor of the house. She would just call a servant and have them unbolted. Or, better yet, she would go for a walk in the garden. She crossed to the door and tried to open it.

It was locked.

Sophie's apprehension returned. She tried the door again, then began banging on it. After a minute she heard a key turn and saw a wide man standing in front of her.

"Thank you," she breathed with relief. "I seem to have lost my key." She made to brush past him, but the point of a dagger against her throat stopped her.

"I doubt that," the man said. "I would be surprised if you had one, given that my orders are to see that you do not leave this room."

Sophie looked at the man's face for the first time, and her apprehension and queasiness reached a new high. It was one of the men she had seen peering into the cellar at Sweetson's. One of the men who had been at Lawrence's the night she was arrested. One of the men she had assumed was a constable. Just one more man she had been mistaken about.

"You work for Lawrence Pickering, don't you?" she stammered.

"Sometimes," the man conceded, sliding the dagger against her throat. "Now I—"

He was interrupted by a voice from somewhere down the corridor. "Kit," the voice called out. "I'm going to the warehouse now, Kit. Be sure to keep Miss Champion well guarded, so that no one *disturbs* her."

Sophie knew the voice instantly, knew it belonged to a friend, someone who would clear up this misunderstanding and let her out of the room. She opened her mouth to call for help, but the dagger was pressed more forcefully against her throat, silencing her.

Kit smiled at Sophie as he replied to the voice. "It will be a pleasure."

"Good. I will return for her at two bells," the friendly voice went on. "But if I do not—"

"I know," Kit interrupted, keeping his eyes on Sophie and the dagger against her trembling throat. "If you do not, I am to kill her."

Crispin could scarcely stop himself from gnashing his teeth in impatience. He could barely stand the fact that he was sitting in a courtroom, doing nothing, while the counterfeiters went about their business unimpeded. The trial and the evidence that supported it were a complete charade. The entire thing had been designed to ensure that he, the Phoenix, would be detained, so that the counterfeiters would be able to get their operation under way without worrying about being apprehended. He had no doubt that at this very moment sacks of the gold coins were being loaded onto wagons to be distributed to selected agents around the country and exchanged for real English coins. He could just picture Sophie—or was her name Diana?—just picture her—

Crispin was so struck by the thought that popped into his head then that he nearly shouted. Three things kicked into place simultaneously in his mind, and he saw at once that he had *not* been wrong. Not about the counterfeiters. And not about Sophie.

Crispin was no longer in the courtroom listening to his life being bandied about by the foxy advocate, but was in his privy, the morning his bed had been burned, listening to Sophie's terrible story. "*I cannot tell you who he was,*" she had said when Crispin asked her to identify the man, but, unwittingly, she had. He closed his eyes and heard Sophie's voice again, somber, pained. "*So he set fire to the house. He said that our parents' deaths were my fault, that I killed them with my lustfulness.*" She had said, "our parents." Hers... and Damon's. It could have been merely a slip of the tongue—that was what Crispin had taken it for at first—but now, suddenly, with a clarity that stunned him, he knew it was not. It was Damon, her brother, who had tormented her that way. Damon, her brother, that she feared. That she still feared. She had been convinced that he had set the fire that burned the bed and convinced that he had tried to kidnap her from prison. Which meant she did not know he was dead. And that she was not out for revenge, that she had not cheated at dice, that she was not the head of a counterfeiting ring, that she was not anything but Sophie. His Sophie.

The bells of Saint Paul's had just begun to chime midday when Crispin rose to his feet, interrupting Advocate Fox's very interesting discussion about the culpability of the foreign aristocracy, and said, "My lord, I ask permission to address the cour*aaaaaarrrghhhh*."

The first shot, in Crispin's shoulder, turned him around, and the second hit him squarely in the stomach. His mangled body hung in the air for three beats, his face contorted into a horrible mask of pain, and then he collapsed to the floor.

As guards ran out to apprehend the gunman, the bailiff pushed through the crowd that gathered around the body and kneeled next to it. He shook his head as he looked at the blood pouring out of the hole in Crispin's stomach, but he put a finger under Crispin's nose and one on his neck anyway. He stayed that way for half a minute and then, still shaking his head, addressed the chief justice and Advocate Fox. "He ain't moving, he ain't breathing, and I can't feel his heart beating."

"What does that mean?" the chief justice demanded fiercely.

"It means, sir," the bailiff said, standing and wiping his bloody hands on his leggings, "that Lord Sandal is dead."

Chapter Twenty-Three

The verdict was confirmed, half an hour later, by the coroner. "Definitely dead," he pronounced with distaste over Crispin's body. "Take him away."

Using the deceased's cloak as a makeshift shroud, the remains of Lord Sandal were carried through the reverently hushed crowd and loaded onto the back of a cart. It was an unceremonious removal for such a great personage, but the necessity of getting the body out before it began to putrefy in the summer heat meant that the delay that would have been caused by sending to Sandal Hall for a proper equipage was unacceptable. Instead, Crispin Foscari, the famous and infamous Earl of Sandal, was taken from the Courts of Justice in the back of a farmer's cart, hastily hired by the warden. The farmer had been hired, too, as chauffeur, and he had not put the gates of the court far behind him before he cleared his throat.

"Good afternoon, my lord," Thurston said over his shoulder without moving his lips, as if there was nothing the least bit unusual about conversing stealthily with the bloody remains of his dead master laid out in the back of a hay cart. "I trust the shots were not too painful."

Crispin spoke from under his makeshift shroud. "Not too bad. My shoulder hurts a little, but the stomach worked like a dream. I am a bit out of practice on the heart stopping, but it went over all right. I thought the hour of escape would never come. The blood, by the way, was superb. It's not the normal recipe is it?"

"No, my lord. Miss Helena suggested a slightly different combination of ingredients. I am glad it met with your approval, my lord."

Crispin made a mental note to at some point learn more about Miss Helena and the fact that she had apparently captivated his completely uncaptivatable steward. But now he had more pressing things to deal with.

"Have you heard anything from Miss Champion?" he asked, still under the shroud. "Has anyone seen her?"

"I did not get the feeling from your comments last night before your arrest that you wanted any search made for her, my lord."

"I take it there has been no news."

"None, sir. Would you like me to take you home to inquire?"

"No, there is not time for that. Take me—" Crispin hesitated for a moment. What he wanted more than anything was to go all over London looking for Sophie. But he knew he had a duty to perform. "Take me to Saint Martin's Fields. To the warehouse."

"Yes, sir. There are some clean clothes under the straw to your left. I brought both sets, both yours and the set you have been wearing to those secret meetings. And also the scar for the forehead and the tooth blackening."

"I think I will go as myself. There is no need for dissembling anymore." Crispin slipped out of his doublet, taking care not to let his motions be seen over the sides of the cart. "Did the messages get delivered? Were there any problems?"

"No, sir. Everyone is in place."

"They will follow my instructions? It has to be handled exactly as I laid it out." Crispin hated working with others, but on this he had no choice.

"Yes, sir. That has been explained to them." Thurston paused as they came fairly close to an orange-seller's cart, but resumed when they moved past. "Her Majesty herself wrote to wish you luck. She commended you and said that your work on this mission has far surpassed your earlier efforts on her behalf."

"I take it Her Majesty does not think my plan stands a chance of success, then," Crispin said, trying to wriggle out of his breeches without showing signs of life. It was well known that Elizabeth only sent commendations to operatives she deemed were about to die.

"She considers it risky, my lord. Very risky."

"It is the only way to do it, Thurston," Crispin said urgently. "Otherwise we shall never destroy the operation."

"Of course, sir," Thurston replied, and Crispin wondered if there had been a note of doubt in his steward's voice or if he was simply imagining things.

There was no question that the plan was dangerous. But it also had the highest chance of success. He repeated this to himself as he lay in the back of the cart, imprinted it on his mind, because he needed to remember it in order to chase out the thoughts and worries about Sophie that threatened to distract him. He had tried during his blindfolded meetings to ensure Sophie's safety by making certain that, one way or another, she would end up in his custody, and he had redoubled his efforts once he learned that his adversaries had spies inside Sandal Hall. Her disappearance yesterday was worrisome, but he knew that she would be fine. The people with whom he had been dealing would not do anything to her, he assured himself, because she was still too valuable to them and because they did not know that he was the man they had been bargaining with. Certainly they would not hurt her before the operation was concluded, and after, with any luck, they would not be in a position to.

Crispin had just resolved this to his satisfaction when Thurston slowed the cart. The bells of Saint Martin's tolled once as they rolled to a stop near a clump of trees.

"I count twenty men, sir," Thurston told the corpse at the back of the cart. "The other detachment must already have left to follow the coins. The counterfeiters began emptying the warehouse this morning, just after news of your arrest was announced, as you had predicted."

"Good." Letting the counterfeiters move their coins out and deliver them to their agents so that the Queen's guards would be able to catch everyone involved in the operation, not just the principals, was the first part of the program—facilitated by Crispin's public arrest and trial, which lulled the counterfeiters into complacency. That part was moderately risky, but not in any personal way. It was this second part, the part that Crispin now had to face alone, that contained the real peril. So far, however, everything was going just as he had planned.

Which made him very nervous. Quashing his uneasiness, Crispin sat up in the back of the cart and brushed the hay from his clothes. "Well, Thurston. I am off. See you in an hour."

"Yes, sir."

The words, words that Crispin had heard a hundred thousand times in his life from his steward, always sounded different to him right before he walked into danger.

Crispin slid from the cart and mingled himself with the trees. He skirted by one contingent of soldiers unseen and rounded the field until the warehouse was in sight. It was a long wooden structure with no windows and only one door, a massive slab attached with huge iron hinges. It had taken Crispin almost an hour the other night to break through it and the complex lock that sealed it, but today, when he reached it, he found it unlocked.

It made a slight noise as he pushed it open, but not enough to alert anyone to his presence. He heard the sound of voices, at a distance, coming from behind a closed door at the rear of the room in which he was standing. He knew from his researches two nights earlier that this larger room had been used for making and storing the coins, but that was not apparent anymore. The place had been emptied. The walls that had formerly been lined with sacks of glittering coins now were bare, and the coin presses that had been arrayed around the room had been dismantled, their parts left in a heap at its center. Around them, indeed covering the entire surface of the floor, was a dark powder that gave off an acrid scent which Crispin knew too well. Gunpowder.

Crispin stood stock-still as he waited for his eyes to adjust. He did not know what kind of gunpowder the counterfeiters had used, but there were several varieties that could be ignited by the slightest friction, say the friction of a man walking across it. If that was the case here, the people belonging to the voices still coming from the other end of the room would have had to leave a path for their retreat. Crispin scanned the floor in the half-light that filtered in through a skylight in the roof and found what he was looking for. It began four arm's lengths to his right. Pressing his body alongside the wall, he crossed the distance on the balls of his feet.

From there, the path led directly to the door at the rear, the door behind which Crispin would find the head of the counterfeiting operation. Knowing whom he would see when he opened the door, he knew he needed to prepare himself well. It was going to be the fight of his life. With this in mind, he pictured the room to himself, pictured the two immense fireplaces that had been used to liquefy the metals so they could be molded, pictured the enormous iron tools that hung alongside each fireplace, pictured the well of liquid quicklime—caustic enough to burn the skin off a man in less time than it took him to say his name—at its center. He made sure he could recall every detail in his mind, should he need it. Then he strode across the floor and let himself in.

. . .

Beauty exalts those who possess it. It raises us up, ~~makes us as gods and goddesses,~~ *endows us with the power of gods and goddesses, with the power of law,* ~~which is the power to make money.~~ *We are above the law, and all those who oppose us will be punished. Those who stand in the way of Beauty* ~~must~~ *will die. Beauty shines when those who oppose* ~~me~~ *her perish.*

Sophie shuddered as she read these words in the journal she had almost tripped over earlier, but she could not keep herself from turning the page.

Passion for Beauty makes men weak.
Passion for Beauty makes ~~me~~ women strong.

Those were the last words in the book. The rest of it was equally strange, all about gold and beauty and blood, but more harrowing was the fact that Sophie knew the hand in which it was written, and knew that it belonged to the voice she had heard earlier, the voice she had thought was that of a friend, the voice of the murderer. Sophie remembered the shocked expressions on the dead faces of Tottle and Sweetson and imagined hers had been the same when she heard that voice, a voice from whom she thought she had nothing to fear, ordering her death. Setting the book aside, she stood up and began pacing the room. It had to be at least a quarter past one by now, leaving her only three quarters of an hour to live, or three quarters of an hour to make her escape. She could hear Kit in the hall outside the door, humming to himself while he sharpened his knife on a whetstone, getting ready for two o'clock.

Her eyes scoured the room for the hundredth time seeking anything that she might use to escape. For the thirty-eighth time, she found herself staring at the large, brass candlestick standing on the table by the side of the bed, and for the thirty-eighth time she reminded herself that it was bolted down and that she could not budge it. Had it not been, it would have been a choice item to use on Kit's head, if she could have convinced him to open the door. But as it was, she would have to somehow lure him all the way into the room and then make him bend down and help her pull it on top of him before she could put it to any use at all. All of which seemed highly unlikely.

She continued her pacing and scouring, trying to focus her thoughts on her escape. Now, now that it was almost too late, she knew who the murderer was. She had heard the voice from the corridor calling for her death, and all the pieces clicked succinctly into place. Suddenly she had seen that Constantia had actually been covering up for someone else. Suddenly she had understood that there was another person who fit, as neatly as Crispin did, the profile of the murderer Constantia had drawn. Someone who would have been threatened by notes referring to the death of Constantia's first husband, threatened enough to kill. Someone who had killed before out of love for Constantia, killed her first husband, and would kill again, kill Lord Grosgrain, and then kill Tottle and Sweetson for the threat their blackmail posed of revealing the crimes to the world. Each of these murders, Sophie saw, had been committed out of love, by someone whose love for Constantia was all powerful. Someone whose happiness was identical to Constantia's.

But even if that person was not Crispin, Sophie knew now that he did not—and would not—love her. There could be no contradicting Constantia's evidence on that front, no way around the fact that Crispin had merely been repeating lines to Sophie to seduce her, lines from someone else's love scene. Probably, Sophie surmised, he had done it to make Constantia jealous, but the motive was unimportant. The life she had dreamed of with Crispin was just that, Sophie knew now, a dream, and an impossible one. If she should manage to escape with her neck still attached to her body—which looked increasingly unlikely—she would not even go to Sandal Hall to burden Crispin with her presence or with the fact that she had won their bet, but would just see to it that the real murderer got what was coming to h—

Sophie's eye fell on the candlestick again, and suddenly she understood how she could use it. Not wasting a minute, she climbed on the bed and began screaming at the top of her lungs.

Kit ran in, brandishing his knife in front of him. "Shut that," he told her menacingly, gesturing in the direction of her mouth.

But Sophie ignored him and continued with her screaming. "A caterpillar," she screeched. "I saw a caterpillar. It went under the bed, it was huge, it went under the bed!"

Kit shook his head at her. "You have more to be afraid of than a caterpillar, Miss Champion," he told her with a glint in his eye. "Half an hour from now, you will be dead. If I were you, I would not spend too much of my remaining time thinking about vermin."

"Please," Sophie begged him with tears in her eyes. "Please just kill it for me. As a last act of kindness for a condemned woman. Please kill the bug. It's under the bed, I know it is." When Kit still did not move, Sophie went on apologetically, "Unless—unless you are afraid of caterpillars too?"

Kit looked at her with utter disdain. Without wasting a word on a response, he wrapped one strong hand around Sophie's ankle to ensure that she could not escape and leaned over and looked under the bed. "Nothing," he sneered, preparing to stand. "I can't see—"

The candlestick, table and all, fell heavily across his back, knocking him out and loosening his grip on her leg. "Leverage," Sophie whispered under her breath with a small smile to the heavens, and then quickly fled through the open door.

Two flights of stairs put her in the entrance hall, where she found the door unlocked. She opened it slowly, wary of guards, and peered into the street. It was completely empty, and the only sound that met her ears was the welcome noise of bees buzzing around the flowering tree she had seen through her window. Looking in both directions, she emerged from the shadows of the entrance into the bright sunlight of the street and turned right.

"Stop the girl," Kit shouted from a window above her, rending the tranquil summer silence. "Stop her, she's getting away."

A dozen men leapt out of the doorways and windows of the surrounding houses and came toward her. They had been waiting for her, waiting for her to try something. Without thinking, Sophie took off, her feet pounding, running as fast as she could go. She turned right, then left, then left again, looking over her shoulder every three steps, her heart racing. They were right behind her, closing the gap, and she pushed herself forward harder. Her legs began to throb, but she did not stop running, right, left, right, right, left, winding around the alleys in this unknown part of London, until she was gasping for air and thought her chest would explode.

They were still behind her but far enough now that she decided to take a chance. She made two quick turns, left and then right, and slid into the first narrow alleyway she found. She slowed her pace now, knowing that there was no way they could have seen her, but she did not stop running. She moved quickly down the alleyway, trying to muffle the sound of her footfalls so as not to give her location away. All she had to do was get to the next street, put that alley between her and her pursuers, and she knew she would be safe. With this single thought, she followed the alley as it wound around, continued down it as it became narrower, and darker, and then, abruptly, came to an end.

"I've got her," she heard one of the men say as she stared at the blank wall in front of her. She was about to try to climb it when a forceful pull on her shoulder dragged her down to earth.

Crispin crossed the threshold of the back room of the warehouse without hesitation and cleared his throat. "Good afternoon," he said amiably to the two people there.

Constantia reacted first, grabbing her companion by the arm and screeching, "Lawrence, what is he doing here?"

Lawrence swung around from the fireplace. In his hands were the papers and books with which he was feeding the fire, the last evidences of the largest counterfeiting ring to ever successfully operate on English soil. When his eyes met his friend's, they were cold and menacing. "That is a very good question my darling asks. What are you doing here, Crispin?"

"Arresting you in the name of the Queen," Crispin explained without preamble.

"The name of the Queen," Lawrence repeated sarcastically. "That certainly sounds mighty. I suppose next you will tell me that you are the Phoenix."

"I am."

"Bah." Lawrence dropped the papers he was holding onto the fire, pushing them in with an iron poker. He spoke without turning. "The Phoenix has fought and vanquished better men than you, Crispin my friend." Lawrence spun around, the poker in his hands, its tip red-hot and aimed at Crispin's throat.

Crispin ducked and passed under the poker, heading for the fireplace. He grabbed the other poker that was lying there with his left hand and had it up in time to parry Lawrence's thrust from behind. Lawrence, wielding the poker like a sword with both hands on one end, ran at Crispin. Iron clanged against iron as the two men went through motions they had practiced together so many times as boys, never thinking they would end by using them against each other as men. The two men were fighting in front of the door now, and Constantia was forced to huddle in a corner as the duel waged on.

They danced around each other, testing, jabbing, until Crispin decided the time had come. With a terrifying holler, Crispin threw himself on top of Lawrence, the poker pressing horizontally across his enemy's chest, pinning him to the wall next to the door. They stayed locked like that, Crispin on top, the poker between them, Lawrence panting beneath it, until Lawrence opened his hand and let his weapon fall to the floor.

"Nicely done," Crispin commended his friend without lessening the pressure on the metal bar that imprisoned him. "But you are no match for me. You are finished, Lawrence. It is over. Your little experiment in counterfeiting is at an end."

"Counterfeiting?" Lawrence asked through his panting. "Look around you, Crispin. What do you see? An empty warehouse. And even that won't be here for very long. Constantia and I are just try-ing to clear away all the debris left behind by her late husband, so we can begin afresh together. I am afraid I don't know anything about counterfeiting."

Crispin smiled at him, a sad smile. "Why don't I tell you about it, then. We have some time before the guards come to take you away, and we may as well spend it in pleasant conversation."

Lawrence's only reply was a snort.

"It was not just counterfeiting," Crispin told him. "It was mur-der too. But all for a common reason. All for love."

Lawrence tried to push the poker off his chest, but Crispin was there, pressing him back. Crispin leaned into him, leaving less than a finger's width between their faces, and the two men glared into each other's eyes.

"Don't try to talk," Crispin admonished him, holding his gaze. "I will tell you the story. It is actually quite interesting. It starts off two and a half years ago, when I broke up your counterfeiting scheme the first time and killed your alchemist, Damon Goldhawk. Of course, I did not know at the time that you were the mastermind behind it, or I would never have let you get away. But I was forced to leave for the continent, and during my absence, you decided to undertake a new operation, this one even more ambitious than the first. You needed a replacement for Damon, so you found the foremost alchemist in England, Milton Grosgrain, and gained a hold over him by using Constantia, the woman you loved. You knew he could not resist her charms—no man can—so you made him fall in love with her and marry her. Then you threatened that she would leave him if he refused to help you revive your counterfeiting operation. He agreed, he could not help himself, and for a time everything went smoothly. But then the blackmail began.

"Lord Grosgrain probably did not see any real harm in the letters when they arrived, letters that raised questions about the death of Constantia's first husband, because their accusations were vague. He was willing to pay the blackmail and be done with it. But not you. You could not be so sanguine. Because you actually had killed Constantia's first husband, and the letters suggested a real peril to you. Only the person who had murdered Constantia's husband would have been upset enough by the letters to kill the blackmailer, and you were the murderer. You planned to kill Richard Tottle, but you knew that you could not do so without arousing Lord Grosgrain's suspicions. So, after making sure you had everything you needed from Lord Grosgrain, had benefited fully from his alchemical expertise, you killed him."

Crispin shook his head in mock sympathy, but his eyes never left Lawrence's. "It must have been quite a shock to you when the blackmail continued even after Richard Tottle's death. But you were committed, and would not be stopped. You killed Sweetson, your new blackmailer, just as you had killed Tottle. And then, finally, you were free to indulge your dual loves—your love of gold and your love for Constantia. You had killed to protect both of them, and now you planned to reap your rewards. But there was one small problem. The Phoenix."

Crispin went on, almost as if he were speaking to himself. "The Phoenix had destroyed your counterfeiting operation the first time around, two and a half years ago, and this time you did not want to take any chances. So you circulated rumors about the Phoenix, made suggestions about his behavior, said enough to make the Queen worry. By drumming him out of favor, you thought you would make him easier to identify, and easier to kill. Unfortunately, you forgot your mythology. The Phoenix never dies."

"This is all terribly interesting and dramatic," Lawrence interjected impatiently, "but it has nothing to do with me. Nor can you prove that it does."

"That, my friend, is where you are wrong. Because there was an eyewitness to all of this. Someone who was there for every act of your macabre play." Crispin turned to look at Constantia now. "You, Constantia, you know all about it."

Lawrence held his breath and watched Constantia, who was cowering in the corner. The expression on his face could have been either hope or fear.

Constantia directed her gaze at Crispin, tears quivering at the corners of her eyes. "Can't you see how he is looking at me?" she asked, trembling. "If I say anything, he will kill me."

"There is no need to be afraid," Crispin told her, soothingly, without moving his body from Lawrence. "His threats will not work anymore. I know that he has manipulated you and made you bow to his will, to his wishes. Isn't that true?"

"Yes!" Constantia sobbed, looking more like an angel now than ever. "Yes, oh, Crispin. It is all true."

Lawrence looked at her hopelessly. "Can't you see that this is a trap, Constantia darling? He has nothing on you, nothing, so long as you do not say a word."

But Constantia ignored his warning. "You cannot hurt me any-more, you monster," she told Lawrence through her tears. "You cannot make me bend to you. You told me that if I loved you, I would have to do what you said. You pretended to be testing my love, my loyalty. You tried to make me wretched, make me vile, make me into a criminal like you. But you couldn't. Oh, Crispin"—she looked at him now—"you cannot imagine the fear, the terror under which I have been living. You were right, he did kill Milton."

"My god," Lawrence cried, and the words seemed to have been wrenched from deep inside of him. "My god, Constantia, you are the counterfeiter."

"Stop, Lawrence," Constantia said, rising and crossing the room toward the two men. "You have called me names for too long now. I will no longer submit to you. You killed Milton. And afterward you liked to make me think about it, about how you had hooked the horse's leg from the alley, about how you had laughed in Mil-ton's face as he lay dying on the pavement, laughed when with his dying breath he said he still loved me." Constantia was shaking, her hands clenched into fists, as she looked at Lawrence.

Then she turned her eyes on Crispin. "You were right about the others as well. He killed them because of the blackmail. And after each of them he reveled in what he had done, reveled in remem-bering how they died, how surprised they looked. If I did not cooperate, I knew he would do the same thing to me. He put his filthy, low-life hands on me, Crispin. He made me call him my lord. He used my body. *My* body." She began to tremble. "I hated him. I told him I hated him, that I wanted to see him dead, and that only made him want me more, made him—" She turned her head away.

Lawrence had lost color as she spoke and was now an almost chalky white.

Crispin was seething. "I will kill you for this, you bastard," he told his former friend. "I will kill you for every way you hurt her."

"Wait, Crispin," Constantia interjected. "It was not just me. He had people, servants, spying on you and Sophie in your chamber to hurt you, too. He made me go to Sophie and tell her about you, about us, tell her lies, use the words you had used with her and pretend you had said them to me, so she would hate you. He wanted to break her heart so that your heart would break. You have no idea what a monster he is, no idea—" She broke off, sobbing.

"Is this true?" Crispin demanded of his friend.

"Constantia," Lawrence whispered in the tone of a man who has just been stabbed through the chest. "Constantia, how could you do this?" His eyes were staring sightlessly at the corner of the chamber where the object of his address was standing, wiping her tears. Soon, Crispin's eyes moved there too.

"Constantia," Crispin told her. "You have already had enough pain for one day. I do not want you to have to see what will happen next. Will you go? Will you leave here if I promise to make sure he can never hurt you again?"

Constantia swallowed hard. "I am so scared, Crispin."

"There is no need. Go outside and wait for me. I will be out soon. As soon as I have finished with him."

Constantia shrank as she neared the door next to which the two men were standing. She pressed herself as closely as she could against the far lintel, then, closing that door behind her, ran across the outer room.

As soon as he heard the sound of the big door clanking shut, Crispin removed the poker from Lawrence's chest. Lawrence did not move.

"I am sorry," Crispin said when the silence between them had stretched. "I wish there had been some other way to show you what Constantia was and what she was doing. I tried to warn you, but I guess there was no way for me to prepare you."

Lawrence swallowed hard, twice, then waved the apology aside. "No. I forced you to do it like this." His words came haltingly. "Remember how I refused to believe what you said about Constantia, refused to believe that she was a counterfeiter? That she was capable of murder? Refused to believe that she was using me or that she did not love me and would turn on me with the slightest provocation?" Lawrence had to stop for a moment to take a deep breath. "I tried to kill you when you told me, if you recall correctly."

Crispin nodded, his hand massaging the place on his neck where Lawrence's dagger had been during their discussion of Constantia two days earlier, when they had arranged the scene they had just acted.

Shaking his head at himself and his stupidity, Lawrence went on. "When you suggested this charade to prove what you were saying to me, I accepted it without the slightest hesitation because I believed in her love so strongly. There *was* no other way to show me what she was, I could not have been convinced of it otherwise. It is too impossible. She is so beautiful. I thought she was perfect. I thought she was good." Lawrence's voice broke here. "My god, Crispin, I loved her so much."

"I know." Crispin put an arm around his friend. "She is very lovely."

"How could I have been such a fool?" Lawrence almost howled. "At first I wanted what she offered, her noble blood, her noble titles. At first I think I wanted her because she had once been yours. But then, later, it became so much more. I would have done anything for her. Anything. I was ready to leave London and run away with her. She told me that she would marry me today, tonight, if I would help her burn down this old warehouse, help her rid herself of her memories from the past so we could start afresh, she said. She said she wanted to be married in France and told me to procure passports for us, and I did as she asked. I never once suspected what she was doing. I had no idea about the counterfeiting, about all this." He waved an arm around the warehouse. "I never even imagined that it existed. But I should have. I should have asked. I should have wondered why she would have anything to do with me." He shut his eyes tight and clamped his jaw. "I was ready to throw away everything I had ever worked for, out of love of her. And she was just using me."

The two men seated themselves on the edge of the quicklime pit. Crispin tried to console him. "You are not the first man to have been fooled by a woman."

"It is nice of you to say so, but how many men allow themselves to be led this far down the path of destruction? Did you hear the hate in her voice when she addressed me at the end? Real hate? She hated me all along. She hated me as she promised to let me marry her. She hated me as she prepared to lay this entire counterfeiting scheme and her murders at my door, hated me even as she used me, and I never knew it." Lawrence jammed his fists into his eyes. "I just loved her more for relying on me."

After a long space of silence, he spoke again but kept his knuckles at his eyes. "You were very good with the poker, by the way. If I had not known any better, I would have feared for my life."

"Not from me." Crispin left his arm around his friend. "Maybe from Constantia."

"So everything you said was true?" Lawrence asked, looking up.

Crispin nodded. "The whole thing, so long as you substitute Constantia's name for yours."

"How did you know it was her and not me? The evidence as you laid it out certainly seems to fit."

"The fact that Richard Tottle was murdered in your club was the principal thing that convinced me it was not you. I could not see you stooping to murder, not even for love, and if something happened to make you kill a man, you would never do it in one of your own clubs. The blackmail, I have to admit, did confuse me a bit."

"Me too," Lawrence confessed. "After you came to my office and told me about the flaming arrows, I had a long talk with Grimley, my deputy. It seems that one night over dinner several years ago I had outlined what I called the perfect blackmail setup, saying, obviously, that I would never execute it because blackmail is a dirty, dishonest crime. Grimley did not have any such reservations and has apparently been putting my ideas into action for some time, even going so far as to blackmail my own Constantia."

"That makes sense," Crispin said, nodding. "I could not imagine who besides you would have developed such a scheme, but I knew you would never blackmail. What did you mean about the flaming arrows?"

"Ah. Those are something a little special that my boys have been working on, under contract for the Queen. It is extremely secret, and there is no chance that anyone but us has them, so when you said you had almost been set on fire by one, I knew that it was someone in my organization. By the way, I think you let me off too easy as a murder suspect. But what made you think of Constantia?"

"Several things. Whoever was behind this had to have great influence over Lord Grosgrain, and there were only four people who could wield such influence: Sophie, Basil Grosgrain, Constantia, and, through her, you. Eliminating you and Sophie left only two suspects, and Constantia was by far the best. She had been around at the time of the first counterfeiting operation, and the need for an alchemist was really the only thing that explained her marriage to Lord Grosgrain. But I did not know for certain that it was her until I met Basil. When questions were posed about his whereabouts at the times of the two murders, he looked tense and scared until Constantia came to his aid and said he had been with her. It was clearly a fake alibi, and after a bit of prodding, he admitted as much. But in doing so he was also admitting that Constantia had no alibi for those times. In other words, Constantia provided him with a false alibi, in order to provide herself with one. When I knew that, I knew everything. I knew that she was the murderer and the counterfeiter."

There was a long pause, and then Lawrence asked, "And then you came to see me. How did you know I was in love with Constantia?"

"Sophie. She saw you in Constantia's dressing room the other night in a fairly intimate posture. She thought it was me at first, but when she explained that she had only seen the man's back, I realized that it was probably you. That and the fact that you were writing all that love poetry the other day when I was in your office."

"I was not," Lawrence said with horror. "Did you go through my desk?"

"No, I saw it on your desk blotter when I rose to go. Not bad, although you might consider that 'Constantia' rhymes better with 'tarantula' than with 'my fancy's doll.'"

Lawrence looked for a moment like he was caught between laughing and crying. "Is that why you let her go, then?" he stammered finally. "For me?"

Crispin grimaced. "I did not let her go. This place is surrounded by the Queen's guards. Or was. Twenty of them. Whose only job was to arrest her."

Lawrence looked at Crispin with shock. "Then you really *are* the Phoenix."

"No." Crispin shook his head. "I was. The Phoenix retired today." He had tried to comfort his friend as much as he could, but he could no longer contain his impatience. "And his retirement won't be worth a damn, my life won't be worth a damn, if I don't lay eyes on Sophie again soon and repair whatever damage Constantia may have done. Let's get out of here."

"What does 'Sophie' rhyme with?" Lawrence asked Crispin mockingly as they rose to leave the chamber. "Maybe with—"

Lawrence's poetic interlude ended abruptly as they opened the door. He and Crispin just stood there for a moment, staring, dumbstruck. They had been so occupied by their conversation that they had not noticed the temperature rising or the popping noises or the strange smell of smoke coming from the other room. Smoke fueled by a dozen barrels of gunpowder carefully strewn to do maximum damage. The smoke of a floor turned into a flaming inferno.

"The fuse. She must have lit the fuse before the guards got her," Lawrence murmured under his breath as they looked at the sea of flames between them and the only way out. "I don't want to make things seem worse than they are," he went on, "but the gunpowder is just the beginning. There are enough explosives wrapped around the rafters to destroy this building, and the larger part of the parish. At least there are if she used half of everything she asked me to get for her."

Crispin gazed at his friend with horror.

"Don't look at me like that," Lawrence ordered. "I already told you. She said she wanted to destroy her husband's workshop so she would no longer be tortured by memories of him. She said it would allow us to start from scratch, with nothing behind us, nothing tying us down."

"I see." Crispin moved his eyes back to the flames and asked coolly, "Any idea how the explosives in the rafters are detonated?"

"Oh, very simply. Their fuses dangle down, so when the flames leap high enough, the first one will be ignited. After that, the roof should fall in and the others will go."

"So we have as long as it will take for the flames to reach the fuses."

"Exactly," Lawrence confirmed. "And I wouldn't worry too much. That one there is only about three-quarters of the way up to the ceiling."

They slammed the door shut and strode to the middle of the room in unison. "The skylight is our best chance of escape," Crispin said, and Lawrence agreed. It was at least five body's lengths from the floor, exactly over the lime pit, which meant they could not attain it directly. They would have to climb up to the rafters, then shimmy along them until they reached it.

"Is there a rope?" Crispin asked hopefully, stripping off his shirt in the melting heat.

"Yes." Lawrence cleared his throat. "In the other room."

They worked without speaking, without needing to. Crispin dragged the table from the wall toward the middle of the room, and Lawrence carried the two chairs over, putting them on top. Like that, with the chairs stacked on the table as a crude ladder, Crispin could almost reach.

"I just need a few more feet," he gasped, stretching as far as he could. And then, as if by magic, he had them. He wrapped himself around the rafter and looked down to see what had achieved this miracle. It was Lawrence who, perched on the first of the two chairs, had boosted Crispin up.

"Go," Lawrence insisted, motioning Crispin toward the skylight. "You go. I will be fine here. I will wait, and you will come and get me."

"Don't be a fool. You know there is not enough time for that." Crispin undid the stays on his breeches and pulled them off with one hand, wrapping them around the rafters with the empty legs dangling down. "Here, grab these," he said, pushing the makeshift rope toward Lawrence.

But Lawrence refused to budge. "Please, Crispin. It is my fault you are part of this. Just go. I will be fine."

Crispin hung by his hands from the rafters just above Lawrence's head. "Damn you, Lawrence Pickering. If you won't come up here, I am going to have to come back down. You are my best friend, despite my better judgment, and I am not going to leave you here to die for love of Constantia Grosgrain."

"Just g—" Lawrence interrupted himself. "What do you mean, 'despite' your best judgment'?"

"Because you are absolutely the most obstinate best friend a man could have," Crispin shouted down at him. "Now grab my breeches and climb up."

After two false starts, a loud ripping noise, and a litany of grunts, Lawrence was dangling next to Crispin. "Obstinate," he muttered as they began to shimmy toward the skylight. "I am not obstinate."

"Are you kidding? If you were not obstinate, you would be working for that deputy of yours."

"You have a point," Lawrence grunted as they struggled to pull themselves along. "But I am not nearly as—"

"Hello?" a voice called from the floor, interrupting them. "Is there anyone here? Crispin? Hello?"

"Sophie!" Crispin and Lawrence shouted in unison.

Sophie tipped her head back and looked up at the ceiling. "What are you doing up there? It must be even hotter than it is down here."

"Sophie," Crispin panted, "how did you get in?"

"Through the side door."

"Side door?" Lawrence growled.

"Yes, just back there." Sophie pointed behind her, confused as to why they were treating her like a demon prodigy. "I will go, if you prefer. I was planning to go anywa—"

"No!" Crispin shouted it. He and Lawrence were madly shim-mying backward, back toward the table. They dropped down, in unison, cracking the tabletop, and leapt off it onto the ground.

"Go, go, go." Crispin grabbed Sophie's arm and began pulling her in the direction she had indicated.

"Wait, Crispin. I *am* going. For real this time. But I just came to tell you that I know who the murderer—"

"Come on," he urged her.

"I am trying to go as fast as I can," Sophie told him, staying put. "I know you are in love with her, so I am sorry to tell you this, but it was Const—"

Crispin picked her up in his arms and was running toward the door when there was an enormous bang and the ceiling came crashing down on top of them.

Chapter Twenty-Four

"*Shh*. Do you hear something?" the guardsman asked his companion. A crew of them—all those who had not been needed to escort Constantia Grosgrain, still fighting wildly despite her manacles, to the Tower gaol—had been combing through the area around the exploded warehouse looking for survivors of the blast. They had found one of them, thrown into a ditch, clothes singed, a bit groggy but otherwise fine, but they had not been able to find the other two. As night neared and nothing new turned up, it was inevitably concluded that the other two had perished. Until now. Both guards stopped moving abruptly and listened.

It was faint, but, with concentration, they could make it out.

"No," a voice said. "I did."

"Oh, no. Certainly not. I did. It was certainly me."

"You must be joking. I—" Crispin stopped speaking as two guards appeared at the edge of the clearing in which he and Sophie had taken refuge.

"We found them," one of the guardsmen called over his shoulder, and soon the sound of a dozen heavy footfalls was heard.

"Um, Crispin," Sophie said from where she had hidden her face in his armpit. "I am not sure you are aware of it, but we are both naked."

"I am aware of it," Crispin said, feeling with his hand for his leggings, or at least one of his boots.

"I believe you left most of your clothes in the warehouse," Sophie reminded his armpit, "and I had to shed mine when we found they were on fire."

Crispin remembered now, remembered stripping off burning clothes and taking refuge in this clearing moments before losing consciousness. He was just looking around for a good-sized leaf, or even branch, when the guards' commander appeared at the opening of the clearing.

"You are wanted, Lord Sandal," he announced formally.

"That is marvelous," Crispin told him, "but I am also wanting. Clothes."

"I am afraid there is no time to procure you any. Your presence is demanded. Now."

"Who is so important that they can't wait a moment while I get some clothes?" Crispin demanded crossly, standing up. "Is it the bloody Queen?"

"Yes, Lord Sandal," said the voice that had given Crispin the false order to retire as the Phoenix thirteen days earlier, "it is."

Crispin and the guards all fell on their knees as Queen Elizabeth emerged into the clearing. Out of the corner of his eye, Crispin could see that Sophie had hidden herself behind a tree but was watching everything.

The Queen stopped in front of Crispin and gave him her hand. The thick gold band with the knot in it, which had signaled that the conversation at their first meeting had been in a form of code and that Crispin was to understand every command preceded by the word "not" as an actual order, had been replaced by a massive, straightforward ruby, which Crispin kissed.

"You may rise, Lord Sandal," the Queen said, adding when Crispin wavered, "Do not worry. We have seen such things before." Once Crispin was standing before her—looking very fine, Sophie thought—the Queen went on. "Your service, Lord Sandal, has been exemplary. You followed Our instructions exactly. You acted clandestinely to uncover and thwart the source of peril to Our kingdom, and you did it in less than the time allotted to you. But there is one instruction you failed to observe."

"I beg Your Highness's pardon, but I—"

"Do not interrupt Us, Lord Sandal. In this single point only did you fail Us." The Queen seemed to grow larger and more imperious. "You have not taken an English bride, Lord Sandal. Your aunts tell me that you have chosen one, but you have not finalized your union, despite their prodding. They even had Our agents issue a warrant to search your house for her, to make you search your heart, but to no avail. However, if they deem her worthy of you, Lord Sandal, then so must We. Marry her, Lord Sandal, marry her soon. With Our blessing. And with Our ring." The Queen slid the ruby from her finger and extended it to him. When Crispin hesitated to take such a rich gem, the Queen leaned toward him and whispered, "You may as well. You already have the matching bracelet."

"And then there she was, the old woman," Sophie explained, leaning her head against Crispin's chest as they soaked in the bath in his garden. It had been ready for them when they arrived at Sandal Hall, already filled with gloriously scented steaming water. "She grabbed me and pulled me into what looked like a pile of rubbish but was actually a hidden door to a small house with an exit on the opposite street. What was stranger than that, stranger even than her being so opportunely placed at the end of an alley, was that she knew who I was, and who you were, and where I needed to go to find you."

Crispin was frowning slightly, running through the inventory of old women in his head. "What did she look like?"

"It is hard to say. She was hunched over slightly and wore a hood. But when she grabbed me in the alley, I was able to see her eyes, and I had never seen anything like them."

"Let me guess," Crispin said, and felt a faint tingling at the base of his spine, "they were gold."

"Yes," Sophie nodded. "How did you know?"

"Because she was here the night of the fire and stayed to help put it out. And I have seen her several times outside of Sandal Hall."

"Who do you think she is?"

"I can't say. We'll have to ask her next time we see her." Crispin's voice was distant, and his eyes were looking past Sophie. Thinking about the fire had reminded him of something he needed to tell her. Something hard.

Thinking about the fire had reminded Sophie of something too. The night of the fire was the night she knew she loved Crispin. If only—

"Sophie," Crispin announced in a strange voice, abruptly breaking into her thoughts. "Sophie, there is something I want to tell you."

Sophie looked at him intently. Her heart was pounding. "Yes, Crispin?"

"Sophie, I—" He broke off.

Sophie smiled up at him, encouraging him, pleading with him to say the words she wanted more than anything to hear. "Yes, Crispin? What is it?"

Crispin took a deep breath and blurted it out. "Sophie, I killed your brother. Damon. I killed him. Two and a half years ago."

Sophie's reaction was worse than Crispin had anticipated. She pulled away from him, a look of painful shock on her face. "What are you talking about? Damon? My brother? What do you know about Damon?"

"I did not do this very well," Crispin stated as much to himself as to her. "I am sorry. Basil Grosgrain told me about Damon. About your past. About who you were before the fire."

"Basil? How did he know?" The look of shock had not receded.

"He hired someone to find out. He had nothing to do with the counterfeiting, but he thought you killed his father and he hired someone to investigate you. He was trying to convince me as well. But what I meant to say, Sophie, is that I am sorry. I understand if, after knowing that I killed your brother, you might feel differently about me."

Sophie stayed very quiet for a time. "How did it happen?" she asked finally. "How did you kill him?"

"He was part of the first counterfeiting operation that I uncovered.

He shot at me, and I had to shoot back. Unfortunately for him, I was the better shot."

"Then he is dead? Really dead?" Crispin nodded. "Thank god," Sophie whispered, so softly that Crispin was not sure he had heard her correctly.

"What?" he asked, a lump forming in his throat.

"I said, thank god." Sophie looked at him again now. "Thank god he is dead. And thank god you survived. I cannot imagine a life without you, Crispin."

"But Damon—" Crispin began.

"Damon was the man who kept me in the attic. The man who tormented me. By the end, he was no longer my brother. He was a monster. I have lived under the shadow of the nightmare he created for years. Until you came along."

"Then you do not want to leave me?" Crispin asked cautiously.

Sophie shook her head. "Crispin, I never want to leave you."

"But before, you pulled away from me like you hated me," he pointed out.

"You surprised me. I thought—I was expecting you to say something else."

"Oh."

Sophie resettled herself in the crook of his arm and listened to the sound of water trickling off the statue of Venus at the far end of the bath and told herself she did not need Crispin to love her. She was repeating this for the tenth time when Crispin's voice roused her from her thoughts.

"About the bet," he began.

Sophie frowned at him. "I do not believe there is anything left to discuss, my lord. The winner is clear."

"I am glad we agree." Crispin sank into the water up to his chin. "Lucky for you, I am a good winner."

Sophie's frown deepened. "It would be lucky for me, if you had won, but since I won you will be made to suffer. I am a terrible winner."

"But I won. You said you knew it was Constantia at noon. I knew hours before that."

"You cannot prove it. And besides, it is moot. I have won."

"You cannot just decree that."

"Yes"—Sophie grinned, her spirits rising—"I can. The Fates were on my side."

"Fates? That is like saying The Aunts were on your side. That is not conclusive."

"Conclusive?" she queried. "I can make it conclusive." She was just about to step out of the bath when Thurston cleared his throat from behind the lavender hedge.

"Good evening, my lord, Miss Champion," Thurston said as if there were nothing the least bit unusual about addressing his soot-covered master and mistress through a hedge. "I took the liberty of removing these from the safe and bringing them to you. I thought you might want them." He extended around the lavender bush a silver tray on which lay two folded pieces of paper, then disappeared.

Sophie splashed to the side of the bath to grab the papers, then seated herself right next to Crispin.

She looked at him seriously. "As I recall, the terms of the bet were that we each wrote down our deepest secret desire, and whoever won got whatever was on their paper. Do you agree, my lord?"

Crispin nodded, equally seriously, and she handed him the paper, neatly folded in fours, on which she had written what felt like years earlier. "Read it," she commanded him.

"'*I desire you to go naked to your next audience with Queen Elizabeth,*'" Crispin read out. Then he looked at her. He was momentarily speechless with surprise.

"You see," Sophie said, bobbing up and down next to him gleefully. "You see, I did win. Because I have already gotten what I wrote on the paper."

Crispin just sat and shook his head. "I can't believe you asked for that," he said as much to himself as to her.

Sophie smiled widely. "Do not forget that you had just made me strip. It seemed only fair at the time. Didn't you wonder why I said I could not marry you until after the bet was settled? I would never want my husband to do such a thing."

"Of course not." Crispin nodded with mock solemnity, looking with slightly misty eyes at his bride-to-be. "It would hardly do. Your husband must be a paragon."

"Exactly," Sophie confirmed. "Now, what did you ask for?"

Crispin shook his head absently and crumpled his paper. "Given that you won, I don't see that it matters."

"Come on, Crispin, show me what you wrote," Sophie said playfully, reaching for the paper, but her playfulness vanished when he resumed speaking.

"I would rather not. I do not think, with our marriage coming up, it would be good for you to know. For either of us. Besides, I wrote it days ago. When we had only just met."

Sophie felt suddenly hollow. After several long moments had passed in silence, she asked, "Crispin, have you ever been in love?"

Crispin nodded but did not look at her. "Once."

"Did it happen slowly? Or all at once like a lightning shock?"

"All at once," Crispin answered without hesitation. "I fell in love with her the first time I set eyes on her."

"Did she love you back?" Sophie asked.

Crispin nodded again. "She said she did. Although I think it took her a little longer."

Sophie wondered about the idiocy of a woman who would not fall instantly in love with Crispin, but kept these thoughts to herself. "Was she beautiful?"

Crispin shook his head. "No. She was beyond beautiful. She was extraordinary."

"Oh." Sophie did not like this woman, she decided. Not at all. "Was she intelligent?"

Crispin smiled to himself. "Sometimes. Other times she could be blind."

"When?" Sophie asked, glad to hear her rival had a weakness.

"Well, when someone was trying to tell her he loved her, for example."

Sophie looked sage. "That must have been hard for you."

"Actually, I found it quite entertaining," Crispin replied, but

Sophie only half heard. A battle was raging in her head, one side telling her it was better not to learn the identity of Crispin's true love, the other knowing that she would never rest until she found out.

"Who is she?" Sophie blurted finally. "I promise not to interfere, if that is what you are worried about, but I cannot live without knowing."

"You honestly want me to tell you?"

"Yes."

"I really do not think this is a good idea," Crispin said seriously.

"Please, Crispin."

"You are sure?"

"Positive."

"Very well." Crispin retrieved the paper he had crumpled and handed it to her.

Sophie took a large breath for courage, then unfolded it with trembling fingers. And felt her heart burst as she read:

YOU

Chapter Twenty-Five

The river garden of Sandal Hall sparkled with the light of almost a thousand candles and torches. Tents of translucent white gauze embroidered with exotic flowers in bold hues dotted the grass, their sides blowing gently in the evening breeze. The sun was just setting, painting the sky pink and purple behind the hushed and expectant crowd facing the wide back door.

Sophie looked down at them from the second-floor window of Crispin's apartments and felt the sudden urge to flee. "No," she said, stepping backward and nearly tripping over her dress. "No, I do not think today is the right day."

"What are you talking about?" Octavia demanded, swooping down to rescue Sophie's hem from being trampled under its unappreciative wearer's feet.

"I think tomorrow might be a better day. Look outside. Doesn't it look like it might rain?"

Emme, seated in the window embrasure, shook her head. "You might be right, Sophie. I think there is a cloud hovering somewhere over the Kingdom of Sweden."

Octavia took hold of Sophie's hand and turned toward her. "Sophie, what is the matter? I thought you wanted to marry Crispin."

"I did. I do," Sophie went on. "But what if he does not want to marry me? What if he is just doing it because he made the promise and is too honorable to break it?"

"A very good point," Emme agreed. "What if he had amnesia when he asked you and forgot that he was already married. Or what if he is not the Earl of Sandal at all but just a cobbler that looks like him and—"

"Enough," Octavia pronounced, struggling not to smile. "Sophie, you know that is not the case. You know he wants to marry you."

"Maybe," Sophie conceded. "But what if the other Arboretti, his brother and cousins, hate me?"

Octavia shook her head. "They won't hate you."

Sophie ignored her. "What if they are all very prim and proper and think that I am unladylike and unmannerly?"

"They would be right," Octavia pronounced matter-of-factly.

Sophie had just turned to her friend, eyes wide with disbelief, when there was a knock on the door. Before anyone could say anything, a blond head, followed by a small body, appeared.

"Are you Miss Champion?" the blond head asked in slightly accented English. When Sophie nodded, she rushed toward her, smiling enormously. "I am Bianca. Your sister-in-law. I could not wait to meet you. You are even more beautiful than Crispin described, and he used many, many adjectives. Not to mention the letters from Lawrence Pickering. Your dress is spectacular, extraordinary." She turned toward the other two women in the room. "You must be Octavia and Emme. I have heard so much about all of you I—"

"Don't be alarmed by my wife," Ian said, striding into the room. "She always talks this much when she is excited."

"May I present, Ian, Crispin's brother and my husband," Bianca introduced. Noticing the other three tall men who had unceremoniously pushed their way into the room, she continued, pointing to each in turn. "And Miles, Tristan, and Sebastian, Crispin's notorious cousins."

"You know very well that we prefer the word 'illustrious,' Bianca," Tristan chided her. "We would not want Miss Champion to get the wrong idea about us."

"Please, call me Sophie," Sophie just managed to say, completely overwhelmed by her new company.

"Sophie," Sebastian repeated with a nod and a smile, then leaned toward her confidentially. "Tell us, Sophie, is it true that you were wearing a mustache when you and Crispin met?"

After hesitating for a moment, Sophie nodded.

"And that you saved a dozen women from prison?" Bianca wanted to know.

"I—I suppose," Sophie stammered, fairly certain that neither talking about her tendency to wear male hairpieces nor talking about her prison record would improve her standing with the Arboretti.

"I didn't save anyone when I was in prison," Bianca confided, clearly in awe.

"You did come home with a new steward," Ian pointed out, his mock exasperation overlaid with loving amusement. "But I don't suppose Sophie wants to spend her wedding day hearing about all of that. There will be years for us to exhaust her with our boring tales."

"Boring?" Tristan was aghast. "Speak for yourself. My stories are never boring."

"Bah. That one about the Raphael painting that you liberated from the collection of the Duchess of Montecastello by feeding her dogs brandy and cookies while you hung suspended by your ankles in her fireplace is definitely boring," Sebastian said with an exaggerated yawn.

Sophie looked from one to the other of the smiling faces surrounding her, and felt—as she had often in recent days—as though she were in a wonderful dream. Someone else's wonderful dream, a dream of such staggering marvelousness that it could never belong to Sophie Champion.

She struggled to find the proper words to tell her visitors how overwhelmed she was, but nothing seemed right. Instead, she managed to come out with, "It is a real pleasure to meet all of you."

"I assure you, the pleasure is wholly ours," Ian replied with an earnestness that gave the words more meaning than mere social niceties. Then he crossed the room toward her and, taking both her hands warmly in his, said, "Welcome to our family, Sophie. We have been waiting for you."

Unbeknownst to him, unbeknownst even to her, Ian had just spoken the words that Sophie had been longing to hear for eleven years.

The group crowding around the base of the main staircase in the entrance hall of Sandal Hall grew silent at a sign from Thurston.

"Breathe," Ian leaned over to whisper to Crispin, who nodded but completely disregarded his brother's good advice. He would not breathe or swallow or even move again until he saw Sophie and knew that she really was going to marry him.

A door on the first landing opened, and Bianca appeared, followed by Helena, then Emme, then Octavia. What Crispin calculated to be roughly six hundred years passed, and then, all of a sudden, she was there.

Sophie seemed to float above them, shimmering splendidly from head to foot. She was an incredible vision, too beautiful to be mortal, blushing too strongly to be anything else. Her gown was of deep ocean blue, and turned her eyes that color too. The skirt was completely embroidered with mermaids and mermen dancing together while sea creatures played among them, their hair and bodies picked out in diamonds and pearls and emeralds to make them shimmer as if underwater. The underskirt was a lighter shade of blue, cut to move like ripples of water, with small diamonds and aquamarines carefully set in so it glistened like the surface of the sea at dawn, and the same stones formed a small bee on the hem of the gown. There was no question that the dress was Octavia's masterpiece, but it was not that which caused Crispin to lose his tongue. It was the way Sophie looked in it, and, even more, the way she was looking at him.

Crispin looked back at her and said in a voice that carried out to the crowds in the streets, "Sophie Champion, I love you."

The cheering that began then did not end until well after dawn. Description of the wedding of the Earl of Scandal to Miss Sophie Champion took up eight pages of the newly reopened *News at Court* ("under the proprietorship of Lady Priscilla Snowden and her sister, Lady Eleanor Nearview, Aunts to the Earl of Sandal"), which featured descriptions of everything from the food that was consumed ("a notable preponderance of orange cakes") to a transcript of the Queen's remarks on the occasion (which included such sagacities as "Very fine wine, Sandal," and "Where do you suppose he had these cushions made?"). A half page was given over to an impromptu monologue performed by a raven named Grip from the window of His Lordship's chambers, apparently on the topic of slugs, and another half to a listing of "Women Claiming to Have Had Their Lives Saved by Sophie Champion." A pageant performed by members of a patriotic association called the Worshipful Hall ("unknown to the Proprietors"), which raised a few eyebrows when all the dancing boys turned out to be dancing girls, received three quarters of a page, but by far the longest segment was entitled "A Report of What Transpired at Midnight."

It was just slightly short of that hour when Thurston, standing in front of a planting shed off to the side of the Sandal Hall gardens, cleared his throat. "Good evening, my lord, my lady," he said, as if there were nothing at all unusual about seeking a renegade bride and groom in the outbuildings of their own garden during their wedding. "I did not like to bother you, but this was just delivered, and the messenger says it is urgent."

Crispin appeared from around the shed first, wiping a smudge of dirt from his ear, and Sophie followed, trying not to blush furiously. She looked over Crispin's shoulder as he slit open the parcel.

Crispin and Sophie,

I wish I could have been there with you to celebrate your wedding, but a melancholy boor who spends all his time licking his wounds is hardly worthy company for such a joyful day. The happiness you know is something I once longed for myself, but understand that I can never have. No one, however, deserves it more than the two of you.

I have sold off all my properties and left the money in a trust to be given to those in need, which I hope you, Sophie, will oversee. All my wishes, all my joys, all my rosy hopes for the future, now reside in you two. Know that when the H.M.S. Phoenix *sails tonight for the wars in Spain, there sails aboard her a captain whose heart is filled with gratitude and love for you both. Your friendship is my most precious possession.*

Please accept the two gifts that accompany this as a token of my deep and undying affection, and in remembrance of where our friendship, Crispin, began so many years ago.

Your humble and faithful,
Lawrence

Before Crispin could ask, Thurston presented him with the large parcel he had been given along with the note. Sophie lifted the canvas that hung over it and let out a gasp.

Standing before her was a painting of such exquisite artistry that it seemed to glow with its own light. In the middle of a seascape, a magnificent woman rose from the water, naked but for her lush hair which wrapped around her, concealing her form but suggesting its magnificence. She stared out of the painting at the viewer, smiling, kind, and very, very beautiful.

Crispin reached down and lifted a rectangle of parchment from where it had been wedged between the boards of the painting and the frame. "*I thought you might like this old piece as it reminds me of Sophie,*" he read from Lawrence's note aloud. "*It's by a long-dead Italian named Sandro Botticelli. According to his son, from whom I bought the painting several years back, old Sandro painted two of them, one called* The Birth of Venus *and this one, which he called* The Water Nymph. *He sold the first one to some Florentine count but kept this version for his private collection because he thought it was superior. I know you probably do not have a place for such an old and useless piece in your grand house—you can see how the left corner is starting to crack—so feel free to use it as kindling or how-ever you see fit.'"*

Crispin shook his head at the note and whispered, "Lawrence, you cad. 'Feel free to use it as kindling.'" Then he looked up at Sophie. "This painting was the masterpiece of Lawrence's collection. My cousin Tristan tried to buy it from him for years. He says it is worth more than all the art he owns put together, more probably than all the art in England."

"It is magnificent," Sophie breathed, mesmerized by the image of the red-haired woman rising from the water.

Crispin had not stopped shaking his head. "It certainly is. But given this trifle, I fear what Lawrence's other present might be." He turned to Thurston and asked with some trepidation, "Where is the other package?"

"There was no other package, sir," Thurston said, looking, for the first time in Crispin's memory, vaguely bemused. Crispin, on the other hand, was relieved. But before either Thurston's bemusement or Crispin's relief could really take hold, a loud explosion was heard, and the sky over the river steps of Sandal Hall lit up with green stars.

Sophie wrenched her eyes from the painting and moved them in the direction of the noise. "Look, Crispin, the other present," she cried, dragging him toward the river. The Thames in front of the house was filled with barges, and from each of them, towers of brightly colored flames were exploding. Some shot high into the air, golden arcs of dazzling sparks; others exploded outward in pur-plish clouds that made the surface of the river seem to be on fire. From this purple cloud emerged first a sparkling golden horn, and then a glittering white unicorn, wearing a fiery red collar from which dangled what looked like a pair of dice. The unicorn reared once, twice, then leapt gracefully into the river. As it vanished, a golden egg appeared on the central barge, growing and growing, and then cracking open with a staggering explosion to reveal an enormous bird, its wings red, its body and head orange and gold, simulated flames lapping at its feet. This Phoenix, for it could have been no other, seemed to double and triple in size until it blazed into a large explosion. Simultaneously, all the barges came alive, awash in white cascades of sparks, and where the Phoenix had been now appeared the letters *C* and *S* in red, moving slowly together and finally entwining to form a single red heart. Just before the firework heart disappeared, a cloud of a thousand live pure-white doves whose wings had been studded with diamonds flew out from behind it, the gemstones glittering wildly in the light from the barges as the birds made their way up and up and up into the sky.

Side by side Crispin and Sophie stood on the river steps of their home, their hands clasped tightly together, their eyes striving to follow the ethereal trail of the last shimmering dove as it disappeared into the night.

For generations afterward, people spoke of the magical summer of 1588 when the Thames exploded in mysterious fiery portents, the *H.M.S. Phoenix* led the English to victory against the Spanish, and three hundred families went from poverty to riches as the sky above London rained diamonds for days.

Epilogue

He was being followed.

There were two of them, both tall. He did not need to turn around as he crossed the hall to know that they were still there; he could sense them.

And hear them.

"Nephew, it is most improper for you to go in there," Lady Priscilla told him as she dogged his heels.

"Extremely indecorous," Lady Eleanor added from the other side.

But Crispin ignored them, mounting the stairs four at a time. At the top he turned, passing by a newly outfitted game room, and hastened toward his apartment. He passed through the library, where Grip was teaching baby Thurston to say "Strip!", pushed open the door of his bedchamber, and rushed toward the center of activity.

Octavia immediately handed him a damp cloth and ceded her place to him. As he reached the top of the bed, Sophie gave another scream, closing her eyes and straining with the effort of pushing.

"You are almost there," the blond woman at the bottom of the bed told Sophie. "Just keep pushing, *carissima.*"

Sophie turned her head and saw Crispin standing beside the bed for the first time, blotting her forehead. "I am never going to let you talk me into doing this again," she told him through clenched teeth. "If you even try it, I think, perhaps, I will kill you."

"Perhaps?" Crispin asked, leaning over to replace the damp cloth on her brow with a kiss.

"Perhaps," she replied, starting to smile up at him, until the smile turned into a grimace and a scream. "Damn you, Crispin," she shouted at him. "How could you do this to me? I am very, ve*rrrrryyyy* uncomfortable."

Crispin looked down at her apologetically. "I am very sorry, Sophie. If there is anything I can do to make it up to you, anything at all, please tell me now."

Sophie screamed again, and the muscles in her neck tightened. "Roast pig," she called out to Crispin.

"I can see the head," Bianca told her sister-in-law. "Just a little more, Sophie, *carissima.*"

Sophie grabbed Crispin's hand and squeezed it until he thought the bones would break. "Spinach soufflé," she hollered out.

"Just one more," Bianca told her. "Push one more time."

Crispin himself was on the point of crying out in agony. "And peaches," Sophie yelled.

At that moment the air was rent by a young girl's cry. A very young, very redheaded girl. A very, very beautiful little baby.

The newest Foscari family jewel.